NEEDLEPOINT:
The poisonous needle that killed Sara Chandler's husband.

NEEDLEPOINT:
The small scrap of embroidered material found near Ted Chandler's body.

NEEDLEPOINT:
The eerie tapestry that hangs on the wall in Sara's father's office.

NEEDLEPOINT:
The fatal injection that killed an innocent child so many years ago.

There's a murderer on the loose. And the killing won't stop until the tapestry is complete.

CRITICAL ACCLAIM FOR *SAMANTHA CHASE*

Also by Samantha Chase:

POSTMARK

needlepoint

samantha chase

TUDOR
TUDOR PUBLISHING, INC.
NEW YORK CITY

A TUDOR BOOK

November © 1989

Published by

Tudor Publishing, Inc.
276 Fifth Avenue
New York, NY 10001

Printed in the United States of America.

Acknowledgments

We are greatly indebted to Charles Kokes, M.D., Acting Deputy Chief Medical Examiner, the State of Maryland, Paul S. Burka, M.D., R. Michael Massanari M.D.M.S., Associate Hospital Epidemiologist, University of Iowa Hospitals and Clinics, for their advice on autopsy procedures, childbirth, and toxins; to Jean Larner, Chief of Police, St. Michaels, Maryland, for local operating procedures; to Joe and Kathy Sykes of Cambridge, Maryland, for Eastern Shore background; to the staff at Harbourtowne Resort for their hospitality, contacts, and information; and to Norman Glick, whose help with research was, as always, invaluable; and to Kate Duffy, whose support has meant a lot to us.

CHAPTER 1

Tuesday, April 4

Ribbons of fog swept across the marsh like mourners in a procession as Ted Chandler pulled onto the narrow bridge.

One of the red warning lights was out, and he had to slam on his brakes to keep from hitting the temporary concrete barrier.

For Christ's sake. Why had she insisted on meeting him out here in the middle of a road project? But then, she'd always been unpredictable. It made him nervous sometimes. But it was exciting, too.

Like the first time, when he'd gone downstairs to get another jug of Burgundy at the Christmas party. He'd heard the door lock and seen her there at the top of the stairs. He hadn't ever thought about starting anything with her. But the way she'd walked slowly down—swinging her hips and watching his face—had made him forget about his wife and the forty-five guests in his living room. Afterward, they'd both gone back upstairs and not spoken to each other for the rest of the evening.

But it hadn't been a passive silence. Vibrations had zinged back and forth between them. When he'd phoned her from the office on Monday, she'd asked him over for an incredibly erotic session. And every other time she'd called, he'd met her wherever she wanted. It was always at night. The playground at the school. The old packing plant down by Kramer's Cove. The graveyard.

That first time had set the pattern. She'd never let him nail her. But she'd always left him feeling sated—and anxious for the next meeting.

He smiled in the darkness. Things were going his way. He had Sara for the home life and for the business contacts. But he gave his wife something too. He earned a decent living. And he was on the edge of finally hitting it big.

Even with the engine idling, it was chilly in the car. Damn, where was she? He'd told Sara he was showing a house in Easton. She expected him back by ten-thirty.

He fiddled with the knob on the radio and brought in a station from Baltimore that played oldies: "She Don't Love You Like I Love You."

It was just the reverse with him and Sara. He loved her, but not the way she loved him. When he'd married her, he'd told himself he could settle down. But a wedding ring on his finger hadn't stopped the ladies from coming on to him.

A figure dressed in black came gliding out of the mist. He drew in a sharp breath. Then he laughed at himself. It wasn't a spook. Just her damn flare for the dramatic.

The passenger door opened.

"You're late," he accused.

Instead of an apology, strong fingers closed around his wrist. He felt surgical latex against his skin.

"Hey—cut it out." He tried to pull away, but the vicelike grip tightened. A hot pain jabbed his right arm. A needle.

He cursed and shoved at the figure beside him.

The hood dropped back from the face, and he gasped.

"What the hell—" The question ended in a gurgled whisper. His voice wouldn't work. In fact, nothing worked.

He could hardly breathe. And he couldn't move. A tide of panic rose in his throat.

"We need to hurry. You've still got to be breathing, so they'll find water in your lungs."

The statement was flat and matter-of-fact above the upbeat tune on the radio.

Ted Chandler was cold and clammy and more afraid than he'd ever been in his life.

God, no—wait. Don't do this to me. His mind screamed the plea. But he could only stare into the darkness, his eyes wide with horror.

He was aware of the glove compartment opening and closing.

"Thanks for leaving the engine on." A hand shifted the gear lever from park to drive. "Good-bye, Ted."

He felt his foot pressed against the accelerator.

No. Help me. Somebody help me. Sara—

The door slammed just before the car shot past the temporary barrier.

Then the cold, murky water of the Choptank River rose up to swallow him.

CHAPTER 2

Thursday, April 6

THE ST. STEPHENS RECORD

Obituary Section

A service of Christian burial will be held Friday, April 7, for realtor Theodore Chandler at the St. Stephens Methodist Church. Interment is immediately following at the church cemetery. Mr. Chandler died April 4 after his car plunged off the Choptank River Bridge.

Born and raised in Baltimore, Mr. Chandler came to the Eastern Shore in 1981 to attend Salisbury State College. A 1985 graduate of that institution, he joined Newhouse Realty the same year and at the time of his death was one of the company's most active agents. In 1986 he was inducted into the Delmarva Peninsula Million Dollar Realty Club. He also served on the St. Stephens Chamber of Commerce, was treasurer of the Tidewater Hunting Club, and gave his time generously to the St. Stephens Volunteer Fire Company.

Mr. Chandler is survived by his wife, longtime St. Stephens resident Sara Chandler. Mrs. Chandler requests that expressions of sympathy be given in her husband's name to the Bay Watchers Society.

Friday, April 7

"May his soul rest in peace."

Sara Chandler's thoughts echoed the words of Reverend Hollingsworth.

Ted's restless spirit was at peace now. At least she could console herself with that. As she turned away from the grave, she felt her father's arm around her shoulders. It was trembling slightly. Reassuringly she reached up to lay her graceful fingers over his. Once she'd been able to rely on Harold Strickland's strength. Not any more.

"I'm all right," she murmured. The words were automatic—but hardly the truth.

Sara tried to concentrate on the sound of her shoes crunching along the gravel path of the little cemetery. Anything to shut out the panoply of thoughts swirling in her mind.

God, why couldn't she just cry? Maybe that would make the sick feeling go away. But she was still too shocked and numbed by the way her marriage had come to an end like a book slammed shut before you'd reached the final chapter. Now she wasn't going to have a chance of making it come out right. Or had she been fooling herself all along? Had there ever really been a chance?

The last thing Ted had said to her was that he was meeting a client in Easton. But the police had pulled his car out of the Choptank River, south of St. Stephens, not north.

The driver opened the doors of the somber black limousine. After her father got in, Sara hesitated for a moment. The salty breeze off the bay blew her auburn hair back from her high cheekbones. She had a sudden image of how she must look standing there beside the car in the late morning sunlight: too thin, the skin drawn across the delicate bones of her face, dark circles under her green eyes, the black dress washing out her pale skin.

Unconsciously she pressed her palm against the slight swell of her abdomen. She hadn't even gotten up the nerve to tell Ted. Now he'd never know.

Abruptly the breeze turned cold. That was why the back of her neck suddenly prickled, she told herself. Yet it didn't just feel like the breeze. She could swear someone's malevolent gaze was boring into her.

She whirled. All she saw behind her was a circle of sympathetic faces—her friends. Ted's business associates from the real estate office and some of the guys from the volunteer fire company, artists who exhibited at her shop, people she'd known since she was a little girl.

"Come on," her younger sister Ginny urged, tugging on her arm. "Cemeteries always give me the creeps."

Had she felt it too? Sara wondered. That sudden chill? The sun-warmed leather of the seat felt good as she slipped into the limousine. The door closed with a decisive thunk.

"I'm glad that's over," Ginny murmured as the big car pulled away.

"Um hum." Pressing her throbbing forehead against the cool window glass, Sara stared out at the countryside. She'd been born and raised here on the Eastern Shore, the flat peninsula between the Chesapeake Bay and the Atlantic Ocean. The familiar scenery was somehow comforting—cattail marshes, peaceful inlets full of pleasure craft and working fishing boats, fields that would soon be lush with corn and soybeans.

Several miles down the road was the Victorian house she and Ted had bought two years ago. The place had been affordable because the previous owner hadn't kept it up.

"I can do a lot of the restoration myself," her husband had promised. Now the copper roofing on the front turret was shiny, and the wooden siding was freshly painted. Inside, only the first floor and one upstairs bedroom had been redone.

Back at the house, she found some of the women from the Methodist church, and a few of her friends from the Bay Watchers, who had come back after the funeral to make coffee and set out platters of food.

Beatrice Pierce tucked a wayward strand of gray hair into the French twist at the back of her neck and came over. A spinster in her mid-fifties, she'd been the feature editor at the local paper, *The St. Stephens Record*, until she retired, the year before.

"Can I get you some food, dear?" she asked.

The thought of trying to gag anything down made a wave of nausea rise in Sara's throat. "Why don't you see if you can persuade my father to have a little something?" she suggested.

She glanced over toward the couch where Dr. Harold Strickland had slumped down against the printed cushions. He looked as if he wished he were anywhere else.

When had he gotten so old looking? Sara wondered, her eyes lingering on his steel-gray hair and the deep lines in the parchment of his face. Once his features had been forceful. Now they had taken on a troubled gauntness. Why was he taking this so hard?

She had just started toward him when Kitty Duncan came over. She gave Sara a comforting hug, and Sara hugged back.

Kitty was a tall, large-featured woman who had moved to St. Stephens the year before. Her natural collages had quickly become some of the most popular items in Sara's gallery. She'd been on one of her trips to Florida, gathering shells, sea-polished stones, and other materials, when Ted had died.

"Oh, Kitty."

"I heard about the funeral when I went to stock up on groceries," she said. "I'm sorry I couldn't be with you yesterday and the day before."

"You couldn't have known."

"What can I do to help—"

Her words were cut off by a sharp crash. Both women whirled.

"Oh for Pete's sake, Ralph." Ginny's voice cut through the sudden silence in the room.

Ralph Meekins had dropped to his knees and started sweeping jagged pieces of beige porcelain into a small pile. "Maybe I can fix it," he mumbled.

The crowd parted as Sara drew closer. She could see the top of Ralph's bald head and his square hands frantically gathering the broken shards.

Sara winced as she saw what he'd knocked off the mantel. The key to the city, which Mayor Hudson had presented to Ted after he'd raised so much money for the new fire engine. She was pretty sure Ralph wasn't going to be able to put it back together.

She knelt beside him, her eyes drawn to the blood welling up on his index finger. "You've cut yourself."

"Sara, I'm real sorry." There were tears in his eyes. "I was looking at it, you know, thinkin' about . . ." He stopped abruptly and shrugged uneasily.

A fifth generation waterman who'd turned his hobby of decoy carving into a retirement career, Ralph wasn't a very articulate man. His eyes were moist now.

Sara's own vision swam. The key had meant a lot to Ted—and to her, too. Her husband had been far from perfect. But there were things he'd done for St. Stephens that were worth remembering. Suddenly she was afraid she was going to cry. But not yet. Not in front of so many people. She squeezed her eyes shut. When she opened them again, Beatrice had appeared with a dustpan and broom. And Lois Pennington, her father's receptionist, had brought a clean cloth for Ralph's hand.

Then Kitty was at her side, helping her to her feet. She wanted to escape from the room. People would understand if she wanted to go up and lie down. But she found that an impromptu receiving line had formed in front of her. For the next hour and a half she listened to repeated offerings of sympathy and murmured words about how everybody was going to miss Ted. Her eyes stung, and the muscles of her face ached from trying to keep her emotions under control.

Across the room, Dr. Harold Strickland sat on the sofa watching his older daughter. Later he'd try to tell Sara he was proud of the way she was handling things today. Not now. He grimaced. In a way, this whole nasty mess was his fault. If he and Ginny hadn't been so damn dependent on Sara after their mother had died, she would have accepted that scholarship to the University of Maryland instead of settling for going part time to Salisbury State. Then she wouldn't have been here to fall under the spell of that slick operator, Ted Chandler.

He'd liked Ted at first. The man had fooled him, just like he'd fooled Sara and a lot of other people. Hell, half the town still didn't know the truth.

Well, Sara might be grieving over her loss

now. But in the long run she was better off without the bastard. And now she'd have the money from the insurance policy he'd made Ted take out when they'd gotten married. Accidental death, it paid double for that: $200,000.

He took a long swallow of Scotch. Miss Bea had tried to give him a cup of tea. He'd put it down on the end table and gone to get some of the Chivas Regal he knew Ted kept in the liquor cabinet. It was the only way he was going to get through the afternoon. In fact, it was the way he was starting to get through a lot of afternoons.

Thank God he had Ben Langley working with him now—taking over the major part of the practice. A year ago he wondered why a sharp young doctor like Ben had been willing to settle for extracting fishhooks from thumbs and treating strep throats in a small town. Now he was too grateful to worry about it.

He took another swig of Scotch and closed his bloodshot eyes, but it didn't do any good. An image of the small package he'd found on his desk blotter this morning leaped into his mind.

Someone had left it there, someone who knew what he'd done. Someone who wanted him to know they knew. But what did they intend to do about it? The question made the vein in his temple start to pound.

CHAPTER 3

"I hate needles."

Dr. Ben Langley steadied the ten-year-old boy's arm. "I'll do it fast," he said reassuringly. The words were punctuated by the quick jab of the hypodermic.

Ben ruffled the boy's hair. "Don't play around any more construction projects, and you won't need a tetanus shot for another ten years."

He watched Bobby hobble toward the door and thought about the rusty nail the boy had pulled out of his foot himself before limping to the doctor's office. The kid was tough—just like most of the folks around here.

After making a few notes in the medical file, the tall, lanky physician shrugged out of his white lab coat and reached for his tweed sports jacket. Bobby was his last patient for the day.

He paused to give his dark hair a quick inspection in the mirror by the door. It was getting shaggy again. He'd been planning to get a haircut today. But that was before he'd volunteered to man the office by himself so Harold could attend Ted's funeral.

Ben rolled his shoulders. He was tired. But he hadn't been all that eager to pay his last respects to Sara's husband anyway.

He was so deep in thought that he almost bumped into Mrs. Cooper on the way to his car.

"Sorry," Ben apologized.

The plump little bank teller shook her head sympathetically.

"That's all right, Doc. I guess you're a little preoccupied today." She clicked her tongue. "It sure was a shock about poor Ted Chandler."

He nodded and let her go on about Ted a bit before changing the subject. "Your arthritis better?"

"Those pills you gave me are helpin'."

"Good."

Doc, he thought as he climbed into his car. The title was a mark of the respect he'd won in the community. When he'd first come to St. Stephens, a lot of people had been slow to trust a physician barely in his thirties.

Most of the guys in medical school with him back in L.A. would have laughed at the kind of practice he'd chosen. And two years ago when he'd started as a resident in Santa Barbara, he'd been thinking in terms of specializing in diseases of the rich. That was before he'd known he had to get as far away from California as he could.

For a moment his jaw tightened. He was proud of what he'd accomplished here. But what if everything he'd worked for came crashing down around his ears? He slammed the gear lever into reverse. That wasn't going to happen. He wouldn't let it.

By the time Ben arrived at the Chandler house, only a few cars were still parked in front.

Ben stopped for a moment beside the antique hallstand that Sara had found at an auction. She kept a whimsical collection of old bonnets and scarves on the hooks. One was a pink boa, and he reached out to touch the silky feathers a bit uncertainly.

Sara was standing beside the dining room table putting rolls into a plastic bag. She kept stopping after every two or three and staring off into space.

When she glanced up and saw him, a storm of emotions swept across her face . . . sadness, vulnerability, maybe even guilt.

He was hoping to see something else as well.

"I thought you weren't coming."

"My last patient just left." He came over and put a hand on her shoulder. "How are you holding up?"

"Okay I guess."

He looked around the room. "Where's Harold?"

"Ginny took him home about an hour ago."

Their eyes met in unspoken understanding. No need to spell out that Harold Strickland hadn't been in any shape to drive himself.

Before the silence became uncomfortable, Sara cleared her throat. "I should go thank the ladies before they leave."

"Sure."

"There's coffee. And some cake." She gestured toward the sideboard.

Ben poured himself half a styrofoam cup of coffee. He didn't really want any, but it gave him something to do.

In a few moments, the women came through, carrying empty serving dishes and gathering up their pocketbooks. Several stopped to exchange greetings with the young doctor.

"A real shame," Lois Pennington murmured.

"Maybe it's for the best," Beatrice Pierce said under her breath.

Ben muttered something noncommittal that he hoped covered both points of view.

After the ladies had finally closed the front door, he turned expectantly back toward the kitchen. When Sara didn't emerge, he put down the coffee cup and went looking for her. She was leaning with her elbows on one of the kitchen counters, her chin cupped in her palms.

"You need to get some sleep."

She straightened slowly. "I won't be able to."

"Do you want me to give you something?"

"No!"

"Sara, don't think you have to get through this without any help."

"It isn't that." She opened a drawer and started noisily putting away cutlery from the dish drainer.

He gently lifted a spoon out of her hand.

"Maybe you should get out of here for a little while."

"I—"

"Doctor's orders."

Sara gave him a half-smile. "That's one of Dad's favorite lines."

"I know. I picked it up from him." He turned her toward the door. "Where would you like to go?"

A deserted stretch of shoreline leaped into her mind. "Swan Point."

"Where?"

"A place we used to go swimming and berry-picking when I was a kid. A friend of my family owns the place. It's down near Tilghman Island."

He took a light jacket from one of the hooks by the back door and draped it over her shoulders. It didn't go with the black dress, but what did that matter?

Once he'd helped her into the passenger seat of his Blazer, she sat with her hands clasped in her lap. Other than giving a few directions, she didn't speak.

"Turn here."

There was a No Trespassing sign on one gatepost and a No Hunting sign on the other.

Ben eyed the warnings. "You say this place belongs to a friend of your family?"

"Miss Jane." She used the local term of address and then clarified it for Ben. "Mrs. Brittingham. It's all right. Ginny and I have permission to come here whenever we want."

The road was badly rutted. Through the trees, Ben could see an old plantation-style house that must once have been elegant. Now it looked like it needed a good paint job. The lane wound past it and ended abruptly at a little beach.

As soon as Ben stopped, Sara opened the door and scrambled out. Sensing that she wanted to be alone, he didn't follow immediately.

Blackberry brambles caught at her skirt as Sara made her way down the uneven path to the beach.

She had't been there in a long time, but it was just the way she remembered—untouched, wild, waves lapping gently against the narrow strip of beach. Across the water, the sun was a glowing red ball in the west and the low-hanging clouds were shot through with pink and violet.

She had just slipped off her shoes and wiggled her toes into the sand when the evening quiet was shattered by the roar of an engine. Not Ben's car . . . a motorcycle!

Her head jerked up as she remembered how often that sound had knifed through her consciousness recently. Mostly late at night when she'd lain in bed waiting for Ted to come home. A lone motorcycle, roaring past. And sometimes she'd heard the engine stop. Once or twice she'd gotten up and tiptoed, shivering, to the window. But when she'd peered out into the darkness, she hadn't seen anything but the bare branches of a tree silhouetted against the moon.

Now she looked up at a solitary figure straddling a sleek, black machine. His leather outfit, too, was black. A visored helmet masked his features with an opaque shield that made him look like a storm trooper from a science fiction movie.

Let me see your face. Why don't you come out from behind that visor. But the words stayed locked in her throat.

She wanted to turn away. Instead she stood there facing him, feeling his hostility washing down on her like icy surf whipped up by the wind. It chilled her to the bone.

CHAPTER 4

She might not be able to see his face, but she was sure she knew who he was—one of those damn kids who'd been shooting bald eagles for fun.

Sara clenched her fists at her sides. She'd been outraged when she'd read about it in the paper. There were so pitifully few of the beautiful birds left. She'd headed the Bay Watchers committee that had talked to Police Chief Dailey about what could be done.

They'd offered a reward for information, and an anonymous tip had implicated the cyclists. But nobody was actually caught.

After that, the cyclists had made a point of roaring past Sara's gallery so loudly that the stoneware in the window rattled. And someone had bombarded the front door with raw eggs and bird seed. But gradually the harassment had tapered off—except for the one rider, whom she kept hearing late at night.

Now, as if to mock her, he revved his engine. The wheels spun, and then the powerful machine plowed across a stand of fragile sea grass.

The deliberate gesture was suddenly a focus for all the pain Sara had locked inside herself since the police chief had come to tell her about Ted. She'd taken the news with deathly calm. Yet the anguish had been growing within her like a storm system building over the bay.

Without warning, the force of the tempest broke. Sara started shaking her fist as she ran barefoot back up the path.

"This is private property. You have no right to be here, you bastard," she shouted.

For a moment the figure sat there like a specter, looming over her. The impenetrable shield of the dark visor, and his arrogant posture, fueled her anger.

She wanted to crack through to the flesh and blood underneath. Wildly, she looked around for something to hurl at him. Spotting a smooth rock, she stopped to pick it up. But at the same time, with a corner of her mind, she watched herself—aghast.

Halfway to the road, she almost collided with Ben, who was rushing toward the beach. Before she could heave the missile, he grabbed her arm. Her eyes focused on him in confusion.

"Easy. Take it easy, Sara," he soothed, grasping her by the shoulders.

Up on the road, the menacing figure on the bike regarded the trembling woman on the beach and smiled a secret smile. In a way, he wished she could see his face, but it was too soon. Instead, he raised his gloved hand in a mocking salute.

When the time was right, he'd let her know who he was. Until then, there would be the pleasure of playing with her like a marlin on a steel line. He'd let the tension go slack so she'd think she had a chance to get away. Then he'd jerk up on it again when she least expected it.

He revved up the motor, feeling the throb of the powerful machine between his legs. After one last satisfied look, he roared away.

"Let me go." Tears were already streaming down Sara's cheeks. "People like him won't be satisfied until they destroy every bit of natural beauty along the shoreline."

When Ben pulled her into his arms, she stopped fighting and sagged against him. The rock dropped from her fingers. "I can't—I just can't—" She was still struggling for control.

His fingers gently massaged her back. "You've been through a lot. Go ahead and let it out, honey."

They stood there on the beach. Her shoulders shook. He quietly offered support. As the sun sank into the water, the wind picked up and began to whip around them.

Ben's hands stroked up and down her arms as he felt her shivering in the light nylon jacket. After a time, she brought her sobs under control and fumbled in her pocket for a tissue. But she couldn't look up to meet his gaze.

"Let's get back in the car." He took her hand and led her up the path.

When he'd closed the doors behind them, she sank back against the seat. "I'm sorry," she finally murmured. "I guess you realize that wasn't just about that damn cyclist."

"Yes."

"I haven't come apart like that in years."

"You're entitled."

"I'm going to get through this, Ben."

"I know."

"You're probably thinking—well, it was a bad marriage, but it's all over. And she can forget about Ted Chandler and pick up her life as though he never existed."

"That's not such a bad idea."

"I wish it were that easy." She knit her hands together in her lap. "Ben, I haven't talked about this with anyone else."

Something in the tone of her voice made a hollow space open at the base of his throat. "What's wrong?"

She swallowed convulsively. "It's not something wrong—I mean—I'm pregnant."

"What?" The question came out as a startled exclamation.

"I went to an obstetrician in Cambridge. I hadn't told Ted yet."

"Why not?"

She shook her head. "I guess I was stalling—trying to find a good time. We'd argued about kids before. He— he— wasn't ready for a family yet."

Ben hoped she couldn't see his tight expression in the gathering darkness. "What are you going to do?" he asked when he was sure he had his voice under control.

"I've thought about it a lot. Despite everything, I want this baby."

He wanted to make her explain it all to him. Instead, he covered her cold fingers with his warm ones.

George Newhouse sat bolt upright in bed. Sweat was pouring down the back of his neck like a rainspout during a storm.

He'd been dreaming about the letter of agreement ... on cream paper, with those nice sharp characters you got from an IBM executive typewriter. It was right in his pocket. And he was laughing in old Miss Jane's pasty white face. At first she'd pulled her shawl around her old-lady rounded shoulders and started crying. Then she'd straightened up her shriveled body and begun to laugh back. A high, braying sound that had set his teeth on edge.

"It's too late. So just shut the hell up," he'd shouted and reached in his pocket so he could pull out the letter and wave it at her. But his fingers had closed around empty air just before he'd woken up sweating.

Jesus Lord. It was just a dream. Then he remembered Ted had said something about pulling the Brittingham file. He should've checked on that today at the office. But everyone had been flapping around like geese in hunting season since the news about Chandler had hit.

The grandfather clock down in the hall struck twelve. But he had to make sure that damn letter was in a safe place. What if it was at Ted's house? What if Sara got her hands on it? Jesus!

He swung his sinewy legs over the side of the bed and stood up. Trying to tell himself he was getting spooked over nothing, he pulled on the pair of gray trousers he'd left on the chair. Then he crossed to the bathroom and splashed cold water on his hot cheeks.

His eyes were bloodshot, but his face looked tanned and fit. So did his body. He'd been captain of the Saints, the football team, back in sixty-two. And he still kept himself in shape. Not like some good ol' boys he knew, with their beer bellies, guys who didn't get any more exercise than walking to the refrigerator during a commercial. He might be forty-five, but he could pass for ten years younger.

Yeah, but it's not going to do you much good without the dough to enjoy life, he reminded himself.

The thought made his heart start to pound. "Oh for God's sake, cool it," he muttered to himself. "You've planned this too good for things to get fucked up now." But even as he uttered the assurance, he knew that it was the little things you can't plan that can trap you in the end.

In the garage, he stopped and looked at the motorcycle. Although it wasn't as souped up as a lot of the other ones in town, it still gave him that youthful image. But not tonight. Better take the car.

He couldn't stop thinking about Ted as he nosed his big Oldsmobile through the dark streets. He remembered when he'd hired Chandler. What a hustler. And as slick as goose grease.

Him and Ted. At first it had been fun showing that boy the ropes. But somewhere along the line he'd started feeling afraid that his protégé was going to take over. There'd been times when he'd thought about kicking him out. But he couldn't. The son of a bitch knew too much.

Well, all those little problems were solved now—just like magic. The best part was that he wasn't going to have to split the proceeds from the Brittingham deal with good ol' Ted. If there was any deal.

Stop it! he commanded himself. *The letter's safe. It has to be.*

When he reached Newhouse Realty, George glanced up at the lighted sign. The name brought in business. People got a chuckle out of the pun. But he wasn't laughing as he parked in the private lot behind the office. After quietly closing the side door, he reached for the light switch in the reception area. Then he drew his hand back. Instead, he waited until he'd closed the door to his own office before turning on the light.

His fingers were shaking so badly that it took him three tries to get the combination on the filing cabinet right. Inside were his confidential files—the ones that his secretary never saw.

Abbott, Arnold, Bradford, Brittingham. He pulled out the folder and began to riffle through the contents.

Jesus Lord. It wasn't here. Heart thumping, he made himself go back through the papers slowly. The crisp cream-colored sheet was clipped behind the appraisal of the property that Ted had commissioned.

George collapsed back into the leather chair beside his desk, his fingers clutching the letter.

After a moment, he folded it carefully in thirds and stuck it in the pocket of his jacket. First thing in the morning, it was going into the safe deposit box.

Ben Langley sighed and sat up in bed. Wearily, he massaged his eyelids with his thumb and finger. He'd thought he could get to sleep. He'd been wrong. On the ride home in the car with Sara, there hadn't been much to say. After making sure she was going to be all right by herself, he'd headed back to the beach house he'd bought last winter. The irony was that Ted Chandler had gotten him a really good deal on the waterfront property. It had been built by a well-to-do Baltimore couple about ten years ago as a vacation retreat. When they'd retired and moved to Florida, interest rates had been high, so they'd settled for less than their asking price.

Wearing just his pajama bottoms, he padded downstairs and looked out the window over the bay.

There were a lot of things he liked about the house—the view from the long deck facing the water, the Jacuzzi on the patio; the galley kitchen that wasn't too hard to keep clean.

He still didn't have a lot of furniture. Really, the place needed a woman's hand.

An image of Sara's house brought a slow smile to his lips. The warmth . . . The personal touches, like the collection of crazy hats on the coatrack and the bowl of seashells on the coffee table, the paintings and sculpture by local artists whose careers she was building. It was a real home instead of just a place where someone could watch T.V., heat up frozen dinners in the microwave, and flop into bed at the end of a hard day.

Had Ted Chandler realized how lucky he was to be married to a woman who could make his life so warm and comfortable? If he did, he had a strange way of showing his appreciation.

There was only one bottle of liquor in the house. A fifth of Johnny Walker Black Label that one of his patients had given him last Christmas—a local Maryland product, the man had explained.

Ben hadn't used alcohol as a crutch since that mess back in Santa Barbara. After he'd seen what it was doing to Harold, he'd vowed to stay away from the stuff permanently. But now he needed something to take the edge off the knife wound that Sara had unwittingly inflicted.

He took a swallow of the amber liquid, letting the warmth trickle down his throat, calculating the amount of time it would take before it reached his brain.

A baby. That certainly changed things. For the past few days, it had been hard to keep a somber expression on his face. He'd figured that Sara would turn to him and that they'd get married after a suitable period of mourning. But did he want to raise Ted Chandler's child? Would the baby be a constant reminder of the past?

His fingers clenched around the tumbler. He didn't realize how tightly he was holding it until the plastic cracked under the pressure and a sharp splinter gouged into the palm of his hand.

CHAPTER 5

Sunday, April 9

There were certain pay phones he liked to use when he wanted to make calls that couldn't be traced. One was across from Frazer's Seafood Market where the streetlamp had burned out and hadn't been replaced. There were two down by the dock. And another one was out at the baseball field in Bayside Park.

It was four in the morning, but a police car was cruising slowly along the street that bordered the marina. Waiting in the shadows until it had passed, he turned around and headed for the park. The single headlight of the motorcycle cut through the gloom as he roared up the narrow track toward the equipment shed. The road was badly rutted, and he had to swerve several times to miss a couple of monster potholes. *The city council should keep the place up better*, he thought with disgust.

After taking off his helmet and hanging it over the end of a handlebar, he combed his fingers through his hair. He hated the way the helmet matted it down.

For a moment he stood breathing in the cool night air. Then he looked up at the sky. There was only a sliver of moon, but the wind had blown away the clouds and left a black dome above him, studded with brilliant points of light. Out here in the country you could see a billion stars. Like when he was a kid. He'd loved to lie in the cool grass and look up at them. They'd filled him with wonder. Tonight they made him feel powerful—as if he were on the verge of fulfilling his destiny.

This morning, his horoscope had agreed. "Stress your confidence, purpose, direction. Victory!" it had said.

After depositing a quarter in the pay phone, he dialed quickly. The call was answered on the second ring.

"Hello?"

He recognized the sleepy voice at once, but he didn't say anything immediately.

"Hello?"

A pulse in his temple started to pound. But he took a deep breath and let it out slowly—as much to calm himself as to show that he hadn't hung up.

"Who's that?"

"You don't know me."

"What do you want?" There was an annoyed edge to the question.

"I know about what you and Ted have been up to." His voice was a hoarse whisper.

"Ted who?"

"Oh come on. Ted Chandler. Who do you think?"

The quick intake of breath on the other end of the line brought him a surge of pleasure that was almost physical. He hadn't realized until this moment how satisfying this part of it was going to be. And, damn, it would have been so easy to have missed the opportunity. But Ted just hadn't been able to keep his mouth shut when he was into something good.

"Get lost."

"You don't really want me to do that."

"What do you mean?"

"I'll call you back soon, and we can talk about it in more detail."

"Wait—"

"I'll be in touch."

The cool demeanor he'd maintained during the phone call snapped. Suddenly he felt like Superman. He'd better get what he wanted out of this—or else. Instead of hanging up the phone, he crashed the receiver into the cradle—once, twice, over and over until the plastic came apart in his gloved hand.

Monday, April 10

Phil Dorsey paid for a box of Old Time Spruce Gum and checked the Coca-Cola clock on the wall of McGuire's Drugstore. He had time for a cup of coffee—if he opened up the hardware store across the street a couple of minutes late.

The group in the little restaurant at the

back of the pharmacy smiled and nodded as he ambled toward them.

"How've you been?" Lois Pennington asked, moving over to make room for him at one of the round formica tables where local residents often gathered for meals and gossip.

"Gettin' a summer cold," Phil allowed.

Jodeen Crane, of the sharp eye and quick tongue, moved her chair out of sneezing range. "Keep it to yourself," the Acme checker muttered.

Cheryl Keene caught Phil's eye and struggled to suppress a grin. She and her boss Leonard McNaught from *The St. Stephens Record*, and Kitty Duncan, rounded out the morning's coffee klatsch.

"So how was Sara?" Phil asked.

"The poor child looked all washed out when she came back from the cemetery. But she's holding up better than you might expect," Lois reported.

Jodeen wiped up her remaining over-easy egg yolks with a triangle of toast. "Well, I could have told her she was makin' a mistake when she married that Ted Chandler. The way things were headin' in that marriage, they were going to hit rock bottom one way or the other."

Lois set down her teaspoon with a clatter. "No matter what shape the relationship was in, losing your spouse like that has got to throw you for a loop."

"That's the truth," Leonard muttered. He'd been through a messy divorce the year before.

"But I'll bet she's going to be better off now without him," Cheryl added quietly.

The waitress, who'd come over to refill several cups, nodded.

There was a moment of silence punctuated by the aroma of fresh-brewed coffee. Although Ted Chandler had done some good things for St. Stephens, he'd managed to rub a lot of old line residents the wrong way. Still, as the son-in-law of Dr. Harold Strickland, he'd been tolerated. And there'd been a grudging admiration for the way he could sell anything from a boathouse to a tobacco barn for a profit.

"So what brings you out so early this morning?" Lois asked, turning to Kitty.

"Ant traps."

"Nasty little pests," Jodeen commiserated.

For a while the conversation turned to the burgeoning summer insect population and beach traffic—equally noxious seasonal annoyances. But finally it returned to a more interesting topic—people. There were currents and eddies swirling through life in St. Stephens. Sooner or later the flow of words always swept the prime gossip into McGuire's Drugstore, like the flotsam from a shipwreck washing up on a beach and there for the picking.

Thursday, April 13

THE ST. STEPHENS RECORD

Community Services

Adopt a Pet
Rocky, a mixed-breed boxer-retriever, needs a home. A great guard dog and

good with children, too, he's just one of the many loving pets currently in residence at the Talbot County Humane Society shelter in Easton. The society urges local residents to consider opening their homes and their hearts to one of the many dogs or cats currently housed at the shelter. For more information, call the Humane Society at 555-2121.

Volunteers Needed
The Dogwood Nursing and Convalescent Home is looking for volunteers to spend an hour or two a week with residents. You can make a big difference in an older person's life. Contact our director of volunteer services, Margaret Ready, at 555-2222.

Sara sat at the Governor Winthrop desk in her living room writing thank-you notes to the people who had sent flowers and made contributions to the Bay Watchers fund in Ted's name. She appreciated the gesture even if Ted wouldn't have.

George Newhouse, the owner of the real estate agency where Ted had worked, had sent a large fruit basket. Looking up, she could see fruit flies hovering around the over-ripe apples and pears. As soon as she finished this letter, she'd have to sort through the stuff and decide what could go in the refrigerator with the rest of the food people had brought and what should be pitched out.

Sara sighed. Most of the fruit was going to

go bad anyway. Maybe she could take some down to the nursing home when she stopped by to see Miss Jane again.

She was just reading over the simple but caring card Kitty had sent when the doorbell rang. She pushed back the desk chair and went to see who was there. The sight of Police Chief Marcus Dailey on the front porch brought a sudden tight jab to the pit of her stomach, as if a muscular hand had squeezed her insides.

The last time he'd been here was in the middle of the night, when he'd come to tell her about Ted. Now what did the man want?

He was standing ramrod straight, the way he always did when he met the public.

She opened the door several inches. "Is this a business call?"

"I'm afraid so."

The solemn words made the phantom hand squeeze her stomach tighter. But she stepped aside and ushered him into the hall. "What can I do for you?"

"The contents of Mr. Chandler's car have been released." Dailey held out the cardboard box that had been tucked unobtrusively under his arm.

"Oh." Somehow she hadn't expected to get anything back. The car itself had been a total loss. Not only was the electrical system ruined, but Mr. Woodward from State Farm Insurance had volunteered that hitting a riverbed was like slamming into a tree going thirty miles an hour. He hadn't offered any more details when he'd seen the blood drain from Sara's face.

Dailey put the box on the side table. After

he'd gone, Sara stared at it for a long moment. Finally she lifted the lid. Pregnancy had heightened her sense of smell. Now the dank odor of mildew and murky water made her gag.

Even after almost a week, the maps were still slightly damp. Sara plucked them out between thumb and forefinger and dropped them in the lid of the box. Under the tire gauge was a wad of gas station receipts. The ink had run, making it impossible to read the imprint or the signatures.

She was about to put the maps back on top when she noticed a strand of maroon wool sticking up along the side of the Ford owner's manual. Curious, she dug down for the source and encountered a piece of needlepoint canvas. Had this really been in Ted's car?

Puzzled, Sara stared at the brownish-red background. The color of dried blood. She shuddered. What an ugly hue. But maybe the water had changed it.

In the center of the canvas was an elongated beige shape, squared off at the end. Sara squinted at it, trying to imagine what it might be. The handle of something? A tool? She didn't have a clue.

A large needle dangled from the end of the beige thread. Sara carefully wove it through the canvas so it wouldn't fall out.

Suddenly she felt confused and strangely edgy. Her mother had done needlepoint. In fact, one of her pictures used to hang in Dad's office. It showed the contents of a doctor's medical bag: a stethoscope, one of those rubber hammers they used to check your reflexes, a thermometer, a hypodermic.

But her mother had been dead for fifteen years, and her father had taken the picture down. Besides, this was much smaller than hers.

So who did it belong to? The woman Ted had been seeing? But why had she been stupid enough to leave it in the glove compartment?

Sara stood staring with distaste at the box on the table, wishing Dailey had just pitched the contents.

She wasn't going to keep the smelly, waterlogged stuff. She carried the box to the back porch and dumped it in the trash. Then she went back in and started to wash her hands.

But after she'd dried them, she couldn't stop herself from going outside again and staring at the trash can. After taking a deep breath, she lifted the lid and retrieved the needlepoint canvas. Even as she wondered why she felt compelled to save a piece of unfinished, ruined stitchery, she slid it into a plastic food bag and secured the end with a yellow twist-tie.

Now what was she going to do with the damn thing, she wondered with a little shudder of distaste. Certainly she wouldn't put it in her scrapbook.

There was a drawer in the laundry room where she kept string, thumbtacks, and other odds and ends.

Sara rearranged some of the junk so she could put the plastic bag beside a box of electrical fuses. The mess in the drawer was just the kind of thing Ted was always fussing at her about.

She was pressing a loop of extension cord down so she could close the drawer when her hand froze in mid-push. All at once a feeling of finality struck her in the chest, as though *she'd* crashed into a tree at thirty miles an hour. Sucking a gulp of air into her lungs, she sat down heavily on the wooden stool by the washtub.

All week long she'd been walking around in a sort of a fog, doing and saying the things that were expected of her. But now there was no one here to face except herself—and reality.

Ted wasn't going to fuss about the drawer— or anything else ever again. Her husband was dead and buried.

CHAPTER 6

Monday, April 24

She'd needed to get back to work, Sara thought as she sorted through a bin of watercolors in her gallery, The Bayside Collection. She'd just gotten in some stunning new ones, which meant she had to reduce the price on the old stock. When the bell over the front door jingled, she looked up and was surprised to see her sister, Ginny, standing in the doorway.

"Classes over early?"

"My sociology prof didn't show." Ginny's plain, freckled face broke into a grin.

Was that really the truth, or was her little sister skipping school? She sighed. Ginny had only been five when their mother died. Sara, who'd been eleven, had tried to take over. But she didn't feel she'd done all that great a job.

"Hey, I like these." Ginny stepped back to inspect a group of stark black-and-white photographs of the town's historic buildings and almost tripped over one of Ralph Meekins's duck decoys.

Sara rescued the strikingly lifelike blue-winged teal and set it on the counter.

For two weeks, she hadn't been able to do anything more constructive than bundle up Ted's clothing for Goodwill. Yesterday she'd come down to the gallery and started rearranging the stock.

Ginny wandered restlessly over to a display of weathered boxes that held a collection of Kitty Duncan's natural collage sculptures. "You sell much of this stuff?"

"Yes."

A year ago Sara had wondered if people would pay what Kitty was asking for polished stones and driftwood. But there was something so compelling about the way the young woman combined the colors and textures of natural objects that they'd sold well right from the first. In fact, Sara had doubled her order last time.

As Ginny passed the cash register, she reached for one of the business cards Sara kept in a Lucite holder. Humming to herself, she began to flex it back and forth between her thumb and forefinger.

"I—uh—need to talk to you."

"What's up?"

"School is sooo dumb. What would you think about my not going back?"

"Ginny, an education is important."

"You didn't finish college. If you think it's so great, why don't you take some classes?"

Sara walked slowly over to her antique rolltop desk and perched on the edge. Maybe this was the time to tell her sister about the pregnancy. "I might do that later. But right now, I can't."

Ginny looked at her curiously.

"I'm going to have a baby."

"Holy shit!" The business card snapped out of Ginny's fingers, and her eyes riveted to Sara's still-flat stomach. "You don't look pregnant. Are you sure?"

"I've been to the doctor."

"Not Dad—or Ben."

"No. I would have felt funny going to Ben."

"Yeah."

"I haven't told Dad yet."

Ginny laughed mirthlessly. "He'll probably fall apart."

Sara didn't know how to answer. She'd put off telling him she was carrying Ted's child. Was it the instinct to protect her unborn baby? Somehow she could hear him begging her to get rid of it. Hadn't she dreamed something like that? She shoved the thought into her subconscious before it had a chance to take on any real substance.

"Are you happy about it? I mean—now." The younger woman's voice dropped in pitch, and her eyes took on a soft, unfocused look.

"Oh, Ginny. I always wanted children. This means more to me than you could guess."

Ginny grinned. Crossing the space that separated them, she wrapped her arms around her sister.

Sara squeezed back.

"You got a lot of practice babying me."

"I didn't mind."

As the news settled in, a bemused smile played around the corners of Ginny's lips. "A baby. Gee. I guess I'm going to be an aunt," she murmured. "When are you due?"

"October."

"At least I won't have any problem getting back in time," Ginny muttered.

"Huh?"

Ginny shrugged her shoulder. "I've signed up for this Caribbean cruise at the beginning of July. While I'm down there I'm going to think about what I want to do next. That's what I really came in to tell you about."

Sara stared at her sister. The last thing in the world she would have expected from Ginny was something like this. "Isn't a cruise pretty expensive?"

"Dad's giving me a loan."

"He is? But you don't have any way to pay him back."

"Maybe I'll get a job."

The feeling of unreality persisted. "How did you ever come up with this crazy idea?" Sara asked.

"It's not crazy! In fact, somebody suggested—" she broke off in mid-sentence.

"Somebody?" Who could possibly have put this bizarre notion in her sister's head?

Ginny plowed on enthusiastically. "Haven't you seen those commercials on T.V. where they show everybody having such a good time? I sent for some brochures. It's easy to make friends on a cruise."

"Ginny, that's all just hype."

Before Sara could protest further, her sister started talking excitedly about the itinerary.

Sara was only half listening. She'd never seen Ginny look so bubbly—which did make her feel good.

Yet even as she watched Ginny's animated face, a voice in the back of her mind kept whispering, "Don't let her go."

Why was her scalp prickling as if icy fingers were roaming over the back of her head? Sara wondered. Maybe because Ginny was so inexperienced. Sara was just nervous about her sister going off on her own. But the trip might be good for her. It might teach her to be more independent.

Sara swallowed and forced a tentative smile onto her face. "It does sound like fun," she heard herself agreeing. "If you really think you can handle it."

"You fuss over me too much." Ginny's fingers pleated a fold of her wrinkled cotton skirt. "Maybe after school lets out you could help me go shopping for some cruisewear."

"All right."

"And we can get you some maternity clothes."

Sara nodded. What with telling Ben and her sister, the pregnancy had taken on a new reality, which brought a whole bunch of new anxieties.

Everything was going to be all right, she told herself. Yet she couldn't shake the feeling that fate was toying with her—like a cat that lets a little animal get away and then grabs it again before it can scurry to safety.

God, what's wrong with me? She was worried about everything all of a sudden.

Just because my husband had a terrible accident, it doesn't mean something's going to happen to Ginny or the baby, she told herself.

But she couldn't shake the nagging thought: bad luck comes in threes.

CHAPTER 7

Wednesday, April 26

Leonard McNaught, the editor of *The St. Stephens Record*, looked up. *The Record* was the town weekly. For daily news, there was *The Star Democrat*, published in Easton. "Miss Bea, it's good to see you again."

Beatrice Pierce smiled across the cluttered desk at the young man who'd taken over as editor. He was only forty, but he was growing into the responsibilities of the job.

"Cheryl said you'd called. Something about using the morgue to do some research for a book."

"If that's all right."

"Sure. What kind of book are you working on?"

"A history of St. Stephens." The lie came out smooth as honey.

"I bet this old town has some stories to tell."

"I'm sure."

Cheryl came in and handed the editor a stack of paste-ups. He rolled his eyes. "These have to go to the printer by four."

"I certainly do remember the four o'clock rush," Beatrice commiserated. "So I won't keep you any longer."

Leonard never had been very organized, she thought as she turned and headed toward the room in the back where a hundred years' worth of *St. Stephens Record*s was kept—along with files of articles and photographs, arranged by subject.

Let Leonard and the rest of the staff think she was writing some stuffy old tome, with dates and facts that nobody except the old biddies at the Historical Society would ever look at. This was going to be something completely different. A novel that would make *Peyton Place* look like *Rebecca of Sunnybrook Farm.* She'd been planning it for years. But seeing Harold Strickland at the funeral had spurred her to action.

There was a lot of gold to be mined out of this town. Everybody thought she was so prim and proper—and nice. Ha! It was going to be incredibly satisfying taking her revenge on St. Stephens. Lord, the scandals that simmered just under the quiet surface of this respectable little town ... sex, political corruption, sweetheart land deals, murder.

Of course, a lot of what she wanted to use wasn't in the papers. But the articles would jog her memory. And she knew a couple of people who'd be glad to help her.

Now let's see. Where did she want to start? Ted Chandler was certainly tempting. He was going to provide a lot of material—even though she'd have to change his name. Then there was some stuff farther back that she wanted to check too.

She pressed her lips together for a moment as a pang of guilt shot through her. Just so Sara didn't get hurt. Sara had been so nice to her. That poor woman deserved a better shake out of life than she'd gotten.

Thursday, April 27

THE ST. STEPHENS RECORD

Calendar of Events

New Exhibit at Bayside Collection
Talented local artist Kitty Duncan announces a new showing of her sculptures at The Bayside Collection. Her work incorporates natural objects such as shells, stones, and feathers. Many of her new pieces include materials collected during a recent trip to Ft. Myers, Florida. The Bayside Collection is open daily, 10 a.m. to 5:30 p.m.

Conservationist Group Meets
The Bay Watchers Society monthly meeting will be held at the Town Hall, Sunday June 4, at 7:30 p.m. Biologist Herb Knuppel from the Blackwater

Refuge will give a slide show on endangered species, and local duck carver Ralph Meekins will talk about some of the best area locations for bird watching. Orders will also be taken for wild birdseed.

Police Log
The pay phone at Bayside Park was vandalized some time late Sunday, April 9. The Talbot County Recreation Department is offering a $50 reward for information leading to the arrest of the party or parties involved.

Even though it was a hot night, his palms were icy as he pulled up to the phone down on the wharf. He'd almost made the call last night. But his horoscope had advised him to put off financial negotiations.

Today he was supposed to remain firm in his convictions and finish what he'd started. Well, he'd never intended anything else. Romance would play a major role. That had made his eyes twinkle.

He looked up and down the deserted dock. A cruise boat had pulled out around eight o'clock. It wouldn't be back until after eleven. Until then, the area would be dead as a body trapped in a car at the bottom of the river.

He dialed the number and waited. He'd pictured himself calm and in control. But as the phone rang, he could feel his heart starting to thump the way it had last time. What if no one was home? What if he didn't get the money?

Finally, on the fifth ring, the phone was answered. "Hello?"

"It's me again."

"What do you want?"

"Fifteen thousand dollars. In small, unmarked bills. Tomorrow."

"You're out of your fucking mind."

"Oh?"

"I don't have that kind of money laying around."

"How long would it take you to get it?"

"I'm not going to."

"Then I'll take my story to Leonard McNaught. And you'll be in the toilet with your friend Ted."

"Let me think about it."

"No. I'll give you until May 17th. That ought to be plenty of time. You can leave it just after dark, in a plastic garbage bag, at the old graveyard at Jester's Corner. Beside the stone that says Elzey. The one that's lying on its back. You know where that is?"

"The old graveyard? Yes."

"The Elzey stone is in the back left corner."

"How do I know that this will be the end of it?"

"You just have to take the word of a gentleman." He laughed and hung up. Then he stood there shaking beside the pay phone.

Friday, April 28

"For God's sake, why didn't you tell me?"

Sara tried to compose her features before she turned to face her father. "How did you find out?"

"Ginny. You didn't think she could keep it a secret, did you?"

"Dad— I was going to—"

"Jesus Christ. I thought it was like erasing the slate when you buried Ted. I thought you were going to be able to start over."

"I *am* starting over."

"But now you're going to be saddled with his kid."

Sara's jaw firmed. "I'm not going to be saddled with anything."

Harold Strickland's expression became hopeful, and she hurried on. "I mean—I want this baby. And you're not going to make me get—"

The blood drained out of his face, and he sat down abruptly. "Make you what?"

Sara swallowed. She didn't want it to be this way between the two of them. "Dad, this is your first grandchild," she whispered. "Can't you be happy about that?"

"Maybe I can try—for you." But he looked down at his hands so she couldn't see the bitterness in his eyes.

CHAPTER 8

Tuesday, May 16

Instead of climbing the short flight of steps to the front porch, Sara stood with her hands on her hips, surveying the six-inch grass. The unkempt look of the front yard was depressing. But the four-acre lot was too big to take care of on her own—especially in her present condition. She was going to have to find someone to mow it.

Just one of the new little problems in her life. She wandered around back, to her garden plot. Beside it was a single tire track across the grass. Panic suddenly surged in her throat like morning sickness. My God, had *he* been here while she was at work? She clenched her fists so hard that her nails dug into her palms. Why couldn't that bastard just leave her alone?

Sara took several deep, calming breaths.

Probably this was just the reaction the guy wanted. He wasn't really going to do anything to her. He just enjoyed getting her upset. Well, if she didn't play his game, he'd get tired of coming around.

Forcing the motorcyclist out of her mind, she turned back to the garden.

Usually by this time she'd planted tender leaf lettuce, spinach, and tomatoes. In the summer, she loved to come out and pick what she needed for a salad just before dinner. And weeding the garden in the evening had always been a good time to think back over the events of the day and make some plans for tomorrow. But this year she hadn't had the energy to plant anything.

A sprinkling of red drew her attention to the edge of the garden. Strawberries. She'd forgotten all about them. Stooping down, she pushed aside some of the leaves and saw dozens of the plump, red berries.

Smiling to herself, Sara went back inside. For a moment she stood in the silent hallway feeling a sense of freedom. She could do anything she wanted, with no deadlines. If she didn't get around to fixing dinner until late, so what.

Upstairs, she changed into a pair of old slacks with an elastic waist that still fit. Then she pulled on an oversized tee shirt and tied her hair back with a cotton bandanna.

Before she left the bedroom, she stopped in front of the mirror. Ginny might have said she wasn't showing yet, and that was true when she was dressed. But she was acutely aware of the way her body was changing. She stroked her hand over her middle for a minute, measuring the slight swell. She hadn't felt the baby move yet, but she knew it was growing inside her.

Maybe Dad would come around. Maybe he'd be happy for her. But even if he wasn't, she wouldn't let him spoil this.

The late afternoon sun was still warm when Sara brought a ceramic bowl outside and plopped down on the grass beside the berry patch. There were more strawberries than she'd thought. In fact, there were enough so that she could eat one for every three or four she dropped into the bowl. They were sweet and juicy. Delicious.

Sara was enjoying this simple pleasure when suddenly she realized she wasn't alone. There was a startled moment as she eyed the pair of brown loafers and long legs beside her. Shading her eyes, she looked up and then let out the sharp breath she'd drawn in.

"Ben." She wiped her berry-stained fingers on her slacks and started to push herself to her feet.

"Don't get up." He hunkered down beside her. "I guess I should have called. But I was passing by and thought I'd stop. I hope that's all right."

"Don't be silly. It's good to see you."

They hadn't talked since the day on the beach. A couple of times she'd thought about calling him, but she'd always put the phone down. She'd found out in the weeks after Ted's death that the people who really wanted to keep in touch made the effort. Now she realized how much she'd missed Ben.

"I've been thinking about you. How are you doing?" he asked.

"Pretty well."

She wasn't sure what else to say. He knelt there, looking at her. Then, as if he were slightly ill at ease, he reached over, pulled a plump strawberry off a nearby plant, and popped it in his mouth. "These are great."

"We could go in and have some with—" She thought for a moment. "Milk. I don't have any cream."

"You've made a sale."

He picked up the bowl and helped her to her feet. Together they started toward the house.

"You look good."

Her cheeks bloomed with the same tinge as the berries. "Thank you, Dr. Langley. But I know I look like a mess."

"No. There's a glow about you. Pregnancy must agree with you."

Sara laughed. "You wouldn't say that in the morning."

"Been sick?"

"Some."

"What does your OB-GYN say?"

"Nothing to worry about—unless it gets worse." She pulled off the bandanna, stuffed it in her pocket, and fluffed out her hair with her fingers.

"It should be easing off soon." He lifted the latch and opened the screen door. "Who are you seeing?"

"Dr. Birch."

"He's got a good reputation."

Ben leaned against the counter as she

washed the berries and began to remove the hulls.

Sara saw him watching her. For a moment his dark gaze tried to capture hers, but she looked back down at the strawberries. "If you really want to go whole hog, there's some ice cream and pound cake in the freezer."

"You've discovered my weakness."

"A sweet tooth?"

"Um hum."

Sara set the ice cream on the counter to soften. Then she got out the foil-wrapped package of cake and sliced off two frozen slabs. She opened the door of the toaster oven and set them on the rack.

Fishing up the cord where it dangled down beside the counter, she started to slide the plug into the socket. As the prongs connected with the electric line, there was a loud pop and a blue flash. At the same time, the overhead light went off.

Sara jumped backwards and yelped, pulling the plug back out of the socket. Ben sprang forward and grabbed her by the shoulders. "Sara! Are you hurt? Did that give you a shock?"

She struggled to catch her breath. "I don't think so. Just startled." She stared at the appliance. "I don't understand. It was all right this morning."

"Well, you'd better not use that again until you have it checked out."

"Don't worry, I won't."

He reached over and flipped the switch on the lights. "Looks like it tripped the circuit breaker."

"Unfortunately, I don't have circuit breakers."

"Fuses?"

She nodded.

"Do you have any?"

"I think there's a package in the utility drawer."

"Can I help you?"

Sara laid a red marking pen and a half-full envelope of lettuce seeds on the counter. "I really do remember sticking a package of fuses in here," she muttered as she pulled out the plastic-wrapped needlepoint canvas.

"That smells like swamp water. What are you saving it for?"

Her stomach clenched. "Nothing. Okay?"

"Sure."

A moment later she dug out the fuses and held the package up triumphantly.

When she opened the cellar door, Ben looked surprised. "I didn't think houses around here had basements."

"A few do." Sara tried the switch at the top of the stairs. The light didn't come on. "Must be on the same circuit as the kitchen," she muttered as she got a flashlight from under the kitchen counter.

"Let me go first."

The stairs creaked as she followed Ben down. The cellar was cool, musty and unfinished. The flashlight played on spiderwebs and little piles of dust as Ben swept it around the large room.

"I'm glad you're here. I never liked this hole in the ground very much." Sara realized she was whispering.

"Yeah."

"Ted spent a lot of time down here with his tools. But I don't come down unless I have to."

Sara pulled the metal door open and studied the fuse panel. "Well, Doctor. You can at least assist."

He laughed and trained the flashlight so that she could remove the burned-out fuse and replace it.

"I should have left the light on." As Sara stepped back she bumped against Ben. She didn't immediately draw away.

Upstairs, neither one of them had been sure what to say. Down here in the shadowy basement, words weren't quite so important.

His arm came up around Sara. She closed her eyes and leaned back against him, conscious of the way his warm body contrasted with the cool, damp air.

His fingers smoothed along her arms. He'd told himself he was coming over here to talk about Harold. That was a legitimate excuse for seeking Sara out. But as soon as he'd seen her sitting on the ground, totally absorbed in picking strawberries—and eating almost as many as she put in the bowl—he'd known he didn't want his problems with Harold Strickland to intrude on the visit.

He'd stayed away from Sara for as long as he could, testing himself—trying to find out if he had just been wanting the forbidden.

Well, that sure wasn't it. He still wanted her—more than ever now that she didn't belong to another man. But he still couldn't find the words to come right out and ask how she felt about the two of them. Not when her husband had been dead less than two months.

Yet the unguarded way she was standing in his arms told him that the attraction wasn't all one-sided. He closed his eyes and skimmed his lips over the top of her hair, breathing in her clean, healthy scent.

When she didn't move, it took a lot of will-power to keep from bending to kiss the tender skin of her neck.

For a moment Sara let herself bask in his touch. There was more than just physical attraction between them, wasn't there? She thought so. But it was hard to trust her instincts—after they'd been trampled on for so long.

She cleared her throat. "We'd better go back upstairs before the ice cream melts all over the counter."

"I forgot about it."

So had she—until her mind had started scrambling for an excuse to pull back from the intimacy of the moment.

There was an awkward silence as they came back up into the lighted kitchen.

"Listen, if you'd rather I left—"

"No." Her fingers compressed the softened sides of the ice cream box. "It's dinnertime. We shouldn't be having dessert first."

"That's right." He looked at the shortcake makings. "I hope you're eating better than this."

She couldn't hide the guilty look on her face. "I really haven't felt much like cooking."

"Why don't you let me take you out?"

"Ben, I'd like to. But—"

"Sure."

"Really. But I promised to visit Miss Jane at the Dogwood Nursing Home. She's the lady who owns that beach we visited—Swan Point."

"Yeah."

Sara looked at the uncertainty in Ben's eyes. Did he think she was just making an excuse? If she didn't say something else now, he might not ask again. "But I'd love to go out later in the week—if you still want to."

"Friday night?"

"Yes."

"Then I'll let you get ready for your visit."

"Wait."

He looked at her questioningly.

"I've got time before I have to change. We might as well have the shortcake for dinner. And I'll start reforming my eating habits tomorrow."

Bobby Craig leaned his bike against a fence with a No Trespassing sign tacked to the top. Shielding his eyes against the late afternoon sun, he squinted at the old house.

The guy who lived there was pretty mean. Last week he'd come out waving a shotgun when he'd seen Josh Morris and Bobby sneaking down to the crick out back. The fishin' there was great, but Josh was a chicken. He wouldn't come back here anymore—even to get the fishing poles they'd dropped.

Well, he was braver than Josh. That was how he'd mashed that nail in his foot at River Meadows. Josh had dared him to go upstairs in one of the houses they were building, and he'd done it. At least Josh hadn't blabbed to his mom—and neither had Dr. Langley.

They'd ditched the fishing poles at the edge of the field out in back. Maybe the guy hadn't picked them up.

Bobby's gaze flicked to the old house. It looked pretty bad. The paint was peelin'. And one of the upstairs windows was broke. The old Atwater place, people called it. But he didn't remember anyone named Atwater ever living in it.

There were houses around here that looked worse. But something about this one gave him the creeps. He sure wasn't going to come here trick or treating on Halloween.

Today there weren't any lights or signs of activity. Maybe nobody was home.

Cautiously, he started poking through the waist-high chicory and Queen Anne's lace. No fishing poles. But he did find some good stuff. A piece of old snake skin that might even be from a copperhead. And a little round blue-metal tag that said "rabies vaccination" and the current year. Some dog must have lost it.

After stuffing the skin and the rabies tag into his backpack, he looked around again. The fishing poles could be in the garage. Dropping down to the ground, he began to creep up on the old building commando-style. When he reached the weathered siding, he eased up so that he could look in the window.

He was surprised to see a German shepherd lying on the concrete floor. A short length of rope tied it to a wooden post. Brown ears pricked up, and a long tail thumped against the ground when the dog spotted him.

Bobby stared back at the dog. It looked scared. Maybe the people who lived here had beaten it or done something else bad. Why was it out in the garage? If he had a great dog like that, he'd want to keep it with him. There was no way he could put his sudden conviction into words. He only knew that, all at once, it was real important to get that dog out of there.

Yeah. Why not?

His eyes flicked to the door. It was fastened with a big old padlock.

When his fingers twisted the cold metal, the dog started to bark.

For a moment, Bobby froze. Jeeez, what if he got caught here? His ass would be grass for sure.

With a fearful glance toward the house, Bobby turned and dashed across the field. From the shelter of the trees, he looked back at the old Atwater place. The dog was quiet now, and the house still looked deserted. But he couldn't take a chance. He just couldn't.

His mom would say he'd done the right thing by not breaking in there, he told himself. But his chest felt tight as he climbed on his bike and peddled away.

After Ben had driven away, Sara went back into the kitchen and eyed the toaster oven. It seemed to lie there on the counter like a coiled snake, ready to strike at her again. It had been a wedding gift, so it wasn't that old. Maybe she could have it fixed.

Then the reality of the close call she'd had

smashed into her. If she had gotten a shock, the baby could have been hurt.

She closed her eyes and stood with her arms crossed protectively over the new life growing inside her. Nothing was going to hurt her baby. She wouldn't let it.

Vividly remembering the blue flash, she made sure once more that the toaster was unplugged. Then she snatched it up, marched to the back door, and dropped it in the trash with a decisive thunk.

CHAPTER 9

Wednesday, May 17

Ginny Strickland flopped down on her bed and picked up the pile of glossy travel brochures from the nightstand.

She'd been looking at them a lot, daydreaming about the trip. There were pictures of the exotic ports she'd be visiting: the Bahamas, with long stretches of sandy beach and coconut palms; Martinique with white stucco buildings set off by vines covered with purple and orange flowers. She wondered what they were called.

A picture from the cruise ship showed a young couple with their arms wrapped around each other. The woman was smiling up at the man and holding a glass of white wine. She'd have to let go of the guy to drink it.

Ginny's eyes danced down the list of activities. Eight great meals and snacks a day! Luxurious service. Entertainment. Singles cocktail parties.

Maybe she'd meet somebody special. She could stand up against him like that with her arms around his neck, a wine glass balanced between her fingers.

Downstairs, the front door opened and then closed. Ginny dropped the brochure she was holding and ran to the window. It was almost dark, but she could make out the figure of her father hurrying down the walk to the car.

She worried her bottom lip between her teeth. He was leaving again without telling her where he was going. He'd done that so many times lately, and she didn't know what to say to him.

You'd think he had a secret life or something. He'd even put a lock on the old garage. But there was nothing but junk in there anyway. Who'd even want to go in?

Where was he going now? It flashed through her mind that she should follow him. For a moment her fingers clenched the smooth wood of the windowsill. She'd never admit how worried she was—or how shut out her father was making her feel. But if he caught her sneaking after him, he'd freak out. Then maybe he wouldn't come up with the final payment for the cruise.

Shuffling slowly back across the room, she plopped back down on the bed. Her father had changed so much over the past year and a half. She couldn't tell how he was going to react from one minute to the next. It was weird the way he'd acted when she first mentioned the trip. A couple of years ago he would have gone into his routine about the way money didn't grow on trees. Instead, he'd agreed right away, almost like he was trying to get rid of her or something.

She pursed her lips in thought. These days she couldn't figure him out. Sara didn't have to live with him anymore. Lucky her.

He was drinking a lot more. First it had just been in the evenings. But now she was beginning to wonder if he was sneaking a drink or two between patients.

God, what was she going to do? She just couldn't take it anymore. She wanted to get out of this house, out of this town. Maybe she really would meet someone on the cruise who would be her ticket to somewhere better. Yeah, maybe. For a few minutes, she stared dreamily into space, threading her fingers through her thin auburn hair and piling it on top of her head.

Then she got up and took her diary out of the empty Russell Stover Candy box in the bottom of her nightstand. Opening the book, she began to write a very romantic scene.

She could almost see the dimly lit lounge on the cruise ship, the air hazy with cigarette smoke, a band playing light rock music, a table piled high with all sorts of little hors d'oeuvres. Like in the pictures she'd just been looking at. Like in one of the romance novels she read when she was supposed to be studying.

She'd be wearing a sexy red cocktail dress. Some gorgeous guy would be watching her from across the room, gliding closer and closer, and then making his move.

"You're shy, aren't you?" he'd say.

In her fantasy, she smiled up at him myste-
riously, through her mascara-thickened lashes.
She'd spent hours at the beauty salon on the
boat that afternoon having a complete makeover.

"I've been looking for someone like you all
my life," he murmured. "Someone real."

"Me too."

Before he took her in his arms, she set down
her glass of white wine. They started to dance,
and it was more romantic than any scene
she'd ever read. Then, magically, the clock
was striking midnight, and she realized with
a little start that they'd been absorbed in each
other for hours.

She looked up at him. "I don't want it to
end."

"Your cabin or mine?"

"Yours."

Somewhere during the fantasy, Ginny had
stopped writing it down. She got up quickly
and locked the bedroom door. Then she changed
into her prettiest cotton nightgown, turned
off the lights, and slipped under the covers.

She and her lover were in bed together. His
name was . . . Chad.

She turned her head on the pillow and
reached out to stroke his face. In the darkened
room, she couldn't see his features. But she
knew he had thick brown hair and blue eyes
the color of the Caribbean.

"Is this the first time for you?" Chad whispered.

"Yes."

"Then we'll make it something you'll never
forget."

His lips pressed against hers, and she opened her mouth so that she could feel the silky rasp of his tongue. "You're so sexy," she murmured. "I'm so glad you picked me out of the crowd."

"You're driving me wild. I can hardly wait to possess you." His hands skimmed languidly across her breasts, and she shivered as delicious sensations rippled through her body. With a helpless little moan, she surrendered to the pleasure of his caresses.

He drove a couple hundred yards up a dirt road into the loblolly pines and cut the engine. For a moment his gloved fists clenched the handlebars. If everything went as planned, he'd have the money soon. This wasn't usually his style. But you had to seize the opportunities that came along. Especially when you needed quick cash.

Good lunar aspect coincides with creativity, travel, change, variety, speculation. When he'd read the Astrograph in the *Star Democrat* that morning, he'd gotten a surge of confidence.

He peered through the trees at the burial plot and congratulated himself once again on the location. It was perfect. Not just for the symbolism—although that was important. People stayed away from weed-choked old graves and fallen tombstones—especially at night. Nobody would be around to get in the way.

But he'd planned it all out carefully, just to be on the safe side. There was a crumbling stone wall back in the woods. He'd spent a lot of time there watching the area and making sure he was right about the place.

Now it was almost dark. Quickly, he lowered the kickstand and hurried to the ancient stone wall, where he settled down to wait.

This whole thing was so tricky. Thank God he didn't have to do it all himself. He had an ally living in town. A person no one would suspect was helping him.

He started to laugh. It was a choked, hollow sound that shattered the twilight stillness and sent half a dozen sparrows flapping out of a nearby tree.

For a moment his vision blurred, and he heard a roaring in his ears like someone had clapped huge seashells to the sides of his head. He had to flatten his hands against the stone wall to anchor himself to reality.

Don't think about anyone else until you get back home, he told himself. *You're the one who's here now. The one who's in charge. And you've got to concentrate on success. You can accomplish anything you want, if you put your mind to it. Take it one step at a time. Just one step at a time.*

He leaned his head back against the cool stones and took several deep breaths. A few minutes later, he heard the purr of a large, expensive car. As the gray-and-chrome vehicle pulled into view, he scrunched down out of sight.

Inside the black gloves, his hands were sweating. After a moment, he took a cautious peek over the top of the wall.

In the dim light he could just make out a hesitant figure standing at the edge of the deserted burial plot. Clenched in his fingers was a large plastic garbage bag. It looked bulky, like it was full of money.

The son of a bitch was going to follow instructions!

Still he held his breath until the mark started walking toward the back left corner of the weed-choked acre. It took only a moment to set the bag down beside the specified headstone.

"Well, here's your blood money. I hope you're satisfied," an accusing voice shouted into the darkness.

He didn't answer. And he waited for fifteen minutes after his victim had gotten back into the car and driven away before he stood up and went to retrieve the bag. When his hand closed over a stack of bank notes, he felt his chest swell. He'd done it. He'd pulled it off. Now he was all set to go ahead with his nasty little plans for Ginny and Sara.

CHAPTER 10

Thursday, May 18

As soon as he put his hand on the door of the old garage out in back of the house, the German shepherd started to bark.

"Shut up. Or you're not going to get any dinner."

The dog couldn't understand the words. But it must have caught the tone of his voice. The barking quieted to a whine.

When he stepped through the door, the animal was crouched in the corner, ears down and tail flat. Just where he'd tied it. The damn thing had knocked over its water bowl again. It cocked its head to one side and regarded him expectantly.

"Good boy." The words almost stuck in his throat. "Good Bruno."

When the dog heard its name and smelled

the food in the bowl he'd brought, it started to wag its tail.

Some clown had given it a German name before getting tired of it and dropping it off at the pound in Easton.

Christ, that place! It had been awash with pee and disinfectant. And he'd had to go back three times to get what he wanted.

He hadn't been able to ride the motorcycle, so he'd had to risk driving the car. He'd pulled a hat down over his head so no one would recognize him.

Three hellish trips to Easton. And not just any of the mangy mutts they were trying to get rid of would do. It had to be a big dog, of course, and weigh at least a hundred pounds. About the weight of a slender young woman. Ginny Strickland to be exact.

The second time, he'd almost settled for one that was gray and black. But the coloring was important. He wanted an undercoat of brown, with gray across the shoulders and on the ruff.

Just like—Hunter.

He stopped and shuddered. It was as if it had happened yesterday . . . the barking, the snarls, the feel of those teeth sinking into his thigh.

He pressed his hands over his ears and struggled to bring the tremors under control.

The dog whined again, and its head jerked up. "I'll take care of you in a little while, Bruno," he promised. "Want your dinner, boy?"

Bruno sat up and barked.

He'd skipped feeding the shepherd last night

so it would be good and hungry this afternoon. He was pretty sure it wouldn't notice the sedative. Now he set the dish down on the cement floor and pushed it toward the animal.

The beast was so ravenous that it started to devour the food at once. While he watched it eat, he thought about the woman from the pound, the dumpy old bat with the gray hair like a cottontail on top of her head. She hadn't even questioned the name and address he'd given her.

"I'm so glad we had the dog you wanted."

"Um hum."

"I feel so happy when they go to a good home. We were going to have to put the poor thing to sleep tomorrow."

"I'm glad I got him in time."

She'd made him wait while they gave the stupid dog rabies and distemper shots, for God's sake. As soon as he'd gotten home, he'd pitched the rabies tag across the field in back of the house. What did he need the damn thing for, anyway?

After the dog finished wolfing down the meal, he filled the water dish.

Bruno slurped up some water and then lay down.

"That's right, Bruno. Just relax."

He watched the dog for a moment. Then he stepped outside to get the supplies he'd left in a metal box on the old table by the door.

His laboratory was a converted bathroom upstairs. Before he'd crossed the yard, he'd taken out a sample of the toxin he'd produced a month ago. The equipment and growth medium had come from a lab supply company in Baltimore.

He'd gotten the idea from a talkative lab technician. The guy had told him everything except how to do it. But he'd learned the techniques from a college microbiology textbook and lab manual. The secret was in making sure you didn't let the temperature get too high or too low, and in keeping any air out of the bottles. Of course, you had to be damned careful with the stuff.

It had taken him a couple of months to perfect the process. Now he had it down pat. Growing the stuff . . . The safety procedures . . . Concentrating the toxin . . . It had worked perfectly.

First he'd tried it on mice and hamsters. Eventually he'd needed something bigger. If he'd been a student, he would have gotten an A on the project. But he'd never run a test to find out how long the poison stayed potent. Now that he had the money for his trip, he was going to have to figure out how to pack the stuff.

After so many years, it was all coming together. If they realized what was really in his mind, they'd lock him up and throw away the key. But he'd known he had to keep his private thoughts hidden. And he'd fooled them. Just like he'd fooled everyone in St. Stephens.

He couldn't repress a little giggle. He could feel the excitement coursing down his veins, like the time when he was a kid and had gotten an electric shock from the old radio in the living room.

Bruno's head was down on his paws now, his eyes half closed.

He'd debated for a long time about doing it like this. There would have been more pleasure in it if the dog had been fully awake. But this was safer.

Quietly he approached the listless animal. He was ready to spring back outside the range of the rope if the dog made any threatening move. But when he reached out a cautious hand and ruffled the fur of its neck, it only turned its head toward his palm. A wet tongue licked across his wrist.

"Good boy. Good, Bruno. Good, Hunter."

Suddenly, it wasn't Bruno. It was Hunter. That other son-of-a-bitching dog. The one that had torn a piece out of his leg fifteen years ago.

It took every ounce of self-control he possessed to keep from jabbing the needle viciously into the dog's flank. Instead, he was gentle as he pressed the plunger. Then he took the stopwatch out of his trouser pocket.

It was only fifty seconds before the dog's body went rigid. He picked up a paw and it flopped back down on the floor when he let it go.

The animal stared at him stupidly. Just like Ted had.

Seventy seconds until its breathing became labored.

Two minutes before its heart started to spasm.

CHAPTER 11

Friday, May 19

Sara didn't want Ben to see her sitting in the living room waiting for him to arrive. So she went back to the kitchen and started clearing half-empty boxes of cereal and stale crackers out of the pantry.

When the doorbell rang, she dumped a package of seasoned bread crumbs into the trash can and brushed off her hands. Then she smoothed down the skirt of her yellow sundress. She'd picked it because it still made her waist look slim.

She was a little breathless as she ushered Ben into the hall.

He regarded her with appreciation. "You look lovely."

"Thank you. It feels good to get dressed up." Her fingers played with the delicate shell necklace Kitty Duncan had brought her from Florida.

Ben seemed different too. He usually looked a little rumpled, as if he didn't think much about his appearance. Tonight he was wearing a crisp navy blazer, gray slacks, and a light blue Oxford-cloth shirt.

"I've made the reservations for six-thirty."

"Good."

Outside, he helped her up into the Blazer. Fifteen minutes later they pulled into the parking lot of the Harbor Watch Restaurant. It was out on a large estate along the Miles River that had been sold and subdivided into expensive building lots bordering a golf course. There was an inn, as well as the restaurant, on the riverbank.

When Ben had called the night before and asked her where she wanted to eat, Sara had thought of this place at once. It catered to tourists and businessmen who scheduled seminars and golfing holidays at the resort. So she wasn't too likely to meet anyone from town.

As they waited for the hostess to seat them, Sara glanced a bit nervously toward the brick and polished-wood bar and was glad she didn't recognize anyone.

She could name a number of people who wouldn't think it was proper for her to be going out to dinner with another man so soon after her husband's death.

Then she turned to Ben and saw the smile in his eyes. She smiled back. Was there anything immoral about being happy for a change?

The hostess showed them to a window table

where they could look out over the sailboats plying the broad river. Closer to the water's edge, a pair of swans bobbed along on the waves.

"This is nice," Sara said after the waiter had taken their orders.

"Do you sail?" Ben asked as she leaned forward to watch a majestic-looking ketch.

"Everyone who grew up around here has webbed feet. When I was a teenager, I used to crew on one of the log canoes, for the races at Perry Cabin."

"Rowing?"

"No. They're small sailboats put together from logs. The early settlers copied some of the Indians' techniques."

They stopped the conversation while the waiter brought bread and butter. Then Sara began to explain a bit about the area's traditional craft.

Ben sat back and listened. He didn't really care much about boats. But he was enjoying hearing her talk and watching the play of expressions across her face.

She was enthusiastic, animated, and more beautiful than he'd ever seen her. He'd been right. Marriage to Ted Chandler had put a damper on her natural *joie de vivre*.

A little wave of uneasiness lapped at his mind. Then he gave himself a mental shake. Why was he doing this to himself? Her husband was out of the picture for good. Things were going to work out for him—if he just didn't mess them up.

"But they know a lot more about it than I

do at the Maritime Museum. Haven't you ever been there?" Sara asked.

"What?" Ben looked a little chagrined.

"The Maritime Museum."

"I keep meaning to stop by."

"We could go some afternoon—" She broke off the sentence, wondering if she sounded too eager.

"I'd like to."

They waited while plates of crab cakes, baked potatoes, and steamed vegetables were set before them.

"I've been doing most of the talking," Sara murmured when the waiter had departed.

"I like to listen."

"Probably one of the things that makes you a good doctor."

"How do you know I'm any good?"

"Come on, Ben. This is a small town. You're a prime topic of discussion in the mornings down at McGuire's Drugstore when the Main Street merchants are sitting around having coffee."

He looked a bit disconcerted. "I am?"

She grinned, and her voice mimicked waitress Patty Trice. "You should have seen the way Dr. Langley patched up old Tom Cunningham. He saved that man's arm."

He shook his head. "I didn't do anything any other doctor wouldn't have done."

"Nevertheless."

Ben forked up some of the crab cake. "This is pretty good. I never had crab cakes before I came east."

"That's right. You're from California."

"Bakersfield."

"So why did you come all the way across the country to go into practice?"

Damn. He'd set himself up for the inevitable question. Some day he'd think of a glib response. "I just needed a change of scenery."

Sara pushed at a sliver of carrot on her plate. She could tell by the tone of his voice that he didn't want to pursue the subject, and that piqued her curiosity. But she wasn't going to do anything to spoil the good mood of the evening.

"Sometimes I think about what would have happened if I'd gone away to college."

He reached out across the table and covered her hand with his. "I'm glad you're here now."

She looked up and was momentarily startled by the intensity of his gaze.

Turning toward the window, Sara saw that the sun had set while they'd been eating. She hadn't even noticed.

"I'd better not have dessert," she said to Ben after the busboy had taken their plates.

He looked disappointed.

"But you can."

"I wasn't thinking about dessert. I hate to have the evening end."

She nodded. "I do too. But I've got to get to the shop early. Saturday is my busiest day."

Outside, the wind from the river had turned nippy, and Sara shivered. When Ben slung his arm around her shoulder, she snuggled against him.

"I'd like to do this again soon," he said as he helped her back into the Blazer.

"So would I."

Mist was rolling in, and Ben drove carefully down Route 33, his headlights probing into the swirls of whiteness.

Inside the restaurant Sara had felt warm and cozy. Now the trees on either side of the road seemed to disappear into a shadow land of unreality. And tendrils of vapor reached out toward the car like witches' fingers. Sara huddled on the seat, hugging her arms around her shoulders.

"A little spooky, isn't it?" Ben muttered.

She struggled to keep a tremor out of her voice. "It can get like this around here."

"Yeah."

All at once she couldn't shake the sensation that something was going to happen. Something bad. No, that was ridiculous, she told herself sternly. Being pregnant had changed her responses to a lot of things. Now she was just reacting to the fog. It was making her claustrophobic.

The mist was even thicker on the side road that led to Sara's house. She leaned forward, peering into the misty darkness. "There's my mailbox."

She felt a tremendous surge of relief as the Blazer turned in at the familiar landmark. Safe at home . . .

But a few seconds later, Ben slammed on the brakes.

Sara jerked forward. Only the seat belt kept her from hitting the dash.

Ben swore under his breath. "Sorry! Sara, are you all right?"

"Yes. What happened?"

"I saw something in front of the car. An animal. I'd better have a look."

He backed up so that the headlights were focused on a lumpy gray and brown shape in the middle of the driveway. It looked like a dog.

Ben got out of the car and stood for a moment staring at the still form. Sara watched him squat down beside it, feeling for a pulse in its neck.

"Poor thing. Did a car hit it?" she asked, coming up beside him.

"I'm not sure."

"Is it—?"

He nodded. "It's dead. Do you recognize the animal? Maybe it belongs to a neighbor."

Sara studied the gray and brown markings. It was a fine-looking German shepherd, but not well groomed. And it wasn't wearing a collar. A dead dog. Back there in the fog, had she somehow gotten a premonition of this lifeless form lying in her driveway? "I haven't seen it before. But I have neighbors I hardly see, either." She gave a nervous little shrug. The dog looked so pitiful lying there. Was it lost? Had it died alone, in pain? Feeling a sudden wave of sympathy for the animal, Sara stooped down and reached to smooth her fingers across the coarse fur.

Ben pushed her hand away. "In your condition, you'd better not touch it. You don't know what it died of."

"I guess I wasn't thinking."

She stood up and took a step back as Ben reached down and lifted one of the dog's paws. Sara could see that it was stiff. When he checked the other paw, he got the same response. "That's odd."

"What?"

"Rigor mortis."

She'd heard her father use the term. It referred to the chemical changes that took place in the muscles of the body following death. They stiffened. And then they gradually relaxed again some time later. She couldn't remember how long that took.

"Doesn't that always happen?"

"Yes. But never right after expiration. The dog certainly wasn't in the middle of the driveway when we left for dinner."

"Maybe he crawled here."

Ben turned to her, an unreadable expression on his face. "Maybe. But, Sara, unless I'm mistaking cadaveric spasm for rigor, this animal's been dead for at least twelve hours."

"Then how—?"

He shrugged. "It's almost like it died somewhere else and was dumped here."

She shuddered. Had someone deliberately disposed of a dead dog in front of her house? Who would do a sick thing like that? A cold chill swept over her like a wind blowing from an open grave. An image of a black motorcycle and faceless rider flashed into her head. The shepherd was strapped across the back of the machine.

No, that was stupid. You couldn't drive a motorcycle down the highway with a dead dog on the luggage rack. Or could you? In the fog . . . ?

She shook her head. She was conjuring up phantoms out of the mist. Nobody would go that far over the business with the eagles . . . unless they were crazy.

Stop it, she commanded herself. Probably someone had just picked her driveway at random.

"Let me take you inside."

"Yes." All at once she wanted to lock the front door behind her.

Ben waited until Sara got back in the car before pulling the stiff body to the side of the drive. They made the short trip up to the house in silence. Sara could hear the blood pounding in her ears.

"Do you have a couple of large plastic bags?" Ben's voice seemed to come from far away.

With an effort, she nodded. "I'll get them for you." She hurried into the house and began to rummage under the sink, glad Ben had given her something to do. She could hear him washing his hands in the laundry room.

When she offered him the bags, he put them down on the table and turned to her. His arms came up to draw her close, pressing her head against his shoulder. "Don't let this upset you."

She gulped, feeling tears brimming in her eyes. Instead of focusing on her own apprehension, she concentrated on the shepherd. "That poor dog. It was a handsome animal. It just needed someone to take care of it."

"I know." His voice was soothing.

"It seems like you're around to pick up the pieces every time something bad happens to me."

"I don't mind."

He looked down into her upturned face, wanting her to know that he felt more than he'd told her. Then suddenly he was lowering his head. His lips brushed over hers. It was his first overt move toward possession.

She could have drawn back. But she didn't.

His arms went around her tightly, pulling her against the hard wall of his chest. Then his lips were moving over hers.

"Sara," he muttered against her mouth.

She couldn't answer. Had she ever been kissed with such warmth and reassurance? Yet at the same time, there was an underlying passion that stirred her senses to life.

When he finally raised his head, she was still clinging to his shoulders.

"Oh, Ben." She shook her head, trying to clear her thoughts. "I—"

"Sara, I remember what I felt when I first met you. It was a real kick in the stomach when I found out you were married."

As she tried to speak, he pressed his fingers gently against her lips. "All I'm saying is that I haven't suddenly started caring about you. It's been there for a long time. But I couldn't say anything."

"I guess I knew."

"But you weren't the kind of woman who would be disloyal to her husband."

"That's right." She swallowed around the lump in her throat. "Ben, four years ago, I made a big mistake when I married Ted Chandler. I guess, for the past year I'd been emotionally distancing myself from him." She sighed. "He was so wrapped up in himself, I don't think he could tell."

"Sara—"

"Let me finish. I was working up my nerve to talk to him about a divorce—before I found out about the baby. Then I decided I should give it one more try. But all the soul-searching and all the rationalizing didn't mean anything when he died like that. The shock shattered all my logic."

"He hurt you, didn't he?"

"Yes."

"Physically?"

"He didn't beat me—if that's what you mean."

"Then what?"

"Ben, I can't talk about it with you. Not yet. And I can't help being—afraid—to—trust my feelings."

"Sara, I'm not going to push you into anything you're not comfortable with. I just want you to know you can count on me."

Somehow, his words and the things she'd told him unlocked a flood of emotions. "Ben, when you kissed me just now, it felt right. But I don't like being—dependent." She stared up at him, hoping he understood. It was so hard to open up to someone again.

A slow grin spread across his face. "I can work with that."

She gave him back a shaky little smile. When he kissed her again, there was a new openness in her response—and in his. When his tongue stroked along the sensitive skin of her inner lips, she couldn't hold back a shuddering little sigh of gratification.

The sound was like a bolt of pleasure shooting through him. He wanted to keep holding her, to keep kissing her, to shift her body so that he could cup her breasts. He'd fantasized about this for so long that the reality had a lot more potency than he had any right to expect from a first kiss. Which meant that if things went any further, it was going to be damn hard to stop.

He drew in a deep breath and stepped back slightly. "It's late. And you have to get up early. I'd better go."

She blinked. "I—yes." She didn't want him to leave. But the feelings he'd created were so intense that she wasn't entirely comfortable with them.

"I don't like the idea of your being alone. Not after finding that dog."

In the heat of the kiss, she'd forgotten all about the poor animal. Now she closed her eyes for a moment as she remembered the lifeless body. "I'll be all right."

"Lock the door."

"I will."

Ben walked slowly down the steps. After climbing into his car and closing the door, he sat in the darkness. Sara had told him she was afraid of her own uncertainty. Yet she'd turned to him anyway.

Needing to let his own elation out, he bounced his fists lightly against the steering wheel. Then, suddenly, the good feeling was replaced by a tightness in his chest.

For a long moment he sat staring into the fog—thinking about the dog and the things he deliberately hadn't told Sara. Damn. He wanted to put their relationship on an honest footing. But what if he told Sara his secret? Would the warmth he'd just seen in her eyes change to suspicion—or even loathing?

Well, he sure couldn't stay here all night worrying about it. If he didn't drive away soon, she was probably going to come out here to find out what was wrong.

With a sigh, he started the engine and turned the car around. At the bottom of the drive, he stopped and carried the plastic trash bag over to the shepherd. No blood. No froth around the mouth.

He supposed there must be some agency that did autopsies on dogs. But how did you arrange for one?

CHAPTER 12

Monday, June 12

The kettle whistled, and Beatrice Pierce carefully poured hot water over the tea leaves in the strainer. The green and white Royal Worcester teapot was one of the few possessions she'd inherited from her mother.

She remembered how strange it had been, going back for the funeral in 1958. All those black faces. And the choir wailing a gospel rendition of "Shall We Gather at the River." She'd felt like a visitor to another planet.

In St. Stephens, she belonged to the United Methodist Church. And she hadn't gone out of her way to make friends with the black folks in town. Sometimes, when she felt their eyes on her back, she suspected that they knew. But no one had ever said anything.

When the tea was steeped just the way she liked it, she set the pot on a tray and carried it to the settee in the bay window. Her narrow, two-and-a-half story house was on Chestnut Street—right in the historic district. Her mother had left her enough money for a nice down payment.

It was amazing how a college degree and a careful schooling of your speech patterns could change your whole life.

Maybe today she wouldn't have tried to cross the line. But thirty-five years ago, when she'd arrived at the University of Pennsylvania as a scholarship student, she'd gotten a glimpse of a whole other life from what she'd ever even imagined. She'd seen right away what a difference it made whether you were black or white.

And since her skin was light enough to pass for white, she'd decided she'd be a fool to tell people about her real background.

Her mother had been a white man's housekeeper and his mistress—and had borne his child. Of course, he hadn't married her—or acknowledged his daughter. But he'd given Libby Pierce enough money to set herself up in business as a seamstress.

Libby had worked hard to give her daughter every advantage that she could—nice clothes, time to study so she could make herself a better life, even piano lessons.

She'd been sad when her daughter had announced she wasn't coming back home to Harrisburg after college. But in the end, she'd been proud of the genteel life her daughter had made for herself in St. Stephens.

The calico cat, lying in a patch of sunlight,

lifted its head sleepily when Beatrice sat down. Reaching over, she stroked the silky fur.

"Do you want a piece of cookie, Ramona?"

The cat stood up, arched its back, and glided over. Her mistress broke off a piece of sugar cookie, set it on a napkin, and watched the cat make short work of the treat.

Beatrice had sent her mother pictures and written long, enthusiastic letters about her new life in St. Stephens. But she'd never invited Libby to visit, and she'd never told her it had only been half a life. She hadn't talked about the high-school principal who had wanted to marry her and raise a family. She hadn't let on how she'd lain in bed weeping into her pillow after she'd turned him down because she'd pictured their children with dark skin and frizzy hair.

She could just imagine how St. Stephens would have reacted to that. One thing about the community; it was small-minded, tight knit, and wrapped in its traditional values like they were the American flag. Oh, on the surface everyone was friendly. She was in the church auxiliary. She'd even been an officer in the Business and Professional Women's Club. But after more than thirty years in town, in some ways she was still an outsider.

Yet there was something about her manner that made people talk to her. She liked to think folks told her things they wouldn't say to anyone else. That was one of the reasons why she'd been so effective as the feature editor of *The Record*.

"Is that good, sweetie?" she asked the cat softly.

Ramona looked at her, eyes hopeful.

"I'm sorry, sugar plum. But you can't have any more today. Not if you want to keep your nice, svelte figure."

The cat, who was used to the routine, nestled against her mistress' hip and began to purr.

Beatrice stirred cream and sugar into her tea and took a sip. For a moment, her eyes lit on a miniature picture of Ramona. She'd painted it herself. For awhile she'd thought she might have a second career as an artist. Sara had taken a few of her pictures on consignment. But only one had sold, and Sara hadn't asked her to do any more. She'd been disappointed. But that didn't matter now. She had a lot more chance of making it as a writer than as a painter.

"I'll bet you want to hear some more about my book. There's so much material I can use. Like all the hanky-panky Ted Chandler was into," Beatrice murmured as she scratched tenderly under the cat's chin.

For a moment her eyes stared unseeingly out the bay window. Handsome, confident, charming Ted Chandler. He'd come here as an outsider too. And he'd recognized her for one. What had she been to him? A novelty? A needy older woman? For awhile it hadn't mattered. Upstairs in her four-poster bed, he'd made her feel like she was thirty-five again.

She clenched her teeth together, trying not to remember the things she'd whispered to Ted . . . more than she had to any of her other lovers. Like George Newhouse. That man put up a good front. But he was a little sick, if you asked her.

Her thoughts turned back to Ted. She shouldn't have had any illusions about a man like him remaining faithful to one mistress. After awhile she'd realized he was more interested in information than in sex. Pride had made her the one to put an end to the foolishness with smug Mr. Chandler.

"Do you remember I was telling you about Swan Point, that old estate along the Miles River?"

The cat didn't answer.

"You remember old Miss Jane promised it to the conservation people as a bird refuge? Sara Chandler must have told her husband about it in confidence. Well, Ted just couldn't stand the idea of a prime piece of real estate like that going to the ducks. So he got in contact with Miss Jane's nephew. And they cooked up a deal with Newhouse Real Estate to develop it."

She paused and took a sip of tea.

"Ted was going to make his money by selling off the individual lots, once the property was rezoned. Now his partner, George Newhouse, will get all the money—if everything's finalized before the story leaks to the conservationists."

Beatrice bit off a piece of cookie and chewed contemplatively.

"Do you suppose, when people find out about the dirty deal, they'll wonder whether Sara or one of the other conservationists got wind of the scam? Why, they might even think one of them murdered poor old Ted. Or was it George, do you think? So he could keep all the money for himself?"

Beatrice laughed, and then her expression sobered. "The one person I wouldn't want to get blamed for it is Sara." She sat there stroking the cat and staring off into space, a preoccupied look on her face. "Of course, we're only talking about fiction," she finally murmured. "So I can make it come out any way I like."

CHAPTER 13

Thursday, June 22

"Are you sure you don't mind closing up the gallery this evening?" Sara turned to Ralph Meekins. Usually she didn't see the decoy carver for weeks. But he'd been by the shop regularly since Ted had died—asking if there was anything he could do to help her out. At first, she'd assumed he was trying to make up for the ceramic key he'd broken after the funeral. And she'd tried to assure him she wasn't angry.

But he'd kept showing up anyway. One thing about Ralph, there was no use coming out and asking him a direct question. He never had much to say. And he went about things in his own peculiar way.

She'd known him since she was a little girl. In fact, he was the one who'd gotten her interested in the Bay Watchers organization. Once, when she'd asked him how he got such lifelike effects with his decoys, he said, "When you spend a lot of time watching birds, you pick up on little details."

There was no false modesty about Ralph. He was hard working, honest, a little gruff, and a little secretive. She'd always sensed his feet were anchored in Maryland bedrock. Maybe that came from generations of wresting a living from the bay.

Last week she'd asked if he minded watching the shop while she went home and took a nap. He'd seemed pleased at the request.

Today, she and Ginny were going shopping on the Western Shore. She needed maternity clothes. Ginny was looking for some cruisewear.

"Don't trouble yourself about it. You and your sister just have yourselves a fine time." For Ralph, it was a long speech.

"I appreciate your minding the gallery for me."

"Ain't no trouble." For a moment, the lines softened in his weathered face. He was in his mid-sixties, Sarah knew. Years of crabbing and oystering had added at least a decade to his wrinkled visage. As the bay's harvests had declined, he'd turned to his hobby for a source of income. Sara had featured his work for the past several years. Now his duck carvings went for five hundred to a thousand dollars apiece. Even at those prices, she had trouble keeping them in stock.

As Sara was telling him which framing orders were due to be picked up that afternoon, Ginny breezed in.

"Almost ready?" she asked.

"Be right with you," Sara told her.

Ginny turned to Ralph. "I saw a busload of city folk down by the marina. At the rate they're walking, they should be hitting this place in about half an hour. Think you can handle them by yourself?"

City folk and *outsiders* were two of the more innocuous terms locals used when referring to the tourists and weekend residents who swarmed over the area all summer. Most townspeople had ambiguous feelings about the influx. The outsiders brought in money, but they also clogged the roads and waterways, bought up the choicest property, and disrupted the peace and tranquility of the area.

"Reckon I can handle things," Ralph mumbled under his breath.

Sara didn't comment as she headed toward the bathroom at the back of the shop. Ralph and Ginny mixed about as well as oil and water, but she'd learned from experience that there was no point in trying to smooth out the relationship. They simply didn't understand each other.

Quickly, she washed her hands and applied a bit of lipstick. She was pleased with her reflection. In general, she was feeling pretty good, and it showed. But she was probably going to have to make another pit stop before or after the Bay Bridge. One of the things she'd discovered about pregnancy was that her life was organized around plumbing facilities.

As they pulled out of the parking lot behind the drugstore, Ginny tossed her purse into the back seat.

"Oh, Sara, I just can't believe I'll be in the Caribbean a week from Saturday. I can hardly wait." She cleared her throat. "Will you look in on Dad? And, you know, have him over to dinner."

"Of course—if he'll come."

Ginny fiddled with the dial on the radio. Then she glanced sideways at her sister. "Dad's been acting pretty weird lately."

"You mean the drinking? Is it getting worse?"

"Yeah. But it's not just that. Sometimes he leaves the house—and I don't know where he's going. It's like something is eating at him—something he doesn't want to talk to anyone about."

Sara nodded. She was worried about her father too. They were going to have to do something, but what? Automatically, she glanced in the rearview mirror as she changed lanes. Several car-lengths behind her was a black-leather-clad figure on a motorcycle. The shiny plastic visor of his helmet covered his face. Sara's foot trembled on the accelerator and the car lurched forward.

"What?"

"That guy on the motorcycle again."

Ginny looked back over her shoulder. "Yeah. I think I've seen him hangin' around."

Sara shot her sister a sharp glance. "Has he been bothering you?"

"What do you mean?"

Sara shrugged. "I don't know. Watching the house? Following you?" God, that sounded paranoid.

"No, I don't think so. He's just been around."

The rider trailed them for a few more blocks.

Then, as Sara watched, he turned off at Baker's Mill Road, and she felt some of the tension go out of her shoulders.

"So let's stop at that outlet mall right before the Bay Bridge," Ginny suggested.

"All right."

Ralph Meekins glanced nervously out the shop window. He'd expected a quiet afternoon. But the street was crowded. Probably a lot of people off the boat would be coming into the gallery.

He paced to the door, then back to the cash register. Sara needed the business—now that she was a widow and on her own. But there was something clawing at the corner of his mind like a crab clutching at a chicken neck. This was the fourth time he'd been here this month—and the best opportunity he was going to have. When Sara had told him she was going home to take a nap, he'd pictured her changing her mind and popping into the store. But she was going to be away for hours today.

Finally, after hesitating a moment longer, he stalked to the door again and flipped over the sign that said "Back in a few minutes." Then he hurried toward the little office at the rear of the gallery, where Sara kept her records.

"So how are you and Ben getting on?" Ginny asked.

"Fine—I guess." She could feel a flush spread across her face. She was four-and-a-half months pregnant, and Ben Langley was courting her as if she'd never been married. After she'd decided it was all right, she'd found she was enjoying the experience—dinner together, Sunday afternoons down by the river, a trip to Annapolis.

"Sara, you're so lucky. All you have to do is look at Ben and you can see that he's crazy about you. He'd be a good father for the baby," she added softly.

"But I'm not going to rush into anything this time."

"Why not? I'll bet he's a better lover than Ted."

"Ginny!"

Her sister giggled. "Well, is he?"

"We certainly haven't—and that isn't any of your business, anyway."

Ginny folded her arms across her chest and slumped down in the seat. Sara still thought she was a baby. Well, she wasn't. And to prove it she was going to find herself a man on the cruise. A man so wonderful that everyone else would be jealous.

Ralph stood looking at the old metal cabinet behind the desk, where Sara kept her records. As he stood there, staring at the scarred and dented drawers, his palms grew cold. He felt like a damn sneak. But there was stuff he had to know. And he couldn't think of any other way.

Before he could change his mind, he crossed the office and opened the top drawer. The file he wanted was right in the middle.

There was a standard consignment agreement at the front, and after that, notations in Sara's neat handwriting: dates, descriptions, prices, a social security number . . .

Ralph's brow wrinkled. He'd just pulled the folder out of the drawer when he heard the bell over the door.

Tarnation! Someone had ignored the sign and come right in. Damn old fool. He should've locked the door!

His heart started to pound as he hurried around the desk. He was in such a rush to get the file back in its proper place and the drawer closed that he jammed his index finger. Cursing, he pressed it against his lips.

"Sara? You forget somethin'?" Ralph glanced up and saw the tall figure of Kitty Duncan filling the doorway. In his guilty mind, she seemed to loom over him like an accusing wraith.

The sculptor's blue eyes bored into him, and he froze. Suddenly he felt as though his head were glass and she could see right into it.

"Ralph, are you supposed to be back here skulking around? What are you up to, anyway?"

"I—uh—I—" He stopped and shrugged. "Came back to get some price tags."

Kitty looked around the office and then glanced back over her shoulder. "Where's Sara?"

"Shopping trip." Ralph felt a bead of cold sweat drip down the back of his neck. He wasn't cut out for this kind of deception.

"Sara's not going to be back today?"

"Ain't likely."

"I'll call her tomorrow."

Ralph's heart was jumping like a bullfrog now. Did Kitty realize what he was doing? And if she did, what was she going to do about it?

CHAPTER 14

Thursday, June 22

THE ST. STEPHENS RECORD

Business Briefs

Considering a career in Real Estate?
Newhouse Realty is looking for enthusiastic new agents interested in
cashing in on the area's expanding
home-buying market. Newhouse is
known for its friendly atmosphere and
its staff that goes that extra mile. If
you'd like to join the team, come on
in and meet owner George Newhouse.
The company will be holding an open
house for prospective agents on Saturday, from 11 a.m. to 2 p.m.

People Section

> Bon voyage to lucky Ginny Strickland,
> who will be off to the sunny Carib-
> bean for a fun-filled cruise. Ginny, we
> wish we were going with you.

You could fool some of the people all of the time and all of the people some of the time. But the one person it was dangerous to fool was yourself. And that meant sometimes he had to touch base with the one person who kept him sane.

He drummed his fingers against the top of the motorcycle helmet that rested on the coffee table. "You're the one who suggested the cruise to Ginny in the first place," he said in an even voice.

"Because you wanted me to. But, dammit, now I feel left out."

"We've been over it so many times." He tried to keep any hint of defensiveness out of his voice.

"I won't be there to share the moment when you do it."

"I know. But we talked about that. I have to do this alone."

The other person's long fingers were knit together. "Because your horoscope says so?"

He didn't answer.

"Sometimes I think you put more faith in the alignment of the planets than you do in me."

"How can you say that? We're in this together. We've been in it together for a long time."

"I don't know. Sometimes I feel like you're taking over control."

He sighed.

Looking down, the other person picked up the square of needlepoint canvas and began to stitch. "It's almost finished."

He peered at the carefully worked design. "This is even better than the last one. Just like the picture he used to have in the waiting room."

"Do you think he knows?" The words were barely above a whisper.

"I think he suspects."

Several more stitches were silently completed. "I want to hurt him—as much as he hurt you."

"I know." He gnawed on his bottom lip for a minute. "But we've got to be careful. We can't take a chance on anyone figuring out what we're up to."

"So I just have to wait until it's over?"

"This time."

"But you're going to need me when you come back for Sara."

"Yes."

His companion smiled.

"I have almost everything ready for the trip."

"What about the—poison?"

"It's all set."

There was a nod of satisfaction.

"I'm going to worry all the time you're on that ship."

"I know. But there just isn't any other way."

The occupant of the chair leaned back comfortably. "You haven't told me about this afternoon."

"It was just like the other time—when I broke into Sara's house."

"I hope you didn't do anything juvenile again—like that stupid stunt with the toaster oven."

His face reddened. "I wanted to scare her."

"But what if you'd killed her? We agreed. It's supposed to be with a needle."

"Just shut up about the toaster oven. I'm tired of hearing about it." His ears were ringing, and his head had started to throb. He squeezed his eyes shut and tried to breathe slowly and deeply.

For a moment, there was a tense silence in the room. Then he cleared his throat. "You're not angry at me, are you? I can't take it when you get angry at me."

"I'm not angry. I love you. I always will."

He swallowed convulsively. "And I wouldn't be alive if it weren't for you."

"You haven't finished telling me about this afternoon."

"Right. Well, I left the motorcycle down the road in the woods and walked around back. The window next to the back door was wide open."

"What did you find out about Ginny?"

"She keeps a diary hidden in a candy box in her nightstand drawer."

"And?"

"She's really looking forward to the cruise. There isn't going to be any problem getting close to her. Getting her to trust me. I'm just the guy who can make her dreams come true. Right before I put her to sleep permanently."

CHAPTER 15

Monday, June 26

Ginny raised her face and took a deep breath of the tangy breeze blowing off the water. "I always loved coming to Swan Point. I'm glad you suggested this."

Sara reached down and plucked a wild daisy. As she stared out over the water, she stroked the soft petals against her cheek. Near the shore, a brood of fuzzy ducklings bobbed along behind their mother.

She and Ginny walked a few yards farther along the narrow beach. Since Mrs. Brittingham had gone into the nursing home, hardly anyone came here.

"How's Miss Jane?" Ginny asked.

"Going downhill." Sara sighed. "I stop by to see her every couple of weeks."

"Isn't she about ninety-five by now?"

"Ninety-seven. This place means so much

to her," Sara added. "We talked about the bird refuge again last week. I guess when she sees me, it makes her think about it."

Ginny nodded, picked up a twig, and tossed it into the water. "Mom used to pack a picnic when we came here, didn't she? Country ham sandwiches—right?"

Sara swallowed around the lump that had suddenly formed in her throat. "Country ham. Old-fashioned potato salad. Lemon cake."

"Yeah. I remember her lemon cake. It was real good."

For a moment the two sisters were silent. Sara watched the mother duck turn to make sure her brood was following. She knew how the duck felt. She'd been turning around to check up on Ginny for more than ten years. But tomorrow Ginny was going away, out of her reach where she wouldn't be able to watch over her.

A shiver played down Sara's spine. Even though she'd tried hard to talk herself out of it, she just couldn't shake the apprehension that seemed to sweep over her every time she thought about the trip.

"I'm finally all packed," Ginny said. "I couldn't decide whether to take the green and white knit outfit or the blue one, so I stuck them both in." She went on to describe most of the contents of her three bags of luggage.

Sara only half listened as she pulled a couple of petals off the daisy. If Mom were alive, she'd be having a mother-daughter talk with Ginny now. But some of the things she'd be telling her were hard to say.

Sara sat down on a large rock and cleared

her throat. "That nightgown you bought at Victoria's Secret while I was in the maternity department at Macy's—"

"Don't you just love it!"

"It's very pretty. But it's the kind of thing I bought before I went on my honeymoon."

The younger woman's chin tipped up. "So?"

"Ginny, anything I say is probably going to sound old-fashioned to you. But I can't help worrying about you going off on your own like this."

"I can take care of myself."

"But you don't have a lot of experience with people. I mean, with men."

"So what? Everybody has to start somewhere. And you have to admit that I'm getting a pretty *slow* start."

"That's why I'm worried. There are guys who go on cruises—guys who are looking for defenseless women."

"Oh, come on!"

"You might meet someone really charming—who could turn out to be a con man."

"You mean like the guy you married—good old Ted?" Ginny shot back.

Sara winced. "That's not fair."

"All right, but he wasn't exactly what he seemed."

"No," Sara admitted in a low voice. "But I wasn't the only one he took in. Just about everybody in town thought he was wonderful. You even told me how much you liked him."

"At first."

Sara stared out across the water, her eyes focusing on a cabin cruiser speeding by in the distance. "We all make mistakes," she said quietly. "And some of them can ruin your life."

When her sister didn't reply, she turned back to face her. "Ginny, I love you. And I just keep having these feelings about the trip. I don't know. Maybe it's just my pregnancy hormones kicking in." She laughed nervously and smoothed a hand across the slightly rounded curve of her abdomen. "I was naive when I met Ted, and he took advantage of that. I was a small-town girl, and he was a guy from the big city. I don't want you to make the same mistake I did."

"I won't."

"Just promise me you'll be careful. There are so many things to worry about these days. Getting pregnant. AIDS. Drugs."

Ginny came over, sat down, and put her arms around Sara's shoulders. "I know," she whispered. "I know more about stuff like that than you think I do." She swallowed. "Sara, I love you too. I never really told you—did I? I guess I never thanked you for taking over when Mom died either."

They hugged each other fiercely. When they finally broke apart, Sara's eyes were misty.

George Newhouse picked up the can of Bud Lite from the holder in the cockpit and tipped his head back. The cold beer sliding down his throat felt wonderful in the heat from the June sun.

He never indulged in more than two lite beers a day. Not if he wanted to keep his size thirty-eight waist. He'd given up cigarettes ten years ago. He ate a lot of seafood, and he worked out at the gym three mornings a week.

Unconsciously, he stroked one of the lines that creased his forehead. That was one thing about the motorcycle—his face didn't show. In fact, when he was all suited up in his leathers, you couldn't tell he wasn't a nineteen-year-old.

With an easy one-handed turn of the wheel, he steered the thirty-foot Pleasure Craft toward the shore. The boat handled like a well-trained filly.

The little cruiser had been a present to himself on his forty-fourth birthday. Last fall he'd taken it out for some mighty fine sea-duck hunting. This afternoon he was treating himself to a little fishing. But he'd decided to swing by Swan Point first. Just to have a look at his future gold mine. After the deal went down, he'd be able to pay off the bank loan on the boat.

George shaded his eyes as he gazed out across the water toward the low-lying land. The Point was coming up on the right.

The sight of the shoreline made his chest swell with proprietary pleasure. Now that Chandler was out of the picture, this place was all his. He'd put the letter of agreement in his safe-deposit box. As soon as that decrepit old lady in the nursing home kicked the bucket, he could make his move.

George gave the wheel a little squeeze. All his life, he'd been right on the edge of the big time. Shit, if he'd only been able to lay his hands on enough bread to buy in on that big condo deal in Ocean City, he'd've been rich by now. Or that resort complex down the road. He'd bailed out when the place looked like it was going belly up. Jesus, why hadn't he thought of selling off the land bordering the golf course as building lots for $100,000 apiece?

Well, he still might have a little cash flow problem, but he was finally in the right place at the right time—thanks to dear departed Ted. Nothing was going to stand in his way this time. Chandler had come to him with the tip because he hadn't been sure how to put that big a deal together.

So George had gone out and found the investors. Nobody else was going to make as much as he was. But none of them were going to be unhappy with their share of the profits, either.

A minute later, he cut the engine and looked over toward the beach.

Then his eyes bulged out. Good God, who was that prowling around on his property? It looked like two women.

As the boat bobbed in the water, he grabbed a pair of field glasses out of the cockpit and trained them on the two seated figures.

The profile of Sara Chandler came into focus. And Ginny.

His fingers gripped the barrels of the binoculars. What the fuck were they doing out here?

He'd convinced himself Sara wasn't going to be a problem. Maybe that was a big mistake. Maybe the widow had somehow found out about his plans. Ted could have left some incriminating notes—or even let something slip. He should have thought about that.

He swore under his breath. This thing was

just too big to let Ted's widow screw it up. He'd better find out what she was up to and right away. If he didn't like what he discovered, he'd have to stop playing around and take care of the bitch.

He turned the boat around and headed back toward the harbor. There wasn't all that much time. He had to find out what was what on the Swan Point deal before he went out of town on that other little business.

Sara pushed the wheelchair along the macadam path. "Shall we stop over there?"

"Yes dear."

She pulled the chair to a halt beside a bed of fragrant roses and stooped to adjust the knit shawl around Miss Jane's humped shoulders. The gnarled old hands clutched at Sara's for a moment, and Miss Jane winced.

"What's wrong?"

"My arthritis. Some days are worse than others. But seeing you is a real tonic," she added as Sara sat down on a wooden bench facing her friend.

"It's a treat for me, too. I love talking with you about the old days. You know, I was out at Swan Point this afternoon."

Miss Jane's watery eyes took on a dreamy look. "Did you get up to the house to see the new sun room?"

The sun room. Sara knew it had been added more than twenty years ago. But that was the way it was with Miss Jane. Sometimes she got things a little mixed up—like the past and the present. Sara always handled the lapses by ignoring them.

"No. Ginny and I just walked along the water. We saw a mother and her baby ducklings."

"Oh, the dear little things. All fuzzy and yellow. I used to feed them."

"Um hum."

"So Ginny's going off on her trip."

Sara nodded.

"Now don't go worrying about that girl. She's going to be fine. My nephew Jonathan was a hell raiser when he was growing up. And look how he's settled down. He's even taking an interest in my affairs."

"Oh?"

A squirrel scampered up a nearby tree, and the old woman's attention flitted to the small silver-gray animal. "Look at that cute little thing. I wish we'd brought some nuts to feed him."

They watched the squirrel until it disappeared into the leafy branches. "You were telling me about Jonathan."

"I'm letting him have the house out at Swan Point after I pass on."

"I didn't know that."

"Don't worry, dear. It's important to keep the family home up. But Jonathan understands about the bird refuge. He's not going to interfere with my plans in any way."

CHAPTER 16

Wednesday, June 28

Harold Strickland was in the middle of checking Mrs. Dunbar's blood pressure when he heard the commotion in the outer office.

"Dr. Strickland. Emergency." Lois Pennington rapped on the door of the examination room.

Harold's fingers clenched for a moment on the black rubber bulb. God, Ben was out of the office. Was he going to be able to handle whatever it was?

Schooling his features to look controlled and confident, he strode down the hall after Lois. She ushered him into the first room on the left.

Paula Hobart was cradling her three-year-old daughter, Mary Alice, in her arms. The child was limp and unmoving as Paula pressed a disposable diaper to her face. Both the diaper and the mother's blouse were soaked with blood.

As he took in the scene, a feeling of calm descended over Harold like a powerful drug kicking into effect. He'd been a doctor for over thirty-five years. He'd seen plenty of head trauma. He could handle this. Gently, he transferred the unconscious child to the examination table and adjusted the light over her head. "What happened?"

"We were at the playground. I was changing Ryan, and when I looked up, Mary Alice was running toward the swings." The woman stifled a sob.

"Sometimes it's so fast, there's nothing you can do."

"I left the baby with Theresa and drove right here. Doctor, is she going to be all right?"

"Yes." Harold's voice was deep and reassuring as he began to clean the angry-looking gash. The wound was below the little girl's left eyebrow. Lucky, he thought. A few millimeters lower and she would probably have lost her sight in that eye.

"It's not as bad as it looks," Harold reassured the mother. "Head wounds bleed a lot."

Mary Alice stirred and began to cry.

"Take it easy," Harold soothed. "We just have to sew you up, and you're going to be good as new."

Harold got out a hypodermic to give the child a local anesthetic. The little girl's eyes riveted on the needle. Then she started to scream.

Another memory leaped into Harold's mind, and his hand faltered. Then, with sudden clarity, every medical mishap he'd ever suffered came rolling through his mind like a newsreel. Not so long ago, he'd been able to convince himself that the episodes were just part of a normal medical career. Every doctor lost some patients. But recently he'd seen the same vivid scenes almost every night: Old Mrs. Jennings. Little Keith Thomas. His own wife.

DR. STRICKLAND LOSES PATIENT TO PERITONITIS

DR. SENDS BOY INTO ANAPHYLACTIC SHOCK

DR.'S WIFE DIES AFTER—

He clamped down on the memory. Christ, he needed some Scotch.

What if he messed up Mary Alice's eye? What if he blinded her? He couldn't sew her up, but he had to.

"Close your eyes, and it'll stop hurting in a minute."

"Nooooo." The refusal ended in a loud wail that probably carried into the waiting room, maybe out into the parking lot.

Harold could feel a film of cold sweat bead across his forehead. For a moment he wanted to smack the little girl, smack her hard—make her stop screaming. Then his hand began to shake as he realized what he was thinking. My God, he was a doctor. You didn't smack a patient.

At that moment, Ben Langley stepped into the room. He'd just come back from an emergency Caesarean at the hospital, and he hadn't even taken off his sports coat.

"Can I help?"

Harold turned to him like a drowning sailor who'd suddenly been tossed a lifeline.

Quickly Ben washed his hands. "This procedure always goes more smoothly when you have assistance," he said over his shoulder to Paula before turning back to Harold. "You hold the head, Doctor, and I'll administer the anesthetic."

The older man's blue-veined hands came up to frame Mary Alice's face. Before she could move, Ben had given her the pain-killer.

He waited until the medication took effect. Then he got out the suturing kit. "You'd advise about fifteen stitches, wouldn't you?" he asked.

Harold nodded and automatically began to dab at the blood still oozing from the wound.

Ben carefully closed the gash. "She's going to be good as new in a few days," he said, lifting his head toward Paula.

"Oh, thank you, Doctor. Thank you." The young mother looked from Ben to Harold and back again.

"I'll give you a sheet with some instructions," Harold said gruffly. "And you'll need to bring her back in ten days to have the stitches out. Make the appointment with Dr. Langley."

He turned and left the room.

CHAPTER 17

Sara had decided to keep things simple for dinner—tossed salad with lots of fresh crab and shrimp, French bread, and fresh fruit with ice cream for dessert. When the doorbell rang, she was washing the salad greens.

She glanced up at the clock on the back panel of the stove. Ben wasn't due until eight. It was only seven-thirty. Had he decided to come over early? After drying her hands, she took off her apron, gave her hair a quick inspection in the hall mirror, and went to open the door. Her smile of anticipation faded as she looked out through the glass panel. It wasn't Ben on her porch.

"George. This is a surprise. I haven't seen you in a long time."

"I meant to stop by, but business has been jumping. You know how it is with real estate in the summer."

He was wearing white Bermudas and an aqua cotton knit shirt, which set off his deep tan and the powerful muscles of his arms and shoulders. He must have just showered and shaved, because she could smell his cologne. It was strong and musky, and in her present condition, it made her want to gag.

Sara waited for him to tell her why he'd picked this evening to visit. He didn't immediately enlighten her. In fact, he was staring at her middle. On her shopping trip with Ginny, she'd bought three soft cotton-jersey tent-dresses that could be worn alone or as jumpers. Although she hadn't made any announcements about her pregnancy, she knew the soft fabric of the dress outlined her changing figure.

George cleared his throat. "I didn't realize you were— How are you feeling?"

"Fine." She hoped he'd drop the subject. "Would you like to come in for a moment?" she asked, wishing he'd decline.

"I would, if it's not puttin' you to any trouble."

"Well, I am having company in a little bit." She didn't like the speculative look in his eye.

"I guess I should've called first. But I thought I'd just take a chance on stoppin' by. I won't keep you but a moment." He gave her a hearty smile that revealed a mouth full of teeth so perfect that she'd always thought they had to be capped—or false. But the heartiness didn't quite reach his eyes. It was typical of George, she thought. He and Ted had been hunting buddies as well as business associates. Her husband had told her more than once that

George had taught him a hell of a lot about the real estate business. But there was something about the man that had always made her uneasy. She wondered what Ted would have thought if she'd told him about the way George had tried to stick his tongue in her mouth when he'd kissed her good-bye at the Christmas party. He'd been loaded to the gunwales. But that hadn't made the pass any less disgusting.

"Me and my secretary were going through our records and realized there are some papers we can't locate. They're all—uh—related to Ted's listings. I know he used to take things home sometimes—"

"And you think the things you're looking for might be in Ted's office upstairs?"

"I was hopin' so."

"Is it something urgent?"

"Not urgent. But if I could just take a fast look-see."

"Well—all right."

"I'll be quicker than a sailor on shore leave." He ended the assurance with a little laugh.

Sara turned away, wishing she could take back the permission. She didn't like being alone with George—especially upstairs in her house. But Ben was on his way over. Trying not to let her misgivings show, she started up the steps.

She wouldn't have been comforted by George's thoughts as he followed her up to the second floor. In fact, he was mentally fondling her bottom. Pregnancy had filled her out nicely. So the widow Chandler was in the family way. If that didn't beat all. He guessed it must be Ted's. She wasn't the kind to fool around.

The bitch. She'd put him down in front of a bunch of people at the Christmas party. That was just one of the things that made him madder than hell. Women didn't put George Newhouse down and get away with it.

He remembered that hunting trip last year when he and Ted had started off by killing half a bottle of bourbon to keep away the chill. Next thing you knew, they'd gotten into exchanging stories about women. He'd told Ted about his ex-wife, who'd been like a block of ice in bed and had taken him to the cleaners with her alimony suit. After sympathizing, Ted had said that Sara wasn't the type to file for divorce, and that she damn well knew she'd better be accommodating.

But she did have her hang-ups, which, as far as he was concerned, gave him the perfect right to find excitement in other places.

"Damn right," George had agreed.

Sara reached the top of the steps and glanced over her shoulder. The calculating look in George's eyes made her take a quick step down the hall. "In here."

She turned on the light and gestured toward the desk. "I guess I should have thought about calling you," she apologized. "Most of the papers he brought home would be over there."

George looked at the neatly stacked folders. Ted had been that way at the office, too—obsessively tidy. That was a help. "This won't take too long."

Should she leave the man up here alone? Sara wondered, unconsciously edging toward the door. In the small room, George's cologne was stifling.

Before she could decide, the doorbell rang. *Ben.*

"Excuse me."

"Sure." George straightened. "I see some of the stuff I'm looking for." He gestured toward the locked file cabinet. "But do you happen to have the key to that?"

The doorbell rang again.

"I don't know."

As soon as she'd stepped out of the room, George opened the middle drawer of the desk. Paper clips, pencils, pens, breath mints . . . no key. It wasn't in any of the other drawers either. *Shit.*

He could hear Sara talking downstairs, and a man answering. He strained his ears. When he didn't detect anyone on the steps, he decided to take a chance. Opening the drawer, he removed a paper clip. Quickly, he straightened it out and tried it in the file-cabinet lock—with no success. *Hell.*

Well, he couldn't stay here forever. He'd just have to come back again when no one was home. But that wasn't any real problem.

After scooping up an armload of files, he turned off the light and closed the office door behind himself.

Sara was looking up at him as he started down the stairs. Beside her was the young doctor who had joined her father's practice— Ben Langley.

Well, well, was this a social occasion? Or were they discussing business? He hadn't heard any tongues flapping about the two of them.

Maybe they were being very discreet. It could be the widow Chandler wasn't quite as proper as he'd thought.

Beatrice Pierce leaned back in her chair and rubbed her shoulders. Typing certainly did tire your muscles. But she had a good excuse to stop. There were some details she needed to check on.

She was working in the upstairs bedroom she'd converted to an office. Since she spent so much time in that room, she'd decorated it in a warm country style. The wallpaper and fabric were from Laura Ashley. The furniture was antique pine and oak. On the chest under the window was one of Ralph Meekins's duck decoys.

Getting up, she crossed to the table, where she'd sorted the photocopied articles from *The Record*—and some she'd gotten from the *Star Democrat*—into piles by subject:

Births and Deaths.

Social Events.

Crimes.

Real Estate.

Local Businesses.

Politics.

Scandals.

She'd spent weeks going through the clippings and thinking about her plot and characters, and about what would make the most dramatic impact. Finally, she'd decided to write a family chronicle. It would be about a dedicated but humanly flawed general practitioner and his wife and children—their trials and tribulations. The joys and sorrows of their lives would entwine with the fortunes of a small Eastern Shore town called St. Albans. It wasn't going to be just a shallow exposé. She had much bigger plans now. It was going to be a book with all the emotional drama of *The Thorn Birds* and the unspoiled setting of *Chesapeake*.

First, she was drawing up an outline. The book's action would start about thirty-five years ago, when the fictitious physician moved to St. Albans.

Ramona was sitting on the Births and Deaths.

"I'm afraid I'm going to have to move you, sweetie."

The cat meowed as she picked her up. But the feline closed her eyes and went back to sleep again once Beatrice had settled her on a crocheted afghan on the sofa.

Sitting down beside the cat, Beatrice thumbed through the clippings. Now where was it? She wanted the story about that boy who'd been bitten by a German shepherd and died after Dr. Strickland had treated him. That would make a heart-wrenching episode.

"Newhouse."

"Langley."

The two men eyed each other. George stuck out his hand, and Ben shook it.

"Well, thank you kindly for letting me pick up these records," George said to Sara.

"Did you find what you needed?"

"I did that."

They waited until the real estate man had closed the door behind him and descended the front steps.

"What's wrong?" Ben asked as he took in Sara's expression of distaste.

"Nothing really. I just never liked George very much. He reminds me of the worms we used to use for bait when we were kids. Dirty. And slippery."

Ben watched out the window as the large Oldsmobile backed down the driveway. All afternoon he'd been steeling himself for a discussion with Sara about Harold. But he could see George's visit had upset her. He'd better put off anything serious until after dinner.

The decision brought its own feeling of relief. He didn't really want to talk about Harold yet.

Instead, he slipped his arm around Sara. "If Newhouse bothers you again, I'll go over and beat him up."

She giggled. "Oh, sure. That's just your style."

His lips flirted with a grin. "Well, if he comes into the office, maybe I can give him a painful injection in the rear."

"You're terrible."

"I'll try to reform. What's for dinner?"

"Seafood salad. But George interrupted me in the middle of getting it ready."

"That's all right. I'll help."

"You can set the table and fix some lemonade." She'd already found out that Dr. Langley's culinary skills didn't extend much beyond tearing a tab off a microwave dinner box.

Arm-in-arm, they started down the hall toward the kitchen. Sara rested her head on Ben's shoulder for a moment. She felt comfortable with him—more than comfortable. He'd been easing himself into her life, and more than once she'd marveled at how different their relationship was from what she'd known in her marriage.

When Ted had come home after a day showing property, he'd wanted a drink ready and a hot dinner not far behind. Never mind that she'd had a tiring day too. He'd kick off his shoes in the living room, throw his coat over a chair, and bury his head in the *Star Democrat* while she took care of the domestic chores.

Ben watched her cross to the sink and start slicing cucumbers and sweet red pepper. It was so damn good being here with her like this. The more time he spent with Sara, the deeper his feeling for her grew. She was probably the most unselfish person he'd ever met. And she had a natural warmth that made him realize just how barren his life had been.

She looked so lovely—even graceful. Pregnancy was softly rounding out her body in a way that was driving him quietly out of his mind.

They'd spent a lot of time together lately. Although they'd been getting closer physically, he hadn't pushed things because he was still afraid that if he let himself go, he'd overwhelm her. Yet he'd gotten to the point where he only had to think about her to find that he was aroused.

After fixing the frozen lemonade, he set the pitcher down on the table. Instead of getting the cutlery, he crossed the room and came up behind Sara.

"Do you need to get in the drawer?"

"No." His arms locked around her middle, and he nuzzled his lips against the back of her neck. God, he loved the back of her neck. It was so soft.

"I'm all finished with the lemonade. Anything else I can help with?"

"I've got everything else under control."

"You do?"

As his lips explored the sensitive skin behind her left ear, the paring knife in her hand clattered onto the cutting board.

When he turned her around, she anchored her arms behind him.

"Maybe I was wrong. Maybe I don't have everything under control," she admitted, her voice husky.

"Sara."

His lips took hungry possession of hers. The kiss was long and satisfying and left her slightly dizzy.

As her lids fluttered open, she was almost overwhelmed by the depth of passion in his dark eyes. He was silently offering her everything she'd missed out on before.

She longed to reach out and hug it to herself. But morality had played a strong part in her life. Was it really all right to be falling in love with another man so soon?

"Ben—I—" Her voice faltered.

He squeezed her hand. "I'm on call tonight. So we'd better eat before my beeper goes off."

"Okay."

The conversation was light and easy during dinner. Dammit, he didn't want to spoil things tonight. But the episode with Mary Alice had shaken him up.

"I've got fruit and ice cream for dessert,"

Sara said as she pushed back her chair. "Do you want some coffee, too?"

"Sounds good."

When she got up to put the kettle on, he played with his spoon, feeling his mouth go dry. He sighed. Back in Santa Barbara he'd made an error in judgment, and he'd ended up having to suffer the consequences. He'd told himself he was never going to repeat the same mistake.

Sara came back to the table with his coffee. "Ben, is something bothering you?"

"Sorry. I didn't realize it showed."

"I guess I'm getting to know you better. Are you worried about a patient or something?"

"No. Your father."

The cup Sara was holding rattled in the saucer, and some of the dark liquid spilled. Quickly, she set the coffee cup down on the table. "You mean his drinking?"

"It's more than that. Sara, today a mother brought her little girl in with a gash right above her left eye. I was out of the office, and Lois had pulled Harold out of an exam so he could sew the child up."

"What happened?" she forced herself to ask.

"The kid was screaming, and your father was trembling like a med-school student confronting his first real emergency. He couldn't give the little girl the local anesthetic. I had to come in and literally move him out of the way so I could sew her up."

She sat down heavily in the chair across the table from Ben.

"He's not the same man who interviewed

me a year ago. Something's happening to him," Ben said in a low voice.

"He'll snap out of it."

"Do you really believe that?"

"I don't know. But being a doctor is his life. If he had to give it up, he really would go off the deep end."

"Yes, but he's holding his patients' lives in his hands. What if he makes a mistake and I'm not around to bail him out?"

Sara had been hoping for months that somehow things would get better. Now she wasn't prepared to hear how bad the situation really was.

"Are you sure? I mean, maybe if you hadn't stepped in to help—maybe he would have been all right."

"I don't think so."

"But you're prepared to sit there across from me making a judgment that will put an end to my father's professional life?"

"Sara, I've been trying to cope with this for months now. I've tried to get him to talk about it more than once. When I bring up the subject, he gets this stony look on his face and turns away."

She knew what Ben meant. She'd seen that stubborn, closed expression that sometimes fell across her father's features like a black veil. But she didn't want to get into a discussion about it. Why did everything have to come falling back on her like an avalanche? The icy cold of it was burying her now, making it hard to breathe.

"Your father has to acknowledge that he has a problem so that he can do something about it. If it's just the alcoholism, we can get him into some kind of treatment program. If it's more serious, we'll have to deal with that, too."

"What do you want me to do?"

He turned his palms up. "Just talk to him."

Sara sighed. "I've had years of experience with him. When he doesn't want to listen, he shuts me out just as easily as he does anybody else."

They stared at each other across the table. The wooden surface had suddenly become like a mile of rough terrain, separating them. Finally, Sara pushed back her chair and stood up. Didn't Ben understand anything? Didn't he realize how much she'd had to cope with in the past few months? Ted. The baby. Ginny. Her own guilt. The faceless guy on the motorcycle who dogged her steps like one of the mythological Furies. "I— Ben— I'm sorry. I just can't handle this right now."

"Sara, I'm trying to deal with your father's— disability—without going to a medical review board."

"Oh, so that's what you have in mind? Having poor old Dr. Harold Strickland declared unfit to continue practicing medicine."

"Jesus, Sara. I didn't say that." He stood too. It was impossible not to feel somehow betrayed. "I'm disappointed. I was counting on you to help me. I guess you don't want to face the problem."

"Oh, is that why you've been spending so much time with me lately? So I'll help you out with Dad?"

"Don't be ridiculous."

When she didn't answer, he added, "Do you imagine I brought this up because I thought I was going to enjoy the discussion?"

Sara turned her head away.

"Maybe we can talk about it later," he offered, waiting. When she didn't answer, he walked slowly toward the door.

As Ben's footsteps receded down the hall, Sara stared at the full coffee cup still sitting on the table.

CHAPTER 18

THE ST. STEPHENS RECORD

Calendar of Events

Independence Day Dinner
The St. Stephens High School Booster Club will hold its annual Independence Day fried chicken and crab cake dinner from 4 p.m. until 8:30 p.m. on the Fourth. Entertainment will be provided by the Saints Marching Band and the Drum and Majorette Corps. Adults, $8.50. Students, $6.00. Children under three eat free.

Fireworks
The annual Fourth of July fireworks display will commence at 9:30 p.m. at the city dock. Due to traffic congestion, this year residents are re-

quested not to drive to the dock area.
There will be ample parking at Bayside
Park—with shuttle buses running every fifteen minutes for your convenience.

Saturday, July 1

Ginny adjusted her oversize sunglasses and
reached for the tumbler of passion-fruit juice.

Really, she liked the taste of plain old orange juice better. But you could drink orange
juice any time, and you sure couldn't get passion fruit in the Acme Market on Main Street.

She leaned back on her chaise longue and
looked around the deck. The boat hadn't even
left port yet, but already she felt like she'd
stepped into the pages of a Danielle Steele
novel.

She'd gotten to the Royal Alexandria at
twelve-thirty, dumped her luggage in her stateroom, and gone exploring. There'd been an
opening at the beauty salon, so she'd had her
hair done right away. Fifty dollars for the cut
and set and some makeup lessons, but it was
worth it. Her hair looked fantastic. And you
couldn't even see her freckles.

After the makeover, she'd changed into her
bathing suit so she could catch some sun before dinner. Of course, with her expensive
hairdo, there was no way she was going in the
pool.

Stretching out her legs on the chaise, Ginny
smiled at the waiter weaving his way through
the sun-worshipping crowd. There were al-

most as many staffers on this ship as there were paying customers.

If Sara could only see her now. As she thought about her sister, she stroked her finger up the frosty side of the glass. Sara had always been such a worrywart. Ever since Mom had died, anyway. In fact, she'd looked pretty uptight when she'd driven her to the airport. She hadn't said anything, but Ginny knew Sara was still nervous about this trip. Well, she was here safe and sound. And she was going to have a fantastic time. What her big sister didn't know wouldn't hurt her.

Ginny took a sip of juice. Sure, she'd been a little worried about going off on her own. Who wouldn't be? When almost everybody else from the flight had collected their luggage and she was still standing there waiting for hers to come down the chute at Miami, she'd almost started crying, imagining all those expensive outfits—lost. Then the blue and red case had finally appeared, and she'd felt so relieved she'd sagged against a pillar.

But after that, everything had gone fine. She hadn't even had to worry about taking a cab to the ship. They'd had a limo waiting for her and the half-a-dozen other passengers who had arrived on the same flight from Atlanta, where they'd stopped over en route.

Gosh, what a place for a vacation, a boat as big as a city block. The shopping promenade had all sorts of neat boutiques. And get a load of this pool.

"Is this your first cruise?"

It took her a moment to realize that the

woman on the next chaise was talking to her. Ginny sized her up quickly. She looked like she was pushing thirty. She had big thighs and a roll of fat around her middle. Not much competition, Ginny decided.

"Yes it is."

"Me too. Isn't this exciting?"

"Yeah."

The woman's name was Dotty, and she was from Stamford, Connecticut. Like Ginny, she was traveling alone.

Dotty was pouring out all the fascinating details of her job as a computer programmer when a shadow fell across Ginny's body. She looked up questioningly to see a waiter standing beside her chaise. He was holding a silver tray, on which rested a stemmed glass of white wine. Lying beside it was a perfect red rose.

"For you, miss," he said with a half-bow.

"Like, are you sure?" Ginny looked at Dotty. "Did you order anything?"

The other woman shook her head.

"The gentleman was very specific. It's for you," the waiter said to Ginny as he set the tray down on the table between the two chaise longues.

A little tremor ran down Ginny's spine as she reached out and touched the velvety rose petals. "What gentleman?"

"The one over there." He gestured toward the edge of the pool area. Ginny shaded her eyes, but she didn't see any young men. Was someone playing games with her?

"Oh, how thrilling, a secret admirer," Dotty gushed.

Ginny shrugged, her face impassive. But her stomach was churning with excitement as she took a swallow of the chilled white wine.

Harold Strickland almost didn't stop to answer the phone.

"Dad?"

"Sara."

"Dad, I'd like you to come for dinner tomorrow. We can talk."

"Sorry, I'm busy."

Before she could continue the conversation, he hung up. He was in a hurry. The phone started ringing again as he headed for the front door, but he ignored it. Even though Sara hadn't said much, there was something in the tone of her voice that had put him on the alert. This was going to be one of those "save the father" conversations. Kind of like "Save the Bay." He wasn't going to let her get started on that again.

Out of habit, he closed the front door softly. He'd been feeling relieved at having sent Ginny off on that cruise. He didn't have to wonder what she was thinking every time he slipped out of the house in the evening. Too bad he couldn't send Sara away as well. Damned if he was going to spill his guts to either one of his daughters. This didn't have anything to do with them. No! He wouldn't let himself believe that.

Quickly, he slipped behind the wheel of the car and started the engine. Fifteen minutes later he was turning in between the gateposts of Swan Point.

After cutting the engine, he sat staring at his mottled, blue-veined hands where they gripped the wheel—old man's hands. Scotch had done that. Sometimes he could barely hold them steady anymore.

He looked down the gently curving beach. He and Margaret had been happy here. In fact, they'd come out on that last afternoon and sat here holding hands.

My God, had it really been twelve years since she'd trustingly lain down on his examination table and let him kill her?

He still missed her so much that the anguish could be like a physical ache. Would the guilt and pain ever go away? But he'd had to do it. There just hadn't been any future for that baby.

The sun was a crimson ball on the horizon. Where it touched the bay, it turned the water the color of blood. Gallons of blood.

He closed his eyes and leaned his head back against the leather seat. When he opened them again, almost all of the shimmering redness had faded to gray.

He sighed. For awhile after Margaret's death, he'd felt as if his whole body had had a shot of novocaine. The numbness had gradually worn off, and he'd forced himself to go on with his life as best he could. Maybe if it hadn't been so soon after Margaret, he wouldn't have— He clamped down on the thought like a paramedic applying pressure to a gushing wound.

He could diagnose his present problem pretty well. He was in a profound depression. Maybe even suicidal.

Well, that might be the best way out of the mess he was in now.

Reaching in his pocket, he extracted a rectangle of needlepoint canvas and turned it slowly in his trembling fingers. Another one. It had come in an envelope with the morning mail. No return address.

It was a lot like the last one he'd found on his desk. Only this time there was a pair of initials stitched into the lefthand corner: K.T. He was pretty sure whose they were.

"Focus for you today is on courage, originality, freshness of approach," his horoscope had said this morning.

It was spooky how accurate the stars could be, he mused as he leaned back against the wall and surveyed the party atmosphere of the lounge.

He'd spent a lot of time getting ready for the trip—for this evening in particular. Most of his wardrobe was new. Not the sort of thing he wore around St. Stephens at all. Tonight he was dressed in a soft blue shirt and dark gray pleated slacks that made him feel sexy. He'd gotten his hair styled just before the trip. In his cabin, he'd experimented with a couple of different ways to comb it. Finally, he'd decided it looked best parted on the left side.

A blonde, wearing a sequined dress split up one leg almost to her waist, gave him the once-over and smiled.

A secret smirk flickered around his own thin lips. But when the blonde winked, he felt suddenly unmanned.

Instead of going over, he moved quickly away. It looked like it wouldn't take much to have one of these barracudas all over him. But there was only one woman here he was interested in tonight.

"Champagne?" a passing waiter inquired.

"Thank you." He lifted a long-stemmed glass off the silver tray and chugged down half the bubbly liquid. Back in St. Stephens he'd been so sure he could pull this off. Now he was beginning to realize that it wasn't as easy as he'd thought. After wiping his sweating palm on the cocktail napkin that came with the drink, he slipped a hand into his pants pocket and tried to look relaxed.

Ginny was on the other side of the room, talking to the same dumpy little woman she'd been with at the pool. But he'd be willing to bet that it wasn't going to be hard to pry her loose from her new friend. Not after the kind of steamy stuff she'd written in her diary.

Ginny had stopped hesitantly in the doorway a couple of feet from him when she'd first arrived. At least he knew she was as nervous as he was.

But he still had the advantage. He'd read her private fantasies. He smiled to himself. She'd even found herself a red dress like the one she'd written about in the diary. And she was wearing his rose in her hair.

He looked across the room at her. It was as if leaving the Eastern Shore had transformed her. Back in St. Stephens, he hadn't had much to do with her. He'd thought of her as homely and gawky.

This afternoon, the beauty parlor on board had done something to her that was close to magic. She'd always worn her fine, wavy hair too long. Now it was cut short and softly fluffed about her round face. In fact, she looked more appealing than she ever had.

Oh, Lord. What if some other man picked her up before he made his move?

As he took a step in her direction, he felt a pair of eyes on the back of his neck. When he turned, he caught a tall, narrow-hipped man checking him out with more than just casual interest. The guy looked like a fag.

He pressed his hand against the silky hair of his mustache. My God, did he look like a pansy or something? He'd tried to go for a casual resort style. But he didn't have a lot of experience with that sort of thing. Had he gone too far?

Trying to dismiss the distraction, he turned his attention back to Ginny. At that moment, she happened to glance up and discover that he was staring at her. For a split second, his legs felt like limp spaghetti, and he was afraid they might collapse under him. Then he locked his knees and raised his head slightly as he gave his quarry a slow, provocative smile.

When she smiled shyly back, he began to weave his way across the room in her direction.

She was going to die. He was coming over. Now what was she going to do?

"Hi."

She tipped her head and looked up at him through her lashes. He was kind of cute, in a quiet way, and the dark mustache reminded her of *Magnum P. I.* reruns.

Ginny touched the rose in her hair and saw his eyes follow her hand. Was he the one who'd sent the flower and the white wine? She was too timid to ask.

"Hi." She answered his greeting in a half whisper.

"You're shy, aren't you?"

She gulped. "Yes."

"Well, so am I."

"But you came over here."

"Because I decided I had to meet you."

"Oh."

Dotty had been taking in the exchange. "Well, I think I'll go over and get a drink. See you later, Ginny."

"Sure. Okay."

The plump woman moved in the direction of the bar.

"Your name is Ginny."

"What's yours?" She toyed with a piece of cheese from the buffet table.

He'd thought about telling her his name was Chad. But that would have been too much. "Keith," he said huskily.

"I like that. Where are you from?"

"Out West."

She looked at him uncertainly for a moment. He reminded her a little bit of someone she'd seen before. But who? Unconsciously, she twitched her shoulder. "I'm from St. Stephens, Maryland. You've probably never heard of it."

"You're right. What's it like?"

"Soooo boring." She didn't want to sound stupid. "Uh—what's your sign?" she asked brightly.

He grinned at her. "Gemini. Are you into astrology?"

"Sometimes. I'm a Cancer."

"Then you're sensitive, a great collector of possessions, and very romantic."

"How did you know?"

"I've made a study of it."

"Oh wow!" Lucky. She'd hit on a subject he really knew a lot about. For the next ten minutes, she listened avidly while he told her about how the stars influenced everything you did.

"I'm doing all the talking," he finally said. "Is this your first cruise?"

"Yes. Isn't it great? This ship is something else, you know?"

"Um hum. But it's all new for me, too. And it would be a whole lot more exciting if I had someone to share it with."

"It would?"

He was looking right at her. Could he see how her heart was thumping? She had to stop herself from glancing down at her chest. Instead, she studied his face. There was an intensity about his gaze that frightened her for a moment. But she could see he was a little bit nervous, too. That gave her the courage to ask, "Do you want to dance?"

"I'm not all that good."

"Neither am I," Ginny admitted.

"Then let's give it a try."

He reached for her hand. The first electric contact of his fingers against hers sent a *zing* all the way up her arm. She glanced sideways at him, wondering if he'd felt it too.

They made their way to the small dance floor, where a dozen couples were already gyrating to a rock number. As she started to move with the music, Ginny closed her eyes for a moment. This was what she'd dreamed about—and more than she'd dared hope for.

CHAPTER 19

Ginny stood nervously in the middle of her cabin. At one o'clock, when the band had finally quit, she hadn't been sure what to say. So she'd asked Keith to come down here with her.

When he'd hesitated, she'd wondered if she'd blurted out the wrong thing. But she'd read that guys liked it when a woman let them know what she wanted.

As soon as they'd closed the door, Keith had excused himself and ducked into the bathroom.

She heard the toilet flush and then the water running in the sink. After that, there was an endless moment of silence from the other side of the door.

Her heart was thumping the way it had when he'd first come over to her. No, harder, really.

When Keith stepped out into the tiny cabin again, she forgot to breathe for a moment. He stopped a few inches from her, gazing down into her face. His eyes were bright, almost feverish in their intensity.

"This is the first time you've been with a man, isn't it?"

Ginny tried to swallow, but her throat was too dry. "Yes."

When he didn't make a move, she stood there uncertainly. What was she supposed to do now? Maybe he'd think it was sexy if she undressed him.

When she reached shakily for the top button of his shirt, his fingers wrapped themselves around her wrist. "Ginny, please don't."

"Keith—I—"

He looked down into her eager face. He hadn't thought that things were going to go this fast. "I have to tell you something," he muttered.

"What's wrong? Did I do something wrong?"

"No. It's not you." He swallowed. "This is hard to talk about. But you need to understand why I can't—why we can't— Ginny, I was in this fire not so long ago. There are scars on my body—scars I'd be embarrassed for you to see yet."

Sudden moisture blurred her vision. "Oh, Keith. I'm so sorry."

"It's okay. I've learned to live with it. But I'd feel better if you didn't touch me—touch my body with your hands."

She gulped.

"Does that turn you off?"

"No—I guess not. It's just not what I expected."

"I know." He hesitated. "But I can touch you."

"Oh, yes."

He reached behind her and, with surprising dexterity, unhooked the snap at the top of her dress. She felt the zipper slide down her back, and then the dress was pooling around her ankles. Almost before she realized what Keith was doing, he put his hands on her arms and spun her around, dragging her up against him so that her back was pressed against his chest. As he cupped her breasts, she drew in a sharp breath and closed her eyes. She was trembling with a mixture of fear and excitement. No one had ever caressed her this intimately before.

"You're not afraid of me, are you?" he whispered, his hot breath fanning her ear.

"Oh, Keith."

He began to stroke her breasts through the lacy fabric of her bra, brushing his fingers back and forth against the hardening nipples.

She braced her feet against the floor and threw her head back against his shoulder.

"Do you like what I'm doing?"

She couldn't answer. With her eyes closed and the breath hissing in and out of her lungs, she dragged his hand down to the waistband of her half-slip.

Tuesday, July 4

Sara knew a phone call wouldn't do. She had to talk to Ben in person. After checking in with his answering service to make sure that he was home, she'd spent the morning making barbecued chicken, potato salad, and blueberry muffins. Maybe if she came over with a holiday picnic, he'd accept the peace offering, she decided as she packed the food in an ice chest.

She'd been feeling so good the other night, that it had taken her by surprise after dinner when Ben had brought up the problem with her father. She just hadn't stopped to censor her reaction. Really, she knew Ben was right. But her own frustration level had kept her from admitting it gracefully.

After stowing the chest of food in the car, Sara headed for Ben's house. She'd never been there before, but she knew where it was—out on Stephens Mill Road.

The wood-and-brick house was set well back from the road. When Sara pulled up beside Ben's Blazer on the parking pad, she didn't immediately get out of her own car. What if she'd fixed lunch and come all this way and he didn't want to talk to her?

Should she even take the food out of the car? she wondered. Finally, she brought the cooler up to the wooden deck and set it by the front door.

No one answered the bell. Then, as Sara was about to try again, the door swung inward.

"Sorry, I was out back." When Ben saw who was on the deck, he closed his mouth abruptly and gazed at Sara quizzically.

She looked up at him, her heart turning over. He hadn't shaved that morning, and he was wearing a pair of cut-off blue jeans, a faded burgundy tee shirt, and a pair of old tennis shoes with no socks. All at once, she wanted to reach out and smooth the ragged threads hanging from the frayed edge of the denim. Instead, she pressed her palm against her own thigh.

He cocked his head to one side.

"Hi," she managed.

"I guess I didn't expect to see you."

"I guess not."

He continued to look at her, his expression a mixture of speculation and wariness.

Sara could feel the air conditioning wafting out through the door into the July heat. It felt good, and she wished she could ask him to invite her in. Her hand fluttered as she gestured toward the ice chest. "I brought a Fourth of July picnic over. I thought we could eat it while we talked."

"Oh."

"I guess the food was just an excuse. I really came to say I was sorry for jumping all over you like that when you started talking about Dad."

For a terrible moment she thought he wasn't going to accept the apology.

"I'm—sorry, too." He stepped away from the door. "Come on in."

When she picked up the ice chest, he took it out of her hands. "Let me."

Sara relinquished the burden and followed him down the short hall.

One large room spanned the back of the house. Floor-to-ceiling windows along its length provided a magnificent view of the bay. But the room itself was almost spartan in its lack of furnishings. There was only a corduroy sectional couch, a glass coffee table in need of a good Windexing, and a wall unit with a television and a stereo unit. The man had been living here for a year; he might as well have been camping out, she thought.

Ben set down the ice chest and straightened. He shrugged as he took in the expression on Sara's face. "I guess I don't have your knack for turning a house into a home."

"Oh, Ben."

They each took an uncertain step forward. Then he was closing the gap between them, pulling her into his arms. For a long moment, they just clung to each other.

"I didn't know how much I'd miss you," she finally whispered.

"I did."

She threaded her fingers through his hair and brought his face down to hers. Their lips met in an almost frantic kiss that was more an acknowledgment of deep feeling than an expression of passion.

Afterwards, Sara rested her cheek against Ben's chest.

"Don't do that to me again," he finally muttered.

"Do you mean lash out at you when you're trying to be honest with me?"

"No, I mean act as if you don't trust me."

"Oh, Ben, I'm so sorry." Her arms tightened around him fiercely. After a moment she mumbled, "I guess it was a case of shooting the messenger."

He laughed, and she smiled as she felt the vibration against her cheek.

It was as if a twenty-pound weight had been

lifted off her body. Yet there was another, still pressing her down. "I did try to call Dad," she said in a low voice.

Ben angled Sara slightly away from him so that he could look down into her face. "And?"

"He hung up on me."

Ben sighed.

"What are we going to do now?" Sara asked.

Keith didn't break his stride as he wiped a bead of sweat off his forehead. There was a jogging track that ran around the edge of the upper deck. Back home, that was the way he kept in shape. It was nice not to have to change his routine on the Royal Alexandria.

Most of the other passengers were enjoying a lavish brunch in the dining room. He and one other runner had the track to themselves.

His arms and legs pumped as his jogging shoes slapped against the green carpet. Then his stride faltered for a moment, and his hands clenched into tight fists. None of this was as simple as he'd assured himself it was going to be.

For a moment, the bright sunlight around him faded to gray, and a point right above his right eye started to throb with an agonizing intensity.

He staggered and almost lost his balance. My God, how long could he keep this farce up?

"Hey, buddy, you all right?"

It took a tremendous effort to pull himself back together. "Yes. I just need a drink of water."

He left the track and clutched the railing,

leaning over into the wind. It dried the perspiration on his face and helped clear his thoughts. Suddenly the scene snapped back into focus.

Tonight was the gala Fourth of July celebration. He and Ginny were going to watch the fireworks together. That would be the perfect time to kill her.

Ben gave Sara a level look. "Even though Harold won't talk to either one of us, I think he's acknowledged in his own mind that there's a problem. Lois mentioned to me that he asked her to do some rescheduling."

"What does that mean?"

"He's told her he wants to ease up on his work load. She's just supposed to give him the routine stuff. And I'm going to take the sick calls."

"Good." Sara approved.

"That's better for the patients. But it doesn't really do anything for him."

"I know."

"At least he took some kind of step—on his own."

"Yes."

She stood there in Ben's arms, feeling better than she had in a while. Dad didn't talk about his problems. But he had a way of working them out for himself. Maybe things really were going to be okay.

When Ben's fingers began to knead her shoulders, she closed her eyes and let her body relax against his. Neither one of them made a move to separate. By slow degrees, she felt another kind of tension blooming between them.

His touch became more sensual as his hands followed the length of her spine and then trailed farther down as he cupped her bottom. This time when he kissed her, she felt a slow heat begin to build in her center.

Her breathing was ragged when he finally lifted his head again. So was his.

"Ben—"

"If you want to stop, tell me now."

She heard the tautness in his voice. "Ben, I'm—fat. My body's starting to look like a ripe pear."

His chuckle was low and throaty as he stepped back and stroked the budding roundness of her abdomen. "My God, woman, is it possible you don't realize how sexy you are?"

Her eyes searched his. They'd been building toward this for weeks now. As the heat of his touch turned her molten, she allowed herself to surrender to the pleasure of the caress.

He led her down the hall to the bedroom. But when they stepped inside the door, he stopped and muttered an expletive. "Sorry, I wasn't expecting company."

She followed his gaze to the king-size bed. A relatively narrow area was cleared for sleeping. The rest was piled with medical journals, books, newspapers, and two empty coffee mugs.

She started to laugh, and he joined her as he began to clear away the clutter. "I guess you haven't been bringing anybody else here."

"There hasn't been anybody I want to bring to my bed. Just you."

After drawing the drapes, he took her hands, bending her fingers so that he could press her knuckles against his lips and then nibble gently at them.

Her thumb stroked against the stubble on his cheek.

"Maybe I should go shave. There's a bathroom right across the hall you can use."

"Thanks."

He was tall and lean and naked when he came out of the bathroom to find Sara waiting for him under the covers. After slipping into bed beside her, he took her in his arms and gently held her against the length of his body, caressing her back and shoulders and giving her time to feel comfortable before he began to explore her feminine secrets.

She'd never felt more cherished, had never been aroused with such a mixture of skill and tenderness.

In the dimly lit room, he whispered endearments as he caressed her, sighed with pleasure as her hands moved over his body in turn.

When they were both more than ready, he entered her carefully and then bent to brush his lips against hers.

"All right?"

"A lot more than all right."

There was only the sound of their labored breathing after that—until she called out his name. She hadn't known a sexual climax could be so intense—or so sweet.

CHAPTER 20

Ginny woke and stretched luxuriously. This was so *great*—no classes, no reason to get up early. Then she peered bleary-eyed at the clock on the bedside table.

One-thirty. Jeez, she'd have to hustle if she was going to meet Keith for brunch at two.

Quickly she stepped into the compact bathroom and adjusted the water taps in the shower stall.

As she began to soap her body under the hot water, she thought about the way Keith had touched her last night. It made her feel all tingly and hot again.

His hands were so knowing and sensitive. It was like he was bringing her flesh to life.

When they'd come down to her cabin that first time, she'd been frightened. She'd never slept with a guy. But Keith hadn't pushed things that far.

Did he love her?

She hoped so. He was so tender and sweet— and so smart . . . her fantasy love come true.

For just a moment, a shadow crossed her features. Poor Keith. He'd been hurt, and not just by that fire that had scarred him. She sensed there were things he was holding back from her, things that sometimes made him seem a little bit strange. But she didn't care about that. He was the first guy who'd ever been interested in her, and she wasn't going to blow it.

Turning off the water, she began to towel her hair dry. There were two more days to the cruise. Before it was over, would he trust her enough to share his innermost thoughts?

She wanted him to spend the night in her bed—and let her touch his body the way he touched hers.

Ben and Sara ate the picnic lunch out on the deck overlooking the water. She hadn't bothered to put her sandals back on, and she stretched out her legs on an extra chair. The sunshine felt good. Out on the blue water, two sailboats skimmed along the waves.

"You have a great view."

"Yes, I do."

Ben's eyes weren't on the bay. They were on Sara, and she flushed slightly. When he reached across the round table to cover her hand with his, she turned her palm over and linked their fingers.

"I'm glad you came over. This is a lot more

fun than going to the high school chicken and crab cake supper."

"You bought a ticket?"

'Um hum."

"So did I. From a student who came to the gallery selling them last week. But then I didn't want to go by myself. I wanted to be with you, even though I wasn't sure you wanted to see me."

"I did. But it was frustrating that we couldn't have an honest discussion about Harold."

"I know. Oh, Ben, I do want a relationship where we can be completely open with each other. It's just that being that way with someone is still hard for me."

He took a bit of blueberry muffin and chewed slowly. She was giving him the opportunity to bring up his own carefully hidden past. But what they had together was still so fragile. He couldn't take the risk yet. He didn't want to lose her.

"It's new to me, too."

"I want you to understand why I was so upset Wednesday night." She swallowed. "After Ted died, it was awfully hard to accept that I wasn't going to get any emotional support from Dad. But I still kept hoping. Then, when you started telling me what was going on with him at the office, I had to let go of one more illusion."

"I didn't know."

"How could you?"

They sat in silence for awhile.

"Can you let me take some of it off your shoulders?" he finally asked.

"I don't know; I'm so used to holding all my problems inside."

"It's not a free offer. There are strings attached. I need you, too."

"I like that."

He took her hand and stood up. "How about a nice relaxing dip in the bay?"

"I didn't bring a bathing suit. I'll bet I don't even have one that still fits."

"Wear your jumper. We'll throw it in the dryer before we go into town to see the fireworks tonight. But, you know, there's no one around. If you don't want to get your dress wet, you can take it off."

She giggled, feeling younger and more carefree than she had in years as she unstrapped her watch and laid it on the table. "Ben Langley, you have a very naughty mind."

"But you love it."

Keith had dragged one of the chaise longues off into a corner by itself. "It's almost time for the fireworks. We should have a perfect view of the show. And we can have some privacy, too."

Ginny's eyes widened. "Privacy? What exactly do you have in mind?"

"Wait and see." He lay down on the chaise and pulled Ginny into the vee of his legs. Then he threw a light blanket over the two of them.

Ginny snuggled back against him. Under the blanket, she pulled his hand up under her green knit top. She'd gotten to know the kinds of things he liked to do. Now there was an added thrill to the excitement. Wouldn't it be neat to make out with all these people walking around?

"Fireworks over the harbor are a St. Stephens tradition," Sara told Ben as they pulled up behind her store. "And since I've got a private parking space, we don't have to worry about the shuttle buses from the park."

He took her hand as they crossed Main Street, and they saw several residents note the gesture. He felt Sara tense for a moment. But she didn't pull away, which meant that, by tomorrow, everybody in town would know that the young doctor was courting the new widow.

He was glad she cared more about holding his hand than about what people would think. As for himself, he felt like shouting it from the top of the lighthouse down at the Maritime Museum.

What a day so far. After they'd fooled around in the water, he'd taken her back to bed. This time, it had been long and lazy, and then explosive. The fireworks tonight were going to seem pale by comparison.

He'd heard her talking on the phone when he'd gotten out of the shower. She'd told him she was arranging a surprise. As they walked along the wooden pier, she stopped in front of a small motorboat called The Ruby Tuesday.

"Is this yours?"

"She belongs to an old friend. We're borrowing her for the evening. The key ought to be—" Sara opened a fishing tackle box and rummaged around. "Here."

"I hope you know how to drive."

"Pilot. And yes, I do. Come on, we want to get out in the river before the show starts."

As Sara expertly steered the small craft out of the congested harbor, Ben hummed the Rolling Stones song with the same name.

"I didn't know you could sing."

"I only have a limited repertoire."

A few minutes later, Sara cut the engine again. "Here we are."

Ben looked around at the dark water and the reflected lights of the town. "Nice."

"Um hum."

"Let's get comfortable." He arranged some cushions, sat down, and held out his hand.

She let him pull her into the vee of his legs and leaned back against his chest.

"This is cozy."

"Um hum."

The night was hot and sultry. As they waited for the fireworks, the boat drifted gently on the water. But Sara could tell that Ben wasn't entirely relaxed. "What's wrong?" she finally asked.

"Nothing."

"Ben—"

"Dammit, I can't help it. I keep thinking about you and Ted."

She tried to pull away, but he held her against his chest. "I haven't been thinking about him at all," she said.

His laugh was hollow. "I can't stop wondering: if her marriage was so bad, why was she sleeping with him?"

She sat there stiffly, her bottom lip between her teeth. Then she bowed her head slightly.

"You know, I keep telling you things I've never told anyone else. I found out after we got married that Ted was a man with a strong libido. When he wanted sex, he wouldn't take no for an answer."

Ben swore under his breath.

"A lot of the time, he didn't seem to care whether I responded or not."

"Did he— I mean—"

"I guess it wasn't rape. Usually, anyway."

"The bastard."

Her fingers dug into his knees. "Ben, before this afternoon, I didn't know how much different it is when someone cares about your pleasure as much as his own."

He pulled her back against him and pressed his cheek to the top of her head. "Sara, I love you."

Her heart was pounding hard, but at the same time, a new bud of promise had begun to unfurl inside her. "Oh, Ben— I feel that way too. But I was afraid to say the words—because it's just been so hard to rely on anyone except myself."

"Honey, I can understand that now. It's lucky I didn't know what he was putting you through. I couldn't have stood by without doing something."

"There wasn't anything you could do—then."

"But now there is. I'm not going to let anybody hurt you again. I mean it."

There was something so achingly sweet about the softly whispered pledge that her eyes brimmed with tears.

*   *   *

It was almost time. He only had to keep up the game for a little longer. He could do that.

What would she want to hear?

"Ginny, will you marry me?"

Her heart stopped for a moment and then started up in double time. She tried to squirm around to face him, but he held her captive between his hands and his body. "Oh God, Keith, yes. Of course."

One thumb lightly caressed a pebble-hard nipple. The other traced the lace at the edge of her panties. "I never thought it could be this way with anyone."

"Neither did I," she gasped. "But Keith, you're driving me crazy. Please—I have to—"

"Be patient. You have to wait for the fireworks."

"How can I be patient when you're touching me like that?"

He laughed, his hot breath burning her ear.

Minutes later, the first shells burst into the star-filled sky.

He drew in a shuddering breath. It was all rushing to completion so fast. His destiny— and hers.

"Keith, you promised," she moaned.

"Yes, I did." His lazy touches turned to the sure strokes he knew she liked best. He felt powerful, more powerful—and more real—than he ever had in his life. *Real.* She'd used that word in her diary.

All at once he was quickening the pace, sending the girl in his arms shattering into a million sizzling points of light. As she writhed in his arms, he felt an answering release in his own body.

Still panting, she sagged back against him.

He struggled to catch his own breath. "How do you feel?" he finally managed.

"That was so nice. This is the happiest night of my life."

"I'm glad." For a moment, the scene around him blurred, and the spot above his right eye began to throb again. Oh, God. He couldn't lose it now. As he struggled silently against the pain and dizziness, one hand continued to stroke Ginny possessively. She'd become his touchstone to reality.

"Keith, what's wrong?"

He struggled to hold his voice steady. "I'll be all right in a minute."

With the other hand, he unzipped the tote bag that he'd set on the deck beside the chaise.

"What are you doing?"

"Nothing."

She felt the prick of the needle in her thigh.

"Ouch," she gasped. "Keith—what—?"

"Shhhh— It's all right, little Ginny. It was written in the stars long before either one of us was born," his voice soothed. Holding her, he felt the first shudders of panic. She tried to twist toward him. He held her firmly for several heartbeats—until the paralysis crept over her.

"I promise it won't hurt, Ginny. And it'll be over real quick."

He kept holding her, stroking her, murmuring tender reassurances even as he felt the life force slipping from her body.

The finale of the fireworks came with a burst of shell after dazzling shell. They drew all eyes to the heavens—except his and Ginny's.

Quietly, he picked her limp form up in his arms and made his way to the rail. For a moment longer, he held onto her. Then he let go and cast her onto the dark waters.

CHAPTER 21

Thursday, July 6

He'd slipped into town in the small hours of the morning and driven straight home from the airport. The narrow bed upstairs where he slept was neatly made—just the way he'd left it. It had taken him a long time to fall asleep.

He didn't get up until mid-morning. After staggering over to the dresser, he stood staring at his face in the mirror. The mustache was gone. It had just been for the cruise. But he'd liked the way it had made him look. He reached up to stroke his smooth upper lip. Then he flattened his palm against the cold, hard surface of the mirror. Raising his fist suddenly, he smashed it into the mocking reflection and watched it crack and splinter. The image that stared back at him was distorted now. The way it should be. For long moments he stood there gripping the edge of the dresser.

Finally, he turned away and headed for the stairs to the attic. Whenever he had doubts, he'd go up there where the acoutrements of Keith Thomas's life were stored in boxes.

As he stepped into the large, low-ceilinged room, a spiderweb glued itself to his face, and he cringed as he slapped it away.

Reaching out, he pulled a chain hanging from a rafter. Nothing happened. He'd have to remember to change the bulb next time he came up. But what did it matter? Enough sunlight streaked in through the dirty window for him to see what he was doing.

He looked around at the boxes and trunks covered with dust and at the possessions he'd taken out and left sitting around. Maybe, when he had time, he'd straighten it all up again. Or maybe he could get her to do it.

Sometimes he liked to unfold the clothes he'd worn when he was a little boy. Other times he'd page through the books his mother had read to him—*Babar, The King's Stilts, Curious George.*

Today, he got out his toys. His marble collection was in an old mayonnaise jar. He unscrewed the rusted top, took out a few of the glass spheres, and held them up to the light. Then he set the jar down and picked up his slingshot. He'd killed squirrels with it. Maybe he could get some now.

Pocketing the weapon, he went downstairs and wandered out to the woods behind the house. He wanted to be alone, but it didn't work out that way.

"I'm glad you're back." The voice was soft and welcoming.

"Yes." His face was a study in cast iron. Stooping, he picked up a couple of stones and pulled back the rubber band in the slingshot.

It broke. "Ouch." He shook his hand where the rubber had stung him.

"What's wrong?"

"Nothing."

"Ginny's dead, isn't she?"

"Yes."

"Then why aren't you happy?"

He shrugged. "This time, it doesn't feel as good as I thought it would."

They sat down on the old log that had fallen across the path that twisted through the woods.

"If you want to stop—"

"No! I don't want to stop. It's just that—"

He pulled off a strip of rotting bark and began to shred it. "If you don't understand about Ginny, I can't explain it to you."

"Try."

"I've never—" He stopped abruptly. "I think she was in love with me."

"That makes it even sweeter."

His vision misted. "But I got so close to her. I felt something for her, too." He ground his fist against the bark. "It wasn't like that smug, self-indulgent bastard Ted."

"But the sins of the father—"

"I know."

He stared off into the trees, watching a flock of little birds flutter from branch to branch. They were yellow and gray. He wished he knew what they were called. But he hadn't had much time to learn things like that—the names of birds, the names of the different kinds of clouds, how to have normal relationships with people.

He'd missed so much. It wasn't his fault; he'd been cheated. When he spoke again, the fire had crept back into his voice. One fleeting moment of remorse over an insignificant girl wasn't going to make him lose sight of his reason for existence. "We've come this far. I want to finish."

"Then Sara's next." There was a moment of hesitation. "If you want me to do it for you, I will."

"No, I'll do it. Soon."

A rustling sound in a tangle of honeysuckle near the creek made his head bob up. An animal?

No. He caught a flash of white fabric through

the woods. It must be one of those blasted kids who'd been poking around the place. No telling what they'd been up to while he'd been gone.

"Get him!"

In the next second, the person he'd been talking to was wiped from his consciousness, as if an eraser had swept across a blackboard in his mind.

He leaped up and sprinted after the fleeing figure. Jesus. Had the little snoop been close enough to hear anything? And would he understand any of it? What *exactly* had they said? Too bad the slingshot had broken. He should have brought his gun out here instead. From now on he would.

The kid crashed through the underbrush and tripped over a root. For a moment, he lay sprawled on the ground.

Christ, he had the little brat now, he thought as he closed the distance between them. He could almost feel his fingers squeezing the scrawny little neck.

Frantically, the boy pushed himself up and scrambled back toward the road, where his bike was propped against a tree trunk. With a frightened glance over his shoulder at his pursuer, he hopped on the seat and started pedaling toward town.

A bike couldn't outrun a motorcycle. Quickly, he dashed back toward the garage and threw the rickety wooden doors open. No time for his helmet and leathers. But when he roared out onto the winding drive, the kid was nowhere to be seen.

* * *

Bobby Craig lay panting in the underbrush. When the motorcycle thundered past his hiding place, he scrunched down farther into the raspberry brambles, where he'd thrown himself as soon as he'd passed the first curve in the road.

His arms and face were scratched and bleeding. Crushed raspberries stained the front of his shirt. But he wasn't thinking about any of that. What should he do now? Stay hidden? Or try to make it back to the highway?

Better lay low. That crazy man might come back. But what if he got off his motorcycle and started beating the bushes? Bobby shuddered. If that guy caught him, he was dead meat for sure.

Saturday, July 8

The deplaning passengers came down the jetway, singly and in twos and threes. Some had obviously been on vacation. Some were in Baltimore on business. Others were just passing through on their way to somewhere else. But Ginny wasn't among them.

Where was she? After hesitating for a few moments longer, Sara slipped through the door and made her way up the jetway. The flight attendants had already gathered their hand luggage together. One of them glanced up with a slightly impatient expression that she quickly suppressed. "Can I help you?"

"I was looking for my sister—Ginny Strickland. She's supposed to be on this flight."

The woman checked her passenger list. "I'm

sorry, but Ginny Strickland didn't join us in Atlanta."

Sara pulled out her wallet and extracted a print of Ginny's high school yearbook picture. "Do you recognize her?"

The woman studied the picture. "We had a hundred and twenty-five people on this flight. But I don't think I remember her. Sorry." She pursed her lips. "Why don't you check with the ticket counter. Maybe there's some mix-up about her arrival time."

"Thanks."

A hollow feeling had been growing in Sara's chest as she'd watched the last of the passengers file out. Now she felt slightly disoriented as she made her way back up the pier. Pulling the itinerary out of her purse, she studied the computer printout as she walked. This was the right day, and the right time.

Disorientation gave way to dread as she waited for the ticket agent to check his computer.

"Your sister didn't reconfirm her flight."

"She probably wouldn't have thought of that," Sara muttered.

"She also didn't check in at Miami, or switch to another flight." He stroked his chin. "It was a K class, no refund ticket."

Sara's fingers clenched around the strap of her pocketbook.

"Does your sister have any friends in Miami? Maybe she decided to stay and visit. Or perhaps she went home with someone else?"

Sara realized she'd been gnawing at the inside of her cheek. "I don't think so. But thanks, anyway." As far as she knew, Ginny didn't have any close friends outside of St. Stephens. *Could she have made friends with someone on the ship?* she wondered.

Crossing the concourse, she sank down heavily on a bench and stared at the board with the arriving and departing flight schedules. All around her, people were lugging bags to the counter and hurrying to make their planes.

Where the hell was Ginny? Was something wrong, or was this just some stupid stunt? How many times had her sister said that she'd give anything to get away from St. Stephens for good? Maybe she'd gone and done it. Or maybe she'd just missed the flight and was stuck in Atlanta. In that case, she would have called.

Struggling to control her growing anxiety and exasperation, Sara checked her watch. It was almost five o'clock. Maybe she could catch Ralph before he closed up. But when she phoned the gallery, the decoy carver told her that he hadn't heard from Ginny. She drew a similar blank with Lois, Harold's receptionist.

"If she calls, get her to tell you where she is," Sara instructed in a calm voice. However, as she hung up the receiver, her legs started to shake with reaction. Suddenly all the bad feelings she'd had about letting Ginny go off on this trip came rushing back toward her like a tidal wave.

"Will Sara Chandler please pick up a yellow courtesy phone."

Thank God.

It took a moment to locate one of the phones. "This is Sara Chandler. Is there a call for me?"

"One moment, please."

The voice that came on the other end of the line was Ben's. "Sara. Is Ginny with you?"

"No. She wasn't on the plane."

There was a moment of silence on the other end of the line. "The cruise line just called. She didn't remove her luggage from her stateroom."

"She didn't? I don't understand. What's going on, Ben?"

"They're trying to check that out. In the meantime, they wanted to know where to ship her things. I—uh—told them to send them to your house."

"To hell with her things. Where is she?"

"Sara, they don't know."

"Maybe she's on another flight. I'm going to wait here and see."

"Honey, do you want me to come up there?"

"Ginny could be here any time. Then we'd miss each other."

"But if she's not, you can't stay there all night."

"I know."

"I'll be waiting up for you."

Sara hung around until the last flight from Atlanta or anywhere in Florida arrived. As each one came in, she had Ginny paged. And she kept walking back and forth between the entrances to the gates, anxiously watching the deplaning crowds. Ginny wasn't among the passengers.

Around ten, she made one more call to Lois at home. Still no word. By then, Sara was so tired that she could hardly stand up, and the straps of her sandals were cutting into her swollen feet like the tentacles of an octopus wrapped around a blowfish.

Wearily she drove back to St. Stephens. It was almost midnight when she arrived at Ben's. He was wearing a pair of pajama bottoms, and his hair was tousled, but she could tell he hadn't been asleep.

When he saw her face, he took her in his arms and hugged her tightly. "She wasn't on any of the flights."

"No."

"Come on in and sit down." He steered her to the sofa and made her put her feet up. When he saw how red and swollen they were, he slipped her sandals off, cushioned her feet in his lap, and began to massage them.

"It's like she's vanished." As she finished the sentence, her voice cracked. "Oh Ben, I'm so worried. I never should have let her go."

"She's not a child, Sara."

"I know—but—" She had leaned back and closed her eyes, but they suddenly jerked open again. "Does Dad know?"

"Yes. I stopped by his place around nine. He was—"

"Drunk."

"I'm sorry."

Ben continued to stroke her aching insteps. "There's no point trying to talk to him now. Maybe we'll have some good news in the morning."

Sara closed her eyes again and tried to relax. It didn't take much persuading to get her to stay the night. Having Ben's arms around her was incredibly comforting. In the early hours of the morning, she finally fell asleep.

Even though she wasn't hungry, Ben made her eat some cereal and drink some juice for breakfast.

"Do you want me to call the cruise line?" he asked.

"I'll do it." But she was glad that he pulled his chair up beside hers as she made the call.

While she waited to be put through to the purser on the Royal Alexandria, Ben took her hand. As the conversation progressed, she found she was clutching with the tenacity of a high-wire artist gripping a balance pole.

Basically all she learned was that an investigation was in progress. If Ginny had gotten off at one of the ports of call, she hadn't taken anything with her. Her passport was with the other belongings she'd left in her cabin on the Royal Alexandria. The whole package was already on its way to St. Stephens via UPS.

"You realize, Ms. Chandler, that your sister could simply have decided to—uh—go off on her own. Or with a companion."

"Yes," Sara admitted in a low voice. "But I can't help worrying that she might have fallen off the ship or something."

"That's highly unlikely."

Looking down, Sara saw that her nails had made four reddened half-circles in Ben's hand. Swallowing, she eased up on the pressure.

"Ms. Chandler, I'm sure that your sister's going to turn up safe and sound," the purser was saying. "But we'll do everything we can to determine her whereabouts. If she should contact you, please let *us* know immediately."

"Of course."

As Sara hung up the phone, she realized she

was saying a silent little prayer. *Please, God, let Ginny be all right.* But she didn't feel any closer to finding her sister than she had the day before, at the airport.

"I'd better tell Dad."

"Yes."

Again, Ben waited while she called.

Her father picked up the phone on the second ring. "God damn you. Why are you doing this?" The question was almost a sob.

"Dad, it's Sara."

"Sara?" He sounded confused.

"I'm calling about Ginny."

"She's dead."

Sara sucked in a strangled breath. "You mean someone called—?"

"No."

"Then what are you talking about?"

"I was wrong. God help me. I was wrong."

"Dad?"

"Don't you understand anything?" he said as if he were speaking to an idiot. "She's dead. Just like your husband. Just like you're going to be." His voice cracked, and he started to sob. But Sara had already dropped the phone. As it hit the wooden surface of the table, it shattered the silence of the room like a gunshot in an echo chamber.

CHAPTER 22

Ralph Meekins had lived in the same little one-story wooden house all his life. It was on a narrow country road on an inlet off Harris Creek. Probably he could get a pretty penny for the property. But he didn't see any point in selling. He was comfortable here. A couple of wood stoves kept the place cozy in winter. In summer, there was almost always a breeze off the water to cool things down.

After his mother had died back in sixty-two, he'd converted her bedroom into a workshop. Now, neat racks of tools lined the walls. On the shelves were several decoys in various stages of production.

Ralph put down the pin-tailed duck he'd been working on, took off his glasses, and rubbed his eyes. Then he gave the decoy a critical inspection. He'd almost finished shaping the slim, graceful body. Soon he could start adding color. But that would have to wait.

It was getting so he couldn't work more than a couple of hours at a time without his shoulders aching or his vision blurring. But this was the height of the tourist season, and he'd promised Sara some more pieces.

Outside, he could see a single headlight cutting through the darkness—a motorcycle, or a car with one beam on the blink. He watched the shaft of light turn the corner and head slowly up the narrow road toward the Baileys' house. Maybe it was somebody visiting them.

Or, maybe not. There was no telling who might come snooping around. He got up and stretched. Then he turned off the light, closed the door, and shuffled into the small sitting room. After staring out the window into the blackness for a moment, he began to circle the room, drawing the shades. He didn't want to broadcast his personal business to anyone. 'Specially this business.

He'd been collecting the evidence for almost two months now—records from Sara's gallery, observations he made in his notebook. But he didn't quite have the clincher he needed.

The stuff he was saving was in an Acme supermarket bag under the settee, in back, where the springs and the lining sagged. When he stooped down to fish it out, he got a crick in his back and had to flop down on the faded rug until the pain eased up.

Lord a'mighty. It was criminal the way a body fell apart when it got old. When he was feeling better, he pulled out the material and spread it in his lap.

The woman he'd been checking up on was living a big lie. He'd suspected that for awhile. But he hadn't been able to prove anything.

He brought his knuckle to his mouth and worried the skin between crooked, discolored teeth.

He'd wondered what she and that man of hers were trying to pull off. Now he was beginning to think it might be murder. If he hadn't been out in an old duck blind with his binoculars, watching a family of canvasbacks, he would have been fooled too. But he'd seen her with Ted, all right. The image of what they'd been doing right out there in the open made him want to puke.

He really ought to warn Sara, or maybe tell Chief Dailey. But he couldn't prove anything yet. Right now, all he had was a nasty story and some suspicions. Maybe when those papers came from Social Security, he'd have enough proof to make someone believe him.

CHAPTER 23

Wednesday, July 12

A summer shower pelted down on Sara as she climbed the steps to the front porch. Over the drumming of the drops on the roof, she could hear the phone ringing inside. Frantically, she fumbled with the key and finally got the lock to open.

Ginny. That had to be Ginny. Or maybe it was about Dad.

Sprinting down the hall to the kitchen, she snatched the receiver off the hook. But it was only a lawn-care service, offering a special deal for the remainder of the summer. Sara said she didn't have a lawn, then hung up.

She glanced at the new answering machine she'd gotten, just in case Ginny or someone else with important information about her sister called while she was out. There were no messages.

Sinking down onto the chair beside the kitchen table, Sara automatically reached down to ease her wet sandals off. It seemed as if her feet had been swollen since the day at the airport.

As she massaged her instep, she closed her eyes for a moment. God, the last few days . . . they would have been unbearable without Ben.

First Ginny, then Dad. She'd known he was going to take it hard. But she hadn't expected him to crack up. After she'd dropped the phone, she and Ben had rushed over to Dad's house. They'd found him sitting in the middle of the kitchen floor with a dozen half-full medicine bottles scattered on the linoleum around him. He'd already been awash with whiskey. On top of the liquor, the pills were enough to paralyze a water buffalo. But Ben had taken him into the bathroom and made him throw up. The hospital had finished the job with a stomach pump.

"Why?" Sara had asked him as he'd lain pale and still in a hospital bed. He'd turned his head away.

"What did you mean about Ginny and Ted?" she'd persisted.

Tears had leaked out of his eyes and down the sides of his ravaged face. But he hadn't said a word—to her or anyone else. Now he was in the psychiatric wing of the hospital, under observation.

As far as Sara could tell, he'd withdrawn into a private world of his own. He hadn't spoken to anyone at the hospital. When she'd first gone over to see him, he hadn't even acknowledged her presence. After the first few visits, Dr. Clifton had suggested it might be better if she didn't come back for several days. She'd wondered if it was for Dad's good or if the doctor was worried about the effect the visits were having on her.

The phone intruded on her thoughts again, and she snatched it up before the first ring stopped. This time it was Judy Wooters, Sara's new assistant at the shop. She was one of Ben's patients. When she'd mentioned to him that she was looking for a part-time job, he'd sent her over. For half a minute, Sara had resented Ben's interference. Then she'd silently conceded he was right. She did need some help running the gallery. And she'd quickly come to appreciate Judy. Not only was she reliable enough to tend the shop on her own, but she had an upbeat, cheerful attitude that was just what Sara needed.

"I'm sorry to bother you," Judy said over the phone. "But I have a customer here who wants to have Kitty Duncan make up a collage centerpiece to match her dining room wallpaper. Does she do special orders?"

Sara sighed and struggled to focus her mind on business. "Kitty hasn't done anything like that for us before. But I'm sure she would. Why don't you call her?"

"I tried. She's not home."

"Take the customer's name and get an idea of what she wants done."

"All right."

Sara rolled her shoulders as she looked toward the refrigerator. Sometimes she had a glass of milk when she came home in the afternoons. Today, all she wanted to do was flop down on her bed.

Sandals in hand, she started for the steps. But about halfway up, she stopped and took a deep breath. A hint of aroma drifted down toward her. It was faintly musky, faintly spicy.

A cleaning product? she wondered. Perfume? No. It was nothing she used.

A little shiver slithered down her spine. She sniffed the air again, feeling suddenly as if she weren't alone in the house.

All her muscles tensed as her eyes flicked to the top of the stairs. Everything was quiet as a tomb. But the upstairs hall was dark, and she couldn't see into the shadows. For a moment it was all she could do to keep from turning and fleeing through the front door. Then she gave herself a mental shake. She'd been through so much lately. But she wasn't going to crack up like Dad.

Decisively, she flipped on the light. Then, with newly resolute steps, she climbed the stairs. The lingering scent was stronger on the second floor. Sara let it lead her down the hall toward Ted's old office. When she opened the door, the musky smell hit her full in the face, and she gagged. The reflex made her realize what she was smelling. George Newhouse's cologne! She remembered how it had made her sick when he'd come to the house to look at Ted's files. Now it was doing it again. But it had been days since George had stopped by. That was before Ginny had left for the cruise.

A stab of pain knifed through Sara's temple. No. Don't let this set you off thinking about Ginny again. Think about George.

Deliberately, Sara looked around the room. The door and windows had been closed, and the heat beat against her in a scented wave. Had the smell of George's cologne really hung around in here all this time?

Or ... The unspoken question hung in the heavy air as thickly as the stale fragrance. Could George Newhouse have come here while she was out? But why would he pull a trick like that?

She pursed her lips, thinking about the way he'd acted when he'd been here. He'd tried to keep things casual. But she'd sensed the tension underneath his smile. Had he come back after something secret? Evidence, perhaps, of something he and Ted had been cooking up and hadn't told her about? And how might he have gotten in?

Sara wiped a trickle of perspiration from her neck as her eyes made another slow inspection of the room. Nothing looked out of place. But she couldn't remember precisely where the piles of papers had been set. Probably she should check the filing cabinet. Crossing the rug, she gave the top drawer a pull. It was locked. Where was the key? And even if she got the drawer open, would she know what she was looking for?

The questions made her head throb. Without realizing she'd taken a step, she backed away from the metal cabinet.

Then she turned and strode out of the room, closing the door with a decisive click behind her. This whole little fantasy about George

Newhouse was ridiculous. She might not like the man very much, but she couldn't seriously imagine him breaking into her house. It was the rain. The dampness had brought back the scent of the cologne, and her overactive sense of smell had picked it up. That was all.

She shook her head. Maybe she ought to lie down and put a cool washcloth on her forehead. She'd probably feel better after she took a nap.

With Harold in the hospital, Ben had to make the most of every spare moment. He'd gotten into the habit of asking Lois to bring him back a sandwich and a Coke from the drugstore at the end of her lunch hour. While he ate, he opened his mail.

Today, there was a large manila envelope among the drug company ads and the medical journals. When he opened it, he found a lab report from the Veterinary School at Cornell University.

Ben took a bite out of his crab-cake sandwich as he read the attached note from Harry Cahill at the local veterinary clinic:

> "I couldn't determine the cause of death of that dog back in June. So I sent a tissue sample to the vet school at Cornell. What do you think about this? Maybe the lab made a mistake in the analysis."

As Ben scanned the computer printout, his eyes narrowed. According to the lab at Cornell, the dog had died of a massive dose of

botulism toxin. Getting out his toxicology text-
books, Ben looked up the bacteria. Because
botulism grew in an anaerobic, or airless,
environment, it wasn't really all that com-
mon. Mostly it was found in food that had
been improperly canned at home, although it
could sometimes contaminate commercially
processed foods.

Ben glanced at his sandwich, shook his head
in distaste, and pushed it to the side of the
desk. He wasn't hungry anymore.

Leaning back in his chair, he thought about
the implications of the lab report. As far as he
knew, there hadn't been any human cases of
botulism poisoning in the county. So where
had the shepherd ingested the stuff? He'd
looked like a stray, which meant he wouldn't
have been too choosy about what he was eating. Maybe he'd gotten into some discards
from a packing plant. Smoked fish and sau-
sage were possible sources. Or the animal could
have dug up some spoiled canned goods at
the dump—very spoiled canned goods, judg-
ing from the level of toxin in the animal's
system.

Ben stroked his chin, remembering how upset Sara had been about the dog. Should he
tell her about the lab report? She'd be interested. But sharing the information wouldn't
solve the puzzle of how the dog had ended up
in her driveway. In fact, it just added to the
mystery.

As far as he knew, Sara had forgotten about
the incident. And she had so many other problems to deal with right now. Why bother her
with this? Better just to let dead dogs lie.

*   *   *

The slight flutter in her abdomen brought her back from a shallow sleep.

The baby. She remembered the thrill of feeling those first butterfly-light movements a few weeks ago. The little kicks and stirrings were getting stronger, but they still filled her with a sense of wonder. Reaching down, she stroked her fingers across the taut skin.

"I see it's not *your* nap time," she murmured with a little smile. Recently, she'd begun talking to the baby when they were alone together. Maybe it was silly, but it gave her a sense of connection with the life growing inside her.

She was hoping for a girl. "We'll finger paint and make beautiful doll-house furniture and bake cookies the way Aunt Ginny and I did when we were little," she crooned. "You'll like Aunt Ginny. And she'll love you, too." To think that the baby might never get to meet her aunt was just too painful.

Sara stroked her hand in slow circles across her tummy and closed her eyes. "You're going to be a fine, healthy little girl—or boy," she whispered. "That's the important thing." Her hand stopped moving. What if the baby did have some medical problem?

Missing toes. That wasn't so bad. You could keep your shoes on. But what about something like a heart defect? Or mental retardation? Her fingers clenched the bedspread. Deliberately she forced herself to relax again. Probably every expectant mother had thoughts like this.

As Sara was willing her mind to stop manufacturing things to worry about, the doorbell rang.

"Just a minute," she called. The bell sounded again as she hurried barefoot down the stairs. Her hair was tousled, but at least she'd lain down wearing her jumper.

The brown-uniformed UPS man had set a duffel bag and a fold-over valise on the porch. They were the blue and burgundy set Ginny had bought for the trip.

"There's a pullman case still in the truck," he told Sara.

After she'd signed for the luggage, he carried the suitcases into the living room. For a long time after he'd gone, Sara stared at the blue and burgundy plaid. The irrational thought kept running through her head that if she opened the luggage, she'd never see her sister again.

Finally, she hauled the pullman case up on the sofa. It was silly to be superstitious. Besides, there might be some clue inside that could help the authorities find Ginny.

She knew her sister had packed neatly. But it was obvious now that someone had just taken handfuls of her belongings and stuffed them into her luggage. When she unzipped the case, underwear, shirts, and shorts came spilling out, like merchandise haphazardly piled on a bargain-basement table.

Sara picked up a red, white, and blue knit shirt and smoothed her finger across the yacht club emblem on the breast pocket. Ginny had been thrilled when she'd found it on their shopping trip, because the red had been a perfect match for the shorts she'd already bought. Now it was so crumpled it would need to go through the laundry before Ginny could wear it again—if she ever came home to wear it again.

A film of tears glazed Sara's eyes, and she blinked to clear her vision. Ginny was coming back. When she did, her older sister would have all her clothes washed and neatly folded for her. She was going to take care of Ginny, just the way she had since they'd been little.

Sara lay the garment bag on the floor. As she pulled on the zipper tab, another thought struck her. Ginny must have been wearing one of her new outfits when she disappeared. Maybe she could figure out which one. At least, that way, she'd have something concrete to tell the cruise company—something they could add to their case file.

She'd called them again yesterday just to check in and see if anything was happening. Both the captain and the purser were unavailable, because the Royal Alexandria was out of port. Sara had been shuffled around to several offices and finally put through to an administrator named Mrs. Koppelman, in the customer service office.

"I'm going to be your point of contact," the woman told her. "My personal extension is 715."

"Have you made any progress?"

"We don't have missing person cases often. But The Royal Star Line is taking this very seriously."

"I'm relieved to hear that."

The woman had told her the company was circulating a picture of Ginny taken at dinner one evening to authorities on the various islands the ship had visited. Perhaps someone would recognize her, Mrs. Koppelman had said soothingly. Sara had hung up clinging to that hope.

Stacks of her sister's belongings began to pile up as she sorted through the jumble in the suitcase. Sara put clothing on the sofa, tossed shoes on the floor, and set miscellaneous items, like Ginny's hair dryer and jewelry case, on the coffee table. In the pocket of a short denim skirt was a white business card with the name Dorothy Griffin on it. She was a computer analyst and lived in Stamford, Connecticut. Ginny must have met her on the ship. Had they made friends? Would Ms. Griffin be able to tell her anything?

Sara didn't want to get her hopes up. But maybe the woman could give her some sort of lead. Sara glanced at her watch. It was a little after four. Probably Ms. Griffin wouldn't be home yet. But she could call in a few hours, she thought as she set the card aside on the coffee table.

A green and yellow flowered bag of toilet articles caught Sara's attention next. It was open, and a tube of toothpaste was sticking out of the top. Some of it had smeared onto Ginny's fancy nightgown. Had she worn it for some man? Sara closed her eyes for a moment and dragged a deep breath into her lungs. It was so easy to let her imagination run wild. In fact, she'd been doing that a lot lately.

Automatically, she tightened the cap on the toothpaste and pushed it back into the bag. As her hand slipped through the zipper open-

ing, her fingers encountered a small rectangle
with a stiff, woolly texture. Even as she pulled
it out, her heart started to pound. No! It
couldn't be. Yet it was.

Her eyes were agog with astonishment as
they focused on the piece of needlepoint canvas in her hand. The background was in dull
red, like dried blood. The picture in the center
was beige and gray. It showed a hypodermic
with a drop of white liquid oozing from the
tip of the needle.

Sara's fingers prickled, as if the picture of
the needle had somehow pierced her flesh.
With a moan, she flung the canvas across the
room.

CHAPTER 24

Sara stared at the needlepoint canvas where it had landed against the leg of a chair. At first, she simply felt numb. Gradually her mind began to function again. Scattered thoughts leaped into her head and mixed with others like ingredients in a recipe for witches' brew. Her husband was dead. Ginny was missing. There'd been a needlepoint canvas in the glove compartment of Ted's car. Now there was one in Ginny's cosmetic bag ... a horrible coincidence, or something she could figure out? Could Ginny possibly have gotten interested in needlepoint? Sara's eyes clouded as she thought about her sister. It was hard to picture the restless teenager sitting still for such a time-consuming craft.

Then a more painful thought shot to the surface of her mind. She'd assumed the needlepoint had been left in Ted's car by the woman he was seeing. Had Ginny been involved with her husband? Her heart stopped for a moment at the thought. No. Ginny hadn't even liked Ted. At least that was what she'd said. Or had that been a cover-up to throw Sara off?

She worried her lower lip between her teeth. She'd almost always been able to tell when her sister was lying. Besides, Ginny was so naive about men. If she'd been having an affair with an experienced guy like Ted, it would have been hard to keep up her unsophisticated image, wouldn't it?

But there had to be some reason why this piece of stitchery was here in her sister's luggage. Maybe Ginny had found the half-finished canvas in the pantry drawer and taken it with her. But why would she want to do that? And would she really go to the trouble of finishing it?

Sara scrambled to her feet so quickly that her head started to spin, and she had to lean down and clutch the arm of the sofa to keep from falling back down. When the dizziness passed, she hurried down the hall toward the kitchen.

There was a momentary feeling of relief when she found the needlepoint where she'd stuffed it into the utility drawer. With shaky fingers, Sara undid the twist-tie and slid the canvas out of the plastic bag. She'd forgotten how faded it looked and how musty it smelled. Holding it in her hand again brought back all the old horror she'd thought she'd put behind her months ago. She wanted to shove it back in the drawer. Instead, she brought it back to the living room.

The other one was on the floor where she'd hurled it. With her jaw clamped tightly shut, she picked it up and put the two pictures side by side on the coffee table.

They were the same size and the same color, if you made allowances for the water damage to the one that had gone into the river with Ted. Now that she had its mate, she could see that the first was an incomplete version of the same design. Except for the drop of liquid at the end of the needle, both of them were a lot like the old picture that had hung in her father's office. What was the connection? It looked as if someone had made two copies. But why?

Perhaps Harold could tell her something. If she could just get him to talk to her.

Should she show the needlepoint pictures to him? Sara pressed shaking fingers against her lip. Maybe carting this stuff over to the hospital wasn't such a good idea. Her father had tried to commit suicide. There was no telling what might set him off again.

Elmo McGuire came out from around the prescription counter and ambled over to the little restaurant area at the back of the drugstore. His bony hand reached for the top of a rock-maple chair at one of the round tables.

"How you folks doin'?"

Kitty Duncan, Phil Dorsey from the hardware store, and Lois Pennington all looked up. Cheryl Keene and Jodeen Crane moved over to make room for him.

"Thanks. My feet are killing me." Elmo dropped into the empty chair. When Patty Trice, the waitress, came over with a cup of coffee, he stirred in milk and sugar.

"You ought to try some of those cushion inserts you're selling over there in aisle four," Beatrice Pierce suggested as she set her tote bag on the floor beside the remaining chair.

Elmo chuckled. "Those fool rubber things never worked for me."

After sitting down, Beatrice picked up the tote bag and cradled it on her lap. Hidden inside was a little tape recorder. She couldn't sit here taking notes. But her memory just wasn't what it used to be, and she didn't want to miss any tidbits that might come in handy for her book. Lately she'd been dropping by the pharmacy two or three afternoons a week. Joining this group was like watching a soap opera. The good stuff was rehashed often enough that you could pick up the gist by tuning in every couple of days.

"So, is there any news about Harold?" Phil asked Lois.

The receptionist pursed her lips. "The poor man. He's still not talking to anyone."

"A shame when someone's mind just up and snaps. But you can understand it in a way, with his girls doing him the way they did." Jodeen tisked and picked up her knitting. "That Ginny, running off without a by-your-leave. She must have broken his heart."

"Maybe she didn't run off. Maybe something happened to her," Cheryl suggested. She'd been a year ahead of Ginny at St. Stephens High School. "You just can't be sure what kind of people are going to show up on one of those cruises."

Lois and Phil nodded their agreement.

"But Sara." Jodeen deftly switched to a juicier line of gossip. "Pregnant and her husband in the ground only a couple of months—and now she's havin' an affair with—" She caught Lois's stony look and took a quick sip of her coffee.

"Pregnant?" The question came from Kitty Duncan. She wasn't really one of the regulars. But she did like to drop by McGuire's, since the pharmacy crowd was better than a jungle telegraph for relating important local doings.

"Where have you been, girl?" Jodeen asked, leaning forward in her seat. "I thought you and Sara were pretty thick."

Flustered, Kitty lowered her dark lashes over her china blue eyes. "I guess I haven't seen her recently."

"Well, she's not flapping her mouth about it, that's for sure. And she's not very big yet—even in those knit jumpers she's been wearing lately." Jodeen's face took on a speculative look. "Say, when's she due, Lois?"

"Oh, I'm sure if you go talk to her, she'll tell you anything you want to know."

The conversation dropped off for a moment, and Beatrice jumped in with a question to keep the right stuff flowing. "So, do you think the baby's Ted's?"

"I guess we'll know when it's born and we can count back and see if he was still livin'," Cheryl giggled.

"That don't prove nothin'," Phil put in. "We'll have to see who it looks like."

"Your mind is in the gutter," Lois muttered. "You've known Sara since she was a little girl. She wouldn't have been running around on Ted."

"Well, she had to know he was running around on her," Phil insisted.

Beatrice looked down into the amber liquid in her teacup, wishing she hadn't gotten everybody thinking along these lines. When she and Ted had been seeing each other, they'd been very discreet. But the mudslinging was getting a little too close for comfort.

"If it was me, I'd want to get back at him," Phil insisted.

"That's you. Sara's different," Lois shot back.

"But you've got to admit, it would have looked a little better if she'd waited till after that baby was born before taking up with Ben Langley," Cheryl murmured.

Lois stood up. She'd needed a break. Now she wished she'd just gotten a cup of tea and brought it back to the office.

Mrs. Kensey-Smith pursed her lips. "For three-hundred-and-fifty thousand dollars, I expected a garage and an eat-in kitchen."

"Property values have really shot up around St. Stephens," George Newhouse reminded her, struggling to keep his growing impatience from bleeding through into his salesman's voice.

"You can see why," he added. "Look at this view." He ushered the well-heeled matron out onto the screened porch and swept his arm proprietarily toward the Miles River. At least the damn rain had stopped. Waterfront property never showed well in bad weather.

"Well, this *would* be nice for summer entertaining. But I wouldn't want to make a decision without seeing a lot more homes. What about one of those houses with the two wings coming in toward the center, out on Tilghman Island? Wasn't there one of those in your current listings?"

"It's a block from the water. And it needs a lot of repair work. But if you want to see it, I'll be glad to take you out tomorrow."

"I think we have time to squeeze it in this afternoon."

"Of course." George opened the door of his black sedan and held it while the rich old bitch slipped into the passenger seat. Hell, she could afford anything around here that struck her fancy. But she was looking for a bargain, and she wasn't going to give up until she'd seen every house on the market on this side of the Bay Bridge.

George started the engine and backed out of the driveway of the pretty little telescope house Mrs. Kensey-Smith had just rejected. As he drove toward Tilghman Island, he automatically went into one of his Chamber of Commerce speeches about the area.

"See that Victorian house over there?"

Mrs. Kensey-Smith craned her neck.

"It's where that author, Ryan O'Flanagan, lives."

"Really. I loved his last book."

"Yes, he's good, isn't he?" George had seen the movie, in case she asked any questions.

"On your left is Senator Hogwood's estate."

"Oh, my. I didn't realize I'd be keeping such famous company."

"Um hum." George made an effort to keep up his celebrity tour, but it was growing increasingly difficult to concentrate.

Thank God he'd finally gotten back into Ted's study. He'd tried last week, but Sara had changed her schedule, and he'd driven right by her coming down the road to her house. That was too close for comfort, so he'd laid off for a few days and finally gone over this morning.

A dog darted across the road, and George slammed on the brakes. His passenger jounced forward.

"You should have seen that animal. Where is your mind, Mr. Newhouse?"

"Sorry. I was—uh—thinking about a house you might want to see. Something special."

"Oh, yes."

Actually, he'd been thinking about Sara Chandler. Jesus, it was lucky she hadn't gone through the slew of Brittingham stuff in the file cabinet. And not only that, Ted had had a folder with notes on *him*. He'd known the guy was willing to stoop to blackmail. He just hadn't figured how systematic the bastard had been.

The papers were burning a hole in the trunk of his car right now. But he hadn't had a minute to go through them properly. Not when he'd had to rush back to the office and meet Mrs. Kensey-Smith. She hadn't wanted to deal with one of his agents. She'd insisted on having the head of the company show her around. And she was too well connected with a lot of potential clients back in Baltimore for him to risk insulting her. So he smiled blandly and drove on—thinking about how he'd like to dump the rich old bitch off the drawbridge when they crossed the Knapp Narrows onto Tilghman.

CHAPTER 25

Sara dialed the number on the business card and waited tensely while the phone rang—once, twice, five times. She was about to give up when a breathless, nasal voice answered.

"Hello?"

"Is this Dorothy Griffin?"

"I broke my nail getting to the phone for this? Whatever you're selling, I don't want any."

"I'm not selling anything, Ms. Griffin. Please don't hang up. My name is Sara Chandler. I hate to bother you, but I need to ask you some questions about my sister, Ginny Strickland."

The voice on the other end of the line warmed up several degrees. "Oh, yes, Ginny. I met her on the cruise."

"Oh, I'm so glad I found your business card in her luggage. When did you see her last?"

"What is this about?"

Sara sighed, imagining how she must be coming across. "My sister didn't come home on her flight. Apparently, she's been missing since the fifth or sixth of July, and I'm terribly worried about what might have happened to her."

"Oh, my. Yes, I see. What did you say your name was?"

"Sara Chandler. I'd appreciate anything you could tell me."

"We got to talking that first day, around the pool. Ginny seemed like such a nice girl at first. Then she got all wound up with that Keith Thomas guy. I think if he'd asked her to jump off the ship, she would have done it."

Sara's heart gave a little lurch. She'd finally located someone who might have important information about Ginny's disappearance. "Ms. Griffin, please. Anything you remember could be important."

"Well, your sister and I decided to go to the welcoming cocktail party together. That's where she latched onto that fellow."

"You say his name was Keith Thomas? You're sure?"

"Yes. Ginny told me several times. And I have an uncle named Tom—so it was easy to remember."

Sara reached for a notepad and scribbled the name.

"After she met Thomas, she spent most of her time with him. Even when they weren't together, she was talking about him. Honestly, I don't know why she was so taken with the fellow," Dotty continued.

"What did this Keith Thomas look like?"

The older woman thought for a minute. "Slender. Kind of average looking. I guess his best feature was his hair. It was dark and thick. I got the feeling he used some kind of mousse or something on it to keep it under control."

Sara felt her excitement mount. Finally, she was getting somewhere. Realizing she was forgetting to write things down, she started to scrawl across the pad. "Dark hair?"

"Yes. Dark brown. And he had a dark mustache."

"Anything else?"

"He wasn't very tall. Maybe five seven or eight."

"Did you see the color of his eyes?"

"Brown—I think."

"How old was he?"

"In his late twenties or maybe early thirties."

"What else can you tell me?"

Sara could feel the hesitation on the other end of the line. "Please. Any little thing you remember could be important."

"Well—I don't like to tell tales. But he and your sister really carried on something awful on the Fourth of July."

"You saw her on the Fourth of July?"

"I walked past them on the deck. The two of them were lying together on a chaise, right out in public—" Dotty paused. "Are you sure you want to hear this?"

Sara didn't, but she had to find out everything she could. "Yes. Go on."

"They were practically making love in front of everyone. There was a blanket over top of them, but it was pretty plain that he had his hands all over her. And from the look on her face—well, I couldn't watch. I just walked by them without saying anything."

Sara had wrapped the telephone cord so tightly around her finger that it had started to throb. When she realized what she was doing, she unwound the coil. "Thank you," she managed.

"I'm sorry."

"No, that's all right. I need every detail I can get. At least I know she was all right on the evening of the Fourth."

"I had no idea Ginny was missing. When I didn't see her after the fireworks I assumed, you know, that they were down in one of their cabins."

"Oh."

"Who else have you talked to?" Dotty pointedly changed the subject.

"You're the first real lead I've gotten," Sara told her and then quickly summed up what had transpired since she'd gone to meet Ginny at the airport.

"Oh, you poor thing," Dotty sympathized. "You must be going through hell."

Sara didn't mention how her father had taken the news—or about the needlepoint.

"Did you see her or Keith after the night of the Fourth?"

"I don't think so. But I had met this guy from Chicago, and the two of us weren't paying too much attention to anyone else."

"I understand. But Ms. Griffin, if you think of *anything* else, please call me—collect." She gave the woman the phone numbers of her home, the shop, and Ben's office.

"I will," Dotty assured her. "Please let me know when you locate your sister. I'm going to remember her in my prayers tonight."

Dotty hung up the phone and tapped the pink polished nail of her index finger against her teeth. That poor woman must be frantic.

Ginny must be quite a handful. She'd enjoyed passing the time with her—until she'd gotten so wound up with that Keith Thomas. Closing her eyes, she concentrated on bringing the man's image back to mind. She hadn't looked at him all that closely, because she hadn't liked him very much. He'd been strange, out of focus somehow. What was it that made her feel that way? Nothing came to her immediately. But she'd put it in her background memory and let it process. Eventually, her mind would retrieve the information.

Maybe if she hurried, she could still get through to Mrs. Koppelman at the cruise line, Sara thought. There was no need to look up the number. She'd memorized it days ago. But her hand was shaking as she dialed. This time, she had a real lead. They'd probably try to tell her that passenger information was confidential. But even if it was, she'd make them give her this Keith Thomas's phone number.

"You have reached the offices of The Royal Star Line. Our office hours are nine a.m. to five p.m. If you want information about a cruise, please leave your name and number after the sound of the tone, and one of our agents will get back to you—''

Sara listened to the message, her fist clenched around the receiver in frustration. *Damn.* She was going to have to wait until tomorrow morning to call up Keith Thomas and confront him with what she knew.

Greasy junk from fast-food places gave George Newhouse indigestion. So, after his wife had split, he'd gotten into cooking.

On his way home, he stopped at the pier and bought a nice fresh croaker, which he had filleted right on the spot. Down the road, he picked up some field-ripened corn and tomatoes from a produce stand.

The first ear of corn he shucked had a worm burrowed down into the kernels. With a grimace, he threw it into the garbage and opened up another.

After pulling the tab on a Bud Lite, he seasoned the fish with a little olive oil, dill, and lemon juice and put it under the broiler. But while he was looking at the stuff from Ted's file cabinet, the damn croaker started to burn. The next thing he knew, the smoke detector was clanging. By the time he yanked the battery out, he was seething like a hill of red ants that had been stirred up with a stick.

Cursing, he threw the charred fish in the trash, chugged down the can of beer, and opened another as he went back to the Brittingham folder.

Jesus, this thing was really getting to him. He'd thought the deal was in the bag. Now there was all this junk bobbing to the surface like dead bodies from a sunken ship.

He flicked through the folder, his motions jerky. Most of the contents duplicated material he already had at the office, which meant Ted had been keeping his own records on the deal. Had he been worried about getting cheated or something?

In the middle of the file was a yellowing ad from the Acme Market. When he flipped it over, he found a news story about the Bay Watchers. It had been published three years ago. Beside the text was a picture of Sara, Miss Jane, and some old guy standing on the shoreline. The caption read, "Estate going to the birds. Sara Chandler and Ralph Meekins are shown site of future bird sanctuary by owner Jane Brittingham."

Probably the story had gone right by him at the time, because it was before Ted had broached the idea of grabbing the property. But his rookie agent must have been thinking about it back then, because he'd saved the article.

George squashed the empty beer can in his fist. Two had been his limit for years. Now he got up and opened another. Sara and Ted must have been married less than six months at the time the picture was taken, which proved that the wily bastard hadn't wasted any time getting his ducks lined up.

As he studied the photo, his eyes were drawn to the man standing behind Sara and Miss Jane. Ted had marked him with a circle. Why?

George's gaze flicked rapidly down through the article—catching the gist. That's right,

Meekins was the old coot who made those duck decoys Sara sold in her shop.

Could Meekins have found out about the Brittingham deal? Had Ted stumbled onto something like that? He hadn't said anything. But that was par for the course with Chandler. He would have tried to control the damage and then laughed about it afterwards. Only this time, he hadn't gotten the chance.

George's face was flushed, and his underarms were dripping with sweat. He'd worked damn hard for this opportunity. And he'd sunk a bunch of his own money into the deal. Jonathan Brittingham III's cooperation hadn't come cheap.

By God, nothing was going to keep him from striking it rich this time. His mind churned. Whatever it took—he'd do it. Screw the old lady. Maybe he ought to knock her off before the deal went belly up.

Or Meekins . . . He could pay him off to keep his mouth shut. And if he wouldn't keep quiet, he just might have a little accident with one of his carving knives.

Then there was that arrogant lawyer, Jonathan Brittingham. What if he changed his mind and decided to live in the house and keep the estate intact after all. There wasn't any written agreement between him and Jonathan. Well, maybe he'd just better make sure the house was in no shape to occupy.

With all the patients who needed to be seen, office hours stretched until almost seven. After the last case of summer flu left, Ben leaned over the sink and splashed cold water on his face. He hadn't felt this stressed-out since those thirty-six-hour shifts he'd done as an intern.

How had Harold handled the practice by himself? Well, it hadn't been quite this busy. And he knew from Sara that the man had been a workaholic. Maybe that was part of the reason he was in such bad shape now. He'd burned himself out.

If the old man didn't come back, he was going to have to get some help. A nurse practitioner, at least, to take care of the routine cases Harold had been handling and to answer questions over the phone. Stuff like that was sucking up too much of his time. Maybe, whatever happened, they should consider taking on another physician.

Opening the door of his Blazer, he climbed inside and started the engine. Usually, after closing up the office, he headed right over to Sara's. Now that she'd let him into her life, he felt as if he was part of a family again. He'd missed that.

He came from four generations of wheat and alfalfa farmers in the San Joaquin Valley. His parents had only had two children—himself and his sister Becky. Dad had been determined his son would carry on the Langley tradition. But Ben had always been more interested in patching up the animals around the place than in planting or harvesting the crops. He'd taken horticulture courses at UC Davis. But he'd also made sure he had a lot of lab sciences, too—to keep his options open.

The light at Route 33 turned red, and he hit the brakes a little too hard. *Damn.* He'd better pay more attention to his driving. But he hadn't thought about his family in months. And he couldn't turn it off on command.

He cringed, remembering the look on his father's face when he'd finally gotten up the nerve one evening at dinner to broach the subject of going to medical school.

Dad had just stared at him like he'd told him he wanted to be on the first spaceship to Mars. He'd chewed and swallowed the bit of pot roast in his mouth and said that Ben could do whatever he damn well pleased—but he'd have to find a way to pay for it himself.

Ben had looked over at Mom, but she had her eyes fixed on her plate. He couldn't remember a time when she'd had the guts to buck her husband.

Ben's grades had been good, so he'd been able to get a partial scholarship and some loans. But once he'd made his choices, he felt as if he wasn't really one of the family anymore. Even Becky had been afraid to act friendly, in case she brought her father's wrath down on her own head.

That was one of the reasons the Santa Barbara trouble had hit him so hard. There hadn't been anyone to share the burden.

The car behind him honked. Ben jammed the gear lever into first with twice the force it needed and lurched forward across the intersection.

Santa Barbara. He was going to feel it hanging over him like a cloud of poison gas until he told Sara. But what if she didn't understand? What if she closed him out, the way the folks had?

He wanted to turn around and drive back

to her house. All at once, he ached to hold her and feel her arms reassuringly around him. But he couldn't. Not tonight. He'd promised himself he'd go over to Easton again and check on Harold's progress—if there was any.

Until Sara's father had tried to commit suicide, they'd felt relieved that he'd at least acknowledged his drinking problem. And they'd both been hoping things would get better. But that was before Ginny vanished. The news had shattered him.

Why was he so upset? Was there some missing piece of information that only Harold possessed? Or had Ginny's disappearance triggered a private nightmare that didn't have anything to do with reality?

He had so much weighing him down right now. Logic told him to dismiss Harold's warning of death and disaster as the ravings of a crazy man. But the nagging fear that there might be something to it simply wouldn't go away.

Twenty minutes later, Ben greeted the head nurse in the psychiatric wing of the hospital.

"Mind if I have a look at Harold's chart?"

"Of course not, Doctor."

Thoughtfully, he studied the latest entries. The medical work-up had uncovered some liver damage. Otherwise, Dr. Strickland's physical health wasn't too bad. But his mental state was another matter. He was on anti-depressants. But so far, he was still completely withdrawn. The psychotherapist who'd been trying to work with him had made absolutely no progress.

"I'm going down to see him," he told the duty nurse.

"Don't expect much."

Through the reinforced glass door of room 210, Ben looked in at the forlorn figure on the bed. Harold was dressed in the striped pajamas Sara had brought over several days ago. Gray hair stood out on his head in unruly tufts. His watery eyes appeared to stare at some spot on the ceiling. The only signs of life were the shallow rise and fall of the old man's chest and the restless activity of his right index finger. It stroked in a circle around his narrow lips—which were red and irritated. Had the nurses put anything on that? Ben wondered as he opened the door and stepped inside. The room was hot and fetid.

Ben took a shallow breath. "Hi. How are you doing?"

The older man's lids fluttered briefly. At close range, Ben could see that the whites of his eyes were shot through with red streaks.

Besides the almost imperceptible quiver of the veined eyelids, there was no acknowledgment that Harold had been addressed. The finger stroking across the lips didn't pause in its circular journey.

Ben dropped wearily into the room's single wooden chair. "Everyone who's come to the office has been asking about you. And there's a whole stack of get-well cards out at the nurse's station. Do you want me to bring them?"

Harold didn't respond to the gambit. Ben shrugged and kept on talking. "I never realized how hard it was to carry on a practice like this single-handedly. How did you do it all these years?" He waited a beat and then went on to talk about some of the patients he'd seen that day. But after five minutes of one-sided conversation, he sighed, resisting the impulse to reach over and yank that incessantly stroking finger away from the reddened mouth.

"Harold." He forced his voice to remain calm. "I know you're in some kind of private hell. But no one can help you unless you let us."

When the blue eyes didn't waver from the ceiling, Ben clamped his teeth together. Maybe Harold was beyond salvage. But what about Ginny? And what about Sara? With a muttered curse, he reached out and grasped the man's shoulder. It was bony. A corner of his doctor's mind wondered how much weight the old man had lost. But that was the least important of his questions right now.

"All right," Ben growled. "Something's been eating at you for months. Something so terrible that you had to numb the pain with whiskey. Now you're in so much agony that you want to turn yourself into a vegetable. But the rest of us need to know what this is all about. Did you find something out about Ginny? Did somebody call you? Send you a message? What?"

For the first time since the visitor had come into the room, the restless finger paused in mid-stroke.

"What the hell were you talking about that night we found you half dead in the middle of the kitchen floor?" Ben persisted. "If Sara's in danger and you don't tell me about it, I'll never forgive you. Do you understand?"

The tip of Harold's tongue touched his raw lip, and he winced.

"Dammit," Ben growled. "Say something. What do you know that you're not telling? About Ginny? And what the hell did you mean about Ted?" He swallowed convulsively, afraid to ask the next question but knowing he had to. "Is Sara next?"

The old man's face changed. It was a little like watching a swimmer coming up to the surface through layers of blue water. Harold blinked. For the first time, he focused on Ben as if he were suddenly aware he wasn't alone in the little room.

"Please," Ben begged, leaning over the ravaged form on the bed. "What are you afraid of? What is it you can't face?"

Tears welled in the bloodshot eyes, and the vacant stare was replaced with a mask of almost unbearable anguish. "Harold, we can get through this together."

The lips moved. The hoarse, unused voice croaked a single syllable. "No."

He'd wrung a response from the man. It wasn't what he wanted, but it was something. "Harold, please. Trust me."

The old man didn't move. For heart-stopping seconds, Ben was afraid he was going to slip down into the deep blue layers of mental anesthetic again. Then the lips moved and the scratchy voice rasped something unintelligible.

"What?"

"Needle—"

"What about a needle?"

"Needle—point."

"I don't understand what you mean."

Harold's eyes glazed over again, as though an invisible film of blindness had silently coated them.

"Don't—" Ben's fingers dug into the waxy flesh of the old man's shoulder. There was no response. "You selfish bastard. You can't do this. Come back, damn you."

The restless index finger began to stroke across his lips as if there'd been no interruption in its progress.

CHAPTER 26

Thursday, July 13

THE ST. STEPHENS RECORD

FRONT PAGE NEWS ITEM

Historic Mansion Damaged by Fire

The Historic Swan Point estate escaped serious damage in an early morning fire Tuesday night. Quick thinking on the part of Captain Tom Postwell of the cruiser *Roundabout* is credited with saving the mansion. On the way back to harbor, a crew member saw the flames and informed the captain, who radioed the volunteer fire department.

According to Fire Marshal Lew Rucker, damage to the mansion is estimated at $10,000. "We don't have any suspects, but it looks like the work of vandals," Mr. Rucker said. "The blaze was apparently set with charcoal lighter fluid—which could have been purchased at a number of locations in town."

The property has been in the Brittingham family for over 200 years. But the house has been unoccupied since owner Mrs. Jane Brittingham entered a nursing home last year. Reached for comment, Jonathan Brittingham III denounced the vandalism.

"It's a crying shame that some people don't have any respect for our country's heritage," Mr. Brittingham said. He has posted a night watchman at the property to discourage further malicious mischief.

Calendar of Events

Historical Society Sponsors Graveyard Tour

Learn more about your ancestors or simply delve into the rich history of St. Stephens. Join the Talbot County Historical Society at their monthly meeting on Friday, July 21 at 7:30 p.m. The program will feature a guided tour through some of the area's historic graveyards. Participants will have the chance to make a gravestone rubbing. The walking tour starts at the St. Stephens Methodist Church Cemetery. Bring your curiosity and

your comfortable shoes. For more
information, contact the Society at
555-3754.

At two minutes after nine, Sara called Mrs.
Koppelman at The Royal Star Line.

"I'm sorry. She had a doctor's appointment
this morning. She should be in around ten-
thirty," the secretary explained. "Do you want
me to have her call you?"

"Yes, please. I'll be at my gallery." She gave
the receptionist her number. "Tell her it's
important."

Sara hung up feeling frustrated and edgy.
She couldn't do a damn thing until Mrs.
Koppelman returned her call.

As she paced back and forth in the kitchen,
her stomach started to churn. During the past
few weeks, she'd been getting indigestion if
she even thought about spicy food. Now, even
though she'd had only a cup of herb tea and a
bran muffin for breakfast, her chest began to
feel as if she'd swallowed a bottle of Tabasco
sauce.

When she opened the bathroom cabinet, she
discovered she was out of the antacids the
doctor had said she could take. At first she
hadn't wanted to take anything, because she
was afraid it might hurt the baby. The doctor
had understood her concern and had been
very reassuring.

She decided to make a swing by McGuire's
on the way to the gallery. After pulling into
the parking space in back of The Bayside Collection, she walked the half-block to the drugstore. Intent on her mission, she headed directly

to the back of the store, where a whole shelf of stomach remedies was displayed near the pharmacy counter. *Probably for tourists who OD on steamed crabs*, she thought wryly.

Elmo McGuire, who was bringing out a prescription as Sara waited to pay, eyed her purchase and shook his head knowingly.

"I sell a lot of that stuff to the ladies in waiting," he told her.

Sara nodded. She hadn't actually spoken to Elmo about the pregnancy. But apparently the word had gotten around town. And why not? She was definitely showing.

"I have had some heartburn lately," she admitted and realized again how bad she felt. Tearing open the package, she unwrapped two tablets, popped them in her mouth, and began to chew.

"Sorry to hear that. Any word on your sister?"

"Nothing concrete," she mumbled around a mouthful of lemon-flavored chalk. She didn't want to go into what she'd learned. If she did, it would be all over town that Ginny had run off with some guy she'd picked up on the cruise ship.

Elmo disappeared behind the counter again, and Sara turned toward the door. Some of the regular patrons were still sitting around in the coffee-shop area. She hadn't joined them since Ginny's disappearance, and she didn't really feel like eating or chatting now. But when Cheryl said hello, she stopped for a moment.

Everybody wanted to know about Ginny and

Harold, and they made sympathetic noises when she didn't have any good news to report.

Then Phil Dorsey changed the subject. "Well, anyway, you do have a happy event to look forward to."

"Yes, I do."

"Too bad Ted didn't live to see his child," Jodeen put in, her knitting needles clicking sharply. The statement would have been solicitous, except for the slight emphasis on the word *his*.

Sara winced. She'd lived in St. Stephens long enough to recognize the subtlety of local innuendo. So Jodeen was wondering if the baby was Ted's. They'd probably all been sitting around hashing over the subject.

A whole array of retorts leaped to her mind. *Ted didn't want a baby anyway. He wouldn't have made a very good parent. It's none of your damn business who the father is.*

She settled for a dignified, "Yes, it is," before she turned away. The bell over the door jangled as she made her exit.

"A little edgy, isn't she?" Jodeen sniffed as she watched Sara's retreating figure through the window.

"Give her a break," Cheryl muttered.

"Dr. Langley. I have Dr. Clifton on the line."

"Thank you."

A cheerful voice boomed over the phone. "Ben. I heard you stopped in at the hospital last night. I expect you're calling about Harold."

"Um hum. He doesn't seem to be making much progress."

"You're right. If the anti-depressants don't

do the trick in the next few days, I'd like to try ECT."

Shock therapy. Ben cringed as he pictured Harold's body strapped to a table, shuddering in the throes of an electrically-induced grand mal seizure.

"In severe depression, it's the optimal treatment."

"There isn't anything else you can try?"

"As you pointed out, he's simply not responding to drugs and psychotherapy."

"What about the accompanying memory loss with ECT?"

"It's often quite mild. Usually it doesn't last for more than a few weeks."

"Harold's not competent to sign the forms, so I assume you have to get Sara's permission."

"Right. I hope you'll help her make the right decision."

Sara tried to occupy her mind with paying some of her monthly bills. But it was impossible to concentrate on bookkeeping.

Restlessly, she got up and walked back to the storeroom. On a corner shelf were two of the little cat paintings Beatrice had brought in last year.

They had a certain charm. But technically they weren't very good. And they hadn't sold—even when the price had been reduced. She would have sent them back long ago if she hadn't been worried about hurting the older woman's feelings.

But what about her own feelings? She wished she could grow a protective crust—like a pond iced-over in the winter. Except that she wasn't that kind of person. Hurts went deep. Ginny—Dad—and now she had to worry about what people in town were whispering behind her back.

At that moment, the baby moved. "We don't care about the gossip. We know the truth, don't we?" Sara murmured.

The baby rapped more strongly against her insides.

"Mommy loves you," Sara soothed and then realized this was the first time she'd said the words aloud to her child.

A gentle smile lit up her face. It was hard to believe, but in a few months she'd be cuddling a baby in her arms. Her baby. She could see herself holding the child to her breast. Rocking it. Letting it know how much she loved it.

The ringing of the phone interrupted her reveries. It was Helen Koppelman from New York.

"You left a message."

"Yes. Thanks for calling back. I got the package of Ginny's things the ship sent," Sara began, tumbling over the words in her excitement to share her new information. "And there was a business card in the pocket of one of her skirts, a card from a woman she'd made friends with—Dorothy Griffin. I called her last night, and she told me Ginny was going around with a guy named Keith Thomas. She saw them together on the Fourth of July."

"Hmm. That's more than we've been able to find out. Just a minute; let me get my passenger list from the July second cruise."

She pressed a button, and Sara found herself listening to a bouncy light-rock tune, followed by a weather report for New York City and then another song. What was taking so long?

"Sorry to keep you waiting, but I was double-checking my list against the computer files. We do have a Dorothy Griffin on the July second sailing of the Royal Alexandria. But we don't have reservations for a Keith Thomas for that date. And his name isn't on the passenger list. Are you sure you have the name right?"

Sara's stomach had begun to churn again. She'd been so certain that she was onto something. "Ms. Griffin told me she was sure because she has a brother named Thomas. But I guess she could have gotten confused. Do you have anybody whose name is close to that?"

"I already checked. There was one person named Keith, but he's a seven-year-old who was traveling with his family. Let's see, there were two men whose first names were Thomas —both of them were with a party of senior citizens from Milwaukee. Did Ms. Griffin say how old the man was?"

"In his late twenties or early thirties."

Sara heard a door open and looked up. It was Judy Wooters, her new employee. "Just a minute," she told Mrs. Koppelman. "I have to give my assistant some instructions." Judy was supposed to get some mail orders ready for UPS. But Sara didn't really want an audience for this conversation. "Let the packaging go for now, and just keep an eye on the showroom. I'll be with you in a few minutes," she instructed.

Judy studied Sara's tense face and nodded. After sticking her purse in the bottom drawer of the file cabinet, she went out to the gallery.

"Sorry," Sara apologized when she was alone again.

"That's all right. I was just about to say that one of the men named Thomas is sixty-five. And the other is seventy-three. Even if they were in great shape, I don't think someone would be that far off in guessing their ages.

"No," Sara agreed bleakly. "But I really don't understand any of this."

"Perhaps your sister's companion gave her a false name."

"Why would he do that?"

"Well—if he had some deceitful purpose, I mean. Mrs. Chandler, I'm sorry. We don't like this situation any more than you do. Of course," she interjected a more positive note, "there *could* be some kind of mix-up in our records."

Sara could hear paper being shuffled on the other end of the line. "I'll double-check our files and call you back later today. And I'll also get in touch with Ms. Griffin. She might remember something else she forgot to tell you."

"Thank you," Sara mumbled. "I'll either be here at my gallery or at home."

"I have both of those numbers."

"There is one more thing I was going to tell you."

"Yes?"

"It's about the clothes you sent back. Ginny's green knit pullover and skirt are missing. So I assume that's what she was wearing."

"That could be helpful."

"I hope something is."

After hanging up, Sara clasped her hands together. Even though it was warm in the office, her fingers were icy cold. She'd been so sure she had a lead when she talked to Dotty Griffin. But there hadn't been anyone on the ship named Keith Thomas. So who in the name of God was the guy who'd given her sister the big rush? And what had he done to her?

When the bell over the front door sounded, Sara didn't get up. Judy could take care of whoever came in. But a moment later, she could hear several voices asking questions. Sara sighed. She'd better go out there and give Judy a hand.

As she emerged from the office, she found her assistant talking to three middle-aged women—the first of a group from a tour bus full of Johns Hopkins Hospital employees who had arrived in town that morning.

Sara had wanted to sit in the back and brood. Actually the brisk tourist business helped take her mind off the mysterious Keith Thomas. For the rest of the morning, both she and Judy were busy showing art works and ringing up sales.

At lunchtime she sent Judy off to eat first. Soon after her assistant left, a young woman with curly red hair came in and started looking at Kitty Duncan's natural sculptures. Kitty had recently begun using colorful feathers in her designs. "I've never seen anything like these before. They're so original. Who made them?"

Before Sara could answer, another voice joined the conversation, "Do you like them?"

Sara glanced up in surprise to find that the sculptor herself had asked the question. She had a half-pleased, half-embarrassed expression on her face.

"Oh, I just love them!" the redhead exclaimed.

"Well, I'd like you to meet the artist," Sara said with a grin. She swept her hand toward the newcomer. "This is Kitty Duncan, one of the Eastern Shore's most unique talents."

"Really? You did these?"

Kitty nodded.

"I just love the feathers. What kind are they?"

"They're from different kinds of ducks and geese. I get them from the nests after they've molted."

Sara stood back and let Kitty bask in the limelight. At the end of the conversation, the woman bought two—one for herself and one for her sister.

When she'd left, Kitty turned to Sara. "That was fun. Maybe I should hang around the gallery more often."

"You're welcome to come any time. I haven't seen you in awhile. Where did you get that great tan?"

"At the beach. I've been on another shell-collecting expedition. I'm going to have another five or six sculptures ready by the end of the week."

"Great. Bring them in as soon as you're done."

"Okay." She looked toward the door and then back at Sara. "I was going to try the luncheon special at the Crab Trap. Want to join me?"

"I've got to wait until Judy's back from lunch."

"That's fine. I can take care of some shopping first."

"See you in about half an hour."

Around one-thirty, Sara and Kitty walked over to the Crab Trap. The rambling old restaurant sat out on a pier between the Maritime Museum and the harbor. She and Kitty threaded their way past tourists, who were snapping pictures and lining up for an afternoon sightseeing cruise.

The lunch rush was almost over, so the hostess showed them right to a table overlooking the harbor. Sara watched as bushel baskets of crabs were unloaded from a work boat.

"I guess our lunch is going to be nice and fresh," she observed.

Kitty nodded.

"Would you like something to drink before your meal?" the waitress asked.

The artist ordered a screwdriver.

"I'd better stick with milk," Sara said.

When the woman had left, Kitty set her purse on the floor. "So how have you been feeling?"

"Better—now that the morning sickness phase is over."

"Why didn't you tell me about the baby?"

"I just wasn't really talking about it."

"But you're happy about it, aren't you?"

"Yes."

Kitty smiled wistfully. "If I could have a baby, I'd be shouting up and down the river."

"You can't?" Sara blurted. "I didn't know."

Kitty fiddled with her spoon. "I had some female problems a couple of years ago—and had to have a hysterectomy. That was before I came to St. Stephens."

"Oh, Kitty, but you're so young."

"Just one of those things."

"I'm sorry."

"Don't worry about me. I'm fine now," she said with forced cheerfulness.

Sara wasn't sure what else to say, and Kitty went on, "I wasn't dating anybody seriously. But, you know, I kind of always had it in my mind that I'd like to have a child."

The waitress brought their drinks and wrote down their luncheon orders. Sara took several sips of her milk. "Maybe you could adopt a child."

"I'm thinking about something like that. But I'm not going to rush into anything."

"You've got your career to establish right now."

"Yes. People do seem to like my work, so that's a plus."

"You're so creative."

"Thanks. But let's stop talking about me. I want to hear about your plans for the baby. Do you need some help fixing up a nursery? I'm great with a paintbrush."

Sara smiled. "Ben said he'd help me put some wallpaper up, but he's been so busy."

There was a pause of several seconds. "I heard you and Ben were seeing each other."

"Then I guess you heard a lot of other stuff, too."

"I don't pay attention to gossip."

234 • SAMANTHA CHASE

"Ben and I—we— I know people are making assumptions. But we didn't—"

"You're lucky you found each other," Kitty finished softly.

"Yes."

The food arrived and both women turned their attention to the meal.

Lunch with Kitty had been a nice break, Sara thought as they stepped out of the restaurant. The sightseeing boat had departed, but another tour bus was unloading passengers.

"St. Stephens is turning into Baltimore's favorite day trip," Kitty remarked.

"Looks that way." Sara's voice betrayed her mixed emotions. "It's good for business. But I miss the peace and quiet, too." She looked out toward a sailboat making for the harbor. "Isn't that—"

The rest of her sentence was drowned out by the roar of a motorcycle. In the next second, it shot around the corner. Kitty jumped back out of the way. When Sara started to follow suit, a cramp arrowed up her leg, and she froze.

"Sara!" Kitty screamed.

But Sara couldn't move. And she was right in the path of the oncoming machine. My God! Was it the same guy who'd been after her for months?

The cycle charged forward like a bull rounding on a matador. She cried out and threw her hands in front of her face, bracing herself for the sickening impact.

CHAPTER 27

Kitty grabbed Sara's shoulder and pulled her back toward the doorway. The sleek black machine skidded past, missing them by inches. Gravel peppered Sara's legs and exhaust fumes stung her nostrils.

As Kitty lost her footing, they both tumbled to the ground. Sara's head crashed against the curb. *You really do see stars*, she thought as tiny dots of light danced in front of her eyes. When her vision cleared, she found herself lying on her side with Kitty leaning over her—her face so close that the features were distorted.

"Sara, Sara." The artist sounded frantic.

"Is she all right?"

"Should we call an ambulance?" The anxious questions came from a group of tourists who had seen the accident.

"Please. Don't make any fuss," Sara begged in a shaky voice as she reached up gingerly to touch her throbbing head. A lump had already started to form, and she winced, wishing the crowd would go away. She looked at Kitty. "Isn't your apartment just around the corner?"

"I think we'd better get over to the doctor," Kitty murmured.

Sara didn't protest as Kitty and one of the men from the crowd helped her to her feet. "My car's right over here," he said. "Let me drive you."

"I don't want to be any trouble."

"No trouble at all."

As Sara leaned back into the sun-warmed seat, she started shaking. "Kitty, it was that same guy!"

"What guy?"

"The one on the motorcycle. After that business with the eagles, he started following me around. But this was the first time he tried to run me down."

"Sara, there are lots of reckless kids on motorcycles who live around here. He had on a helmet. How could you tell who it was?"

Sara closed her eyes and tried to picture the rider. But it had all happened so fast. "I guess I can't be sure," she finally admitted.

"Do you want me to call the police?"

She shook her head. "What would I say? I can't describe him, except for the black leather and the helmet."

"Where to?" the driver asked as he reached Main Street.

Kitty leaned forward to give directions.

Five minutes later, Sara was in the waiting room of her father's office. It was noisy and overflowing with a cross section of St. Stephens' residents—restless kids with poison ivy or summer flu, mothers in for well-baby checkups, older men and women with chronic problems.

Everyone turned in Sara's direction as she limped in, still supported by Kitty.

"Sara! What happened to you?" Lois gasped.

"A motorcycle almost ran us down,' Kitty explained breathlessly.

"Let's get you right into an exam room," Lois murmured.

Sara looked at all the people waiting their turn. "But I hate to—"

Lois took her arm. "Emergencies have first priority. Come on; you need to lie down."

Sara looked at Kitty. "Thanks."

"Do you want me to wait and take you home?"

"I'll be fine."

Lois turned Sara over to Anne Brannock, the new office nurse.

"Your legs look like they've been peppered with bird shot," she clucked as she began to clean the wounds and swab them with antiseptic.

Sara winced. Anne had barely finished swabbing up her legs when Ben burst into the room.

"Lois said you were in an accident. What happened?" His voice had lost the calm professionalism he maintained with patients.

"A motorcycle almost ran me down." The words came out high and shaky.

"Jesus Christ."

Anne quietly left the room and closed the door.

"How do you feel?"

"Not too bad."

Ben checked the abrasions on Sara's legs. "Any other damage?"

"My head."

Gently he probed the bump. "Did you lose consciousness?"

"I don't think so."

"Any vision problems?"

"Not unless you count seeing stars when I hit the ground."

"I'll just have a look at your eyes." As he examined her pupillary reflex, he skillfully led her through a series of questions designed to determine the extent of her injuries.

"Well, you've got a real goose egg. But I don't think it's serious," he finally concluded.

"What about the baby?"

"It's in a nice safe baby-carrier. But we'll check things out just in case."

Sara felt suddenly self-conscious. "A pelvic exam?"

"You're not having any vaginal bleeding—or any cramping, are you?"

"No."

"Then I'm sure everything's all right," he assured her. "But let's have a look at your abdomen." He helped her lie down on the table.

A doctor's touch was supposed to be imper-sonal. Hadn't she bared her middle every month to Dr. Birch without a second thought? But this was different. The man folding up her dress and pushing down the edge of her panties was also her lover.

"Just relax."

Sara could tell from his voice that he wasn't as objective as he was trying to appear.

At first his fingers were a little stiff as they palpitated her abdomen, feeling her uterus and the outline of the baby. A very routine procedure.

"I think everything's okay." His voice was husky, and his hand lingered, his thumb trailing across her taut skin. "Damn." He quickly folded down her dress.

"Is something wrong?"

He laughed. "Not with you—or the baby. But unfortunately, this is turning me on," he muttered.

"Dr. Langley!" The exclamation was part relief that everything was really all right, part satisfaction that the reaction hadn't been all one-sided.

"This is the first time I ever wished the exam rooms had locks."

She laughed, feeling a delicious little shiver.

When his lips brushed against hers, she reached up to circle his neck with her arms. He kept right on kissing her as he pulled her to a sitting position and hugged her tightly against his lab coat. "God, I was scared when I heard you'd been hurt."

She'd been scared too. Now it was comforting to cling to him. "I trust this isn't your standard bedside manner," she murmured.

"Only for you."

The words, and his possessive look, brought her a warm glow. For a few moments he continued to hold her close. Then, from down the hall, a child shrieked, and reality intruded once again.

He sighed. "I guess I need to get back to business."

"I know. And so do I."

"No, you certainly do not. I had Lois call the gallery and tell Judy you wouldn't be back this afternoon."

"Oh."

"I want to keep an eye on you for the next couple of hours."

"Is that really necessary?"

"You're a doctor's daughter. You know the drill for head injuries. You really shouldn't be alone for the next twenty-four hours. So why don't you lie down on the couch in your father's office where we can look in on you every once in a while?"

She wanted to protest, but he was already turning toward the door as the wailing down the hall intensified.

It wasn't so bad being pampered, Sara decided a few minutes later, nestling under the soft blanket Anne had tucked around her. She snuggled into the cushions of the old leather couch that had been in the office ever since she could remember. Her father had given up his pipe several years ago, but a faint smoky smell still clung to the worn upholstery.

For the first time since the accident, she was aware of the baby kicking. That, as much as anything Ben had said, made her feel reassured. She smiled as her hand drifted to her abdomen, where she traced a random little pattern.

"Settle down and let Mommy rest," she whispered.

Anne had pulled the shades, and the room was cool and dim. She could see the tall shapes of the bookshelves, with their medical journals, and the small, old-fashioned refrigerator where her father kept some of his drugs. Being here brought back so many memories.

Her eyes lit on a box of latex gloves, and she bit back a grin. Until just now, she'd forgotten all about the afternoon she and Ginny had been waiting for Dad to finish up and had gotten bored. They'd filled a dozen rubber gloves at the sink in the corner and were having a water fight when Dad had interrupted the game. He hadn't been pleased, and they'd gotten a spanking for that trick.

But there were other times, too. Like the Saturday when she'd fallen off her bike and opened up a gash on her elbow. She'd left the bike by the side of the road and somehow dragged herself down to her father's office.

Her arm had needed stitches, and Dad had taken care of it in here because all the exam rooms had been filled. Because she'd been such a brave little girl, he'd sent his nurse over to the drugstore for a Popsicle. He hadn't even fussed when some of the grape syrup had dripped on the couch.

Somehow, here in his private domain, she felt closer to her father than she had in a long time. *Oh, Dad,* she thought. *Why did everything go wrong? Are you going to get better? Are you ever going to come back here?*

Sara closed her eyes and brought her mind back to the good childhood memories.

The baby had followed orders and stopped kicking. Eventually, Sara drifted off to sleep as well.

Down the hall in exam room two, Bobby Craig jumped when the door opened. He was trying to untangle himself from the blood-pressure cuff he'd been fooling with while he was waiting for the doctor.

"I didn't break it, honest."

"Here let me help you," Ben offered.

Bobby waited while the doctor pumped up the cuff and checked his blood pressure.

"So you're going out for midget football in the fall," he remarked as he got out his otoscope and peered into the boy's ears.

"Yeah, I hope the coach lets me be the quarterback."

"But it would be fun to be on the team— even if you don't get the top job. I played in high school."

"What position?"

"Offensive line. But I wasn't first string. Let's listen to your heart." As he bent toward the boy's chest, he noticed a blue aluminum circle hanging from a metal chain around his neck.

"A dog tag? I guess we won't have to give you a rabies shot."

Bobby laughed a bit self-consciously. "Rad, isn't it? I found it in a field over by the old Atwater Place."

Ben murmured an answer as he moved around to the boy's back. "Take a deep breath and hold it. . . . Good."

Bobby expelled the breath.

"How's your foot?"

"It's been hurtin'. But in a different place."

"I'll look at it before you go. Lie down so I can check your stomach."

Bobby complied, and Ben's fingers probed for the spleen and appendix.

"Doc?"

"Um?"

He'd felt bad about that dog ever since the day he'd found the tag. But he'd been afraid to get that close to the garage again. And since that crazy guy had chased him into the woods, he wasn't stupid enough to go anywhere near that part of town. But what if the police went out there and put that guy in jail for beating on his shepherd? "Isn't there a law about being mean to dogs?"

Ben had moved down to the end of the exam table and picked up the boy's foot. "There sure is. It's against the law to be cruel to any animal. Do you know about a dog somebody's mistreating?"

Bobby reconsidered. Gee, if a policeman went out there, maybe he'd have to tell the guy who ratted on him. Boy, he wished he hadn't started this conversation. He backpeddled a bit. "Well, maybe not mistreating. They had this German shepherd tied in the garage. And he looked—you know—sad."

Ben had just noted that the nail wound he'd treated back in April had healed nicely. At the mention of a German shepherd, his head jerked up.

Oh, shit, why hadn't he just kept his big mouth shut? Bobby wondered. "But maybe they weren't home, you know, and they didn't want their dog roaming around."

Ben nodded. A German shepherd. There were probably dozens of them in St. Stephens. But what had this one looked like? The half-formed question was driven from his mind by the business of the moment as his trained eye spotted a round sore on the boy's sole. "I think I see what's wrong with your foot." His finger probed gently.

"Hey, that hurts."

"I'm afraid you have a plantar's wart."

Bobby's voice was apprehensive. "Jeez. What's that?"

"It's caused by a virus. If we don't treat it, it will grow into your foot and you'll have a hard time walking, much less playing football."

"What do I have to do?"

"I'll give you a prescription. Your mom can put some medicine on the wart every night. That should make it come off. But I'll want to see you back in three weeks to make sure everything's all right."

By late in the afternoon, Sara was feeling restless. She might have driven herself home, but she wanted to wait for Ben.

When she took a peek out at the waiting room, Lois told her there were only two more patients, so they should be finishing up soon.

Back in her father's office, she turned on the light and fished in her purse for the baby name book she'd been carrying around for weeks. It was so hard getting the right one. If the baby was a girl, she wanted to name it after her mother. But Margaret was so old-fashioned. That would have to be the middle name. And what if it was a boy? The only thing she knew for sure was that her son wasn't going to be Ted, Jr. Maybe Brian. Ryan. Aaron. Michael. Or Stephen. She spent fifteen minutes turning back and forth through the dog-eared pages before putting the book away. She still had months before she had to make a decision. Getting up, she rinsed her face at the sink in the corner and combed her hair. Then she sat down at the desk and called the gallery to see how Judy was doing.

"Everything's fine," the young woman assured her. "I'm just getting ready to go home."

"How did you do?"

"I sold one of Ralph's decoys." She sounded proud of herself.

"That's great. Then I'll see you in the morning."

"If you want me to, I can open up."

"Thanks."

Sara put down the phone and glanced over the surface of the desk. Next to the lamp was a framed picture of her and Ginny, taken after her graduation from high school. She studied her own face, noting how young and proud she looked. It hadn't seemed like it at the time, but things had been so simple back then.

Maybe she could take the picture down to Dad at the hospital the next time she saw him.

Her fingers drummed against the sheet of glass protecting the surface of the desk. There'd been another photograph in the office, too. A shot of the four of them the day Ginny had started kindergarten. Dad had removed it from the desk years ago after Mom had died.

It was the kind of thing she'd like to save for the baby.

She didn't remember Dad ever bringing it home. And she couldn't believe he would have thrown it out. So it must still be in the office. Where would he have put it? In the closet? Or maybe in one of the desk drawers?

Her first shock came when she opened the left bottom drawer. At first, all she could see was a pile of medical journals. But when she reached underneath, her fingers closed around cold metal—and it wasn't the frame of a picture.

It was a revolver. Carefully, she withdrew the weapon and laid it on the desk. What in the world was this doing in her father's office?

Like many residents of the rural community, she had a bit of familiarity with weapons. When she checked the cylinders, she found the gun was loaded. After making sure the safety catch was on, she emptied the shells onto the blotter.

What had been in Dad's mind? Was he worried about self-defense? Was this another manifestation of his paranoia? Or had he been thinking of blowing his brains out and decided pills would be better?

She looked down at the drawer. What else was in there? Kneeling on the floor, she began to empty the contents onto the rug. At the very bottom was a manila envelope. From the uneven shape, it didn't look as if it contained just paper. When she reached inside, she knew what she was holding, even before she pulled it out. Still, her eyes narrowed as she stared at the two rectangular needlepoint pictures. Each depicted a hypodermic. In the dimly lit room, they seemed to draw the light from the desk lamp like paintings spotlighted in a gallery. Either that, or they glowed with some sort of internal, evil illumination.

CHAPTER 28

A smile of anticipation curved Ben's lips as he stepped into the room. "Well, Lois is gone. So now we have the place to ourselves." Instead of the playful response he anticipated, there was only silence.

"Sara?" Moving farther into the room, he spotted the revolver lying on the blotter. "Sara?" Two fast steps took him to the desk. Finally he saw her huddled by the open drawer, her face deathly white, her eyes wide and staring.

Jesus! What was wrong? What was she doing on the floor? He hadn't heard a shot or anything like that. Dropping to the rug, Ben reached for her.

"My father murdered Ted."

"What are you talking about?"

"And maybe Ginny, too. I mean, he could have hired somebody."

"Sara, honey, take it easy."

Wordlessly, she reached out her trembling hand.

Ben took the needlepoint canvases and held them up to the light. "What makes you think— Wait a minute. Where did I see something like this before?"

"There used to be one sort of like it hanging in the office. My mother made it. But that's been gone for years. You saw the one in the utility drawer the day we had to change the fuse."

"It was in a plastic bag—and it smelled bad, right?"

"It came out of Ted's car—after they pulled it from the river," she whispered.

"Then how did you get it?"

"Dailey brought me the contents of Ted's glove compartment. I thought it must have been something that Ted's mistress left. I didn't want to look at it, but I couldn't throw it out, either. Then when Ginny's luggage came back from the Royal Alexandria, there was another one in her cosmetic case. And now, here are two more, from the drawer where my father was hiding a loaded gun."

Ben leaned back against the side of the desk and pulled Sara into his lap. He pressed her face against the cotton fabric of his shirt and stroked her hair. "You can't jump— Jesus—"

"What?"

He hesitated.

"You'd better tell me," Sara persisted.

Ben sighed. "You know how Harold's been— completely unresponsive. Well last night," he continued in a low voice, "my frustration level boiled over and I guess he sensed that."

"What happened?"

"He came up out of the blackness long enough to say something. Something he must have thought was important."

Sara gripped Ben's arm.

"There were tears in his eyes, and he said—*needlepoint*."

"I knew it. Don't you see, Ben. He hated Ted. He hated him for marrying me. He thought Ted was ruining my life. And he's the one who made him take out that big insurance policy before we got married."

"But that doesn't mean he murdered your husband. Sara, think about it. The medical examiner ruled that Ted's death was an accident. Now you're suddenly assuming he was murdered. And you don't even know Ginny's—dead." He'd finally said the word she'd been dreading.

Sara began to cry softly. "Oh, Ben," she managed. "Dad was so hung up on that needlepoint picture—especially after Mom died. It was like a symbol to him. If he—if he—really flipped out, he might have left it as a kind of calling card."

"I know he was in bad shape. But murder? He's a physician. For forty years he's been saving lives."

Sara wiped her cheek with the back of her hand. After taking several shuddering breaths, she blew her nose on the handkerchief Ben handed her.

"Ever since Ginny disappeared off the face of the earth, I've been so strung out I don't know what to think anymore." She looked up at him, pleading for understanding. "If the needlepoint doesn't have anything to do with my father, then tell me what it means. For Ted. For Ginny. And now these two in Dad's drawer."

Ben looked at her helplessly. "I don't know what it means. You say there was one in Ted's car and one in Ginny's makeup case? Are you sure Ginny and Ted weren't—" He hated to raise the question. "—seeing each other? She could have left one in his car and taken the other with her."

"I thought about that." Sara shrugged. "Could he have hidden *that* from me? Could she? I just don't know. What if Dad had figured out they were having an affair and wanted to punish both of them?"

"Sara, he's not a murderer."

"He didn't used to be. But what if his mind had snapped?"

She closed her eyes for a moment. "I'm probably sounding pretty crazy myself. I guess you're wondering—how could she suspect her own father of murder. But Ben, he was always so disciplined, so methodical. And now he's totally gone to pieces."

"I understand what you're going through. But honey, we'll work this out together. I promise." Ben stood up and helped Sara to her feet. Harold's office was no longer the cozy refuge it had been earlier. "We can't stay here all night. Come on, let's go back to my house."

"No. I want to compare the other two needlepoint pictures to these two. Then I want to talk to you about Keith Thomas."

"Who's Keith Thomas?"
"I don't know. But I'm going to find out."

Ralph Meekins had picked a hiding place where a tangle of honeysuckle vines grew over the sagging remains of an old fence. Peeking up over the barrier, he trained his binoculars on the Atwater house. Despite the ninety-five-degree heat, he was wearing a long-sleeved camouflage jacket and cap.

Watching people was a lot like watching birds. You made sure they didn't see you, observed behavior, kept notes, and speculated about implications.

A mosquito buzzed near his ear, and he reached up to swat it before it took a bite. Damn pesky insects were thick as ground fog after all the rain there'd been lately. It was no day to be out in the bushes. But from the moment he'd gotten his mail this afternoon, he hadn't been able to think about anything except finding out what in blazes was going on out here.

The letter he'd been waiting for had finally come from the Social Security Administration. He'd written the inquiry on Sara's office stationery. Lord help him, he'd half hoped they'd make a mistake and send the information back to her. Then he wouldn't have to tell her anything. She could figure it out for herself.

But it had come to his house as he'd requested. Now he was going to have to tell her something—and soon. The social security number by itself didn't prove anything. Lots of people changed their names for all kinds of reasons. He needed something more than an old man's crazy suspicions.

He loosened his hold on the cylindrical barrels and flexed his fingers. They were starting to ache. Darn arthritis. He wasn't going to be able to sit out here much longer. If he didn't get what he wanted today, he could come back. That was one thing bird watching taught you—patience. Sooner or later he was going to see something that would spell out what the two of them were up to.

He'd had a hunch about the social security number. He just hadn't expected to get so much information from a series of nine digits. At first, he'd thought it might be a phony, but that hadn't been the case.

He lifted the field glasses again and trained them on a window. Probably the two of them in there had cooked up some scheme to kill Ted. But why? And what was she up to now?

She'd come back an hour ago and gone running into the house like she had something to tell her boyfriend. Or maybe she was hot to get her oil changed. He could believe that—after what he'd seen her doing with Ted down by the marsh.

If the two of them were busy, this might be a good time to do some snooping around. For a moment, Ralph considered getting closer. Then he settled back into the honeysuckle. With his high-powered binoculars he could see as well as if he were ten feet from the porch.

A shape crossed in front of a bedroom window, and Ralph raised the binoculars again. The sun had dipped low on the horizon, and he wished he was on the east side of the house. But there wasn't any good cover along the back edge of the property until you got down by the crick. And that was too far away.

The figure in the window stopped abruptly and gazed out. Ralph froze—all at once feeling as if the roles of hunter and hunted had been reversed. The hair on the back of his neck prickled. It was almost like the guy was looking right at him. Involuntarily, he scrunched farther down into the underbrush and pulled his visor cap down over his face.

CHAPTER 29

Ben studied the four needlepoint rectangles lying on the kitchen table.

"You're right. They do look just alike—except that the first one isn't finished." He rubbed his thumb across the water-stained canvas. "But do you really think your father had either the interest or the ability to make something like this?"

"The one my mother did was from a kit. It wasn't just a picture of a hypodermic needle." Searching her memory, she brought back an image of the framed stitchery. "There were some other things a doctor would have, too— like a thermometer, and a stethoscope. The implements were already stitched onto the canvas. All mom had to do was fill in the easy part—the background."

"Where did she get the kit?"

"From a catalog of decorations for doctors' offices. If you ordered one like it, you could cut out the rectangle with the hypodermic and throw the rest away."

"Do you remember the name of the company?"

Sara shook her head. "I don't even know for sure if it's still in business. But Lois probably does. If they're still around, I could contact them and see if they shipped any of the pictures to my dad. Or to Ginny."

"I'll ask her about it in the morning," Ben promised.

"Thanks." Sara gathered up the pieces of stitchery and stuffed them all into a paper bag, which she shoved back into the drawer. When she turned to Ben once more, her shoulders were sagging.

"You've had a rough day. Don't make it worse by stewing over this stuff. There's probably some perfectly reasonable explanation."

"Like what?"

He thought for a moment. "Like the hospital auxiliary was selling needlepoint pictures to raise money for new bed pans. Your father bought two and stuffed them in a drawer because they were so ugly."

Sara rolled her eyes. "Oh, Ben. That's ridiculous." She couldn't keep a little giggle out of her voice.

"But I made you laugh. And that's just part of my prescription. As your doctor, I advise you to go up and take a hot shower and get into bed. While you're doing that, I'll go out and get some dinner. What do you want?"

Her mind warred between safety and self-indulgence. "Pizza."

"Pizza?"

"With everything."

"What about your heartburn?"

"I'm living dangerously."

He gave her a quick hug and pointed her toward the stairs. "Go on up. I'll phone in the order. Then we can have a picnic in your room."

Ralph Meekins' lips tensed as he listened to the busy signal. After several seconds, he dropped the receiver back into the cradle. At least Sara was home. He could go over there right now. He snatched his jacket off the settee and then tossed it onto the rocking chair. He couldn't just go charging over there like a damn fool. He had to think this through. One thing for sure, he didn't want to be seen at Sara's place by the wrong people.

He always thought better when he was doing something with his hands. In the small kitchen, he made himself a cup of strong coffee and poured in a generous shot of whiskey. He felt like he'd been caught in a rowboat on the water when a storm had suddenly blown up: exposed and vulnerable. And he'd have to paddle like hell to get safely back to shore.

After taking a couple of long pulls on the coffee cup, he reached for the phone again. This time it rang, and he waited expectantly for her to answer.

"This is Sara Chandler—"

"Sara—"

"I can't come to the phone right now. But if

you'll leave your name and number, I'll get back to you as soon as possible."

Dang machine, Ralph thought. He always felt funny when he had to talk into one. What should he do? At the sound of the tone, he cleared his throat. "Sara, I've got to talk to you. It's real important. Call me back as soon as you get home."

Sara stepped out of the shower and reached for a towel. A few minutes later, she was propped up in bed wearing a comfortable nightgown and a silky robe. It wasn't the double bed she and Ted had slept in during the four years of their married life. That was a symbol she'd wanted to get rid of, so she'd had it moved into the guest room and had replaced it with the large four-poster she'd slept in as a girl.

"Feeling better?" Ben asked as he came in the door with the food.

She looked at the concerned expression that he was fighting to suppress. He was really worried about her. On top of that, he'd had a hard day himself. She ought to try and put her anxieties away and enjoy what was left of the evening with him.

She reached back to adjust her pillows. "Yes. You were right, the shower was just what I needed."

"Good." Some of the tautness went out of his features. Then he made himself busy setting the box down on the dresser, taking Styrofoam plates out of a bag, and serving them each a slice of pizza. "I wasn't sure what to get to drink. You can't drink coffee or tea, and they didn't have milk. I hope you like caffeine-free Coke."

"That's fine."

Ben sat cross-legged on the other end of the bed. As he ate his share of the dinner, he tried to look as if he wasn't watching Sara. Thank God she seemed relaxed again.

He was just finishing his last bite of pizza when he remembered the conversation that morning with Jay Clifton. The idea of electro-convulsive therapy for Harold didn't make him very happy. Even if it cured his depression, he might never be able to practice medicine again. However, it was something Sara was going to have to consider.

But not now. He wasn't going to spoil the rest of the evening by bringing it up. Besides, if he did some reading before he broached the subject, he'd be in a better position to advise her.

Suddenly he was swept by a desperate need to touch her. Reaching across the spread, he found her foot through the covers and squeezed it.

Sara looked at him and wiggled her toes. "What are you doing?"

"Did you know that in the Middle Ages doctors sometimes had to protect their female patients' modesty by examining them through a sheet?"

"Really?" She grinned, responding to the sudden lusty quality of his voice. "Are we playing medieval doctor?"

His hand moved up her calf. "Could be. Or maybe I'm just checking your reflexes."

Even through two layers of bedclothes, her

body reacted to his touch. She closed her eyes and scrunched down farther against the pillows. The bed shifted with his weight as his skillful hand continued to work its way up her body, pausing to explore the curves along the way. She'd never engaged in games like this before. Never known that sex could be both playful and erotic at the same time. "You're going to turn this into a medieval torture session if you keep that up," she murmured.

The hand stopped, and she drew in a quick breath—waiting. Supercharged seconds passed, and her lids fluttered open. He was right there beside her, and the dark fire in his eyes told her the time for games was over.

CHAPTER 30

Friday, July 14

"Want me to make you some coffee?" she offered.

"No. Go back to sleep for a little while." Ben leaned over and gave her a lingering kiss that brought her arms tightly around his neck.

"You're making it damn difficult for me to get out of here."

"Sorry."

"I'll see you tonight."

"Ben—" There was a wistful note in her voice that made him sit down on the side of the bed.

"What is it, honey?"

"Dr. Birch recommended that I take prepared-childbirth classes."

"Natural childbirth?"

"I'm not sure I want to go that far. But I want to keep my options open."

"That's a good idea."

"But the brochure says you're supposed to come with a partner."

"Um." He understood how important this was to Sara. "Do you want me to go with you?"

"Oh, Ben, would you?"

He thought about his insanely hectic schedule. "Sure. But if I'm on call—"

"I understand. Maybe the instructor could fill in for you when you're not there." She pushed herself up to a sitting position. "I've been worrying about—you know—labor and delivery—how I'm going to be. Whether I'm going to end up screaming to be knocked out."

He squeezed her hand. "You're going to do just fine. Every pregnant woman worries about childbirth. It's like when men have to go off to war. They wonder about whether they're going to be cowardly in battle."

She smiled tremulously. "I guess I wouldn't want to go into battle, either."

"Not in your condition." He glanced at the clock. "Lois will have a fit if I don't show up in the office pretty soon."

After Sara heard the front door close, she dozed off again until her alarm rang an hour later. Shutting it off, she climbed out of bed and flexed her legs. She was still a little stiff from the accident. But other than that, she was feeling better than she had in days. Ben was right, she thought, as she made her way downstairs to fix a cup of herb tea. She had to keep things in perspective—or she wasn't going to do Dad or Ginny any good. Or the baby, either.

Ben had brought the newspaper in. While she waited for the water to boil, she glanced at the headlines. Then she happened to look over at her new answering machine, which sat on the end of the counter. Since she'd checked it when she'd come home the evening before, she wasn't expecting a message. But the light was blinking insistently. Curious, she pressed the "play" button.

"Sara, I've got to talk to you. It's real important. Call me back as soon as you get home." "Seven thirty-five p.m.," the machine announced before clicking off.

The caller didn't give his name, but she knew it was Ralph Meekins. There was an unaccustomed tension in his voice that made her skin prickle. What was bothering him? He'd never called like this before. Maybe there was more trouble over at the bird refuge. He must have phoned during the ten minutes she was in the shower. Darn. She wished she hadn't missed him.

Was it too early to call now?

When she tried his number, there was no answer. That and the tone of his voice from the recording machine made her draw in a deep breath. Then she remembered Ben's advice. There was no point getting upset over some vague suspicion. Ralph was probably just out on one of his early morning walks along Harris Creek. His constitutionals, he called them. He'd get back to her later if he really had something important to tell her.

But once she'd gotten dressed and climbed into her car, she found herself heading south instead of toward Main Street. No harm in swinging by Ralph's house before going in to the gallery. Maybe he could even give her some of those decoys he'd been finishing up.

It was only a ten-minute drive to the little community where Ralph lived. The area had once been strictly a waterman's village. Now the old clapboard houses along the quarter-mile-wide creek were interspersed with expensive vacation homes.

Only one scruffy-looking dog came out to bark at her car as she made her way up the narrow lane. The sky was cloudless. The sun glinted off the water. Sara squinted into the brightness and pulled down the sun visor as she turned into Ralph's drive.

In the next second, she slammed on her brakes. There was a vehicle blocking her path. A shaft of sunlight bounced off a strip of chrome above the bumper with the intensity of a lighthouse beam, so it was several seconds before Sara realized she had almost run into a blue and white police car. Then, other facts began to register—each with a separate and heart-stopping impact. An ambulance was pulled up beside the police car on the grass. A crowd of neighbors gathered around the porch. And Officer Morris—the Moose—Bramble was positioned by the door. Somehow the scene was a confirmation of all the anxiety she'd been trying to suppress since she'd gotten that message.

A pulse was pounding in Sara's temple as she threw open the car door. She had just taken several quick steps up the gravel drive, when the front door opened, and two men appeared on the front porch carrying a heavy stretcher loaded with a man-size shape.

"Ralph—"

Someone grabbed Sara's shoulder. "He can't hear you. He's dead."

She saw, then, what she hadn't wanted to see before. The lifeless form on the stretcher was sealed in a dark plastic body bag. "No— He can't be dead. He left a message on my answering machine. I was coming over to find out what he was upset about." The words gushed out as if the explanation could somehow wash away the awful reality.

"Ma'am, you're going to have to move your car so we can back this ambulance out."

Sara stared stupidly at the ambulance driver.

"Move your car, please," he repeated.

Nodding numbly, Sara slid into the front seat again and started the engine. Some part of her mind was amazed that she could function behind the wheel. Slowly, she backed out of the drive and pulled the car onto the shoulder of the road. Still stunned by what she was seeing, she watched the ambulance drive away.

Then, on legs that felt like blocks of wood, she headed back toward the knot of neighbors, who were shaking their heads and talking quietly on the lawn.

"What happened?" she managed to ask around the lump that had formed in her throat.

"Someone knocked him off."

"He was murdered?" Sara's question came out as a surprised gasp. She had expected to hear that he'd had a heart attack or something.

"Looked to me like he surprised a robber," a tall, dark-haired man volunteered.

"Jed, here, found him," another neighbor added.

"Went out to get the paper," Jed continued with the story he'd already told a dozen times that morning, "and my fool retriever ran over to Ralph's house and started barkin' like he had a coon up a tree. Couldn't git him away from the front porch. So I finally went over and knocked on the door. It was unlocked. There was stuff scattered all over the living room. And poor old Ralph was layin' in the middle of the mess. The back of his head was all—" He glanced at Sara's white face and switched gears. "I figure he'd been dead half the night."

Sara felt a black wave of dizziness sweep over her. All at once, she knew she wasn't going to hang on to her meager breakfast. As quickly as she could, she turned away. But she only made it as far as the side of the house before she threw up.

Mortification kept her standing with her back to the crowd. She'd given them something else to talk about. And she'd had enough of that lately. Fumbling in her purse, she tried to find a tissue.

"You all right?" The question came from Officer Moose Bramble.

Sara wiped her mouth, but she couldn't wipe away the sour taste. It was as much from the shock of Ralph's death as from having been sick. After taking a couple of deep, calming breaths, she nodded.

Moose led her to the porch steps and sat her down. "You stay right there. I'm going to get you a glass of water."

Sara wanted to get away from the curious stares. There was no reason to hang around. She couldn't do anything for poor Ralph now. But she didn't argue with the officer. Probably her knees were too rubbery to carry her across the lawn anyway. In a few minutes, Bramble was back with a paper cup of cold water. Sara took a cautious sip. It stayed down, and she took another.

"Thanks."

"I've already sent the ambulance off. You going to be all right, Miss Sara?"

"Yes. I'm sorry—I just couldn't help—"

"No need to apologize."

He waited a few moments.

Sara finally filled in the silence. "They said Ralph was murdered."

"It does look like a homicide. How well did you know him?"

"I guess as well as anybody. He sold his decoys at my shop, and lately he'd been helping out around the place." She was still feeling a little dizzy, and she wondered if she sounded coherent.

"Do you know if there are any relatives?"

"He never spoke about anyone but his mother. And she died several years ago."

Bramble gave her a considering look. "I may want to ask you some questions later. You ought to go home and take it easy."

Sara had been hearing that since yesterday afternoon. Straightening her shoulders, she looked up at him. "I have to open up the gallery. I'll be over there if you need me."

*   *   *

It took more time to crack a crab than it did for the news of Ralph Meekins's death to reach the early morning crowd at McGuire's Drugstore.

Phil Dorsey from the hardware store heard it on his Bear Cat scanner on the way into town. By the time Officer Bramble came in for a cup of coffee, Cheryl Keene from the newspaper had already grabbed her camera and headed for the crime scene.

"Say, Moose, are you gonna fill us in on the murder?" Elmo asked.

"Poor old Ralph," Jodeen Crane added, her tone more charitable than usual. "I just can't believe it." The deceased had been an upstanding citizen, and his spreading fame as a master carver had brought him a lot of local respect.

Moose Bramble propped his bulky frame against the soda-fountain counter. He and Police Chief Marcus Dailey were about as different as two law enforcement officers could be. Dailey was an outsider—a transplant from the Midwest. Neat and orderly to the point of obsessiveness, he was a retired army sergeant who ran his department like a military unit.

Bramble, on the other hand, had been born and raised on the Eastern Shore. Still on the shy side of thirty, he had a waterman's instinctive knowledge of the times and seasons. Sometimes he let police matters drift on the current. It wasn't a case of letting his lines go slack. He'd learned it could pay to wait and see what would float his way. "You know Dailey would have my hide if I gave out any privileged information," he answered now, his gaze causally sweeping the small crowd.

Kitty Duncan met his eye for a moment before putting down her cup of tea. "Bad— was it?"

"It's a good thing we don't get much stuff like that around here."

The one listener Bramble couldn't see was George Newhouse, who was standing on the far side of the aisle that separated the coffee shop from the rest of the drugstore. He'd been about to pick up a tube of hair-setting gel when the conversation in the restaurant area had riveted his attention.

"Have a cup of coffee on the house," Elmo offered, sliding behind the counter and picking up the pot. Serving customers in the coffee shop wasn't his job. But Pattie was busy with an order of scrambled eggs and bacon.

"Don't mind if I do," Bramble allowed.

Come on, get back to the murder, George silently urged. He wanted to step around the partition. Instead, he forced himself to wait silently for Bramble's next bit of intelligence.

"You got any leads on who did it?" Beatrice asked obligingly.

"For God sakes, Miss Bea, we just carted the body away a half hour ago. These things take time."

"Well, I'm sure you'll get your man." Phil cast his vote of support for the local lawmen.

Bramble took a thoughtful sip of his coffee. "Funny coincidence," he mused. "Sara Chandler was out there this morning."

"Oh?" Beatrice leaned forward.

"She's getting to be like Jessica Fletcher on

Murder She Wrote. Her friends and relatives are all turning up dead," Jodeen observed dryly.

"That's morbid," Kitty objected. "Her husband had an accident. And we don't know what happened to Ginny."

"Probably Miss Sara just came out to pick up some of his duck decoys," the deputy speculated. "You know, he made them for her shop."

"That's right," Kitty mused. "Too bad for Ralph. His career was just taking off. I guess Ralph Meekins originals are going to be a real collector's item now."

George took the tube of hair gel up to the counter. Ordinarily, he would have stopped to ask the clerk if he had any leads on new people moving to town. Today he didn't bother with any chitchat. And he didn't glance over at the coffee-shop crowd as he left the store. He was thinking about Sara Chandler again. Every time he turned around, there she was, popping up like a bad penny.

Sara would have been surprised to know how closely her thoughts were paralleling the gossip at the drugstore. It wasn't until she'd been in the gallery for fifteen quiet minutes that reaction set in.

She was moving a stained-glass panel depicting a seagull in flight when it slipped through her fingers. Somehow she managed to catch it before it hit the floor. Sagging back against the wall, she carefully set the picture down. She'd almost broken a three-hundred-dollar piece.

My God, people she knew were dropping like flies. Ted. Dad, in a sense. Ralph. Ginny. She blanched. Had she really added her sister to the list?

Yesterday she'd almost been run over by a motorcycle. Was it just coincidence? Or was there some crazy pattern to it all? Then there was the needlepoint she'd found in her father's drawer. Ben had stopped her from thinking about it last night. But she couldn't just drop it. She had to know how her father fit into all this.

She was still struggling to get her fears under control when Judy came in.

"Did you hear about Ralph?" her assistant began.

"Yes."

"Isn't it terrible?"

"I'm going to miss him," Sara said quietly, her eyes misting.

"Are you sure you don't want to go on home?" Judy asked.

"I guess I would like to get out of here," Sara admitted. "But it seems like I'm asking you to hold down the fort by yourself a lot lately."

"You can give me a raise if it would make you feel better."

"I think I will."

As she stepped out of the shop, Sara silently acknowledged that she wasn't returning home. She was going to her Dad's place to search for clues, anything that would point to what had been in her father's mind and what had happened to her sister.

*   *   *

The house was stuffy and dusty, and Sara was overtaken with a fit of sneezing when she stepped into the front hall. After opening several windows, she stood indecisively in the dining room.

Feeling like a burglar, she almost turned and walked out. Then she clamped her teeth together and opened the front hall closet. She had to settle this one way or the other. She had to *know*. There was nothing but a collection of coats—including several of hers that she hadn't bothered to take when she'd gotten married. In a medical supply box on the shelf above them was an assortment of gloves, scarves, and hats.

The drawers in the dining room were much less interesting than the ones in the desk at the office. They contained the usual collection of serving platters, napkins, and tablecloths—most of which hadn't been used since her mother died.

Next she went down the hall to the small room her father used as a den. Like his office in town, it was filled with medical books. On the left, there were two filing cabinets between the narrow windows. Both were filled with tax returns and other personal records—going all the way back to the first year her father had opened his practice. Sara thumbed through some of the folders. She didn't immediately come across anything useful. After forty-five minutes, she had the feeling that, even if she spent hours poring over the papers, she'd have little more than eyestrain to show for her trouble. But she felt she had to at least look at the labels on the folders.

The cabinets were more than forty years old and hard to yank open. Sara's back was beginning to hurt from leaning over by the time she got to the bottom drawer of the second cabinet. *Maybe this was a dumb idea after all*, she told herself. But she'd come to make a thorough inspection, and she didn't like to leave a job half done.

When she pulled out the drawer, it was empty—except for a gray metal box shoved in the back. Sara stared at it. Across the front was a gummed label that said, "Personal and Confidential."

Did it hold the secret she'd come to find? The dull gray surface of the metal gave nothing away. But suddenly she was afraid of what she might discover.

She almost slammed the drawer shut. Instead, she lifted out the box and set it on the faded Oriental carpet. It was lighter than she expected. When she shook it, nothing rattled. There was only the sound of papers rustling against each other.

Records? Letters? Secret tax receipts? Or something more sinister? It was frustrating, yet also a relief, to see that the lid was secured with a padlock.

Sara gave the metal hasp several sharp twists, but it didn't give. She couldn't get it off right now, so she wouldn't have to open it here—alone in this empty house. She could take it home, and Ben could help her decide what to do.

CHAPTER 31

By the time Beatrice returned from her morning errands, the mail had arrived. As she shuffled through the stack of circulars and letters, her hand froze, and the breath caught in her throat. At the bottom of the pile was another one of the manila envelopes she'd come to dread. She'd sent a sample chapter and an outline for her novel to several publishers. Now they were winging their way back like homing pigeons. In the past few days, three publishing houses had already told her that her project wasn't right for their list. She'd tried to stay optimistic. Probably *Gone with the Wind* had been turned down a dozen times before Macmillan finally took it on. Yet each rejection was like ripping a piece of adhesive off of tender skin.

She was tempted to toss the envelope in the

trash without even looking. But her own return address was in the upper left-hand corner. In order to find out what publisher it was from, she had to look inside. After tossing the rest of the mail on the kitchen table, she slit the end of the envelope open with a bread knife.

Dear Ms. Pierce:
We have read your outline and sample chapter with interest. Your work shows promise. Your focus on Dr. Lackland and his family, for example, works well. But you need to broaden the scope of the book by following the stories of some of his patients.

Beatrice's heart had started to pound, and she sank down onto a ladder-back chair. Hallelujah, they liked it. Not everything. But they were giving her suggestions for changes. Of course, they knew more about what would sell than she did. Ramona came padding into the kitchen and began to rub up against the chair-leg. Beatrice didn't even notice.

The doctor is a strong character. But we also need to see his vulnerability. One way is to emphasize his medical defeats and the personal toll they extract. The scene where he loses his wife can be very powerful. But you should include other patients whose deaths he feels responsible for. Like the young boy bitten by the dog.

Go into the boy's family background. Let us know how his death affected the people who loved him. Also, don't be afraid to kill off several more characters during the course of the book. As to your style, I like the nautical images you've used to reinforce the seafaring heritage of the town. Just don't go overboard with this.

The two-page letter went on with more comments about the structure of the story and about Beatrice's style. It was signed by an assistant editor named Donna Patruchio, who invited Beatrice to submit the manuscript when it was completed.

Beatrice's head was spinning by the time she reached the end. When Ramona jumped up in her lap, she scooped up the feline and gave her a breathless kiss.

"They like it. Oh, sweetheart, they like it," she bubbled. "I knew it was good. I just knew it."

She gave the cat a whole handful of her favorite chicken-flavored treats and watched affectionately as she began to gobble them down.

For herself, she got out the can of Almond Roca she kept on the top shelf of the pantry. The candy was her favorite. But she only allowed herself a piece on special occasions. And this certainly qualified, she thought as she unwrapped the gold foil and bit into the nut-and-chocolate-covered butter brittle. It was better than sex.

Then, with reborn energy, she started upstairs to her office. Donna Patruchio wanted to focus on Keith Thomas and his family. They'd moved away after he died. But maybe she could find out what had happened to them. She needed to reread the article about the boy—and do a little more digging into the family background.

Ben looked at the piece of flounder on Sara's plate, noting that she'd flaked it instead of eating it. Then he reached across the table and laid his hand over hers. "I know you must be feeling terrible about Ralph."

She closed her eyes for a minute. "Why would anyone do such a horrible thing to that poor old man?"

"It was robbery. He had some valuable duck decoys in his house."

"They could have gotten some of those out of the gallery, and they didn't rob me. I can't believe it's that simple."

"But your security's better. And the gallery's practically across from the police station."

"You make it all sound so logical. But there's something you don't know."

Ben's fingers closed around hers. "What?"

"Ralph left a message for me on the answering machine while I was in the shower last night."

"He did?"

"I could tell from his voice that he was worried about something. He wanted to talk to me. Oh, Ben, maybe if I'd taken that call, he might still be alive."

"Good God, Sara, don't torture yourself with 'what if.' Maybe he just needed someone to talk to. You've known him—knew him—for a long time."

"And I wasn't there for him."

"Stop it." His hand tightened on hers. "Do you still have the tape?"

"I didn't know it was going to be important. So I just let the machine erase the message. Maybe I even destroyed important evidence."

"Sometimes messages are still there, even when you think they've been erased. Do you have a cassette player?"

"No."

"Well, I do. Let me take it home and play it."

Sara got up stiffly, fumbled with the buttons on the machine, and finally ejected the tape, which she gave to Ben. As he pocketed it, she awkwardly inserted a new cassette into the slot.

Ben watched, wishing he could do something to make her tension vanish.

When she caught the look in his eyes, she gave a little shake of her head. "I'm not going to fall apart."

"If you were, it probably would have been before this."

"Is that a vote of confidence?"

"Um hum."

She came back to the table and stopped beside his chair, leaning over so she could cradle his head against her breasts. "It's not just Ralph. It's all the crazy things that have been happening. Maybe they're all connected."

He sighed. "Sara, I've been thinking a lot

about it too. I don't see any logical way they could be tied together."

"So you think I'm just imagining all this?"

He reached up and pulled her down onto his lap. For a moment, he just held her and stroked his fingers across the back of her neck. but the tightness didn't ease out of her body. "Honey, I know you're under a lot of stress. I wish I could do something about it."

"You can." The words were muffled against the front of his shirt.

"Anything."

"I went over to my father's this morning, looking for something—some evidence that might explain what's been happening."

"You found something?"

"I'm not sure. There was a metal box stuffed in the bottom of his filing cabinet. It was locked." She got off Ben's lap and went to retrieve the box from the utility room. When she returned, she set it in the middle of the kitchen table.

Ben eyed the label. "Sara, your father obviously doesn't want anyone looking at whatever's in there."

"I know. But, don't you see? That's exactly why we have to do it."

Ben felt his chest constrict as he fingered the padlock. "If we break this off, Harold's going to know."

"And if we don't find out what's bothering him, maybe he's not going to get any better."

For a moment he was silent. Harold Strickland had offered him a partnership when he'd needed a place to make a new start. The idea of abusing the older man's trust made him almost physically ill. But maybe Sara was right. And he could see from the lines of strain around her mouth and eyes how important this had become to her.

"I'm going to open it whether you help me or not. It's just going to take me longer to saw off the lock than it will if you do it."

"You might hurt yourself."

Sara shrugged.

"All right. Where's your hacksaw?"

A hand shuffled through the contents of the Acme grocery bag from under Ralph's settee. "Jesus, look at all this stuff. He's even got my social security number. Old Ralph must have thought he was a regular Dick Tracy."

"It's lucky you spotted him in the woods."

"Yeah." He picked up the bird-watching journal and tossed it into the bag with the other papers.

"We ought to burn this stuff."

"Not the journal."

"Why?"

"He's got notes on more than just birds in here. I want to see if he spilled the beans to anyone else."

"I don't like keeping any of this around."

"Then put it out of your mind. I'll worry about it." He changed the subject smoothly. "Why don't you tell me what they're saying in town about poor old Ralph."

"It's all just speculation. Nobody really knows anything. It was a good idea for you to make it look like a robbery. That way, they'll just think the head injury killed him."

"Yeah."

"I just wish you hadn't given him that injection."

"Nobody'll know. It was easier to jab the needle into him than take the chance on his attacking me."

"I understand."

"Relax. We're completely in the clear."

"I hope so."

With a final grating rasp, the hacksaw blade broke through the last eighth-inch of metal. Ben pulled the lock off and set it on the newspaper Sara had spread on the workbench to catch the metal filings. He was sweating from the exertion of sawing with a blade that needed replacing. But he could see Sara shivering in the clammy dampness of the cellar.

"Let's take this upstairs," he suggested.

As Sara followed him up the stairs, her eyes focused on the box under his arm. All at once she felt less sure of herself than she had a half-hour ago. Was she really doing the right thing? But it was too late for second thoughts now that the lock was off.

Ben carried the box into the living room and set it on the coffee table. "Do you want to be alone with this?" he asked quietly.

The question made her realize just how much a part of her life he'd become. "No. Stay here with me."

Conflicting emotions had tied his stomach into a hard knot. This wasn't his business. Or Sara's either, really. They were violating Harold's privacy.

She glanced up at him, and he sat down heavily beside her on the sofa. As he slipped his arm around her shoulder, he knew that she meant more to him than anything else in the world.

Sara gave him one more quick look, then reached for the box and slowly lifted the lid. Inside was a piece of rectangular cardboard with a label like the one on the front of the box. It said: "Fatal Medical Mistakes of Harold Strickland, M.D."

When she saw the name on the first folder—Margaret Strickland—the breath froze in Sara's throat.

"Your mother."

"Yes," she gasped. "She died when I was fourteen. Dad would never talk about what happened."

Ben's arm slipped from her shoulder to restrain her arm. "You can just close this damn box back up and forget you ever saw it."

"No, I can't." Sara shook off his hold and pulled out the manila folder. Inside were a set of medical record forms. The notations were in her father's familiar slanted handwriting. They were neater than they might have been—probably because he was writing about his wife. But the entries were as professionally detached as if he'd been making notes on any other patient.

At first there were just routine entries starting in the late 1950's when her father and mother had first married. As Sara remembered, her mother had worked in the office before Sara'd been born.

Her eyes skimmed down the sheets, stopping to take in some of the details.

> January 14, 1958. Patient treated for
> sore throat.
> January 16. Strep culture negative.
> July 10, 1961. Patient treated for in-
> fected splinter on bottom of foot.
> April 17, 1962. Patient complained of
> early morning nausea and vomiting.
> April 27. Pregnancy confirmed.
> June 2, 1962. Patient suffered a spon-
> taneous abortion.
> Bed rest and light duties recommended.

Sara glanced at Ben. "All these little details I never knew. She was pretty healthy. But she lost a baby before I was born." Unconsciously she pressed her hand protectively against her own abdomen.

"Spontaneous abortion isn't unusual in the first few months. It's not going to happen to you." His voice was quiet, reassuring.

"Look, she got pregnant again six months later." Sara smiled. "That must have been with me."

> January 5, 1963. Pregnancy confirmed.
> Patient referred to Dr. Winters in Cam-
> bridge for prenatal care. Baby girl
> born September 2, 1963. Six pounds,
> five ounces. Eighteen inches in length.

Sara laughed, so caught up in the unexpected family record that she'd forgotten why she had opened the box in the first place. "He didn't drop the dry medical reporting even for his own daughter."

"I guess he wanted a precise record."

There were more entries, including notes on Ginny's birth and the removal of a wart from Margaret's hand.

"This is so interesting." Then she turned the page and her hand clutched on the edge of the paper.

> August 7, 1974. Pregnancy confirmed.
> October 12, 1974. Patient contracted German measles. Probable damage to fetus.
> October 28, 1974. Abortion performed.
> October 28, 1974. Patient died of complications.

There were several additional paragraphs after the entry, the writing stark and slashing across the page.

> The abortion was performed at my insistence because I couldn't handle the prospect of raising a blind, deaf, or retarded child. The patient finally acquiesced to my coercion—but only with extreme reluctance. Abortion was against her moral code. She agreed to terminate the pregnancy only because her marriage was more important to her than her morality. But she didn't want anyone else to know about the culpability and insisted that I perform the procedure in secret at my office.
>
> The patient seemed to be recovering from the D&C. I had to leave her to go out on an emergency call and

came back two hours later to find that she had suffered a massive hemorrhage. Apparently I cut into an artery during the curettage and didn't realize what had happened. If I hadn't left the patient alone, she wouldn't have died. If I hadn't insisted that she have the abortion, she wouldn't have died. Now I have to live with this for the rest of my life.

Tears glistened in Sara's eyes when she lifted her head. "Oh, Ben. Maybe subconsciously I suspected something. I think I woke up in the middle of the night and heard them arguing with each other. But I didn't really know. I didn't know." Then she drew in a sharp, shuddering breath as a forgotten detail leaped into her mind. "I remember getting sick with the German measles and missing school. Mom caught them from me. Ben—I—"

He slammed the box shut, set it back on the coffee table, and pulled Sara into his arms. "Getting sick wasn't your fault. It wasn't anyone's fault. It's just something that happened. You can't blame yourself."

Sara reached for the folder again. Ben snatched it out of her grasp and tossed it across the room. It landed by the door, and the papers fanned out across the rug.

When Sara tried to get up, he held her on the sofa. "Leave the past alone."

"Dad couldn't. Don't you see, Ben? This explains so much I didn't understand. He changed after Mom died. It just broke his spirit. I tried so hard to make everything right. But I just couldn't."

"What a burden to set on a kid's shoulders. I guess it explains a lot about you—too. Why you feel so responsible for your father and your sister."

"Maybe you're right. I never thought about it like that. I just knew I had to try and hold things together."

Despite the magnitude of what she'd just learned, there was a feeling of relief at knowing the truth about one of the most painful chapters in the life of her family. For years she'd been guessing and speculating. Leaning back against Ben, she closed her eyes. "Well, now I know why he was so devastated by her death. But I can't help being angry, too. It's hard to forgive him for making that kind of mistake."

"There's the possibility of error in any medical procedure. It was just damn bad luck that he got an emergency call when he did."

"I don't mean that. I mean the way he forced my mother to have the abortion. Maybe he was right, medically. But she was the one carrying the baby. He should have let her make the decision. That was the real tragedy."

Ben was silent.

"You don't agree with me?" she finally asked.

"You can't sit here and second-guess what happened twelve years ago. Sara, he wrote those final notes when he was feeling devastated —and guilty as hell. I'm not trying to dismiss what happened. But maybe he overstated the case. I don't know what really happened between the two of them, and neither do you.

There's a lot involved in making assumptions about someone else."

The raw pain and starkness in his voice made her lids flutter open, and she turned slightly, so that her questioning green eyes searched his clouded brown ones. They were hooded, and his expression was closed.

"You're not talking about Dad, are you?"

Ben felt his jaw muscles tighten. It was finally time to lay all his cards on the table. Yet it was a terrible effort to respond to Sara's question. "No, I wasn't just talking about your father." His mouth was so dry he could barely swallow. "I was thinking about myself. There's something about me that you don't know. And I never could figure out a way to talk to you about it. But it's been like a gate, holding me back from you. I can see you there on the other side. I can even reach through and pull you toward me. But there's still that barrier between us."

Sara moistened her lips with the tip of her tongue. "You mean before you came here you made a mistake—and lost a patient?"

"No. I made a mistake in judgment, like your father. That's why I never wanted to talk about my residency in Santa Barbara. And why I moved three thousand miles away to a small town in Maryland."

As she waited for him to tell her what had happened, she slipped her arm around his waist.

The reassuring gesture made it easier for him to continue. "In the hospital where I was a resident, someone gave five terminally ill patients an overdose of morphine, and they died. Each time, it happened when I was on duty—on the night shift."

"Mercy killings."

"Yes. But it's still against the law."

"You didn't do it?"

"No. But they suspected me. I was the only staff member in the right place every time."

"Oh, Ben."

"They didn't have any other evidence against me, and charges were never filed. But you can imagine the way gossip spreads around a community hospital. Everybody knew who was under suspicion. I was damn lucky the head of the department gave me a good recommendation when I finished up." His expression was stony.

"What a horrible thing to go through."

"You don't know what a relief it is to finally talk about it."

She swallowed around the lump in her throat. "Did they ever find out who was really responsible?"

"No."

The way he said it made the back of her neck tingle. "You knew?" she whispered.

"Yes."

"Why didn't you say? Why didn't you tell them what you suspected when they started investigating you?"

"It was too late by then. She'd had a nervous breakdown and was in the State hospital at Camarillo."

"Who was it?" Sara persisted.

"A nurse who'd been with the hospital for twenty-five years. Her husband had been terminally ill with a cancer—and in terrible pain.

When I thought about it later, I realized she must have killed him with an overdose of morphine."

"Maybe he asked her to. Maybe they had an agreement."

"That could be true. But after he died, she went on to do the same thing for other patients in pain. I saw her in the ward a couple of times when she wasn't on duty, and I wondered what she was doing there. But you know how it is when you're a resident and you've been seeing patients for thirty-six hours. You just don't have the energy to think about anything besides what has to be done."

"Oh, Ben. The whole ordeal must have been terrible for you."

"Yeah. I was angry—and helpless—and scared. Probably the way it was for your father after your mother died."

Sara laid her head against Ben's chest, feeling the pounding of his heart against her cheek.

"In a way, I kept wondering if I was getting what I deserved. I bet it was like that for your father, too."

"But it *wasn't* your fault. You didn't *do* anything."

"If I'd asked some questions or said something when I first wondered why she was at the hospital in the middle of the night, I might have saved two lives."

"You said the patients were terminally ill. They probably only had a short time to live anyway."

"But morally—ethically—"

"Ben—you're the one who just said to leave the past alone. You were a resident. She was on the senior nursing staff. You weren't supposed to be monitoring her actions."

"Yeah. I know. I've told myself all that over and over." He sighed. "On the Fourth of July, when you said you didn't want any secrets between us, I thought about Santa Barbara. But I wanted you to know me better before I laid a story like this on you. Sara, it's why I was so uptight when we had that first conversation about Harold."

"You already felt bad about sitting in judgment over him—the way they'd judged you in Santa Barbara."

"Yes."

"I didn't know."

"I didn't tell you. With everything that's been going on, it never seemed like the right time."

She circled her arms around his shoulders and hugged him. "I'm glad you told me now. You're a good man. That's why this has been eating at you."

All he wanted to do was hold on to her. And she seemed to feel the same way. They'd been drawn into an emotional whirlwind that evening. The aftermath of the storm's fury brought them a peace that was new and, therefore, precious.

Without speaking, they both eased down onto the sofa until they were lying on their sides, facing, his body automatically shifting to accommodate the swell of the baby. Long moments slid by as his hands stroked her hair and face. Her fingers soothed across his shoulders and down his back. The new feeling of closeness—of trust—was something rich and warm, wrapping them in its healing mantle.

The same thoughts were in both their minds, and their soft whispers echoed each other.

"I love you."

"I need you."

"I'll always be here for you."

"I know."

"I've never felt like this before."

"Neither have I."

His lips brushed against hers, pausing, and pressed more firmly. She opened, welcomed, invited. With sighs and murmurs, tenderness flowed into passion.

CHAPTER 32

Moose Bramble keyed in another setting and waited while the satellite dish shifted positions. He could pick up one hundred and fifty-four channels right in his own living room, and half the time there still wasn't a damn thing worth watching. Even the Playboy Channel was boring tonight.

The dish moved again, and he picked up the local Fox station. They were showing *The Maltese Falcon*. He sighed and leaned back, watching the misty night scenes and harsh shadows flicker across the screen. Everybody who'd played in that film—Bogart, Astor, Greenstreet, Lorre—was dead. Their essence had been reduced to a series of moving pictures captured on black and white film.

But the old movie was stylish. He had to give it that. *The Maltese Falcon* made its point without a sea of blood and guts. Not like the new detective movies. Or like real-life crime, which was apt to be a lot messier than even the new cinematic genre of splash and splat. And you couldn't guarantee that you'd find a solution in under two hours—like good old Sam Spade.

The images moving across the twenty-five-inch picture tube ceased to hold Moose's attention. Instead, he thought again of Ralph Meekins's angular body sprawled in the middle of his living room. Someone had caved in the back of the old man's head like an empty milk carton.

Why?

There weren't many murders in St. Stephens. When there was one, it was usually among friends or relatives.

This time it looked like a robber had been surprised in the act, had panicked and turned on Meekins.

Yeah, robbery was the apparent motive. The old guy's house was sure torn apart pretty good. But if someone had been looking for money, why hadn't he taken the silver coin collection from the top of the bedroom closet? Had the perp gotten scared and run off before he'd finished? Or had he been after something else? What did old Ralph have that was valuable?

Moose sighed, heaved himself out of the recliner, and padded into the kitchen. He took a can of beer out of the refrigerator and a bag of sour-cream potato chips from the pantry, his last one. He'd have to remember to stop at the grocery tomorrow.

Back in the living room, he flipped off the T.V., tore open the bag, and reached for a handful of the chips. His jaw began to work rhythmically as he thought about the murder.

Ben sensed the change in Sara's breathing. "Are you awake, honey?"

"Um hum."

They had gone up to her room some time after one in the morning. Outside the window, he could see only inky blackness, but he didn't want to look at the clock and find out how much remained of the night. Instead, he reached for Sara's hand and brought the knuckles up against his lips. "Marry me."

"Oh, Ben. I want to."

"But?"

"It's too soon. I don't mean for me—for how I feel about you. I mean—"

"You mean this is a small town. And—"

"We both have to live here."

He rolled over onto his back, his eyes staring into the ceiling he couldn't see. "Sara, after the funeral, when you told me about the pregnancy—I was too stunned to know how I felt."

"I understand."

"But I've come to realize how much I want to take care of you and the baby. I want him to grow up thinking of me as his father. I want to *be* his father in every way that counts."

"Ben, I love you so much. And your saying that means so very much to me."

"Then please—"

She pressed the side of her hand against her lips. "I can't. Not yet. It's not just the town,

Ben. It's me. The way I was raised. I wouldn't feel right about it—not so soon."

"One thing about you. When you make up your mind, you don't budge."

"It's part of who I am."

"Yeah. That's part of it for me, too. Where I came from. Who I am."

"What do you mean?"

He sucked in a deep breath. "I told you about the worst thing that ever happened to me. I guess I might as well tell you the rest. Haven't you wondered why I never talk about my parents?"

"Yes, I have."

"When I went away to medical school, they sort of disowned me."

"Why?"

"My father expected—assumed—that I was going to take over the family farm. He made it clear that if I chose some other career besides farming, I didn't have a home with him and Mom anymore."

Sara found his hand again in the dark. "But that's horrible. I can't imagine someone doing that to his son. He sounds like a feudal lord or something."

"You're right. My father's a real throwback, and the rest of the family's so afraid of his wrath that they fall right into line with him." Ben laughed hollowly, glad she couldn't see the pain on his face. "I didn't understand back then. Now I can see that keeping up the family tradition meant a lot to him. But at the time, I resented the hell out of his trying to force me into a mold where I would have been miserable."

"What did you do?"

"I made my choice—and walked away. That's why I have a whopping medical school loan to pay off. Because I had to finance it all myself. At least I had good enough grades to get the money."

They were both silent for several moments. "That kind of rejection must have been devastating," Sara finally murmured. "I mean emotionally."

"Yeah. In Santa Barbara, when they were trying to pin those murders on me, I kept thinking that if I'd just done what my father wanted, I wouldn't be caught in the manure spreader. And I couldn't even go to them for help."

"Oh, Ben. That must have made it so much worse."

"It's been a long time since I felt I could count on anyone," he murmured, turning toward her in the dark. "Or as if I belonged to anyone."

"Ben Langley, you belong to me."

"Not legally."

Sara's hands splayed possessively across his chest. "In every other way a man can belong to his woman."

He closed his eyes, enjoying the feel of her fingers combing through the hair on his chest. "The baby's due in October," he finally said.

"Yes."

"Would it give you enough time— Would you marry me on Christmas Day?"

"Yes."

"It'll be the best damn Christmas present I ever got."

"For me, too."

Saturday, July 15

Cheryl Keene turned on the light and stood looking around the deserted office. No one else was down at *The St. Stephens Record* on Saturday morning. Under ordinary circumstances, Cheryl would have been doing laundry or her weekly grocery shopping. But this was her big chance to show Leonard that she had what it took to be a reporter—not just an administrative assistant. Sure, Leonard had sent Tom Polchek down to police headquarters as soon as he'd learned about the murder. But she'd hotfooted it out to Ralph's while the neighbors were still standing around talking about the morning's excitement. And she'd taken down some great eyewitness interviews. Stuff Tom hadn't gotten—she knew, because she'd heard him talking to Leonard about his story.

After flipping the switch on the electric typewriter, Cheryl rolled a sheet of crisp white paper into the machine. There was a little smile on her face as she typed a headline and her name at the top of the page.

Leonard didn't want to give her a chance to switch to reporting. But she'd edited enough news stories to know what she was doing. Maybe he'd even run her account as the main article, right on the front page. Even if he didn't give her top billing, he'd have to use her material as sidebar.

Digging into her purse, she got out her little blue notebook and flipped it open. Boy, did she have some great quotes. Jed Insley had actually been in the house and seen the body.

She'd start with that. Then there was the stuff about Sara Chandler showing up and pulling into the driveway right in back of the ambulance. She'd use that, too.

CHAPTER 33

Saturday, July 15

The next morning, Ben fixed himself a cup of instant coffee and stood with his hips propped against the kitchen counter, sipping the hot liquid.

Last night had been one of the worst—and one of the best—in his life. He'd told Sara the two dreadful secrets he'd been carrying around like a knapsack full of unexploded munitions. He realized now that, all along, he'd been half afraid she'd reject him the way his father had. Instead, she'd opened her arms and wrapped him in the warmth of her body and her generous spirit. He was damn lucky to have found such a remarkable woman. And even if she wasn't ready to marry him until the end of the year, he knew she loved him and wanted to protect him from any more hurt. He wanted to do the same for her.

Setting down his mug with a clank, he strode into the living room. The metal box that had caused Sara so much anguish last night was still sitting on the rug where he'd put it. Over across the room, the file lay where he'd thrown it. Kneeling down, he scooped the papers back into the folder and shoved them into the box, with the distaste of an orderly handling contaminated hospital waste.

There were other files in the box, but he didn't even glance at the names on the index tabs. God knows what self-accusations Harold's twisted mind had conjured up. Fact or fiction, it really didn't matter. These phantoms from the past had the power to torment Sara, and that had to be his primary consideration.

With the file tucked firmly under his arm, he closed the front door quietly behind him. The cassette from Sara's answering machine was in his jacket pocket. He'd put the file away where Sara didn't have to worry about it. But he'd listen to the cassette later. Maybe it did have some clue about what had happened to poor old Meekins.

Monday, July 17

The lead story in the "People" section of the Sunday *Baltimore Sun* was an interview with Jake Levitt, a private detective who specialized in locating missing persons.

Monday morning, Sara phoned him.

"My name is Sara Chandler, and I read the article about you," she began.

"It's amazing how many people saw the piece. Did you want to discuss a missing relative?"

"Yes. My sister, Ginny Strickland. She disappeared on a Caribbean cruise two weeks ago."

"What can you tell me about the case?"

Levitt listened while Sara outlined what little she knew. "Most of the calls I've gotten have been from people who've been out of contact with relatives for twenty or thirty years and want me to reunite them. Your sister's trail is a lot less cold."

"Then you think you can help me?"

"I can give it my best shot."

They talked about fees—which were high. But, thankfully, Sara had that two-hundred-thousand-dollar insurance policy money sitting in the bank and could afford to pay what Levitt was asking. Just talking to him gave her some hope.

"Your sister's only been missing for a couple of weeks. She was traveling in a contained environment, and the cruise line has the passenger list."

"That didn't do them much good when it came to locating Keith Thomas."

"They don't have much experience with this sort of thing. I do."

"How soon would you be able to get started?"

"As soon as you can send me some pictures of your sister—and the answers to my detailed questionnaire. I can mail it to you this afternoon."

"Could you send it by Federal Express?"

"Of course. And if I need any more information after I look over the material, I'll let you know."

Sara thanked him profusely and hung up feeling more optimistic than she had since the terrible day she'd spent meeting every plane coming in to BWI. Every lead on Ginny and Keith Thomas had petered out. But surely a trained professional would have better success.

Tuesday, July 18

Sara closed her eyes for a moment. "Shock treatment. I don't know, Ben. It sounds so horrible."

"These days it's called electro-convulsive therapy. I don't much like being put in the position of advocating it, but they don't even consider it unless a patient is profoundly depressed. From what Dr. Clifton is saying, it might be the only thing that's going to snap your father out of his present state. The drug therapy just isn't working. In fact, he's getting worse."

"I don't like having to make this kind of decision."

"Honey, I know that."

"Is it dangerous?"

"I did some reading about it. The procedure involves attaching electrodes to the patient's head and passing an electric current through them."

Sara shuddered.

"It's just for a second or less. It causes a seizure. But the patient is anesthetized and given a muscle relaxant first. No one really knows why it relieves depression—but sometimes it really is the only thing that works."

"I can't believe there aren't any side effects."

"The patient always has amnesia for the period immediately following the therapy and can be confused for the next hour or so. Sometimes there's partial memory loss. That usually clears up pretty quickly." *It better*, Ben thought. He was gambling on getting Harold Strickland into a condition where he could answer some questions.

"You're telling me he might not be able to come back to his practice?"

"He certainly can't come back to it now."

"Oh Lord, Ben. I just don't know."

"Do you want to read some of the literature?"

"Yes."

Wednesday, July 19

Kitty had suggested a trip to a design store in Annapolis to look for wallpaper for the baby's room. As they sat at a table with half a dozen books spread open, Sara fiddled with a pencil. Finally she looked over at her friend.

"There are so many patterns. It's hard to make a decision, isn't it?" Kitty sympathized.

Sara sighed. "I thought I was going to be able to concentrate on this, but I can't."

"What's wrong."

"Oh, Kitty, it's my father."

The artist's face grew contemplative. "You haven't talked about him much. How's he doing?"

"Not well. Dr. Clifton wants to try shock treatment."

"Don't let them!"

"What do you know about shock treatment?"

"I—uh—read an article about it once. It was written by a woman who'd been an accountant. The treatment made her forget how to do her job."

"I'm worried about something like that happening to Dad," Sara admitted. "Medicine means so much to him. But Dr. Clifton thinks it may be the only thing that will get Dad out of the hospital."

Kitty's fingers played with the edge of a nursery-room print. "I'm glad I don't have to make a decision like that."

"Unfortunately, I'm the only one who can decide. I'm sorry I dumped it on you."

"Sara, it's all right. Any time you need to talk to me, I'll listen."

"Thanks."

Thursday, July 20

THE ST. STEPHENS RECORD

FRONT PAGE

Neighbors React to Murder of Local Artist

BY STAFF REPORTER CHERYL KEENE

Neighbors of longtime Harris Creek resident and duck carver Ralph Meekins were shocked to learn about his tragic death early last Friday morning.

Mr. Meekins's body was found by a neighbor, Jed Insley. "My dog wouldn't stop barking at his front door. So I went on over there. The door was unlocked, and Ralph was just laying on the floor with stuff strewn all around like a henhouse raided by fox," Mr. Insley told this reporter.

Mr. Meekins sold his popular duck decoys at The Bayside Collection, a St. Stephens art gallery. Owner Sara Chandler was also on the scene the morning of the murder. Mr. Meekins was reported to have left an urgent message on her telephone answering machine.

(see Reaction, page 5 column 3)

Community Services

A white elephant sale will be held on Sunday, July 23, at the St. Stephens High School gym to benefit the Bay Watchers Society. Donations of clothing, household items, toys, books, and furniture should be brought to the gym between 10 a.m. and 2 p.m. Friday and Saturday.

Sara couldn't bear to read the articles about Ralph. Instead, she flipped to the back of the paper, and a community service notice caught her eye—the white elephant sale. Someone from the committee had told her about it weeks ago, but she'd forgotten all about it.

She'd been planning to donate a bunch of Ted's stuff to the sale. Upstairs, she took a final look through the boxes of clothing she'd set in the spare room at the end of the hall. She'd been thinking about using it for a nursery. But it really wasn't as big and bright as the room Ted had appropriated for his home office.

Why not get rid of the furniture? It was all plastic and metal stuff he'd picked up from an insurance firm going out of business. It could go to the sale, and the room would be empty. Then she could start right in with redecorating.

"Do you know any teenagers who want to make some money hauling?" she asked Judy Wooters that morning at the gallery.

"My son Bruce is always looking for ways to earn cash. Let me see if he's available."

In the afternoon, Sara went home and emptied the contents of the desk and the filing cabinet into boxes. By the time Bruce and his friend arrived, she was ready for them to move the furniture down to the pickup truck they'd borrowed.

"Are you sure that isn't too heavy?" she asked as the two boys maneuvered the metal filing cabinet down the stairs. They were eager furniture movers, but a bit inexperienced. If they didn't end up gouging out a piece of the wall, she'd be lucky.

"Naw. Bruce can bench press two hundred and twenty-five pounds."

Sara nodded and went back down the hall to sweep the floor. It was amazing, she thought, how much dirt sifted behind furniture that was never moved.

When the teenagers came back upstairs, they heaved the desk away from the wall.

"This go, too?"

"Yes. And the chair and table." Sara turned toward the now empty wall, dustpan and broom at the ready. In addition to dust, several crumpled phone-message slips and a large manila envelope were shoved against the baseboard.

As Sara turned the envelope over, her brow wrinkled. Written in Ted's authoritative hand were the words "Swan Point." Miss Jane's estate. It certainly wasn't for sale. Why would Ted have had any information on that?

Inside was a large sheet of blue-tinged architectural paper. When Sara unfolded it, she found a site survey of the Brittingham property.

As she stared at the estate layout, her eyes bugged out. The plan showed the property divided into building lots, with notes on drainage. At the bottom right-hand corner was the address of Newhouse Realty and an October date from the previous year.

Building lots? Newhouse Realty? Miss Jane had promised that the estate would be a bird refuge. Had she changed her mind? Sara wondered. And what was Ted doing with this survey?

"Mrs. Chandler?" Her head jerked up.

"Anything else you want done?"

Anything else? Forcing herself to think about the project at hand, she pointed to the boxes

308 • SAMANTHA CHASE

near the door. "Could you carry that stuff down to the basement?"

"Sure."

"No, wait." What other surprises were hidden in Ted's records? Maybe I should go through it."

"Okay by me."

She gave the young men a weak smile. "Let me pay you. And thanks for helping."

As soon as they left, she reached for the phone. Maybe George Newhouse could tell her what was going on. But, in the middle of dialing the number, she stopped and replaced the receiver in the cradle. Ted hadn't said a word about Swan Point to her. But he'd known about this survey for nine months. He and George had been keeping it a secret.

All at once, she remembered when George had come over to sift through Ted's records. He'd been as nervous as a cat who'd knocked over a carton of cream. Maybe he was afraid that his former employee had been careless about leaving evidence around.

Sara's hands clenched in tight knots. Unbelievable as it seemed, it looked like George and Ted had cooked up some kind of deal behind everyone's back to snatch the property for themselves. But Miss Jane had been so sure about her plans for the bird refuge. Or was she so addled that she didn't know what was happening?

The feeling of needing to do *something* made Sara's breath wedge in her chest. Was it too late to get this straightened out? No. The property was still Miss Jane's, and she could decide what she wanted to do with it.

Sara looked over at the wall clock. It was seven-thirty. Visiting hours at the nursing home were over. But they didn't mind when she stopped by to see Miss Jane in the evening. She'd go over and talk to her right now.

CHAPTER 34

Sara's car pulled out of the driveway and sped down the road. Her mind was so focused on Miss Jane and Swan Point that she didn't see the black motorcycle and leather-clad rider parked under the low-hanging branch of a tree on one of the nearby lanes. Five minutes after she'd passed, the engine revved up.

His horoscope had said, "Smooth sailing from now on out." But just to be sure, he'd read the front-page story on Ralph Meekins in *The Record* this afternoon for any hint that he was in trouble.

He'd almost skipped the part about the neighbors' reactions. Who cared what a bunch of hicks thought? But he'd scanned down the column, anyway. It was all drivel, he'd told himself, until he came to the sentence about the answering-machine tape. Then angry red blotches had bloomed on his cheeks, and he'd slammed his fist through the paper. Of all the fucking bad luck. Old Ralph had rushed right home and gotten on the horn to Sara. What the hell had he told her?

Yesterday, Meekins had simply been one less problem he'd had to worry about. Now it was like the son of a bitch had reached out from the grave to grab him from around the neck.

He had to find out what was on that tape. Was it still in the machine? Or had Sara already turned it over to the police? He sure as hell hoped they didn't know about it yet.

He'd decided to take the chance of slipping into Sara's house again before she got home from work. But she'd come back early again—followed by two guys and a pickup truck. They'd spent the afternoon loading furniture.

He'd hidden out at the end of the old hunting road in the woods, feeling the sweat trickle down his back under his leather jacket and wondering what to do.

When the truck pulled away, he'd gotten his hopes up. Maybe she'd leave, too. But no.

So his mind had frantically started to scramble for some way to get her out of the house. What if he called up and pretended to be Ginny and asked Sara to meet her somewhere? She'd come running. Yeah. Except that he probably couldn't do Ginny's little-girl voice well enough.

What about Sara's dad? He didn't have to actually imitate the old guy. He'd just pretend he was someone from the hospital and say the old geezer was asking for her. She'd be in Easton quicker than a thirsty horse that smelled water.

He was about to start the engine and drive to a pay phone when her car whizzed right past him like the devil was after her or something. Jesus, she was in a hurry. He hoped she wasn't just going out to get a quart of milk.

He turned into her driveway and left the motorcycle behind the garage, where no one could see it from the road. The back door was locked, but the windows in the living room were wide open. People were so damn trusting around here. All he had to do was knock out one of the screens and climb in.

After propping the screen back into position, he turned to survey the living room. Now that he was inside, his head was starting to throb. All at once, his vision blurred. Oh, Lord, not that.

Go away, he ordered through clenched teeth. *Not now!*

His body shook as powerful forces warred inside his head. But he was the stronger, the master of his destiny. *He* was the one who'd reached out from the dead. Not pitiful old Ralph Meekins.

He straightened his shoulders and looked around. The answering machine wasn't in the living room. But he remembered seeing it downstairs somewhere. In the kitchen!

It was sitting on the counter near the wall phone. His gloved hand was on the "eject" button when he heard a key turning in a lock. A second later, the front door opened.

He froze, his feet glued to the floor. *Oh, shit.*

He'd made a big mistake. Sara was back. What the hell was be going to do now?

For a fraction of a second, the idea of simply turning and smiling at her flashed through his mind. But it wouldn't work. She'd know something was wrong the instant she saw him dressed like this.

The footsteps were coming closer. There wasn't must time.

I told you so. You stupid fool. You shouldn't have tried to handle this by yourself. The mocking words echoed in his mind.

He'd come too far to let anything gum up the works now. Somehow he got control of his arms and legs again. It seemed like minutes had passed since the front door had opened. He knew it must only be seconds. And there were mere seconds left.

He looked wildly around, realizing he'd never make it out the back door in time. Maybe he could hide in the utility room. No. The basement door was closer.

Leaping inside, he pulled the door almost shut. Musty damp wafted up toward him as he crouched on the landing. In the dark, he could hear the footsteps coming closer.

They were heavy footsteps, he realized with a sudden jolt. It wasn't Sara at all. It had to be a man. Maybe Dr. Langley; they were lovers now. Had she given him a key?

Cautiously, he opened the door a crack and peeked out. His eyes widened as an intruder stepped into kitchen. Good Lord. It was the poor bastard he'd blackmailed into giving him the $15,000 for the cruise. He couldn't suppress a gasp of surprise.

The second man whirled, equally astonished that he wasn't alone. "Who the fuck—?"

The attacker, crouching in the dark, had given himself away. Now, in one frantic motion, he sprang through the door and grabbed for a nearby arm. Surprise was his only real advantage. With a super-human yank, he whipped the heavier man off his balance.

Feet scuffled desperately on the stairs. But a savage kick sent the bigger man hurtling down into the darkness. There was a sickening scream as fingernails scraped uselessly on the railing. It was followed by a loud thud when the heavy body hit the cement floor. A moment later there was deathly silence.

Sara stepped up to the Dogwood Nursing Home's front desk and cleared her throat. The nurse on duty lifted her head from the paperback romance she was reading.

"Would it be all right if I talked to Mrs. Brittingham for a moment?"

The woman shook her head apologetically. "Oh, Miss Sara. I wish you'd called first, before you came over. She was in a lot of discomfort this evening, and we had to give her some pretty strong pain medication. I'm afraid she's—" the nurse searched for the right turn of phrase, "—not going to be very coherent at the moment."

"Oh—I didn't realize. You're right. I should have called. But I just thought—"

"You can come back in the morning. I'm sure she'll be glad to see you then."

"Well, thanks anyway." Sara's shoulders sagged as she turned back toward the door. She'd been so fired up to get to the bottom of the Swan Point mystery. Well, she wasn't going to find anything out from Miss Jane tonight. But maybe Ben would have some ideas.

The leather-clad figure at the top of the stairs flipped on the light and peered down into the basement—half expecting the intruder to get up and come lunging after him like something out of a horror movie. To his intense relief, he saw only a body lying in a broken heap. But just to make sure, he tiptoed down and felt for a pulse. It wasn't beating, and a trickle of blood dribbled out of the open mouth.

Should he get rid of the body? No. This could pass for an accident. No one would have the slightest reason to suspect he was involved. Let the police figure out what this guy was doing at the bottom of Sara Chandler's basement steps.

Standing up again, he gave the body a little poke with his booted toe. The man lying at his feet was a lot heavier and stronger. But it hadn't done him any good, he thought, unable to suppress a smirk of satisfaction.

With a new lilt to his step, he climbed the stairs once more, turned off the light, and made sure the basement door was ajar. Then he crossed to the answering machine, took out the tape, and slipped it into his pocket. After a final look around the kitchen, he retraced his path and secured the screen in the living room window. He'd leave by the front door. But first, he'd have a quick look around to make sure he hadn't forgotten anything else.

Twilight was hovering at the end of the day like a bird ready to settle into its nest as Sara got out of her car. So that the trip wouldn't be a total loss, she'd made a quick stop at the grocery store. They'd had a "buy one, get one free" sale on ice cream, so she'd picked up a couple of quarts of the chocolate swirl Ben liked.

Wishing she'd left the porch light on, so that she could see what she was doing, she shifted the bag to her hip bone and fumbled with her key in the lock.

After setting the bags down on the kitchen table, Sara started toward the freezer with the ice cream. On the way, she glanced toward the cellar door. She didn't like the darkness, looming like a black hole that might suck her in.

Her hand froze in the act of closing the door. There was that smell again, sickly sweet, instantly recognizable, and much stronger than the last time.

A new wave of fear rose to meet her from the blackness, and she instinctively reached inside the door to turn on the light. "Is someone there?" Her voice quavered.

No answer.

She wanted to slam the door shut. Instead, her eyes flicked to the floor below. Lying in a crumpled heap was a man's body. Somehow there was no doubt in her mind that he was dead.

A scream tore from her throat, and she dropped the ice cream she was still holding. The cartons bounced down the stairs, burst open, and landed in a mound of brown and white goo on top of the body.

"Miss Sara!"

The shout came from behind her, and she flattened herself against the wall, partway down the basement steps.

"Miss Sara—what?"

Her head swung around, and she looked up into anxious brown eyes. It took a moment to register who was standing over her.

"Officer Bramble. Oh, thank God." To her own ears, her voice sounded high and strained. She wanted to get away from the dead man below her. But when she tried to make her way back up to the kitchen, her knees buckled. Bramble pounded down the steps and grabbed her arm, lowering her gently to one of the risers.

"It's George Newhouse. I guess he fell down the stairs. He looks like he's dead," she gasped.

"I better check on him."

A few moments later, he glanced up to where Sara still sat. "It doesn't look like he's goin' anywhere." Bramble helped Sara back upstairs and settled her on the couch. "Gotta report this."

She nodded.

When he came back from calling the ambulance squad, the medical examiner, and the Maryland State Police, some of the color had seeped back into her cheeks.

"How did you know it was Newhouse?" he asked, getting out his notebook.

"I smelled his cologne." She shuddered. "You know, when you're pregnant, certain smells really get to you."

"I'll have to take your word for that."

Sara smiled weakly.

"I remembered the cologne from when he was here picking up some of Ted's records."

Bramble nodded. "I need to get a statement from you."

"All right."

"You say you came home and found the body at the bottom of the steps?"

"Yes. I went over to the nursing home to talk to Miss Jane. But she'd been given some medication and wasn't having any visitors. So I stopped by the grocery store and came home."

"You talked to someone at the nursing home and at the grocery story?"

"Yes."

"The Acme?"

"Yes."

"Do you have any idea what Newhouse was doing here?"

Sara hesitated and cocked her head to one side. "What were *you* doing here?"

"Fair enough. I read in the paper that Meekins had left a message on your answering machine."

"In the paper?"

"In one of the articles about the murder. Didn't you tell a neighbor he'd been upset and called you?"

"I—maybe—I can't remember."

"*Did* he call you?"

"Yes." She looked up at the police officer, a

feeling of deja vu sweeping over her. She'd sat on the front steps of Ralph's house less than a week ago, having a very similar conversation. "If you read about the tape in the paper, George probably did, too," she finally muttered. "I'll bet that's what he was doing here."

"You're goin' a little fast for me. Can you back up a ways?"

"I think George Newhouse and my husband cooked up some kind of scheme to get development rights to the Swan Point estate." She paused for a moment, her mind making quick connections. "And I'm pretty sure he was worried that Ralph or I had found out about it. Oh God, do you think he killed poor old Ralph?"

Before Bramble could answer, they were interrupted by the sound of gravel crunching in the driveway. The deputy stood up. "That'll be the ambulance crew." He looked down at Sara. "I don't know how the two are connected— or if they are. But we'll get to the bottom of it."

He studied her face, searching for any signs of guile or concealed emotions. She looked washed out—and worried, which wasn't unusual if you'd just found a dead body at the bottom of the cellar steps. But was there something she wasn't telling him? She'd already tossed out a better lead in the Ralph Meekins case than they'd been able to dig up in the week since the murder. What else did she know?

He switched off the cassette recorder.

"All that trouble. Another man dead. And there's not a damn thing on the tape."

"I can figure that out for myself."

"It was pretty stupid getting caught in Sara's house like that."

"Could *you* have handled it better?"

"Yes. You've been piling up bodies like an undertaker in the middle of a typhoid epidemic."

He waited for several heartbeats before answering. "All right, if you're so smart, you just take care of things any way you want to."

"You're not going to leave me now." She couldn't keep an edge of panic out of her voice.

"I'm tired."

"Wait! This has all been for you. Don't you understand?"

The only sound in the room was the hiss of air as she drew in a sharp breath.

CHAPTER 35

The medical examiner, an ambulance crew, and a lab team from the Maryland State Police had all trooped through Sara's house by the time Ben arrived.

"Sara, what's going on now?" he shouted as he burst into the living room to find Moose Bramble just getting ready to leave. Without embellishment, the patrolman filled Ben in.

He swore under his breath. "Newhouse? What was *he* doing here?"

"It looks like he and Ted worked out some kind of deal to develop Swan Point." Sara went on to tell him some of what she'd pieced together that afternoon. "Maybe that's what Ralph was trying to warn me about," she concluded.

"Newhouse must have read about the tape in the paper—same as I did," Bramble added.

Ben slapped his forehead. "The tape. Jesus. Sara thought she erased it, and I was going to see if I could find the message from Ralph. But with everything else—" he stopped abruptly and glanced at Sara. "I forgot about it."

Bramble looked from one to the other.

"You know Sara's father's in the hospital. We've been hoping the electro-convulsive therapy will snap him out of his depression."

"Um—yes. I understand. But do you still have the tape?"

"I guess it's still in my jacket pocket—in the car."

"I think I've better take it off your hands."

"Sure." Ben retrieved the tape and gave it to the police officer.

"You folks take care now," Bramble said as he ambled toward the front hall. Sara closed the door behind him and sank back against it. But she looked amazingly composed after everything she'd been through. Ben slung his arm around her shoulder and pulled her against him.

"You know what this means?" she whispered.

"I think I came in in the middle of the third act."

She tipped her head up and began to speak rapidly. "It's all over. It wasn't Dad. It was George. It looks like he was behind everything. Officer Bramble found a folder in his car with all kinds of Swan Point information and a photograph of Ralph and me with Miss Jane taken when the article about the bird sanctuary was in the paper."

"Sara—"

She wasn't about to let him interrupt.

"Ralph's picture was circled. There was all sorts of crazy stuff written down on yellow sheets of paper. George had a motive to kill Ted. And it looks like he thought Ralph was ready to blow the whistle on him. Which means he could have killed him to shut him up. Only he didn't know that Ralph had called me."

"But what was he doing in your basement?"

"Snooping around to see if Ted left any incriminating evidence, I suppose. I'm pretty sure he was here once before when I wasn't home."

"Good Lord. Why didn't you say something?"

"I wasn't trying to hide anything. I just didn't realize it at the time. I remember smelling his cologne when I came home one afternoon. But it was raining, and I thought the dampness had brought the smell back from the time he stopped by where you were here."

Ben watched Sara stride back to the living room, her steps full of nervous energy. As he followed her down the hall, he wondered what to say. He understood why she wanted to believe Ralph's killer had been found. Maybe she even needed to believe George had killed Ted. But he wasn't quite so willing to be convinced. "Sara—I hope it's all over."

She rolled her shoulders. "I feel like a thousand-pound weight has been lifted off of me."

He pressed his lips together. There were more questions he wanted to ask—more points that should be brought up. But if talking about them meant shattering Sara's peace of mind, it wasn't worth the price. At least not right now. And maybe, just maybe, she was right.

Friday, July 21

The air had the kind of peaceful clarity that comes when a storm has swept away all the haze and impurities, Sara thought as she pushed the wheelchair along the gravel path. It made her think of renewal and fresh beginnings.

"Shall we stop here?" she asked, leaning down toward the snowy top of Miss Jane's head.

"This is fine, dear. It's so cool under the trees."

"Yes, it is." Sara brushed several acorn shells off the wooden bench opposite the old woman and sat down.

"It's such a nice surprise to see you. I only just finished my breakfast."

"I wanted to come and talk to you—about the bird sanctuary. You didn't change your mind, did you? I mean about Swan Point being a nature preserve."

"Why, goodness me, dear, how can you ask such a silly question? My nephew Jonathan stopped by just last week, and I was talking to him about it."

Sara let out the breath she hadn't realized she was holding. "Miss Jane, I don't want you to get upset," she began gently. "And I hate to be the one to tell you this. But there are some things you should know . . . about Newhouse Realty—and Swan Point."

"Newhouse Realty?" The rheumy eyes blinked. "Why what do you mean, dear?"

"I think Jonathan had some—uh—secret dealings with them last year."

"My goodness. That boy couldn't have been thinking about selling my house, could he? Why, my husband would turn over in his grave if something like that were going on behind my back."

Sara pulled the Swan Point site plan out of her pocketbook and spread it on top of the afghan that covered Mrs. Brittingham's knees. "It's not the house," she corrected.

The old woman peered down in confusion at the large blue sheet. "What is this thing?"

"A scheme for dividing your property into one- and two-acre building lots. Miss Jane, I'm so sorry. But it looks like Ted and Jonathan and George Newhouse had their own plans for Swan Point."

The parchment brow wrinkled. "But I don't understand. How could they? I own Swan Point, not Jonathan."

"Didn't you tell me you signed an agreement with Jonathan?"

"That was just for my house. I mean, I assumed it was. Jonathan had the papers drawn up."

"Did you read the agreement before you signed?"

"Why no, dear. These tired old eyes can't see small print. But Jonathan explained it all to me."

"I think you may want to read it now."

Tears filmed across Miss Jane's eyes and dribbled down her papery cheeks. "I trusted that boy."

Sara patted the old woman's arm. "Oh, Miss Jane, I know you did. And I understand how you feel now, believe me. But it's not too late to set the whole thing right."

The arthritic old woman struggled to straighten her shoulders. "Sara, take me back up to my room. I want to call my lawyer. Right now."

"The first church on this site is believed to have been built in 1662," Marybeth Brownwell of the Talbot County Historical Society intoned as she led the party of eleven people down the gravel path of the old Cedar Grove Burying Ground.

"The word 'cemetery' didn't come into existence until the Victorian era, when people were into delicacy of expression. 'Burying ground' was just too crude. Of course, the people buried here would probably turn over in their graves if they heard the language shouted on Main Street today."

There were some *tsks* and a few polite chuckles. Beatrice Pierce glanced at Cheryl Keene, and the younger woman rolled her eyes.

Beatrice nodded sympathetically. Cheryl was the only one in the group under forty. From the way she was taking notes, it was obvious she was on assignment for *The St. Stephens Record*. So Leonard had taken her on as a reporter, after all. That meant she'd be covering weddings, yacht launches, and Historical Society functions. It was a step up for Cheryl. But Beatrice had had enough of those assignments to last a lifetime—maybe two. She was here by choice this evening—getting local color for her book. She only had to write down the juicy bits of hundred-year-old gossip.

"This is the second grave of the wife of the Reverend Victor Godwin." Ms. Brownwell pointed toward an old-fashioned stone marker.

"Second grave?" Cheryl questioned.

Ms. Brownwell got ready to deliver one of her best stories. "Yes. It seems that, three hours after her funeral, grave robbers dug her up. They were after the antique ring on her finger, but it wouldn't budge. So they cut her finger off."

Someone in the crowd gasped.

"Apparently the pain revived the poor woman —who hadn't really been dead after all. She walked home from the cemetery in her shroud. It was lucky her husband didn't have a heart attack when she came in the front door."

A bank of clouds had rolled in off the water, obscuring the setting sun. Beatrice thrust her arms into the sleeves of the sweater that had been resting on her shoulders and squinted as she tried to read the inscriptions on the headstones. As the tour progressed through the cemetery, she recognized the names of families that had moved to St. Stephens within the past generation. Some names were familiar from stories in *The Record*. In fact, she'd written some of the obituaries herself.

Martha Stanford had died of a heart attack— which she'd thought was simply indigestion from the crab soup at the annual Fourth of July picnic.

Ed Myers had committed suicide. But the family hadn't wanted the facts in the paper. Instead, it had been attributed to a shooting accident while cleaning his hunting rifle.

The next plot belonged to the Atwater family. Beatrice remembered old Mrs. Atwater. She'd been a widow for thirty years and had lived out on the road to Easton. Her daughter had moved out West, but then she'd come back to St. Stephens with her family.

Atwater. Atwater. Good grief. Beatrice stopped in her tracks and stared at the headstone. It was spooky how things ended up being connected in a small town. The daughter. She was the mother of that Keith Thomas boy who'd died.

Unaware that she was being left behind by the rest of the tour, Beatrice began to search the nearby graves. What she found made her eyes widen in surprise. In back of Maude Atwater's resting place was an expensive double headstone in carmine marble, with angels wings spread out protectively over two names.

Keith Thomas. Katrina Thomas

A bond so strong death could not separate them.

So the sister had died young, too. But it was strange to see a brother and sister with a double headstone. And with such a maudlin sentiment. That kind of thing was usually reserved for a married couple.

Yet those children had been very close. She remembered when Keith had died. Then, not long after, Katrina had disappeared. Apparently, she'd succumbed a couple of years after her brother. And the parents' grave was here too. How sad; a whole family wiped out.

The group of history buffs had moved on to

another section of the cemetery while Beatrice pondered the demise of the Thomases. All at once, she found herself standing alone at the center of the now dimly lit graveyard.

There was a flapping of wings and a *whoop, whoop, whoop* above her. Instinctively, she ducked as a dark shape swooped toward her from the eaves of the old church. A bat.

She covered her head with her hands and ran down the path toward the rest of the party. Her terrified shriek was loud enough to wake the dead.

Ben threaded his way through the boisterous Friday night crowd at The Cannon Ball Tavern, named after the single lucky shot that had saved the town from the British during the Revolutionary War. The T.G.I.F. scene wasn't exactly his milieu. Even though he was dressed in jeans and a knit shirt, he couldn't help feeling out of place. But when he'd called Moose Bramble and said he wanted to talk, the police officer had invited him to stop by. And he didn't want to put the conversation off any longer than he had to.

Bramble, who was sitting in the last booth on the right, took a swallow from his tankard of Michelob as Ben slid onto the wooden bench across the table.

"How you doin', Doc?"

"Fine."

The waitress came over, and Moose ordered a refill. When Ben asked for a Coke, the patrolman raised an eyebrow.

"You a teetotaler, Doc?"

"I'm on call tonight."

"Me too. But probably any local disturbance is goin' to originate right here." He drained his tankard. "You know, it takes a lot less precision to lay a drunk out on the barroom floor than it does to patch him up."

Ben laughed. There was something disarming about the man's laid-back country style. But there was a gleam of sharp intelligence behind his hooded eyes, which meant that it was a good idea to stay on your toes around Officer Bramble.

The Moose wasn't in any hurry to get down to business. Instead, he crunched a steady stream of potato chips and kept the conversation on the Orioles and the oyster beds—both of which were having a rebuilding season.

Ben looked down at the carvings on the wooden table as if they could give him a clue about what the officer was really thinking. All he learned was that somebody named Hardy had apparently had a burning passion for someone named Heloise.

Finally tired of playing the waiting game, Ben pushed his Coke away and leaned across the table. "Did you find anything on that tape from Sara's machine?"

"Nope. It was erased, all right. Just like Sara said."

"Damn."

"Hopin' for some easy insights, were you?"

"I was hoping to nail down the connection between Newhouse and Meekins."

Bramble refrained from commenting.

"Sara didn't make up that Swan Point stuff," Ben added. "It looked like Chandler and Newhouse were all set to subdivide the property. Maybe Ralph did find out. Sara says he was acting kind of strange ever since Chandler's car went into the Choptank."

"Um."

"Don't you have an opinion about any of this?"

"I'm keepin' an open mind."

Under the table, Ben's fingers gripped the edge of the bench. "If Newhouse didn't kill Meekins, then there's something else going on, which means Sara could be in danger."

"I haven't ruled that out." Bramble leaned back comfortably in his seat, folded his arms across his ample stomach, and waited a couple of beats. "Doc, what do you know about botulism toxin?"

The blood drained from Ben's face.

"Okay, what is it you're not tellin' me?" Bramble inquired.

"About the dead dog."

"Oh?"

"Sara and I had gone out to dinner—back in June. When we came home, a dead German shepherd was lying across the driveway. I knew it hadn't crawled there, because it was already stiff. And we hadn't seen it when we left. So I asked a local vet to do some lab work. When he couldn't find anything, he sent a sample to the Veterinary School at Cornell. The report confirmed that the dog had died of a massive dose of botulism toxin."

Bramble whistled through his teeth.

"Why are *you* so interested in the exotic toxins?" Ben shot back.

The officer studied him for a moment. "Maybe

we should get the Santa Barbara stuff out of the way before I tell you that."

"You did a background investigation on me?"

"It seemed like the prudent thing to do."

Ben sighed. "Is that damn rotten mess going to follow me around for the rest of my life?"

"Why don't you tell me about it?"

In a flat voice, Ben recounted the same story he'd told to Sara. While he spoke, he studied Bramble's features. But he simply couldn't get a handle on how the man was reacting.

"I can see how it might have gone down like that," the officer finally conceded. "But you probably made a mistake by cuttin' out."

"There wasn't anything else to do. The hospital couldn't prove I was guilty. But I couldn't prove I was innocent."

"Yeah."

"So what do you think?" Ben clenched his hands in his lap so he wouldn't reach up and wipe away the beads of sweat on his forehead.

"I think your patients like and respect you. I think in the year you've been here, you've proved you're a compassionate physician. And I think we wouldn't be having this little discussion if you weren't worried about Sara Chandler."

"I'm going to marry her."

"Ted Chandler's baby and all?"

"Yes."

"There are some folks around here who aren't so sure it's not your pup."

Ben balled his hands into fists and started to stand. Bramble reached across the table and pushed him back into his seat with surprising strength. "Take it easy. I'm not one of them. I just wanted to see if you were ready to defend the lady's honor."

"You like to get a rise out of people, don't you?" Ben accused.

"When it suits my purposes."

"Well, if you're through testing my reactions, maybe you'll tell about me *your* interest in botulism toxin. Or did you just agree to meet so you could pump me for information?"

"I was hoping for a fair exchange. Trouble is, I don't like to get into sharin' unless I feel like I can trust a man." Bramble took a contemplative sip of beer. For the first time that evening, he smiled.

Ben wasn't quite ready to return the friendly gesture.

Bramble set down his glass tankard. "The Meekins autopsy report came back from Baltimore last week. Any fool could see the old man had been bashed over the head. But that wasn't what killed him."

Ben felt as if a frigid wind had suddenly frozen the sweat on his forehead. "Botulism?" he managed.

"A massive dose. By injection."

"Jesus Christ. What in the hell is going on?"

"I don't know, Doc. But there's a good chance it's not as simple as George Newhouse trying to hide a real estate swindle."

"I only ran into him a few times besides that evening at Sara's. He seemed like a slimy bastard."

"Some people got along with him all right. Some didn't. I've found out a lot about Newhouse in the past twenty-four hours. Like I know, for example, he was out of town when Ginny Strickland disappeared."

"He was? You don't think—"

"It crossed my mind, although I'm damned if I can figure out how killing Sara's little sister would fit in. But it turns out Newhouse was at a realtors' convention in D.C. Dozens of people talked to him there. He was trying to raise some money. Maybe he needed additional capital for the Swan Point deal. I don't know."

Bramble went on to relate some other details of George Newhouse's life. "It sounds like he was gettin' kind of squirrelly toward the end," he concluded. "Frantic, I'd say. Like he was afraid of somethin'."

Ben digested the information. "So what does all this have to do with the toxin? I was thinking in terms of food contamination. But I checked with the county health department. There weren't any reports of human illness from botulism toxin."

"According to the state medical examiner, in the kind of concentration they found in Meekins, it had to come from a lab."

"Germ warfare?"

"Well, Fort Detrick, the army base where they make stuff like that, ain't all that far from here. But I'd assume the security is pretty tight. My guess would be, somebody's cookin' up a batch at home." Bramble lowered his voice slightly. "I already checked. Newhouse didn't have the facilities for something like that. You don't either."

"You're sitting there and telling me you searched my house without a warrant?"

"In front of a judge, it would be your word against mine."

"Right." Ben stared at the man across the table. He didn't exactly play fair, but he got results. "And you checked out Sara's place too, I assume."

"As part of the investigation, after the paramedics carted Newhouse away." The police officer paused for a moment as a Roy Orbison oldie blared from the jukebox. "Newhouse had a key to the Chandler front door in his pocket."

"One of the perks of being a real estate agent."

"Yeah. So why did he take off one of the living room screens and then replace it?"

"How do you know he did?"

"The other window sashes were covered with a film of dust."

Bramble had been pretty damn thorough, Ben mused. "Maybe he wanted to make it look like he came in that way," he muttered.

"Could be."

"But you don't think so."

"I told you, Doc; I'm keepin' an open mind. There are things about this case that just don't add up."

The two men sat in silence for a few moments. As the music and conversation of the bar swirled around them, each was lost in his own private thoughts. When he'd called Moose Bramble, Ben had been praying that somehow his nagging fears would be laid to rest by a candid conversation with the police officer. As they'd gotten deeper and deeper into the mess that was swirling around Sara, an icy knot had crystallized in his stomach. In the past few minutes, it had grown to glacial proportions.

"You know," the police officer finally mused, "we don't get many murders in St. Stephens. Maybe one a year. Usually the perpetrator knows the victim pretty well. A husband murdering an unfaithful wife. A friend killing a buddy in a fit of anger. It's pretty easy to figure out what happened. Hell, they usually confess as soon as you confront them. So you get kind of rusty when it comes to real detective work."

"Rusty is the last thing I'd call you, Officer Bramble."

"Yeah, well. I haven't got anything yet. But this is a mighty interesting puzzle, see. Maybe the thing with Ginny fits in, and we don't know how. Then there's the botulism business. I haven't got a handle on it yet, but I'm damn well going to figure out how the pieces fit together." He reached in his pocket and pulled out a notebook. "What do you remember about how that German shepherd looked?"

"Why—it was—you know—just a shepherd."

"Was the coat in good condition? Did it look like a stray or like someone had been taking care of it? What was the background color of the fur? What about the accent color?"

Ben searched his memory. He hadn't figured on having to dredge up these details. "Well, it was nighttime. But I think the main color was brown—with gray across the shoulders."

Bramble took down the information.

"The dog wasn't particularly well groomed.

Maybe it was a stray. But someone would have had to capture it before they could give it an injection."

"Yeah, or maybe they got it from the pound. What was the exact date in May?"

CHAPTER 36

Ben leaned back against the headboard and watched Sara brush her hair. It was a pleasure to simply let his eyes wander over her. Or to imagine taking the brush out of her hand and letting his fingers stroke through those thick, silky tresses.

As if she felt his regard, she looked up, and their eyes met in the dressing table mirror.

"Come over here."

She got up and drifted toward him, the thin batiste of her gown molding her burgeoning figure. "When I see that look in your eye and know I'm still desirable, it makes my heart turn over."

"Oh, you're desirable all right." Damn, he thought as he moved over to make room for her on the bed; he'd give anything if he could simply lose himself in her sweetness and block out the fear that was making it difficult to draw a full breath. He wondered if she was playing the same game. Was she concentrating on the two of them, all warm and intimate in here—when neither one of them knew what lurked in the blackness outside the window?

He didn't want to bring the blackness inside. But there were things he had to talk about. Which meant he had to tread a careful path between scaring the hell out of her and making her understand that the danger wasn't over.

While he pondered exactly what he was going to say, he nuzzled his lips along the incredibly soft skin beside her ear. In response, her fingers played with the hair on the back of his arm.

"Sara, I want to talk to you," he finally muttered.

"About what?"

"Giving me an early Christmas present."

The fingers on his arm stopped moving, and she looked at him questioningly.

"I'm talking about getting married."

"Ben—"

"I know you have your reasons for wanting to wait until the end of the year," he hurried on. "But I have my reasons for wanting to make it a hell of a lot sooner."

"I thought we settled all that."

"That was before George Newhouse ended up in a broken heap on your basement floor."

She sucked in her breath.

"Sara, I'm not going to leave you in this house alone at night. Would you rather I just move in and have everybody gossiping about how we're living in sin? Or would you rather marry me?"

She fought to keep her voice steady. "What do you think is going to happen to me if I'm here alone at night?"

"I don't know. And I don't want to find out."

Sara tipped her head up so she could meet his eyes. "Are you hiding something from me?"

"I don't want . . . to frighten you."

"Then you should have kept your mouth shut."

"I wish I could." He raked his fingers through his dark hair. "Jesus, Sara, I've been back and forth on this like a tennis ball at a championship match." He swallowed. "I had a talk with Moose Bramble tonight."

"I thought you were seeing a patient."

"Yeah, well I wasn't even going to tell you about Bramble if I didn't have to."

"But he changed your mind?"

"He's not discounting the possibility that there's more going on than George Newhouse trying to protect a real estate investment."

"What?"

"He doesn't know for sure."

"Are you saying he thinks I'm in some kind of danger?"

"Not exactly. Sara, I just don't know what to think."

"Then what are you worried about?"

"Nothing concrete. But dammit, Sara, if it had been you at the bottom of the basement steps instead of Newhouse, then my life wouldn't be worth living. Please, for God's sake, just let me be here for you."

She snuggled against him and closed her eyes, wrapping herself in his familiar scent and the warmth of his body. When he pulled her into his embrace, like a child in the middle of a nightmare, she gave a little murmur.

There were questions she should ask. But would it do her any good to know the answers?

Unconsciously, her hand reached down to cradle her middle, and her eyes tried to pierce the darkness beyond the window. Was someone lurking out there? Someone who wanted to hurt her and the baby?

She had tried to talk herself out of the fear that hovered just at the edge of her consciousness. But too many unexplained things had happened.

God, why couldn't all the uncertainty just go away? Why couldn't she be free to love Ben and her baby like any normal human being? Maybe everything would be all right by itself. Maybe Dad would recover. Maybe Ginny would even turn up, with that reckless grin on her freckled face, and explain that she'd just been island-hopping in the Caribbean and hadn't bothered to write.

Sara felt Ben press his cheek against the top of her head. He loved her. Perhaps that was the only certainty in her universe right now. Ever since her mother died, she'd been the one who'd held her family together. It was hard always being the strong one. Was it so terrible to let herself lean on Ben Langley's strength for a change?

He wanted to be here with her. And she

wanted him here. Maybe she didn't have to think past that decision. Maybe in ten years they could look back on the way he'd railroaded her into marriage and laugh.

"All right, I'll marry you," she whispered.

"Oh, honey, it'll be the best thing that ever happened to both of us."

Neither of them was capable of saying any more. For endless heartbeats they simply held each other.

Monday, July 24

The red-brick single-story building that housed the police department and the town office was one of the few modern structures on Main Street.

The police department had two public rooms —and a small private office in the back for the chief.

Officer Moose Bramble had one eye on the door to the chief's inner sanctum as he finished his phone call to the New York offices of The Royal Star Line.

"Thanks for your assistance. And I'd appreciate it if you could send me the passenger list and some general information about the Royal Alexandria." Damn! Here came the chief. Bramble replaced the receiver in its cradle and looked up to see the square-jawed face of Police Chief Marcus Dailey staring down at him.

"We don't have much budget for long distance. If you're planning to arrange a cruise, do it on your own nickel."

"This is related to the Newhouse investigation."

"I thought I told you, we're not putting any more manpower into that case. When a man falls down the steps and breaks his neck, you don't have to do a two-month investigation to find out what killed him."

"But you might want to know why he was sneakin' around somebody else's house."

"I thought we had that all figured out."

"Maybe."

"Bramble, let it rest. There's no way a passenger list from a cruise ship has anything to do with Swan Point." As Dailey saw it, St. Stephens was a pretty peaceable town—partly because he and the rest of the seven-man police force had been hired by the city fathers as a visible symbol of law and order. Running rowdies and vagrants off the street, catching speeders, and policing the business district were the main duties of the department. No need to poke a stick under the surface and stir up any more mud than necessary.

"It's the passenger list from the ship Ginny Strickland was on when she disappeared."

"The Caribbean isn't exactly in our jurisdiction."

"But the two things could be related. Ginny Strickland is Sara Chandler's sister."

"Jesus, I know that!" The police chief fixed Bramble with a frigid stare. "When the town council asks how we've been spending our funds, I don't want to have to explain how one of my patrolmen has been flapping around making extra work for himself."

Bramble gave it one more try. "What about the Meekins investigation?"

"You're the one who's convinced Newhouse didn't kill the old geezer."

"Yeah."

"You got any leads on that? Found out who's cooking up deadly chemicals in their kitchen? Botulism toxin." He snorted. "Maybe the medical examiner's office in Baltimore got Meekins's report mixed up with someone else's. I heard of cases like that before."

"Sure," Bramble muttered under his breath.

"What's that?"

"Nothin'." Bramble sighed, shuffled the papers on his desk into a pile, and shoved them into a folder. There was no use arguing with Dailey when he was in this kind of mood.

Hands on hips, the chief watched for a moment. Then, as if he were satisfied, he started toward his private office. But when he reached the door, he turned back toward Bramble. "What I suggest is that you get on out to that stretch of Route 33 where that little hill hides the patrol car from the speeding tourists. You've only got a few more days to fill your quota for July."

Officer Bramble nodded and reached for his navy blue Stetson. If he was going to continue with this little investigation, it was going to have to be on his own time.

Sunday, July 30

Harold Strickland's lined face broke into a broad grin as his daughter opened the door to the hospital lounge. "Sara! It's so good to see you." He looked behind her to where Ben Langley stood, a little way back. Ben was trying not to reveal his tension as he observed the scene. Harold called out, "And Ben. Thank you for stopping by."

Tears glistened in Sara's eyes as she took in her father's renewed health. True, he'd lost weight, but the deep-etched anxiety was gone from his face, and his expression was serene. She'd made the right decision, and something had worked out the way it should for a change. The shock treatment had cured her father's depression. "It's so good to see you, too, Dad." She smiled as she clasped him in her arms.

He hugged her tightly. "Oh, Sara. What would I have done without you?" Then he drew away abruptly. "You're pregnant."

"Yes. Don't you remember?"

Harold's expression became perplexed. "No, no I don't." He smiled sheepishly. "I'm afraid there're a lot of things I don't remember. But Dr. Clifton says the memory problem is only temporary."

Sara glanced back at Ben. He raised his eyebrows a fraction of an inch and shrugged slightly. Before they'd come into the lounge, the doctor had talked glowingly of Harold's recovery and had casually warned them to expect some memory loss—particularly for recent events. But she couldn't help being disappointed—and shocked. How could her father have forgotten about something as important as the baby?

"They tell me I can leave here in a few

weeks," the old man was saying. He beamed. "It'll be good to get back home again."

"I was hoping you'd like to live with us," Sara cut in, changing the subject quickly.

"Oh, you don't want an old man around the house." Harold scratched his head. "Now refresh my memory. When did the two of you get married?"

"Ben and I—we're—not married yet. We're getting married on Wednesday."

Harold stared pointedly at Sara's bulging middle. "It looks like you two put the cart before the horse."

Sara felt color flood her face. "The baby's not— Oh, Dad, don't you—?"

"Sara, it's all right," Ben interjected. His voice was calm and steady, but his insides were churning. Had he lost the desperate gamble? How much had the old man forgotten?

Sara took a deep breath and tried to regain her equanimity.

"If you fill in the gaps, maybe I'll remember," Harold added with determined cheerfulness. But was there a shadow of worry behind his eyes?

As Sara forced a smile, her mind was reeling. Dad didn't remember her husband. Or her husband's death. Somehow she couldn't bring herself to go into all that right now, so she let Ben take over and tell Harold about how well the practice was going.

"So why didn't that sister of yours come to see me?" Harold asked suddenly.

"She's on a trip."

"Oh, yes. Right."

Did he remember that, or was he just faking it?

They talked for half an hour. It seemed like an eternity. When Ben pointed out that they had things to do, she gratefully stood up to leave.

"Oh, Ben," Sara muttered when the door to the lounge had closed behind them. "There's so much of his memory gone. And the loss is so selective. If he can recall taking you on as a partner, why can't he remember Ted? And he even commented on the illnesses of some of his patients."

"Sara, I can't give you any answers. But at least he's calm. He's not suffering anymore. His intellect's intact. Huge chunks of memory may well come back. That's what Dr. Clifton said. It may just take a little longer with Harold than with other patients."

"Yes—but—do you think he'll ever be well enough to go back to work?"

"I don't know."

They stepped outside, and the bright July sunshine was suddenly mocking.

"I guess I'll figure out how to cope with this," Sara murmured. "But it's not just the memory loss. It's Dad's personality. He was always so meticulous and precise. He seems so different now. I'm not exactly sure how to relate to him. Mom's death—" She swallowed. "—the abortion. I guess I understand how it could have happened. I wonder if he even remembers that now."

Ben reached down and squeezed her hand. "We all just have to do the best we can."

When they reached the Blazer, he opened

the car door and helped Sara up to the front seat. As he walked around the back of the vehicle where Sara couldn't see him, he gritted his teeth for a moment. He'd kept the conversation with Harold light and pleasant for Sara's sake. And afterwards he'd put as good a face as possible on things.

He hadn't figured on the old man's suffering this kind of massive memory disturbance. Christ, he sure as hell was going to have a little chat with Clifton Monday morning. How many treatments had they given Harold, anyway?

He'd been counting on asking Dr. Strickland some pointed questions when he could get him alone—questions like what the hell he'd been babbling about that night they'd rushed him to the hospital to have his stomach pumped.

Well, it looked like that line of attack would be a waste of time. Whatever demons had been haunting Harold Strickland appeared to have been vaporized by the same electrical current that had zapped his memory.

CHAPTER 37

Monday, July 31

"What brings you here, Officer Bramble?" the woman behind the desk asked nervously as she eyed the nameplate on the front of Moose Bramble's blue shirt. The County Animal Shelter was run according to strict guidelines, but sometimes they did get complaints.

"I need to ask a few questions about a dog you might have placed with a family back in April or May?"

"I can check the records. What breed was it?"

"A German shepherd."

Bramble got a drink of water from the cooler and took a seat while the woman checked through her log book. In the back of the building, a large dog started to bark and was joined by a chorus of shrill yaps from some of the pound's smaller inmates.

"Is it a question about a rabies vaccination?" the clerk asked when the noise had leveled off. She was a slender woman with iron gray hair and old-fashioned pointy glasses. "All our dogs and cats are required to have an inoculation before they go to a new home."

Bramble leaned back in the wooden chair and stretched out his long legs. Right now, he was supposed to be giving out parking tickets or laying low for speeders. But Police Chief Marcus Dailey was on a fishing trip to the Outer Banks. And what the chief didn't know wasn't going to hurt him. "No, ma'am. I'm looking for someone who might have taken this particular dog."

"Um." The clerk went back to the log. "We had five German shepherds in April and May." She clucked her tongue. "I'm afraid we had to put two of them to sleep. But we did place three with new owners. One went to a Sam Partridge from Nevitt. One went to the Trusted Security Company in Cambridge. I think they wanted him for a guard dog. The other one was taken by a Keith Thomas."

Bramble's face didn't change expression, but tumblers were clicking in his mind. Keith Thomas. For someone who was dead, the guy sure got around. "I'll need Mr. Thomas's address."

"It's right here. Three fifty-two Walnut Street."

Bramble copied down the address, along with a phone number and the rabies tag number that had been issued to the dog before it left the premises. "Do you know who handled the transaction with Mr. Thomas?"

The clerk looked at the initials at the bottom of the entry. "T. H. That would be Thelma Hart. She won't be on duty until Friday. Do you want her address?"

"I'd be obliged."

"Miss Hart is one of our volunteers. But she's a bit eccentric."

"Thank you for your help."

As he climbed back into his cruiser, Bramble felt a little jolt of satisfaction. Maybe he was actually getting somewhere with this investigation. First he'd talk to Ms. Hart. Then he'd go back to St. Stephens and check out the address on Walnut Street.

Thelma Hart lived in a white clapboard cottage, west of town. The first thing Bramble noticed when he pulled into the driveway was that the lady liked to bring her work home. He could count nine cats lounging in the yard and on the porch. Some had long hair. Others were ordinary alley cats. A white Persian, a gray tabby, and a Manx scattered as he climbed out of the car. The rest looked at him disdainfully.

A buff-colored longhair came over and rubbed against his leg as he knocked on the door.

Several minutes passed before a short woman with a powderpuff of snowy hair piled on the top of her head responded to his repeated pounding. She was wearing a faded green housecoat. When she opened the door, he caught a definite aroma of ripe cat box.

The woman eyed Bramble's blue uniform. "You're not local. So my neighbors didn't send you to complain again."

"No ma'am." He could believe Ms. Hart

wasn't exactly the toast of the neighborhood. God knows what kind of toll her menagerie had taken on the local bird population. Inside, he could see more cats, curled up on tables and chairs as if they owned the place.

"I'm trying to locate a man who took home a dog from the Animal Shelter back in May."

"Oh, yes. Come in."

"I'm fine out here."

Ms. Hart sniffed and stepped onto the porch. An orange tabby slipped out with her and began to wash its face industriously.

"The man's name is Keith Thomas, and he adopted a German shepherd named Bruno."

Ms. Hart tapped a fingernail against her teeth. "Back in May. Keith Thomas. Yes, I do remember him."

Bramble pulled out his notepad and waited tensely for some kind of description.

Instead, Ms. Hart began to muse, "It's a real pity when an owner abandons a pet. That's why I volunteer down at the shelter. I'm always so pleased when someone wants to adopt one of our poor babies. The cats especially. Sometimes, if there's a cat I've taken a fancy to and nobody wants her, I bring her home myself."

"You say you remember Keith Thomas?" A gray tom made a tentative swipe at Bramble's leg with its right front paw, and he gave it a dangerous look. Luckily, Ms. Hart didn't notice.

"Oh ,yes. Now let me see. Funny, he seemed sort of afraid of the dog. Like he thought it was going to bite him or something. But he was sure Bruno was the animal he wanted.

Maybe he needed a guard dog. I got the feeling he didn't like paying for the rabies vaccination."

Bramble stood with his ball-point pen poised above the paper. "What did he look like?"

"He had a brown coat with gray highlights."

"I mean Thomas."

"Oh, yes, Thomas." She closed her eyes. "Well, he was short and slender, with dark hair slicked back from his face. Clean shaven."

"Can you remember anything else?"

She pursed her lips. "His hands were small. I noticed that when he hooked the leash to Bruno's collar. And he had a sort of a pretty-boy face. Not very masculine, if you know what I mean. Maybe that's why he was wearing a leather jacket and boots."

"Um. Anything more?"

"I don't believe so. But you could leave me your card. Did Keith Thomas mistreat Bruno?"

"We suspect he killed the dog."

"Oh, my goodness. How terrible. Then I certainly hope you find him and hang him by his fingernails."

I hope we find him too, Bramble thought as he headed back to his cruiser. A gray tabby jumped down off the hood as he reached for the door handle. Was it the same tabby he'd seen when he first drove up, or another one? he wondered.

If he hadn't been in his cruiser, he would have been caught in one of the department's speed traps on his way back to St. Stephens. The first thing he wanted to do was check out that address. Walnut Street was just at the edge of the downtown area. And it wasn't

354 • SAMANTHA CHASE

very long. It shouldn't take much time to locate the house.

He turned off Main Street onto Walnut and began looking at the numbers. Three fifty-two was on the second corner. In front of the porch railing was a small wooden sign that said: Doctor Harold Strickland and Doctor Benjamin Langley. Office hours by appointment.

Bramble tipped back his blue Stetson. If Ms. Hart's description was anywhere near correct, neither Ben Langley nor Harold Strickland had picked up that dog. But Keith Thomas had given their office address. Now that certainly was an interesting development.

Ben and Dr. Clifton had their little chat about Harold at lunchtime. Ben had been careful not to lose his temper or question the psychiatrist's judgment. Clifton had responded to his careful questions by accentuating the positive. But the bottom line was that nobody knew how quickly Harold's memory would return.

Ben had hung up the phone very carefully— to keep from slamming the receiver into the cradle. He hadn't bothered reporting the conversation to Sara. After dinner, he'd told her he had some office-related business to take care of and had gone back to his own house. The box she'd taken out of the filing cabinet drawer was sitting in the coat closet where he'd stashed it.

He'd promised himself he wasn't going to dig into the box again—and not just because he didn't want to invade Dr. Strickland's privacy. He didn't want the past to cause Sara any more pain. Maybe all the mess was really over. In that case, he didn't have anything to worry about. But if it wasn't and the answers just happened to be in this box, then he'd never forgive himself for not checking.

It might have been a nest of rattlesnakes instead of a collection of patient files the way he gingerly lifted the lid. Not knowing exactly what he expected to find, he began to thumb through the files: Pete Ditchfield, Dennis Hamlin, Carolyn Sutcliffe. None of the names meant anything to him.

His fingers came to the last file and froze. *Keith Thomas.* Jesus. Wasn't that the name of the guy who was supposed to have been romancing Ginny on the cruise ship? He sure as hell hadn't expected to find his record in here.

With a jerky motion, he pulled the folder from the box. After taking a deep breath, he flipped it open and began to read. It belonged to a boy who had first come to Harold at the age of 11. At the beginning were the usual routine entries. Ben read rapidly.

June 5, 1970. Physical exam. 5'3", 97 pounds
Patient healthy and developing normally. DPT booster. Penicillin allergy.
January 10, 1971. Allergic rash treated with cortisone ointment.
March 15, 1973. Asian B flu virus. Recommended bed rest, Tylenol, fluids.
November 10, 1974. Patient bitten by dog.
Laceration of thigh required 28 stitches. Patient given tetanus and penicillin injections.

Ben's fingers crumpled the edges of the paper. *Jesus. Why hadn't Harold checked the patient's record for allergic reactions?* The answer came in a flash of his physician-trained ability to pull together disparate pieces of information into an inclusive diagnosis. Harold Strickland had lost his wife under terrible circumstances only a few weeks before Keith Thomas was injured. In the depth of his guilt and anguish, he was in no condition to be making life-and-death decisions. Yet, as the only doctor in town, he'd been forced to keep seeing patients.

Ben knew the kind of thing he was going to read before his eyes swept farther down the page. It was the same sort of entry Harold had written after Margaret Strickland's death. Only this time the cause of death would be anaphylactic shock, not a severed artery.

> After they patient received the penicillin injection, his family was anxious to take him home and made him comfortable in the back of the family station wagon. By the time they arrived home, he was experiencing angioedema, bronchospasm, and cardiac arrhythmia.
> They immediately drove back to the office. I did an emergency tracheotomy and administered a shot of adrenaline, but it was already too late to save the patient.

The boy had died of a severe allergic reaction to the penicillin injection. During the ride home, when nobody was monitoring him, his whole body must have turned into one massive hive. His throat would have closed up, and his heart would have started to beat irregularly. Probably he had suffocated. Even though Harold Strickland had taken the right emergency measures, he was the one who had precipitated the crisis in the first place by not checking for drug allergies.

There was more to the report. But it wasn't about Keith Thomas.

> The patient had a twin sister, Katrina Thomas, who was visiting friends at the time her brother died. When she learned about what had happened, she went into an uncontrollable rage and attacked this physician—smashing objects around the office and at one point trying to stab him with a hypodermic needle.
>
> December 10, 1974. God help me, this time I'm not just responsible for a boy's death. Apparently he and his sister had an extremely close relationship, and the loss has caused a psychotic break. She's been taken to a private mental hospital in Baltimore, but the prognosis is guarded.

Ben felt emotionally drained as he slowly closed the folder. Keith Thomas. Was it just a coincidence that someone with the exact same name had gotten involved with Ginny just before she'd disappeared? And if it wasn't a coincidence, what did it mean?

First he'd better call Bramble and fill him in—on the medical record and the possible tie to Ginny. Then he'd have to go home and talk to Sara.

CHAPTER 38

Sara was in the living room, working on a pair of baby booties, when she heard a car in the drive. There'd been a time when she'd welcomed visitors. Now her stomach clenched as she waited for the doorbell to ring—or the key to turn in the lock.

"It's me."

Ben. He understood how she felt. Now, when he came in, he always let her know right away that it was him. "I'm in the living room."

She'd become an excellent judge of Ben Langley's expressions. His face had assumed that guarded look he got when he had something to say but didn't want to worry her. "You might as well tell me," she prompted, setting down her knitting.

He dropped onto the sofa beside her. "Yeah. Well, maybe I'd better start with a confession."

When her eyes grew round, he hurried on. "I was—uh—counting on asking Harold some pointed questions. But after Sunday—well—I don't know when he's going to be able to tell me anything. So I got out that box—the one with the medical records on your mother."

"The one you wouldn't let me look in."

"I changed my mind. Somebody had to check."

"And you found—?" Sara could hear the tension in her own voice.

"Something strange." Ben took a deep breath. "There was a fifteen-year-old boy who died in 1974 after your father gave him an injection of penicillin. His name was Keith Thomas."

"The same name as the man Ginny was supposed to have been going around with before she disappeared."

"Yes."

"What does it mean?"

"I don't know. But I was thinking. Is there someone in town who might remember the case?"

"Jodeen Crane, the old busybody who's always down at McGuire's Drugstore. When it comes to St. Stephens, she's got a mind like an encyclopedia—especially if there's a nice juicy scandal involved. But I'm not going to ask her a damn thing." Sara's eyes were clouded. "You say the boy died after a penicillin injection. Was my father at fault?"

"Sara—what does that matter now?"

"Was he at fault?"

"Yes. It was only a few weeks after your mother died. I guess he wasn't—" He closed the distance between them and wrapped her in his arms. For a few moments, she buried her face against the front of his shirt. Then she raised her head again. "Did you bring the records home?" she asked in a flat voice.

"No."

"Then I guess you'd better tell me the rest of it."

"All right."

Tuesday, August 1

Beatrice Pierce finished the word she was typing and reached for the phone on her desk. "Hello."

"Miss Bea, it's Sara Chandler."

"Oh, Sara. How are you doing?"

"Not too badly, everything considered."

Beatrice clucked her tongue.

"I was—uh—calling to ask a favor."

"What can I do for you?" the older woman inquired cautiously. Sara didn't have any idea she was working on a book, did she? No, of course not.

"Last night, I was thinking—uh—this is—" She took a deep breath. "I was wondering if you remembered anything about a boy named Keith Thomas."

"Oh, my."

"Then you do remember."

"It's funny you should bring him up now. I just saw his grave a few days ago."

Sara couldn't repress a little shudder. "Do you remember what happened after he died? The part about his twin sister?"

"You mean her attacking your father?"

"Yes."

Beatrice repeated the same facts that Ben had reported from the medical record.

"I don't suppose you know what hospital Katrina went to."

"I'm sorry. The family kept that private." Beatrice wished she had that information herself. What had they treated the girl for, exactly? And had she recovered from her madness? Maybe she'd even committed suicide. That would certainly add a bit of spice to the book.

"I don't suppose the family is still in town."

"No. But I do know that the mother's maiden name was Atwater. She was from around here."

Sara thought for a moment. "I don't remember her. I was wondering if you knew what happened to Katrina after she went into the hospital."

"Well, if you'd asked me a few days ago, I wouldn't have been able to tell you a thing. But I just found out that she passed away."

"She's dead?"

"Why, yes." Beatrice gave a background summary of the Historical Society's recent graveyard tour. "There's a double gravestone in the Cedar Grove Burying Ground. She and her brother are in adjoining graves."

"Could you tell me where the plot is located?"

"My goodness, why this sudden interest in the Thomas family?"

"I—" Sara swallowed. What was the point of keeping Ginny's shipboard relationship a secret now? "Apparently, my sister met a man on the cruise ship with the same name as the boy who died. I was wondering if there might be some way that tied in—"

"She did? How very strange. Spooky, don't you think?"

"Yes."

If you were going to visit a cemetery, it might as well be in the bright morning sunlight, Sara thought as she got out of her car and stood before the wrought iron gates of the Cedar Grove Burying Ground. So many graveyards had walls and bars—probably to keep the public out. It certainly couldn't be to keep the dead in.

The thought made her want to turn around and head downtown to the gallery. Instead, she pushed open the gate and stepped inside. Was it her imagination, or was it ten degrees cooler in here? Maybe it was from the shade of the huge old oak trees that had grown up inside the wall.

Quickly she started down the main path. The only sound she could hear was the crunching of her own sandals. Even the birds were silent this morning. Or maybe the caretaker shooed them away, so they wouldn't mess on the headstones. One of the pebbles from the path lodged under her right foot, and she paused to dislodge it, steadying herself against a white marble cross. She was beginning to feel unwieldy—even if Ben did keep telling her she wasn't really all that big. She certainly hadn't had a robust enough appetite to gain much weight. The bulge that made it hard to bend over was all baby.

Beatrice had given her good directions. It

took less than ten minutes to locate the carmine double stone that marked the graves of the Thomas twins. Sara stood staring at the names. Keith and Katrina.

Her father's medical report had mentioned that the brother and sister had an extremely close relationship—so close that Katrina had been devastated by Keith's death. And Beatrice had confirmed that. But it was still odd to see them buried here together like a married couple.

Sara took several steps closer and ran her fingers across the cold surface of the headstone. It was almost new—with none of the weathering you saw on older stones. Who had put this one up?

A cloud drifted in front of the sun. The sudden feeling of being watched sent a shiver down Sara's spine—just like on the day they'd buried Ted. Only then she'd been with a crowd of people. Now she was alone. Struggling to keep her movements from being jerky, she turned and looked behind her. The burying ground was silent and empty.

Were the dead watching her? All at once she started running awkwardly back toward the gate.

CHAPTER 39

Wednesday, August 2

It was a quiet wedding ceremony in the study of the Reverend Boyd Hollingsworth at the St. Stephens Methodist Church. The bride wore a light-blue maternity dress and carried a bouquet of pink roses and baby's breath. The groom wore a satisfied smile and his navy summer suit. The only invited guests were Kitty Duncan, Beatrice Pierce, and Harold Strickland, who had a special hospital pass for the occasion.

"I'm so glad things have worked out like this for Sara," Beatrice whispered to the bride's father as the happy couple were greeted by the minister's wife.

"Yes."

"It's just a little soon after Ted."

"Ted?"

"I knew you didn't like her first husband. Neither did I."

"Um—yes."

"But the way he was killed."

Harold turned sharply toward Beatrice. His brow furrowed in concentration. "The way he was killed," he repeated to himself.

"I can see why you wouldn't want to think about it."

Before Harold could answer, the Reverend Mr. Hollingsworth cleared his throat. "Well, friends, I think we're ready to begin."

Thursday, August 3

"I understand congratulations are in order."

Sara turned toward the entrance to the drug-store. Just her luck that Jodeen Crane was coming out when Sara was on her way back from the Acme with some sugar for the coffee and tea cart she kept in the gallery.

"Why yes, thank you," she acknowledged pleasantly.

"I heard your father was able to attend the ceremony. How nice."

"Yes. We were so pleased."

"I'll bet he's tickled pink about the baby."

"Yes."

"Have you thought of a name?"

"If it's a girl, we're going to call her Alyssa Margaret."

"Margaret. For your mother."

"Yes, If it's a boy, I haven't quite decided. But I like Michael Brian."

Jodeen didn't comment. Her face had taken on a faraway look. "I remember when my Thad was born. I was in labor for thirty-six hours. It was agony. I thought I was going to die." She began to recount the grisly details of twenty-five years ago as if they were last month.

Sara began to edge away. This wasn't the first time recently she'd been treated to a recitation of pain and suffering. What was it about pregnancy that drove other women to bring out horror stories of labor and delivery? Like men exchanging old war stories—they got more gruesome in the telling. At least, she hoped that was the case.

"I can hardly wait," Sara murmured with a little shudder. Was it really going to be that bad?

Friday, August 4

"Being able to relax during the first stage of labor is very important, because it conserves energy for transition and delivery," Holly Westbrook, R. N., told the prospective parents who had assembled in the recreation hall of the Methodist Church. "But don't feel you have to get through labor and delivery without any medication—unless the two of you decide that's what you want to do." She paused. "Even if you think you want natural childbirth, you can always change your mind if the going gets too rough."

It was strange being back here so soon for a labor and delivery class, Sara thought. She and six other pregnant women were lying on the floor. Each had her head on a pillow and one bent knee resting on the other. Husbands sat beside their wives, waiting for instructions.

It was the group's first meeting, and everyone was a bit self-conscious. But Sara felt particularly awkward. She'd wanted to take the class, but she knew that her pregnancy and recent marriage were hot topics of conversation around town. For a moment, she glanced at the woman next to her. Sally Porter had been a year behind her in high school. And the husband of another woman had been in her class. In fact, she knew half the people here. The rest were newcomers to St. Stephens.

"We're going to practice some breathing techniques for early labor," Holly advised, and Sara pulled her mind back to the business at hand.

"There used to be a time when all a man could do while his wife was in labor was chain-smoke and pace back and forth in the waiting room, waiting to be told he had a son or a daughter. Now the father's right in the labor and delivery room with his wife, coaching her through some of the most important hours of their married life."

The instructor looked around at the men. "Daddies, you need to know just as much about the breathing relaxation exercises as your wives. It's your job to make sure the Mommies get the rhythm right when they're under the stress of labor. So let's start with deep chest breathing, which is useful for the early first stage of labor."

Ben gave Sara an encouraging smile. He'd seen plenty of women practice this particular breathing technique during his training. But sitting with his hand on Sara's belly added a unique personal dimension for him. Childbirth was rarely easy. In fact, it could be a long ordeal. He was glad he'd found the time to come here with Sara. It was something important he could do—as her husband. And he knew better than the other men here that the more prepared she was for labor, the more control she was going to have—and the less discomfort.

He leaned over and counted her breaths. "You're going a little too fast. Slow down. One . . . two . . . three . . . four."

For a few minutes, the only sounds were quiet counting and heavy breathing in the room.

"Sounds like an obscene telephone call over an amplifier," one of the husbands quipped. Everybody laughed.

After they'd gone though several different exercises, Holly called a break. The husbands hauled the wives to their feet, and everyone congregated around the pitcher of lemonade and the plate of oatmeal cookies the instructor had supplied.

"When are you due?" a pretty blonde asked Sara. She was one of the newcomers to town. Sara hadn't met her before.

"October."

"I'm not due until the end of November, and I'm already a lot bigger than you are. But then, this is our second."

Her husband turned to Ben. "Is this your first?"

Out of the corner of her eye, Sara caught

the sudden interest of Sally Porter and another women she'd known through the church.

Ben reached down and casually linked his
fingers with Sara's. "Yes."

"We waited a couple years before having
Heather. How long have you folks been married?"

Ben started to laugh. "Two days."

The husband looked as if he wished he hadn't
asked the question.

'It's a long, complicated story," Ben told
him. "How old is your little girl?"

"Uh—almost three."

"That's a good age difference," Ben remarked.

A moment ago, Sara had felt like sinking
through the tile floor. Now she began to relax
again. When Ben grinned at her, she smiled
back.

"All right, let's get back to work," Holly
called out. "I'm going to show you guys how
to give your wives a soothing back massage."

Later, after the class was over and they'd
climbed into the car, Sara turned to Ben.
"Thanks for handling that awkward question
so nicely."

"For a split second, I thought about saying
two years. Then I decided, the hell with it."

She rested her head on his shoulder as they
pulled out of the parking lot. "I'm glad you
talked me into getting married."

"Hold that thought until we get home, Mrs.
Langley."

Neither one of them saw the motorcycle
parked in the shadows of the church parking
lot. It had been absent from their lives for
several weeks. Now it had returned.

* * *

"I'm glad you're back, Keith."

"I couldn't stay away from you."

She laughed. "I think you couldn't stay away from Sara."

"Yeah—well—" His lips contorted. "We started this to torture Harold. Now the bastard doesn't even remember why he's being punished."

"Sara's hopeful that his memory will come back."

"What if it doesn't?"

"We can still give him pain. He's going to find his other daughter dead and his grandchild missing. That will send him to the depths of hell."

Saturday, August 5

Dotty Griffin's eyes snapped open.

"Babe, what is it?"

"Just a bad dream."

"You were thrashing around in your sleep."

"Oh, Jerry, I didn't mean to wake you up."

"Not to worry, babe. I like waking up in the middle of the night with you all warm and sweet beside me." His hand stroked down her fleshy arm to the nicely rounded swell of her hip. Jerry Manuelo enjoyed his women plump— and agreeable. When Dotty snuggled into the warmth of his embrace, he smiled in the dark and began to nuzzle his lips against her neck.

Boy, was he glad he'd gotten hooked up with Dotty Griffin. He hadn't even met her until

the end of the cruise, because he'd been romancing another broad. But after the first
few nights, when that woman had been oh so
sweet and docile, she'd turned out to be the
type who wanted to call the shots in bed. He
wasn't going to let that ruin the rest of his
vacation. So he had gone searching for a
woman who looked at lovemaking from the
right perspective.

Too bad Dotty lived in Connecticut and he
was in Chicago. But they'd already spent a
hot weekend together in July. And this one
was shaping up to be just as rewarding.

As Jerry's fingers stroked her breasts, Dotty
arched against him and moaned. He was so
damn sexy—so commandingly masculine in
bed. So what if he was two inches shorter and
fifty pounds lighter than she was? Stuff like
that didn't matter when you were horizontal.

Maybe it was the way Jerry was holding
her now. For a moment, an image from the
dream that had awakened her flashed into
her mind. She was standing on the deck of the
Royal Alexandria watching Keith Thomas and
that poor Ginny Strickland who'd disappeared.
It was the Fourth of July, and they were lying
together on a lounge, waiting for the fireworks.
Only, in the dream, it was different than it
had been. Keith was grabbing Ginny by the
breasts—not under a blanket, but right out
where everybody could see. Then she was
jumping up and trying to get away—only his
arms stretched and stretched to hold her, so
that finally he was pulling her backwards.
She screamed and looked over her shoulder.
When she saw Keith's face, she screamed again.

It wasn't the same. Somehow it had changed into a woman's cruel countenance. No, that was crazy. It was just the distortion of the dream.

Jerry felt the woman in his arms tense. "What is it, babe?"

"The nightmare. I can't get it out of my mind."

"Oh, poor little dumpling. Don't worry. I'll make you forget all about that nasty dream."

And he did.

CHAPTER 40

Thursday, August 31

Ben set down the mail in the front hall. The two women in the living room were so engrossed in their conversation that they hadn't heard him come in. Sara and Kitty. They'd been together so much lately that he was starting to feel jealous.

"It must be difficult for Ben to be excited about the baby," Kitty was saying.

The sound of his name drew him to the door. He didn't like eavesdropping, but he was curious to hear Sara's reaction.

"He's been terrific at those classes. I know he's going to be a good labor coach."

That made him smile.

"But even a man as caring as Ben Langley might have some reservations about being the substitute father to another man's child."

Ben stepped through the doorway. "I think I can handle it."

Both women had guilty expressions on their faces as they looked up.

"Ben, I didn't know you were home."

"Mrs. Jenkins canceled, so I was able to get out early."

Kitty stood. "Well I'd better leave you two honeymooners alone."

"You don't have to leave," Sara protested.

Ben couldn't bring himself to second the invitation to stay.

Friday, September 15

"Sara?"

"I'm upstairs practicing my breathing."

Wearily, Ben climbed the stairs and headed down the hall to the bedroom. It had been a long week, and he wished he didn't have office hours tomorrow. Sara was lying on her side on the bed, with her eyelids closed and her knees bent. *Only a little more than a month to go, thank God*, he thought as he eyed the arm cupped around her now prominent middle.

He leaned against the doorjamb, watching her concentrate. She was practicing upper-chest breathing, which was used when labor contractions began to get stronger. But she'd probably be like most of his patients these days—she'd be ready for some pain relief by that time.

Sara didn't even look up at him. But that was the way it had been recently. The closer she got to delivery, the more she'd turned inward—toward the baby. Well, he'd known that the later stages of pregnancy were tough on the husband. And before he'd insisted that she marry him, he'd convinced himself he could handle that. Maybe, on some level, good old Kitty was right. It wasn't his child sapping Sara's energy and absorbing most of her attention. Despite everything, it was getting harder and harder to cope with the fact that his wife had temporarily stopped meeting his needs. Or was it temporary? Maybe he'd rushed her into a marriage she regretted.

He sighed, and she opened her eyes. "How come you're home so late?"

"A kid put his arm through a window, and I had to stitch him up." He came over and helped Sara sit up. When his hand slid tentatively up under her breast, she moved away. "Kitty was over again today."

Right, Kitty. The two women had become closer than Siamese twins during the past few weeks. It was almost as if Kitty was deliberately sucking up the intimacy that should have gone to him. No, that wasn't fair. It was just that Kitty and Sara were both wrapped up with the blessed event.

"We finished up the wallpaper in the baby's room. I mean, Kitty finished. I'm so clumsy and tired, I'm not much help anymore."

"Um."

"Come and see."

Ben followed Sara across the hall to the nursery. She had read that babies were more stimulated by bright colors than by pastels. When Kitty had suggested decorating the room in red, white, and blue, Sara had gone along with the idea.

"What do you think?"

"It's bright."

"Yes. Kitty's painting the bureau and the toy chest at her house, so I don't have to smell the fumes—and she's bringing it over later in the week."

The bureau and low wooden chest had been in Sara's old nursery and had been stored in Harold's attic. But she and Ben had bought a new crib and changing table, which were already in place.

Sara sat down in the rocking chair by the window. "I had some more Braxton Hicks contractions again today," she told him, referring to the intermittent contractions that were especially noticeable during the later stages of pregnancy.

"When?"

"This afternoon. So I came home. Judy said she didn't mind. Ben, I keep wondering whether I'm going to be able to tell when I'm really going into labor."

"You've got a ways to go yet."

"I guess so. But I don't know—" She smiled and changed the subject. "Judy's so understanding."

"Sounds like she's enjoying working her way into taking over as manager."

"Lucky for me. I really don't remember how I got along without her. She's got a real flare for the business."

"I'm glad it's working out so well for the two of you."

Sara sucked in a deep breath. "I got another report from that detective in Baltimore."

"And I suppose he doesn't know anything else." He wished she could just accept that her sister wasn't coming back. But he understood why Sara couldn't let it go.

"He still doesn't have a line on Ginny," Sara admitted. "But he was able to find out what hospital Keith Thomas's sister was in. A place called Maple Springs. She was discharged as cured, two years ago."

"I guess she didn't leave a forwarding address."

"That's right. Evidently she wasn't interested in getting Christmas cards from the staff."

"And the patient records are confidential, so he didn't get a look at them."

Sara nodded. "But there may still be a way to get a lead on her."

"Sara, she's dead."

"Is she? How do we know that for sure? How do we know anything for sure? I keep thinking about hiring someone to dig up those graves and find out if there's really anybody in there."

"Sara!" After the baby, Keith Thomas and his sister were taking up more and more of Sara's thoughts. Kitty was all caught up in that, too. He'd heard them talking about the Thomas family almost as much as about the baby.

He'd wanted to tell Kitty to leave it alone. But maybe he was the one who was wrong. Maybe it was theraputic for Sara to talk to someone. It was just that it went against his instincts.

Now Sara was talking about digging up graves. When was it going to end? He was tired—tired of being on guard every second when nothing else had happened for months. He just wanted a normal life with the woman he'd married.

When she saw his expression, Sara pushed herself awkwardly out of the chair and came over to circle Ben's waist with her arms and lay her cheek against his chest. For a moment he didn't move. Then his arms came up to embrace his wife.

"Oh Ben, I don't know why I can't—" She stopped. "This has got to be tough on you. I'm not exactly acting like a model wife."

"I'll survive."

"Didn't they tell you in medical school that advanced pregnancy can make women slightly batty?"

"Something like that."

She closed her eyes. "Poor Ben."

"I just need a hot meal and a couple of hours off my feet."

"Uh—I wasn't up to fixing dinner again. Maybe I could scramble some eggs or something. Or maybe you could pick up some fast food."

"No, let's go out. After next month, we're not going to be able to do that without a babysitter."

"Um hum."

"Why don't I see if I can get a table at the Harbor Watch?"

"Like our first date!"

Saturday, September 16

Harold Strickland swung his skinny legs out of bed and padded to the bathroom. He wasn't in a hurry. What did it matter? Saturday. Sunday. Monday. All his days were the same now. He had a beautifully tended vegetable garden out back. Not a weed in sight. And all the clutter was gone from the garage. Probably the most exciting thing he did these days was work on a reproduction of a sneak boat down at the Maritime Museum. He and another old coot, Ken Blades, had started the joint project. Blades, a former waterman who knew a lot about boat building, was teaching Harold the techniques.

Dr. Strickland flushed the toilet and methodically washed his hands. Although he'd told himself he didn't want to go back to the hectic pace of his old life, it was hard to feel useful now. But he didn't complain. Sometimes he'd wake up in the middle of the night. The sheets would be soaked with sweat, and he'd be gasping for breath. His conscious mind had only vague memories of the awful dread that had held him in a vicelike grip before the shock treatments. But his unconscious wasn't quite so handicapped. What had he been so damned afraid of? Maybe it was better not to know.

That's why he hadn't been agonizing over his memory loss—or making an effort to reach back into his recollections. Not being able to remember his own history was frustrating—sometimes infuriating. But it was also a blessing, he told himself.

Back in his bedroom, he glanced toward the dresser. Three women smiled back at him from black and white photographs in identical gold frames: Margaret, his wife; Ginny and Sara, his daughters.

He clamped his lips together. He remembered what he'd done to Margaret. That knowledge was so terrible that it had never left him. Was remorse over her death what had triggered his suicidal depression? Even after all these years, it could have been enough. But the fear kept nagging at him that there was more—that he'd done something to hurt Ginny and Sara, too.

He picked up the photographs of his daughters and sank down onto the edge of the bed, looking into the smiling faces of the two girls.

Ginny. No one knew what had happened to her. Sara. She was great with child now, and so damn vulnerable. He couldn't shake the feeling that he was somehow putting her in danger. The thought made his heart start to thump inside his chest and his skin grow clammy.

God he just wanted to keep on drifting through his days—pulling weeds in his garden and learning to build a boat. But how could he? It was time to make himself face the past. Maybe he couldn't remember by himself. But there was a way to jog his recollection. He'd kept a locked box in one of the filing cabinets in his office. Even if he didn't want to, he was going to make himself confront whatever was inside.

But when he got downstairs, he went into the dining room and stood looking at the cabinet where he kept the Scotch. His hands trembled slightly, and he thrust them into the pockets of his bathrobe. Finally, he turned and strode into his office. Before he could change his mind, he squatted down on the rug and pulled the file drawer open with a clang of metal against metal.

At first he was unable to cope with what he was seeing. Carefully, his eyes probed the dark recesses of the drawer. It was empty. But he'd been so sure the damn box was here. Had he forgotten where he'd stashed it?

Quickly he opened other drawers. The ones on the bottom left and right were stuffed with ancient tax records. The ones above were jammed with folders.

There was no box of patient records. It was missing—vanished. Or had it ever existed?

Now that was an ironic twist, he thought with a little grimace. Had his injured memory conjured up a physical manifestation of his guilt?

His hand froze on the cold metal handle of the file drawer. Or was there a more likely explanation? He'd had a nervous breakdown and been in the hospital for months. Had someone come in here looking for explanations for his behavior? Who might it have been? Ginny?

No, she'd gone on her trip before he'd gotten sick. Hadn't she? It was so damn hard to keep things straight these days.

Well what about Sara? Or Ben? Or some enemy he couldn't even remember?

He shuddered. Why think about enemies? It was bad enough to imagine Ben or Sara opening that box and learning his shameful secrets. Jesus, there was stuff in there he didn't even remember himself.

Was that why Sara sometimes gave him those funny sidewise glances when she thought he wasn't looking? Did she know how her mother had died? Or was his own remorse conjuring up an imagined reaction.

Suddenly he realized that his head was throbbing. For a moment, he cradled it in his hands, pressing his palms against his closed eyelids.

A man shouldn't have to live this way, he thought. When he raised his head again, the first thing he saw was the telephone on the desk. He could call Sara or Ben right now. But how could he ask about something like the box?

He sucked in a lungful of air. Which was worse—knowing or not knowing? And what would the consequences be if he just pretended that everything was all right?

CHAPTER 41

Friday, September 29

Sara's back had been aching all morning—which made her grumpy and out of sorts.

"Maybe you ought to go home," Judy suggested.

"I'm sorry I've been fussing at you."

"Don't worry about it. I know how you're feeling. The last few weeks are the hardest."

"Lucky me."

Finally at noon, after three mistakes on a charge sale, Sara decided to pack it in. Feeling like the Goodyear blimp with rocks in its gondola, she dragged herself out to the car. Just getting around was a major effort now—never mind the problem of slipping into shoes that you couldn't see and that were a size too small.

Thank goodness the temperature had dropped a little now that fall was here—or she couldn't imagine how she'd get through the rest of the month. At home, she set the mail on the dining-room table and shuffled into the kitchen. But the idea of eating lunch made her throat clog. So she climbed heavily upstairs and hoisted herself into bed. Around one-thirty, a crampy pain in her abdomen woke her up. ·

What a time for a stomach virus, Sara thought as she rolled over and tried to get comfortable. At least little Michael or Alyssa wasn't kicking.

The pain eased up a bit, but a half an hour later it was back again. Sara began to wonder if she might actually be in labor—even though it was still almost a month early.

After pushing herself to a sitting position, she reached for the phone and dialed the office number. "Lois, can I talk to Ben?"

"He's got an emergency appendectomy at the hospital. Hold on for a minute; I have another call."

Another pain hit her while she was waiting for Lois to come back, and she clutched the receiver until it subsided. Finally Lois returned.

"Sorry, things are really crazy around here this afternoon with Dr. Langley having to cancel half his appointments," the office assistant apologized. "Is anything wrong?"

"Lois. I think I may be in labor."

"Isn't it kind of early?"

"I know. But I keep having these cramps."

"How far apart are they?"

"I don't know. I've had a nagging ache in my back all morning. The abdominal stuff just started a little while ago."

"I'll leave a message for Dr. Langley to call

as soon as he gets out of surgery. Why don't you see if you can time the contractions? And write down how long they're lasting."

"All right." There was a notepad beside the phone. When the next contraction hit, she jotted down the time: 2:28. The next one was at 2:45 and lasted for 35 seconds.

When the phone rang, she snatched up the receiver. But instead of Ben, it was Jake Levitt, the private investigator from Baltimore.

"Mrs. Langley. I called the gallery, and your assistant said you'd gone home. I hope you're not under the weather today."

She laughed. "Not exactly. I think I'm about to have a baby."

There was a flustered cough on the other end of the line. "Uh—congratulations. I didn't know you were expecting."

"I guess it never came up."

"Why don't I get back to you in a few days?"

"Was there something important you wanted to tell me?"

"Maybe. I've been trying to find out more about the Thomas twins. It turns out that their mother was from the St. Stephens area. Her maiden name was Atwater."

"I already knew—" The sentence ended with a sharply indrawn gasp. This time Sara used deep breathing to get through the thirty seconds of discomfort.

"Listen, I think I better let you go."

Sara glanced at the clock and wrote down "3:04," followed by "Atwater." She hadn't tried checking on the grandparents. Maybe that would lead to something. But her hand was unsteady, and the notation was difficult to read.

Levitt was speaking again.

"Sorry, what?"

"We don't have to discuss this now. I can—uh—put it in a letter."

Sara said good-bye, hung up, and eased back against the pillows wishing Ben would call. As if to answer her silent plea, the phone rang again. This time it was Kitty, who'd been checking in every day to see how she was.

"Oh, Kitty. I'm glad you called. I think this is it."

"You're having the baby? But you're early."

"I know. But I'm sure this is the real thing. I'm waiting for Ben to get out of surgery."

"Sara, you don't want to be alone at a time like this. I've got a couple of things to do at home. Then I'll be right over."

"That would be great."

Sara maneuvered herself to the side of the bed and stood up carefully. When another contraction hit her, she grabbed the bedpost. "3:21," she dutifully wrote down, followed by "35 seconds" and a question mark. How could you time the duration of the damn things when you kept getting interrupted?

Weeks ago, after her class had discussed what to take to the hospital, Sara had packed a small suitcase. Now she got it out of the closet and set it on the bed. Once more, she checked to see that she had everything she needed—for labor, for her own hospital stay, and for the baby. Her labor kit was in a book bag. It contained cornstarch, a washcloth, and a paper bag in case she started hyperventilating

. . . socks for cold feet, a lollipop in case her mouth got dry, a bag of Oreo cookies for Ben. For the hospital, she had several nightgowns, a bathrobe, slippers and toilet articles.

The baby's things included receiving blankets, tee shirts, and a green and white sleeper. She took it out and stroked her fingers over the soft fabric. After all these months she'd finally be holding her own little baby.

Thinking about the ride to the hospital, she slipped into one of her comfortable knit jumpers, with a soft cotton blouse underneath.

When the doorbell rang, she went downstairs. Kitty stood on the porch, looking disheveled and nervous.

"Relax. You look like you're in worse shape than I am," Sara laughed.

"I got here as fast as I could. Did Ben call back?"

"Not yet."

"Then you're still here alone?"

"Yes."

"Good."

"What?"

"I mean, Ben can probably just meet us at the hospital. That'll be a lot easier for him."

"You're right. Come on—" The rest of the sentence was cut off by another contraction. This one was longer and stronger, and Sara sagged against the wall.

"Are you all right?" Kitty asked when it was over.

"I think so."

"Maybe we'd better get you out of here," her friend suggested.

"I probably still have hours to go."

"Why take a chance?"

"I guess you're right. I'll feel more comfortable about things when I get to the hospital," Sara agreed.

"Is your bag packed?"

"It's up on my bed. I—"

"No. You just sit down in the living room and be comfortable. I'll go up and get it."

"We should let Ben know."

"I'll call his office and tell them you're leaving."

"I should call Dr. Birch's office, too."

"You save your strength. I'll take care of everything."

"Thanks."

A few minutes later, Kitty came back downstairs. "Ready to go?"

"Uh hum."

When Sara stepped outside, she saw that the sky had changed. Dark clouds hovered on the horizon like messengers of dread tidings. "It looks like we're going to get a storm."

"Or maybe it will blow over."

Kitty helped Sara into the car and waited while she stretched the seat belt to its limit. "A little more, and I wouldn't be able to fasten it," she joked.

Soon they were heading down the highway toward Easton. The contractions were closer and harder. Instead of trying to time them, Sara leaned back and closed her eyes, wishing it wasn't such a long ride.

"That's right," Kitty crooned. "You just relax and take it easy. We'll be there before you know it."

A few minutes later, Sara felt the car slow,

and she opened her eyes just in time to see
Kitty turn off onto a dirt road. "Where are we
going?"

"I just have to make a quick stop. This is
right on the way to the hospital. You sit tight."

"Kitty—"

Her friend didn't respond, and Sara gave
her a long look. She was leaning forward,
eyes intent on the winding road.

The narrow lane was rutted, and Sara felt
every jolt. She was about to plead with Kitty
to slow down, when they rounded a curve and
pulled up in front of a large, run-down Victorian
house. Sara stared at it in confusion, but Kitty
had already bolted from the car. She opened
Sara's door. "This won't take long."

"Kitty, we don't have time to stop. What if
the storm breaks?"

"Don't worry. I promised I'd pick up some
stuff here. You shouldn't wait in the car."
Kitty reached in the back and pulled out Sara's
suitcase. With her other hand, she took Sara
by the arm and pulled her out onto the gravel
drive. A contraction hit, and she leaned into
Kitty for support.

"It's all right. I'll take care of everything,"
the other woman murmured. "Come on in
and sit down."

The underlying rasp of metal filings in the
familiar voice made a shiver undulate up
Sara's spine. What in the world was wrong
with Kitty? She was acting so strangely.

"Please." Sara tried to dig her feet into the
ground as she glanced nervously at the house.
It was an elaborate structure with a wide
front porch and a balcony under the central

attic window. In her present condition, she was no match for Kitty's command of the situation. With a sense of helplessness, she found herself being propelled up the steps, across the porch, and inside. She whirled as Kitty bolted the door after them. "Kitty, why are we here? What's going on? Where are we?"

"I have a surprise for you," Kitty whispered. "Something really special. Just give me a minute."

"Can't we do this later?"

Instead of answering, her friend turned and dashed up the stairs, leaving Sara alone in the foyer.

Feeling caged in, Sara gulped in a lungful of musty air. The walls of the old house were dingy, the wide floorboards worn. Suddenly she felt disoriented. Was it her imagination, or was Kitty cracking up or something? She fought to hold back a wave of panic. She hadn't been paying attention to their route. Why had they come to this old place?

Sara walked over to a filmy window. It was bolted, like the door. Beyond was an overgrown field that might once have been a lawn. The setting was isolated—probably at least a couple of miles from the highway. What if Kitty didn't come back soon? She couldn't walk back to civilization. Were the keys in the car? Was she in any shape to drive?

Sara had started down the hall to the back of the house, with some vague thought of going back out to the car, when she stopped short. In the empty dining room were the bureau and toy chest Kitty had volunteered to fix up. Both were now painted bright red. There was also red paint smeared garishly on the floor and on the walls, as if someone had taken pleasure in making a mess of the room. Above the bureau hung a smashed mirror. The whole effect set her teeth on edge. Sara had quickened her pace toward the kitchen when she heard heavy footsteps coming back down the stairs.

"Sara—at last."

She whirled to find herself facing a short, slim man with dark hair slicked back from his face and angular features that were hauntingly familiar. He was wearing boots and motorcycle leathers. The proprietary gleam in his over-bright eyes made her take a step backwards. "Who are you?"

"I'm disappointed. I thought you'd know. Remember, we met that afternoon at Swan Point. After Ted's funeral. You were upset. But you shouldn't have been. He wasn't worth it."

Sara shook her head, not so much at the words but at the horrible conjecture teasing the edges of her mind like a vulture circling around a dead animal in the road. Her chest tightened as the newcomer's gaze held hers captive.

"You said you wanted to see my face. And I wanted to show it to you. But it was too soon." The voice was alto, with a slight trembling.

Sara backed away, still shaking her head.

"I'm Keith Thomas." He gave a little lift of his right shoulder. "I've been living here in my grandmother Atwater's house. And I've been waiting a long time to talk to you. It would have been months ago, back in July, except for the baby."

He came forward and grasped her shoulders, his fingers digging menacingly into her flesh.

Sara screamed.

"This is Sara Langley. I can't come to the phone right now. If you want to get in touch with Dr. Langley, please call his office number. If you want to talk to me, leave your name and number after the sound of the tone; I'll get back to you as soon as possible."

"Sara? Are you there?" Ben called into the receiver. Still dressed in his scrub suit, he'd phoned from the hospital as soon as he'd gotten the message from Lois.

When Sara didn't answer, he hung up without leaving a message. Sara was probably on her way to the hospital—or maybe she had already arrived by now, which meant that she would have called Dr. Birch's office.

He'd been carrying her obstetrician's number around in his wallet for the past several months. After fishing it out, he made the call.

"This is Ben Langley."

"Can I help you?"

"I assume you got a call from my wife earlier this afternoon."

The receptionist checked her records. "No, Dr. Langley, I'm afraid we didn't."

"Oh."

"Is there some problem?"

"I got a call from my office saying that Sara thought she was in labor."

"I'm sorry; we haven't heard from her."

"Thanks."

He hung up the phone and tugged the green vee-neck shirt over his head, trying to ignore the rising feeling of panic in his throat. What if Sara were home alone? What if she'd fallen down and was in too much pain to get to the phone? Then he brought himself up short. Calm down, he told himself. You're acting like a frantic expectant father. She'd just forgotten to call Birch. She's probably down in Admitting right now.

Unable to grapple with her fear, Sara pushed herself awkwardly away from the man who called himself Keith Thomas. She looked wildly around. Surprisingly, he didn't reach out for her again. Instead, he stood there looking at her, his expression interested and speculative.

That, more than anything else, made her realize there was nowhere to run, nowhere to hide. "Where's my friend Kitty?" she gasped. "What have you done with her?"

"I haven't done anything to her. She just can't be with us right now."

"Let me out of here."

He laughed. "I can't do that."

"Please. I'm going to have a baby. I have to get to the hospital."

"You're not going to the hospital. I have everything you'll need, right here."

"Oh, my God." Another spasm gripped her, and she doubled over. Keith Thomas grabbed her arm. "Your room is all ready. You'd better come lie down." When she tried to push him away, he slapped her face. "Calm down."

"Kitty! Kitty!" Sara screamed. "Help me! Please help me."

"My sister isn't going to come to your rescue. I'm in charge now."

"Your sister?" She stared at him. At close range, the features were almost identical to Kitty's. His twin sister ... Kitty—Katrina. "But you're both dead," Sara whispered.

"Maybe once, but not now. Kitty brought me back to life." He started to laugh again as he dragged Sara toward the stairs.

When she resisted, he stopped and fixed her with a quelling look. "Stop fighting me. It's going to be a lot worse for you if you don't cooperate."

"Sara?" Ben shouted as he threw open the front door. Her car was in the driveway, but she didn't answer. "Sara?" He made a rapid tour of the first floor, then the second. After that, he checked the basement. Both of them had avoided the underground chamber since George had been found at the bottom of the stairs. Now it made him shudder to search the musty corners of the damp room.

It was a relief not to find her down there. But that didn't solve the mystery of where she was. On leaden feet, he made his way back through the empty house to the bedroom they'd shared for the past few months.

This time, he forced himself to make a careful inspection. The closet door was open, and the packed suitcase was gone. On the table beside the bed was a notepad. Ben snatched it up and scanned the entries. Sara must have been timing her contractions—starting at two-twenty-eight—just after she'd called Lois. Next to one of them was a notation that looked like "A water." Had her amniotic sac ruptured? That took away any doubt that this could be a false alarm.

Ben sat down on the side of the bed and rested his chin on his knuckles. What would Sara have done when she couldn't reach him? She might have called someone else to take her to the hospital. Of course, her friend Kitty.

Impatiently, he thumbed through Sara's phone book, looking for the number. When he called the artist's apartment, he got a recording. "I'm sorry, I'm out of town gathering natural materials for my sculptures. But I plan to pick up my messages periodically. Leave your name and number after the sound of the tone, and I'll get back to you as soon as possible."

Ben slammed down the phone. Damn machines. Didn't people answer their phones anymore?

Next he called Harold, being careful not to alarm the old man. No, Harold hadn't heard from his daughter since yesterday.

Several more calls established that Sara hadn't arrived at the hospital yet. She hadn't called Judy or Lois again. In fact, nobody had heard from her since around two o'clock. It was after four now. A woman in labor couldn't vanish into thin air. Where the hell was she?

The small room was on the second floor of the old house. Inside, there was a narrow bed covered with a white sheet, a rocking chair, a bureau, and a baby's changing-table. Tacked to the wall was a brightly colored astrological poster featuring Gemini, the twins.

The windows were closed, and the air was hot and still. When Sara's fingers grabbed at the door frame, Keith took her by the shoulders and marched her inside.

"See, everything's ready for you. There's even a bathroom." He pointed toward a door on the right. "So you won't have to go anywhere."

She turned to him, her eyes pleading, hoping he wasn't aware of the way her heart was thudding in her chest. "Why are you doing this to me?"

A look of satisfaction suffused his face. "Justice."

"I don't understand. What have I done to you?"

"Nothing. But you're the one who has to pay."

Sara's heart started to pound even harder.

"They shot the dog, you know."

"What dog?"

"Hunter, the dog that bit Keith Thomas. They should have shot your father, too. He was an incompetent, bumbling fool, playing at being a physician. He killed Keith. His daughters have to pay for that crime."

Sara's head was spinning. This was beyond sanity, beyond reason. She'd tried to avoid his eyes. Now she looked up and saw the hatred looming over her. It was all she could do to get words out of her trembling lips. "But—how—? You say you're Keith."

"Weren't you listening? I told you, Kitty brought Keith back to life. I can only share her body."

Sara stared into his contorted face and then stumbled backwards. This was a terrible nightmare. It had to be. But there seemed to be no way to wake up.

"No—" Her legs hit the edge of the bed, and she sat down heavily. "Share her body. Share her body. Oh my God—you—you—are Kitty!"

"No!" He raised his hand and stared at it. "This is her flesh. But Kitty's gone away now. When I tell her she has to go, she does what I say. She wanted to come on the boat with me. But I wanted to handle that by myself."

"The boat—"

"With your sister, Ginny. I pulled it off all by myself. I had a mustache and brown contact lenses."

"You mean—Ginny—you're the one—what did you do to her?" The sentence ended in a gasp.

"She was a sweet girl. It was easy to make friends with her. And she trusted me. She made me wish I really could be a man." He gulped. "But I did make her happy."

It was hard to believe what she was hearing.

His face twisted in pain. "I didn't like killing her. But it was her destiny—my destiny. It was written in the stars." His voice rose on a note of triumph.

The awful words were too much to take in, too much for Sara's horrified mind to absorb. Her sister was dead. With a strangled moan, she fell backwards on the bed. Blessed blackness swallowed her up.

"Take it easy, Doc." Moose Bramble stared at the disheveled figure who had come bursting into the St. Stephens police station just as he'd been getting ready to leave for the day.

"But, I tell you, Sara's in labor. And she's disappeared."

"Disappeared? You've checked with the hospital?"

Moose noted that the other two guys in the squad room were looking on with considerable interest. He stood up, took the doctor's arm, and led him toward Dailey's office—which the chief had vacated fifteen minutes earlier. "Let's go back here where we'll have some privacy."

Ben allowed himself to be steered toward the little room. "I've checked everywhere. She's gone," he muttered. "Or she could have been in an accident. I didn't think of that. Have there been any accidents reported on the road to Easton?"

"No."

"I'm just grasping at straws now. She must have been about to leave for the hospital—and somebody grabbed her."

Bramble's eyes narrowed. Ben Langley wasn't the hysterical type. Even when he'd been put on the spot about that Santa Barbara business, he'd recounted the events in a dispassionate voice. Now he sounded like a man walking a razor's edge. "Maybe you better tell me what happened."

Ben sucked in a deep breath. He was probably coming across like a madman. "Yeah."

"Sit down." The patrolman gestured toward the chair beside the desk. After a moment's hesitation, he shrugged and settled his large frame into the chief's seat.

Ben sank into the wooden chair and raked his fingers through his hair. "I made Sara marry me so I could watch her—protect her. But it's been months since anything strange has happened. You know, I wanted it all to be over. Ralph. Newhouse. Harold. Ginny. But I should have known. Jesus, I should have known."

"What are you talking about?"

"Whoever got them has Sara."

"Take it easy. You don't know that. You're just guessing." But he hadn't liked the smell of this thing from the start. Even as he mouthed the reassuring words, Moose Bramble was beginning to wonder about just what in the hell had happened to Langley's wife. "Let's start at the beginning. Give me facts. You're sure Sara's in labor?"

"I'm not positive. But it's pretty likely. She was timing her contractions. And her amniotic sac had ruptured."

"What's that?"

"Her water's broken. At least that's what she jotted down."

A long, gripping pain woke Sara, and she groaned. Outside, the wind shrieked around the corner of the building.

She didn't want to open her eyes. That would mean acknowledging her surroundings. A soft, damp cloth mopped the perspiration from her forehead. "Ben—"

"It's not Ben. It's Keith. We're going to be here together until you give me the baby. It'll be born right here on my bed."

"Oh, God."

"While we wait for the blessed event, I can answer all your questions. You don't know how much I've been wanting to tell you everything. But I couldn't. Kitty had to be the one to keep an eye on you. She did everything just right—except for that stupid stunt of hiring someone to run you down with his motorcycle. She thought it would throw you off the track."

Sara shuddered as she thought back over her friend's solicitousness. Had it all been motivated by evil intentions?

"I'm going to take good care of you," Keith promised. "We don't want anything to happen to our baby."

Her lids snapped open. "What do you want from me?"

"I just told you. The baby. He's going to replace Keith—really replace him. Kitty and I can take care of him. I'll be the father, and she'll be the mother."

The twisted logic made her skin crawl. But maybe if she kept him talking she could get through to him. Or maybe there was some way to escape, if she could catch him off guard.

"Yes, a baby needs two parents," she murmured.

"I'm glad you approve. Kitty had the idea. After she got out of the hospital, she was going to have a little boy and turn him into Keith." His features twisted into a mask of agony. "But then she had that horrible operation, and she couldn't. She told you about that."

"Yes. Oh, Keith. I'm so sorry. I wanted a baby too. So I understand. I know it must have been—"

"Don't give me that social-worker crap. You couldn't possibly understand!" He cut her off sharply. "All her hopes, her plans. Wiped out like someone smearing blood across the floor."

Sara shuddered. Blood. Like the red paint downstairs, like the background on the needlepoint canvases. "Please, let me go," she whispered. "My baby won't be Keith."

"Yes he will."

"But what if it's a girl?"

"A girl won't do. If it's a girl, she's going to die—right before you do."

CHAPTER 42

Harold Strickland took a step backwards when he saw the two grim-faced men standing on the porch—his new son-in-law, Ben Langley, with Police Officer Moose Bramble.

"What have I done?" he faltered.

"We've got to talk to you," Ben explained as he pushed his way into the house without being invited. "Sara's in labor—and she's disappeared." His voice cracked on the last word of the sentence.

Harold sagged backwards as if he'd been hit in the stomach with the blunt edge of an ax. "No."

"I'm sorry," Bramble muttered.

Ben took the old man's arm and led him into the living room. Harold dropped to the couch. The two visitors took seats opposite him. "You may be able to help."

The aging physician shook his head. "I'm no help to anyone now."

"We think this has to do with the Keith Thomas case," Ben said.

Keith Thomas. At the sound of the name, Harold felt as if a handgun had gone off in his head. He reeled backwards. "Keith Thomas."

Ben leaned forward urgently. "Do you remember him?"

"That name. Was he a teenage boy?" He shook his head. "I don't know."

"Harold, I read your patient records—the ones in the box. Keith Thomas was a fifteen-year-old boy who went into anaphylactic shock after you gave him a penicillin injection."

Bramble turned and stared at Ben. He hadn't heard that part of the story before.

"Oh, Christ," Harold gasped.

"It was fifteen years ago. Right after Margaret."

"You know about that?"

"Yes. But she's not the issue now. You have to remember. The Thomases moved to St. Stephens a few years before the boy died. He had a twin sister named Katrina. She went crazy and attacked you in the office."

"Yes, yes." There was a spark of recognition in the old man's eyes. "I remember that. She snatched the needlepoint picture off the wall and threw it at me." He stared off into the distance. "That's why I knew what it meant when I started getting those pictures."

"What are you talking about?" Bramble asked.

"Needlepoint pictures of a hypodermic needle," Ben explained. "Sara found them in the drawer in his office—along with a gun. There were two others. One was returned to Sara with the things from the glove compartment of Ted's car after it was recovered from the river. One turned up in Ginny's luggage. We thought—we thought it might have something to do with the woman Ted was seeing—"

"Sara got them, too?" Harold started to sob.

Ben came over and gripped him by the shoulder. "Take it easy. Falling apart's not going to help. You have to think. Anything you can remember might be the key to finding Sara."

Harold wiped the back of his hand across his eyes. "I don't—I can't—"

"You remembered about the picture."

"Yes. I guess I did. When you said Keith Thomas's name—" His voice trailed off.

"In Ted's car. And Ginny's luggage," Bramble mused. "It sounds like this whole thing started with Ted."

"Keith's sister. Did she come back? Did you see her around town?"

"I don't know. I don't think so. But wouldn't she be a lot older now? Different?"

Unable to sit still any longer, Ben got up and started to pace back and forth. So many crazy things had happened. Some of them had to be related.

He looked at Bramble. "The guy on the motorcycle. The one who Sara thought was following her around. She never saw his face. Even when he tried to run her over."

"Was he short and slender?" the officer asked.

"I only saw him once, right after Ted's funeral. But that sounds right."

"It could be the same guy who got the dog from the pound."

"Who the hell is he? And what if he has Sara now?" Ben grated.

"He can't be Keith Thomas. I sent for his death certificate," Bramble added.

"You did?"

"Yeah. I wanted to see it—just to make sure there wasn't any mistake."

"What about the sister's?"

"All I know is that she didn't die in Maryland. There's nothing on record in the state."

"His grandmother brought him into the office once," Harold mused.

"What?"

"His grandmother."

"Do you remember her name?"

"It wasn't Thomas."

Ben hadn't seen the woman's name in Keith's file. "Maybe it's somewhere in your records," he suggested.

The contractions were coming every ten minutes now. Keith was timing them with an old-fashioned pocket watch. "This belonged to my great-grandfather," he explained. "It's been given to the oldest son in the family for the past three generations. Soon it will be little Keith's."

Sara didn't reply. It was taking most of her energy to get through the contractions without falling apart. Thank God she'd taken that class. If she hadn't practiced so conscientiously, she'd probably be reduced to a mass of quivering jelly by now.

Hiss. Hiss. She dragged air into her lungs and let it out. The breathing technique was something she could cling to in this melodrama too horrible to be real.

But it was real.

Would Ben figure out where she was? she wondered. She'd scribbled "Atwater" on the notepad next to the bed. But how would Ben know what it meant? Would he even see it? If Kitty had noticed it, she would have torn it up. Sara grimaced. She had to get away. But how? Maybe there was something in her bag she could use. "Could you bring me my suitcase?" she whispered.

"Why?"

"With all this special breathing, my mouth is so dry. They warned me that might happen, so I packed some lollipops. I need to suck one."

Keith brought the bag over and rummaged inside. "I don't see a lollipop."

"It's in with my labor-room stuff." She reached for the bag, and Keith watched closely while she found the candy. After unwrapping it, she stuck it in her mouth. But she had to take it out a moment later when another pain grabbed her. They were getting stronger.

She moved restlessly on the perspiration-soaked sheets. Keith's face swam into her field of vision. "How are you doing?"

The wind had picked up and she could hear it whistling through the walls of the old house. "I should be in the hospital. The baby could die if you don't do the right things for him."

"Are you too hot?" He went over and cracked the window. "There."

The cool breeze played with her damp face. "Thank you."

"I've been reading about home delivery and baby care."

"I know. But I really should be in the hospital," Sara repeated. "Kitty would understand that." She wasn't sure of that anymore. But it was important to maintain the fiction.

"Kitty's not going to help you."

"She's my friend."

Keith laughed. "It was all an act. Everything. She was just helping me."

"I don't believe that."

Keith shrugged and began to rock back and forth in the chair. It was old and squeaky. "Oh, you don't. I guess you couldn't tell she was stirring up trouble between you and Ben. He saw it. But he didn't know what to say. Lucky he's such a nice guy."

Sara swallowed. Ben. *Oh, Ben,* she thought, her eyes misting. And Kitty. The woman had been so friendly over the past few months. She'd been so interested in every detail of the pregnancy. Almost as if the baby had been hers.

Sara shuddered. Kitty had been thinking of the baby as hers all along. Sara was just an incubator. A surrogate mother.

Keith smiled. "But that's not all," he continued. "Let me tell you a little story that may amuse you. Your best friend Kitty was your husband's lover."

"No!"

He began to rock faster. "Well, not in the

truest sense of the word. It amused Kitty to have her little rules about what Ted Chandler could and couldn't do with her body. But she certainly satisfied his perverted appetites. Of course, it wasn't Kitty who met him that last night by the Choptank River. It was me."

Sara struggled to keep from gagging.

"Oh, yes. Your husband was so easy to lead around by the cock." He swallowed. "He wanted Kitty—for—for—kinky sex."

His eyes pinned her to the bed, and she squirmed away toward the farther edge. *Keith* had killed her husband! And the idea of his sister fooling around with Ted Chandler had made him as sick as it made her.

Keith seemed to pull himself back together. "But Ted served our purpose. He was such a good source of information. He couldn't keep from bragging about the Swan Point deal to his mistress. That's how I blackmailed George Newhouse into giving me fifteen thousand dollars. Part of it went for the Royal Alexandria cruise. The rest will support us until Kitty can establish herself as an artist under a new identity." Keith chuckled. "Isn't it amazing how it all worked out so well?"

"You blackmailed George?"

"Yes. And I pushed him down your cellar stairs. He must have been in your house for the same reason I was—looking for that answering-machine tape."

The awful revelations were rolling out like tabloid stories hot off the press. As Sara tried to make sense of it all, another contraction hit her, and she struggled to concentrate on her breathing.

"They're getting closer," Keith approved. "After you've delivered the baby, I'll go get something that will put you to sleep. Just like that dog I left in your driveway."

Sara stifled a gasp.

"I think we should make this a festive occasion."

She watched as he opened the top drawer of the chest, got out half a dozen candles, and began to set them in holders around the room.

Soon his form was shadowed by eerie, flickering light.

"Don't you like the way they set the mood? They make the evening special. Like a ceremony."

"I—"

"And we need music, too." He pulled a child's music box from one of the shelves under the changing-table. It was a small merry-go-round, decorated with faded horses, lions, and giraffes. "This was mine and Kitty's when we were little. I brought it down from the attic for you." He wound it up by turning the canopy on top. When he set it on the changing-table, it began to spin and play a tinkly circus tune.

"Katrina was in a private psychiatric hospital," Harold related. He was trying desperately to dredge up any information that might be relevant. "I felt like I'd put her there, so I used to have them send me reports."

"According to the detective Sara hired, she got out about two years ago," Ben added.

"I wonder if they would have discharged her if she hadn't run out of money. Where would she have gone after that?" Harold's brows furrowed as another memory popped into his mind. In the context, it didn't quite make sense. But maybe he just wasn't capable of making the right connections. He looked at Ben. "You weren't there after the funeral."

"Which funeral?"

"Ted's. I was just thinking about how Ralph dropped that ceramic key and broke it. It just popped into my mind. Maybe that's important."

"A ceramic key?"

"The one the fire department or the mayor or somebody gave to Ted. Everyone was at Sara's house. Ralph picked up the key from the mantle. He dropped it right after Kitty said something about just getting back to town and hearing about Ted's accident. The rest of the crowd was gawking at Ralph. But I was watching Kitty. You should have seen the look on her face."

Ben's head jerked around. "Kitty."

He and Bramble stared at each other.

"My God—we've been looking for a man," Ben grated. "But what if it wasn't a man after all? Remember, it was the sister who wanted revenge."

"A tall woman could pass herself off as a short man," Bramble reasoned. He was already on his feet. "I'm going to send someone over to her apartment."

"She's out of town. I got a message on her answering machine."

"She *said* she was out of town."

For the first time in hours, Ben felt his chest well with hope. "You're not sending someone. We're going over there."

*   *   *

It was hard to think clearly. Every time the merry-go-round stopped, Keith wound it up again, and the tinkly melody was driving her crazy. But she was afraid to protest.

Somehow she had to get away from Keith.

She racked her brain for an escape plan. Two contractions later, she'd come up with an idea. If she could just get him out of the room. . .

"Keith. My mouth is so parched. The lollipop's not enough. I need some ice chips," she whimpered pitifully.

He studied the bulky form of the woman curled on the bed. "That's too bad. Because I'm not going to leave you alone."

Ben stared around the empty apartment. He could barely keep himself from picking up a chair and smashing it against the wall. On the Fourth of July, he'd promised Sara no one would ever hurt her again. What a travesty he'd made of that promise.

"Kitty's sure as hell not here. And it looks as if she left in a real hurry," he growled.

"Yeah." The police officer pointed to the *Star Democrat* on the kitchen table. It was open to the horoscope page. "Today's paper. Either she brought it in just before she left, or she's not really out of town."

"Another dead end," Ben sighed. He strode over to the phone. "I'm just going to check one more time to make sure Judy Wooter hasn't heard from Sara."

Bramble watched the physician dial. A hundred to one, nobody had heard from Sara. Bu if it made Langley feel better to check, he wasn't going to interfere.

"Judy—"

"Did Sara call again?"

"I thought you were going to tell me she'd called you."

"Dammit—no."

"There's something I should have asked before. Did anyone call before Sara left to go home?"

"No. But that detective from Baltimore was trying to get ahold of her early in the afternoon."

"Levitt?"

"I think that's his name. Wait a minute; he gave me his number." She shuffled through some papers. "Here it is—" She read it to him.

"Thanks."

"Ben—call me at home if you hear anything."

"I will."

Bramble cocked an eyebrow. "What'cha got?"

"I don't know. A detective from Baltimore was trying to get in touch with Sara. She had him looking for Ginny. At least he can tell me if he talked to her."

When he dialed the number, he got the man's answering service. "This is Dr. Benjamin Langley," he told the woman on the other end of the line. "Please have Mr. Levitt get back to me as soon as he can. It could be a matter of life and death."

Keith stood, holding one of the flickering tapers in front of his face. "Have you ever thought about life and death?" he intoned. "Someone can be alive, and with just a prick of a needle, they can be dead. You wouldn't believe how fast it can happen."

Sara closed her eyes. She didn't like the turn the conversation was taking.

"Then there's life. One minute the baby's part of you. The next minute, he's a separate entity." He got up, took the washcloth to the sink just inside the bathroom door, and soaked it in cool water. Bringing it back, he laid it across Sara's forehead.

"Thank you."

"You're giving me the most precious gift I could receive. A new life. Kitty gave me something, too. She gave up part of her existence so I could come back. You know, I started coming to her in the hospital. But she couldn't tell anyone. Getting out was the important thing. They never would have let her out if they'd known about me."

Sara tried to bite back a moan. Then she went into one of the mid-chest breathing patterns that was getting her through this ordeal.

"Another contraction? Is it bad? They're only five minutes apart. It won't be so long now."

When the contraction was over, Keith got up and opened one of the bureau drawers. He was holding something against his body so she couldn't see it. "I have something else to show you."

Sara gasped as he held the original needlepoint picture from her father's office.

"I stole it." He answered her unasked question. "I needed it for a pattern."

She shrank away from the art work. "*You* sent them to me!"

"And to your father. It all started with that injection right there in his office. I wanted him to know—and think about me out there stalking him and his daughters. But now the bastard can't even remember what crime he has to pay for." Keith focused on Sara again. "That's your fault! You're the one who let them give him the shock treatment. Kitty knew what could happen and told you not to do it. Why didn't you listen to her?"

"I was only trying to help him—"

"Shut up," Keith snapped. He had begun to sock his fist into the edge of the mattress. "I don't want to hear your rationalizations."

Sara cringed away from him again. She could see a vein pounding above his left eye. What would he do to her if he didn't calm down?

Her eyes focused on the poster. "Is Gemini your sign?"

He looked down at her. "Yes."

"What will the baby's sign be?"

"Libra." His face took on a glow of excitement. "I just realized, I'll be able to write down the exact moment of birth. That way I can have a chart cast."

Sara struggled to keep her own expression from changing.

"But I can already tell you he's going to be artistic—like Kitty." Keith babbled on.

"Yes. Tell me more about him." Talking astrological nonsense was safer than any of the other topics he'd introduced. How had Keith reconciled the difference in his birthday and the baby's? She didn't dare ask.

"He'll be stylish and easygoing. He'll hate distracting objects and clashing colors."

Her son's horoscope as interpreted by a maniac. Or, heaven help her, what if it was her daughter? Her fingernails dug into the sheet, and she fought back a scream of anguish and frustration.

CHAPTER 43

When Ben's beeper went off, he and Bramble were in the officer's squad car heading back to the Langley house to look for any clues Ben might have missed.

"I can patch you through on the radio. What's the number?"

A moment later, Bramble handed Ben the receiver. The answering service reported that Levitt could be reached at his home—which Bramble also dialed.

"Jake Levitt here."

"This is Ben Langley. Did you get in touch with my wife this afternoon?"

"I certainly did. Did she have her baby?"

"I don't know. She's disappeared."

"What?"

"When did you talk to her?"

"About three o'clock. I was calling to tell

her that the Thomas twins' mother grew up in St. Stephens. Her maiden name was Atwater."

"That's all?"

"I'm sorry I can't be of more help."

Ben hung up and stared out the windshield. Then he reached into his pocket and pulled out the slip of paper from the notepad. It said 3:04. The word written after the time was hard to read, but it could be *Atwater*. Jesus Christ, that's what Sara had written down! He'd thought it referred to her membranes rupturing.

"Have you heard of a family called Atwater?" he asked Bramble.

"There are a bunch of Atwaters around here." The police officer tapped his fingernail against his teeth. "But you know who might be able to put us onto the right one—Beatrice Pierce. She knows everybody's business back through the past thirty years."

Ben nodded wearily. "We might as well ask her. What do we have to lose? There have been so many dead ends—Ginny, Harold's memory, the dog."

"Yeah. I went to the pound. When Thomas took the dog, he gave your office as his address."

"The bastard. What else did you find out about him?"

"He had dark hair. He was short. And he didn't like the idea of having to pay for a rabies vaccination. No wonder, since he was planning to kill the animal a couple days later."

It was as if a light bulb had gone off in Ben's head. "A rabies vaccination. Jesus, a kid—one of my patients—was wearing a new rabies tag. He said he'd picked it up in a field." He strained to remember the conversation. "And he was upset about someone mistreating a dog—a German shepherd, I think. I wasn't paying a lot of attention."

"I tell you what, Doc. I'll drop you off at your car. While I go question Miss Bea, you can talk to the kid."

The contraction was over a minute long. For the past few hours, she'd been able to handle the discomfort. But it was getting worse. Soon she wasn't going to be able to do anything but fight the pain.

She looked at Keith. He wasn't going to take a chance on leaving her alone, so she'd thought of something else to try. It was terribly risky. But she didn't have any other choice. This was her last chance, if she was ever going to get away from him.

However, she had to time things carefully. When she was in the grip of a contraction, it held her captive as effectively as Keith. The instant the pain subsided, Sara turned her head toward the madman who was going to kill her and steal her child.

"Keith."

"What?"

"Please—it's getting bad."

"I can see that."

"If you won't get me any ice chips, I need a drink of water."

"All right. I guess if you're not going to be having any anesthetic, we don't have to worry about your throwing up."

As Sara watched him start toward the bathroom, her chest tightened painfully. Could she really pull this off? She didn't know, but she had to try.

The suitcase was on the floor beside the bed. She reached inside. After a moment's fumbling, her hand closed around cold metal. Pulling out a small can, she hid it in the folds of her jumper. "Hurry. Please, hurry!"

He came back across the room.

"I can't sit up by myself. You'll have to help."

When he leaned down toward her, she pulled out the cylinder and pressed on the button. A blast of spray deodorant hit him in the face. He screamed and staggered backwards, but she kept her finger jammed on the button as long as he was in range.

He was cursing and rubbing at his eyes as she pushed herself awkwardly off the bed. A barrel on jelly-roll legs, she forced herself across the room toward the door. There was a tug inside her, and a woosh of liquid ran down her legs. Her water had broken, but her concentration was so focused on getting away that she didn't even notice the gush of amniotic fluid.

Adrenalin and guts kept her going. Behind her, she could hear Keith cursing. Suddenly, his voice changed to a woman's sob. "What the fuck? I'm going blind! Help. Help me."

The pain had driven Keith away for the moment. Kitty was back. Sara hoped Kitty didn't have the advantage of knowing what was going on. And Sara sure as hell wasn't going to stop and explain. She gained the door, threw it open, and slammed it shut behind her in one continuous stroke.

Her fingers brushed against metal. A bolt. Keith must have planned on locking her in here if he needed to leave her alone. Quickly she slid the rod into the bracket. In the next second, the knob rattled and the door shook. Sara forgot to breathe. The bolt held. But for how long?

"Mrs. Craig, I'm sorry to bother you."
"Has something happened to Bobby?"
"Nothing like that. I just need to talk to him."
Bobby Craig's mother shook her head. "He's not here. He's still up at the school at football practice."
"Thanks." Ben turned and sprinted for his Blazer.

Behind Sara, something heavy crashed into the door.
"You bitch. Let me out of here!" It was Keith's voice again. He kept up a steady stream of curses.
Another contraction, like a giant fist, seized her belly, and she whimpered, unable to summon up the energy to pant through it. When it was over, she looked wildly around. He'd expect her to go downstairs and try to get out the back door or a window. But the windows were bolted. She'd have to break one. How long would she have before he burst through the door? Now he was furious. What would he do when he caught up with her? She had to do the unexpected.
All at once, she remembered how the outside of the house had looked. There was a

window in the attic that opened onto a balcony above the porch. He'd never look for her out there. But could she make it down to the ground?

Somehow, she'd have to.

The most efficient way for Moose Bramble to get through the Friday afternoon traffic in town was to turn on the siren. It was still wailing when he pulled up in front of Beatrice Pierce's.

The woman herself was wide-eyed as she answered the door. "Officer Bramble? What's wrong?"

"I don't have time to go into all the particulars. Do you know where the Atwater house is?"

"That rambling old place off the road to Easton?"

"Yeah. I hope so. Can you give me directions?"

"Now let me think. Is it the first turn or the second after the abandoned church?"

It took precious seconds for Sara to pull the sandals from her swollen feet. When she got them off, she tossed them down the stairs, so he'd think she'd gone that way. Then she turned and staggered down the hall, opening doors as she went.

The first one she came to had been a bathroom. Now it was a laboratory. On the table by the sink was a hypodermic needle. For her!

Sara grimaced and staggered on, her swollen body swaying. The third door on the right enclosed the stairwell leading to the attic. Gripping the rail and half pulling herself up, she began to climb.

The locker room smelled like dirty laundry. The mumbled conversations of the tired boys echoed off the metal lockers. Bobby Craig had pulled his jersey over his head and was unfastening his shoulder pads when Ben burst into the changing area behind the gym. When he found Bobby in the crowd, his eyes were drawn to the blue tag still hanging around the boy's neck.

Ignoring the questioning stares of the team members, Ben threaded his way to Bobby's side.

"I have to talk to you."

"Did the coach find out about the beer?"

For a moment, Ben wondered what the kid had been up to. "No. I need your help with something important." He reached for the dog tag. "You said you found this. Where?"

Bobby shrank back.

"Now you're gonna get it," a stocky boy teased.

"I didn't steal it," Bobby defended himself. "It was lyin' on the ground."

"I know that." Ben hunkered down beside the boy and took him by the shoulders. "Bobby, my wife is missing, and I think she might be at the house where you found that dog tag."

The youngster's eyes grew round. "Jeez. You mean the old Atwater place?"

Ben's fingers dug into the boy's arms. "That's right. Can you take me there? Right now."

Bobby snatched up his shirt, vividly aware that he now had the starring role in an adventure story: Dr. Langley asking Bobby Craig to save the day. "Sure."

A flight of stairs had never seemed so endless. By sheer force of will, Sara dragged herself to the top and collapsed panting in a heap on the dusty wooden floor. One more door loomed like an insurmountable barrier. As she lay there looking at it, a terrible rumbling noise seemed to break and swirl around her. It took a moment to realize she was hearing thunder.

The storm.

A vivid picture of herself being blown off the roof by the wind leaped into her mind. She'd be killed. And the baby— No, she couldn't think about that.

Moose Bramble lit out down the highway at ninety miles an hour, siren blaring. The second turn after the abandoned church, Miss Bea had said, although she hadn't been perfectly sure. When he reached the turn, he took the corner on two wheels, but had to slow down on the unpaved surface. The road led back to a cabin by the river. Several nervous retrievers started barking at him when he pulled into the dirt clearing. This sure as hell wasn't a sprawling old mansion. Maybe the guy standing in the doorway holding a shotgun could give him directions.

Sara was reaching for the door when another agonizing contraction gripped her middle. They were bad before, now they had become almost unbearable. Her fingers squeezed the metal as if that would alleviate the pain. As soon as it was over, she twisted the knob.

Locked. Or maybe it was just stuck. She couldn't hold back a little whimper of defeat. How in the name of all the saints was she going to drag herself down the stairs again and past the door to the bedroom?

"Down this way," Bobby directed. "There's a road that leads to the house. But I don't know exactly where."

It was agony for Ben to slow down, but he forced his foot to ease up on the accelerator.

"Right there!" Bobby shouted. "This is where he chased me."

A dead branch was tossed against the hood by the wind, and Ben reflexively slammed on his brakes. "He chased you?"

"I thought he was gonna kill me."

The realization suddenly struck him that he was putting this boy in grave danger by bringing him back here. He glanced at Bobby's excited expression. To him, this was an adventure. But who knew what might be waiting up there? "The house is at the end of this road?" he questioned.

"Around a couple more curves."

"I'm going to let you out."

"Aw, Doc."

"Bobby, I have an important job for you. I want you to run back down the road and stop at the first house you come to. Call the police department and tell them I need help. Tell them where I am. Can you do that?"

"Yeah." The boy started to scramble out of

the car. Ben put a hand on his arm. "Watch out for flying branches."

"I will." In the next second, Bobby was running down the road like a halfback going for a touchdown.

Ben continued up the winding track. Two curves later, he could see the house, silhouetted against the twilight sky. Dark clouds wheeled past, driven by the racing wind.

When he saw Kitty's car pulled up in front of the door, his heart gave a leap of hope. She was here. Logically, Sara should be, too.

In the gathering dusk, the Victorian structure loomed in front of him like the "Addams Family" mansion. The details were obscured by shadows of black and gray—except where one light shone in an upstairs window. It was halfway open. Was that where Kitty was holding Sara?

Instead of driving all the way up to the house, he stopped several hundred yards away, at the edge of the woods. He'd do the rest on foot.

CHAPTER 44

Sara rested her cheek against the door, fighting a sudden spasm of nausea. When she'd come up with this desperate plan, she hadn't realized how sick and weak she was going to feel. It was getting harder and harder to function.

Summoning every ounce of her ebbing strength, she gave the knob the hardest turn she could manage. The door swung open with a groan, and Sara literally fell into the attic.

The relief of getting past the barrier was so great that she didn't even feel the hard thump of her shoulder against the rough floorboards. Pushing herself to a sitting position, she peered into the attic. It was a large, low room, hot and stuffy from the afternoon sun that had beat down on the roof before the storm clouds had begun to gather.

Sara's eyes struggled to adjust to the dimness. A shaft of light had followed her up the stairs; and there was a bit of illumination coming from the far wall.

The window. She'd expected it to be closer to the top of the stairs, but it was all the way at the other end of the room.

As if to emphasize her discovery, a sudden jagged shaft of lightning flashed in the darkening sky beyond the dirty panes.

Another contraction rolled over her, and Sara knew she couldn't spare the effort to get up. Instead, she began to inch slowly between the boxes and trunks scattered around on the rough wooden planks.

When something damp began to pool around her knees, she looked down. Wetness was oozing down the insides of her legs and onto the floor—amniotic fluid. Her waters had broken, and she hadn't even noticed.

A terrible thought struck her, and she looked back over her shoulder. A moist trail followed her across the floor. Was it on the stairs? In the hall? Would Keith notice? If he did, she might have made a fatal mistake.

The realization spurred her onward. Yet she couldn't keep crawling through the contractions that were crashing over her now like giant waves pounding a beach.

Ben cautiously approached the house. It might have been deserted except for that one light.

What had Kitty done to Sara? What would she do if she knew he was here?

And what about the fact that Sara was in labor? Was her life—or the baby's—in danger?

His mouth clamped into a grim line as he forced his mind into more productive channels. After considering several possibilities for getting inside without being detected, he crossed to the large sugar maple growing beside the house. It was swaying in the wind.

Ben hadn't done any tree climbing since he'd fallen out of a jacaranda when he was eight and broken his left arm. Now, without any hesitation, he stripped off his sports jacket and tossed it on the ground. Then he jumped up, grabbed one of the lower branches of the maple, and pulled himself up. After taking a moment to decide on the best route, he began to climb.

It took only a few minutes to reach the level of the porch roof. Just as he clambered onto the slanting surface, an unexpected clap of thunder seemed to burst right over his head. It sent him reeling. For an endless moment, played out in agonizing slow motion, he felt himself slipping off the roof. As his hands and feet scrambled for a foothold, he thought he heard a crash inside the house.

Finally he regained his balance. With a renewed sense of urgency, he began to move as quietly as he could toward the flickering light.

It took several minutes before Sara reached the last of the boxes littering the floor. Stopping short, she panted from the exertion as she took in the broad expanse that still separated her from freedom.

For a moment, she squeezed her eyes shut

in frustration. She hadn't been able to tell from the doorway, but the attic wasn't completely floored. To get to the window, she'd have to crawl across the rafters. Could she do that now—without falling through the ceiling?

Perspiration plastered her jumper to her body as she stretched out a tentative hand toward one of the narrow wooden beams in front of her.

Crash. The sound reverberated through the house, and her hand stopped in mid-reach.

Another roll of thunder? No, that must be the door to the bedroom giving way. Then footsteps pelted along the hall. In the old house, they echoed like drumbeats.

Sara held her breath when they stopped. Had Keith reached the stairs? Would he see the shoes and go down? Or would he see the track she'd left?

He was moving again. Her heart stopped as she realized the steps were getting stronger, closer.

"I know you're up there, you bitch. You might as well come down."

Sara shrank back into the shadows behind a pile of boxes as heavy footfalls thumped up the stairs.

She took a quick look at the window. There was no way to reach it before her pursuer gained the attic. She was trapped.

Was there some way to defend herself? Desperately, she searched the collection of assorted junk that surrounded her. The large chest to her right must have come from a boat. Inside were a fishing net and some navigational instruments. No good.

Next, her eyes lit on a mayonnaise jar full of marbles. Just as another contraction gripped her trembling body, she tilted the jar and sent the glass spheres rolling across the floor.

When the pain was over, Sara peeked cautiously around the box that hid her from view. Keith was framed in the doorway. He'd brought a candle with him, and it was held aloft in his left hand like a beacon. "You can't escape me. It's your destiny . . . like your sister Ginny."

She scrunched down farther into the shadows. "Come out!"

Lightning flashed, eclipsing the candle and glinting off the knife in his right hand. "I'm tired of waiting. I'm going to take the baby now."

Keith began to curse as he held the candle high in the air. Tucking the knife in his belt, he started to tear through the contents of the attic with his free hand. He was only five feet from Sara's hiding place when another contraction hit. It took every ounce of control she had left to keep from crying out. But she must have writhed with the pain.

"*Aha.*"

Sara gasped as Keith lunged forward. He had her now. She and the baby were as good as dead.

But before he reached her refuge, there was a scraping of shoe leather and a clinking of glass. As Sara watched, Keith's feet flew out from under him. The marbles! He'd slipped on the marbles she'd spilled across the floor.

*   *   *

Little drops of rain began to hit Ben as he peered around the frame into the partially opened window.

The flickering light came from half a dozen shimmering candles. They illuminated a bed, a chest, and a baby's changing-table.

It was like a parody of a holy shrine.

His eyes riveted to the empty bed, with its rumpled sheet and the depression of a human body running along the middle. Somehow he knew Sara had been lying there. The intuition was confirmed when he saw the suitcase on the floor.

There was no time to waste—or to consider what he was going to do next. Shoving the window all the way up, he climbed inside. For the first time, he was aware of music. As it slowed, he realized he was listening to the last faint notes of a child's music box. When they tinkled to a halt, the room was plunged into eerie silence.

He was halfway to the door when he saw that it was smashed in. Pieces of a rocking chair lay around it on the floor.

His mind scrambled to draw conclusions. Sara must have gotten away from Kitty somehow. But where was she? Were she and the sculptor playing a game of hide-and-seek somewhere in the house?

He looked at the floor. In front of him was a pool of colorless liquid, flecked with white. It was splotched with two sets of footprints.

He peered out into the hall and saw a trail of footprints, one with shoes—the other barefoot.

Squatting, he scooped up some of the liquid

and brought his fingers to his nose. Amniotic fluid and vernix, the cheesy-looking substance that covered the baby's skin. Jesus, Sara's water had broken, and she was stumbling around somewhere in the house. And Kitty was following her.

Keith fell forward, crashing through the open part of the ceiling just to Sara's right. The impact sent the candle flying out of his hand. It hit the ancient insulation, which began to smolder.

Sara edged away from the smoke. Slowly at first, and then with more authority, it began to billow into the confined space of the attic.

By degrees, it became harder to see, and she looked wildly around. Had Keith fallen all the way through the ceiling of the room below?

If he had, he sounded awfully close to her. He was chanting a steady stream of curses.

"You bitch. You won't get away from me." She could hear a scraping sound on the rafters. He must be holding on with his fingers and scrambling to get better purchase.

An acrid haze was filling the room. Sara's eyes smarted. If she didn't get out of here, she'd suffocate. Coughing, she tried to drag herself back toward the door, but moving now was like trying to make progress at the bottom of the sea. Only it wasn't water pressure that weighted her down. It was pain—squeezing, constricting pain, bulldozing over her.

Her body knew that she wasn't going to make it out of this room. She didn't have the strength to crawl. But her mind told her she had to. Inch by painful inch, she kept moving toward freedom.

The smoke was much thicker now. But she could feel cool, fresh air wafting up the steps—tantalizing her lungs. That, as much as anything else, helped keep her from giving up. But the doorway seemed to float ahead of her at the end of a long tunnel. It might have been miles instead of yards away.

"You bitch," Keith shouted again.

Sara didn't spare a glance behind her. But she could hear Keith's rasping breath, and she sensed he was getting closer. With the small part of her mind that wasn't consumed by the pain, she could picture him struggling to pull himself up through the rafters. First his hands, then his arms, then his head and shoulders.

Behind her, he was coughing, too. Then the sound was drowned out by a series of loud pops, followed by an explosion of heat. The open insulation had reached flash point and burst into flames.

It had been hot under the eaves before. Now, all at once, the enclosed space was transformed into a vision of hell. Flames began to shoot up from the insulation, enveloping the far end of the room.

Her head low to the floor, Sara gasped for breath and dragged herself toward the doorway at the top of the steps. But Keith was crawling toward her, the knife raised.

He smelled smoke. A deadly cloud of the stuff billowed down the stairs as Ben raced upward. When he reached the attic, he choked out an exclamation of horror. The end of the room shimmered in a red-gold haze of flames.

As he watched, greedy fingers of fire began to reach out along the edges of the rafters. In a moment, the whole place was going to go up.

"Sara! Where are you?"

"Ben—" Somehow she managed that one syllable. But the exclamation turned into a gasp of agony as a powerful contraction gripped her.

"Sara, hang on." In the thick smoke, he couldn't see her. But he dashed across the room toward the sound of her voice. Before he reached her, his feet went flying out from under him, and he landed heavily on the attic floor.

For a moment, he lay dazed. All he could feel was the throbbing in his knee. Then he pushed himself up—and his heart froze. Through the smoke, he could just make out the figure of a man closing in on Sara. A knife glinted in his hand.

CHAPTER 45

A vicelike claw snapped around Sara's ankle. She screamed.

"No. Please God. No!" She felt herself slipping.

"You and the baby are coming with me."

He was pulling her back toward the fire and smoke. Her fingers scraped uselessly on the rough boards of the attic floor. She was being dragged down, down, down into a fiery hell.

Then another hand locked onto her wrist. Ben! Her backwards slide stopped. But Ben couldn't pull her forward either. It was as though she was suspended between good and evil—heaven and hell.

"Stay out of this, Langley! She's mine."

In the next second, a whip of fire lashed out and wrapped itself around one of the man's pants legs. Ben heard a bloodcurdling scream. Then the figure jerked and shook its head, as though taking in the smoke and fire for the first time. "Keith! Keith! Where are you? Keith, don't leave me here."

With the last bit of strength she possessed, Sara kicked out at the hand that was dragging her toward certain death. As the grip loosened for a second, Ben yanked her toward him.

"Nooooo!" The maniac who had held Sara rolled away and slapped at the hot flames with frantic hands. Then it was like watching a human torch ignite. The figure spun crazily into the vortex of red-hot flames.

Ben looked away. All his efforts were bent on saving Sara and the baby. Locking his fingers around her wrist, he pulled her back across the smoky expanse of floor. A moment later, the advancing flames licked at the spot where she'd been lying. There wasn't a second to spare if the two of them were going to get out of there alive.

She was dead weight in his arms as he struggled to drag her back across the rough floorboards and toward the doorway. His knees throbbed with every movement, and his lungs burned with each indrawn breath. Behind him, the attic was crackling and shimmering in a yellow-red glow. Then the rafters began to crash to the floor. But he and Sara had made it through the doorway onto the landing.

Somehow he got Sara down the stairs. When they reached the second floor, someone dashed down the hall toward them. For a split second, Ben wondered who it was. Then he recognized the welcome bulk of Moose Bramble.

"You're here," Ben blurted.

"Yeah. After a slight detour. Sara all right?"

"I think so. But we've got to get out of the house. The whole place is going to go up."

Together the two men carried Sara downstairs, out the front door, and away from the burning building.

"What happened to the Duncan woman?"

"She was up there—dressed as a man." He glanced back at the flames licking through the windows of the upper floors. "She must be dead."

"Then Keith's dead, too." Sara said.

Both men turned to her.

"Kitty—Keith—they—" The attempt at an explanation ended in a gasp.

"It's all right. You can tell us about it later."

Behind them the flames leaped higher. With a shuddering crash, the roof collapsed.

Bramble peered at Sara. "We'd better get her to the hospital."

"I don't think there's going to be time for that," she gasped. "I—have—to—push."

"Hang on for a minute. Pant," Ben directed as he considered the best course of action. The wind had died, and only a spattering of rain had come and gone. He'd have more room to deliver the baby outside than in the car.

"There are blankets and towels in the back of the Blazer, and a sheet. Bring them and my medical bag," he directed the police officer. "And turn on the headlights so I can see what I'm doing."

"Right."

Ben carried Sara around to the front of the car. The air felt blessedly cool after the stifling heat of the fire.

"Everything's going to be all right now," Ben murmured. "But we want to try and slow things down just a little. Can you keep panting?"

"I—" Sara tried. But everything was rushing to completion of its own accord. Now that she was safe, it was almost impossible not to surrender to the unrelenting natural process that held her in its steely grip.

She was dimly aware of Ben laying her down on a bed of blankets. But mostly her attention centered on the forces that had taken control of her body. All at once, there was a tremendous increase in pressure that brought on a primal urge to bear down.

Ben knelt over her, talking in a low, reassuring voice as he got her ready. "Not much more to get through, honey. Try to relax between contractions to save your strength. You're doing fine. Perfect. You'll be holding the baby soon."

Even as he spoke to Sara, he was making assessments and judgments. The baby was premature, which meant it probably wasn't over six and a half pounds. That would make the birth easier. But what kind of shape would the child be in? He'd know soon enough.

After rolling back Sara's jumper and stripping off her underpants, he pulled on a pair of rubber gloves from his medical bag.

When he examined her, he could already see the baby's head. He sighed with relief. It was in the right position, facing down.

Burning, stretching, unbearable pressure . . .

Sara couldn't hold back a scream as she bore down again, and then again. It was incredibly hard, exhausting work.

Suddenly, the pain was less.

"That's the head. Perfect. As soon as we get the shoulders, it will be a lot easier for you."

He pulled downward gently to facilitate the delivery. First one shoulder, followed by the other. The torso, hips, and legs came with a gush of liquid.

A high-pitched wail pierced the stillness.

"A girl," Ben said. Sara could see him suctioning the tiny nose and mouth with a syringe.

"We've got to get her warmed up—or her temperature's going to drop."

Sara had begun to shake uncontrollably. "I—is—she—"

"She sure sounds healthy. And angry! She feels the way you would if you'd just stepped out of a nice hot shower into a chilly room." As he spoke, he rubbed the tiny body vigorously with a towel and then wrapped her up.

Next, he wrapped a blanket around Sara. When he laid the infant on Sara's stomach, her arms came up to cradle her daughter. She was exhausted, triumphant, exalted. And the physical relief was almost overwhelming.

"I'm going to clamp the cord and cut it now. "I'll leave it a little long so I don't have to unwrap her."

Neither one of them heard the ambulance or another patrol car arrive. But suddenly they were surrounded by a small crowd of uniformed men.

Ben spoke to the ambulance attendant. "We

need to get the baby into a controlled environment as soon as possible. And my wife's going to need some attention, too."

"Ben—" The thought of being separated made her reach out frantically toward him.

He found her free hand and clasped it. "I'm coming with you."

In the ambulance, he sat down beside her and brushed a damp strand of hair away from her forehead. Her face was streaked with dirt and soot, but she was the most beautiful sight he'd ever seen.

"You were tremendous."

She laughed weakly and wrapped her arm tighter around the sleeping infant. "I don't think I had much choice."

He wasn't just talking about the birth. When he thought about how close he'd come to losing her—losing everything—something inside him tightened and twisted. He wouldn't ask questions now when she needed to rest and recuperate. Yet he couldn't get the awful possibilities out of his mind. What had she suffered today?

The hospital room was full of flowers. Sara lay propped against the pillows nursing Alyssa Margaret Langley.

In the chair beside the bed, Ben watched, his mind filled with a mixture of awe and profound gratitude.

He'd stayed with Sara all night. Sometimes she'd slept. When she'd awakened she'd reached for him, just as she had when the ambulance crew had tried to take her away. He'd made sure he was at her side.

Fingers tightly meshed with his, she'd told what had happened. The story that had unfolded in low, urgent tones was almost too incredible to believe. Kitty. Keith. A desperate need for revenge against Harold Strickland and his family. And so many deaths. Ted. Ginny. Ralph. George. They were all part of a mad scheme—the desperate calculations of an unbalanced mind.

"I thought Kitty was my friend. Keith told me she was trying to drive us apart—that she wanted to hurt me any way she could. Oh, Ben, I'm so sorry I let her mess us up like that."

"Sara, I'm the one who's sorry. I could see it was happening. I didn't know what to say to you."

"I kept lying there on that bed thinking about you. About us. About all the things I wasn't going to be able to tell you."

Her eyes had filled with tears. His had too.

Now he thought about Kitty and Keith Thomas again—the twins who wouldn't be separated. In her anguish, the sister had brought her brother back to life. When it had come to the crunch, he'd left her in that burning attic to face death alone.

But Sara had outwitted both of them. Now the Thomas twins were dead—for good.

Ben drew in a deep shuddering breath.

When Sara looked up and saw the expression on his face, she stretched out her hand, pulling him close to her and the suckling baby. "I love you."

"I wasn't here when you needed me."

"You were in the operating room. You

couldn't do anything about that. And you found me—when I needed you most. There's no way I would have gotten out of that house without you."

"Sara—"

"It's over now. I want to put it behind the three of us."

"I love you, Sara. And you, too." His finger stroked the infant's soft cheek.

"We're a family now." There was no way to make up for the losses she'd suffered. But she had a rich life ahead of her with Ben.

Saturday, September 30

Jodeen Crane bustled into McGuire's Drugstore. "Did you hear what happened at the old Atwater place yesterday?"

Elmo McGuire nodded. "I got it from one of the night nurses at the hospital. An ambulance crew brought Sara and her baby girl in. The way I heard it, the doc delivered the baby himself and wouldn't leave Sara's side."

Jodeen's smile was condescending. "I just knew those two were made for each other."

Cheryl Keene set down her coffee mug. "You did?"

"Doesn't that beat all about Kitty Duncan?" The Acme checker deftly changed the subject. "And to think she sat here all these months steeped in evil."

"Four murders."

"She was dangerous."

"And crazy as a loon."

"You never know what some people are plotting."

Beatrice Pierce nodded silently. That's right, you never knew. But they'd find out soon enough when her book hit the best-seller list.